Praise for
ARCHANGEL

'As the suspense builds, the re—— —— ——e pages ever faster... with Harris's controlling —— —— narrative pedal, the reader has no choice but to ride, ——ailed, towards the plunging abyss' Natasha Fairweather, *Observer*

'The terror of a country in which unstoppable evil and violence are about to be unleashed is well observed and tangible... intense, well-researched and very readable' Michael Hartland, *Daily Mail*

'[Harris's] best book yet and surely establishes him as the true heir of le Carré' David Profumo, *Country Life*

'Harris is a master of background, a setter of places and people that are so gripping in their own right that the plot becomes almost incidental... a book I did not want to end' Philip Knightley, *Mail on Sunday*

'*Archangel* is page-turning entertainment... it rattles along a lot faster than the train from Archangel... blood-curdling, shiver-making, as befits a thriller... shows both prescience and enviable cunning' Julian Rathbone, *Independent*

'Robert Harris confirms his position as Britain's pre-eminent literary thriller writer with *Archangel*' Brian MacArthur, *The Times*

'Harris is one of the very few people writing serious, intelligent thrillers which deal with the great issues of our time' *Daily Express*

'Nerve tingling... nobody is more adept... a talent for heart-poundingly tense story-telling and an ability to conjure up atmospheres almost palpable with menace' Peter Kemp, *Sunday Times*

About the author

Robert Harris is the author of *Fatherland*, *Enigma*, *Archangel*, *Pompeii*, *Imperium* and *The Ghost*, all of which were international bestsellers. His latest novel, *Lustrum*, has just been published. His work has been translated into thirty-seven languages. After graduating with a degree in English from Cambridge University, he worked as a reporter for the BBC's *Panorama* and *Newsnight* programmes, before becoming political editor of the *Observer* and subsequently a columnist on the *Sunday Times* and the *Daily Telegraph*. The film of *The Ghost* – for which he co-wrote the screenplay – directed by Roman Polanski and starring Ewan McGregor and Pierce Brosnan, is due to be released at the beginning of 2010. He is married to Gill Hornby and they live with their four children in a village near Hungerford.

Also by Robert Harris

───────────── FICTION ─────────────

Fatherland   Enigma   Pompeii

Imperium   The Ghost   Lustrum

───────────── NON-FICTION ─────────────

A Higher Form of Killing (*with Jeremy Paxman*)

Gotcha!   The Making of Neil Kinnock

Selling Hitler   Good and Faithful Servant

Archangel

ROBERT HARRIS

arrow books

Published by Arrow Books 2009

5 7 9 10 8 6 4

First published in the United Kingdom in 1998 by Hutchinson
First published by Arrow Books in 1999

Arrow Books
The Random House Group Limited
20 Vauxhall Bridge Road, London SW1V 2SA

www.randomhouse.co.uk

Addresses for companies within The Random House Group Limited
can be found at: www.randomhouse.co.uk/offices.htm

The Random House Group Limited Reg. No. 954009

A CIP catalogue record for this book
is available from the British Library

ISBN 9780099527930

The Random House Group Limited supports The Forest Stewardship
Council (FSC®), the leading international forest certification organisation.
Our books carrying the FSC label are printed on FSC® certified paper. FSC is
the only forest certification scheme endorsed by the leading environmental
organisations, including Greenpeace. Our paper procurement policy can
be found at www.randomhouse.co.uk/environment

Typeset in Adobe Garamond by
MATS, Southend-on-the-Sea, Essex

Printed in the UK by CPI Bookmarque, Croydon, CR0 4TD

IN MEMORY OF

Dennis Harris
1923–1996

and for

Matilda

Prologue

Rapava's story

'Death solves all problems – no man, no problem.'
J. V. Stalin, 1918

LATE ONE NIGHT a long time ago – before you were even born, boy – a bodyguard stood on the verandah at the back of a big house in Moscow, smoking a cigarette. It was a cold night, without stars or moon, and he smoked for the warmth of it as much as anything else, his big, farm lad's hands cupped around the burning cardboard tube of a Georgian *papirosa*.

This bodyguard's name was Papu Rapava. He was twenty-five years old, a Mingrelian, from the north-eastern shoreland of the Black Sea. And as for the house – well, *fortress* would have been a better word. It was a tsarist mansion, half a block long, in the diplomatic sector, not far from the river. Somewhere in the frosty darkness at the bottom of the walled garden was a cherry orchard, and beyond it a wide street – Sadovaya-Kudrinskaya – and beyond that the grounds of the Moscow Zoo.

There was no traffic. Very faintly in the distance, when it was quiet, like now, and the wind was in the right direction, you could hear the howling of caged wolves.

By this time the girl had stopped screaming, which was a mercy, for it had got on Rapava's nerves. She couldn't have been more than fifteen, not much older than his own kid sister, and when he had picked her up and delivered her, she had looked at him – looked at him – well, to be honest, boy, he preferred not to talk of it, even now, nearly fifty years later.

Anyway, the girl had finally shut up and he was enjoying his cigarette when the telephone rang. This must have been about two a.m. He would never forget it. Two o'clock in the morning on the second of March, 1953. In the cold stillness of the night the bell sounded as loud as a fire alarm.

Now, normally – you have to understand this – there were four guards on duty during an evening shift: two in the house and two in the street. But when there was a girl, the Boss liked his security kept to a minimum, at least indoors, so on this particular night Rapava was alone. He threw down his cigarette, sprinted through the guard room, past the kitchen and into the hall. The phone was old-fashioned, pre-war, fastened to the wall – Holy Mother, it was making a racket! – and he grabbed the receiver mid-ring.

A man said: 'Lavrenty?'

'He's not here, comrade.'

'Get him. It's Malenkov.' The normally ponderous voice was hoarse with panic.

'Comrade –'

'Get him. Tell him something's happened. Something's happened at Blizhny.'

'Know what I mean by Blizhny, boy?' asked the old man.

There were two of them in the tiny bedroom, on the twenty-third floor of the Ukraina Hotel, slumped in a pair of cheap foam armchairs, so close their knees were almost touching. A bedside lamp threw their dim shadows on to the curtained window – one profile bony, picked bare by time, the other still fleshy, middle-aged.

'Yes,' said the middle-aged man, whose name was Fluke Kelso. 'Yes, I know what Blizhny means.' (*Of course I bloody know,* he felt like saying, *I did teach Soviet history at Oxford for ten bloody years –*)

Blizhny is the Russian word for 'near'. 'Near', in the Kremlin of the forties and fifties, was shorthand for the 'Near

Dacha'. And the Near Dacha was at Kuntsevo, just outside Moscow – double-perimeter fence, three hundred NKVD special troops and eight camouflaged 30-millimetre anti-aircraft guns, all hidden in the birch forest to protect the dacha's solitary, elderly resident.

Kelso waited for the old man to carry on, but Rapava was suddenly preoccupied, trying to light a cigarette from a book of matches. He couldn't manage it. His fingers couldn't grasp the flimsy sticks. He had no fingernails.

'So what did you do?' Kelso leaned across and lit Rapava's cigarette for him, hoping to mask the question with the gesture, trying to keep the excitement out of his voice. On the little table between them, hidden among the empty bottles and the dirty glasses and the ashtray and the crumpled packs of Marlboro, was a miniature cassette recorder which Kelso had put there when he thought Rapava wasn't looking. The old man sucked hard on the cigarette and then contemplated the tip with gratitude. He tossed the matches on to the floor.

'You know about Blizhny?' he said at last, settling back in his chair. 'Then you know what I did.'

Thirty seconds after answering the telephone, young Papu Rapava was knocking on Beria's door.

POLITBURO member Lavrenty Pavlovich Beria, draped in a loose red silk kimono through which his belly sloped like a great white sack of sand, called Rapava a cunt in Mingrelian, and gave him a shove in the chest that sent him stumbling backwards into the corridor. Then he pushed past him and padded off towards the stairs, his sweaty white feet leaving prints of moisture on the parquet flooring.

Through the open door, Rapava could see into the bedroom – the big wooden bed, a heavy brass lampstand in the form of a dragon, the crimson sheets, the white limbs of the girl, sprawled like a sacrifice. Her eyes were wide open, dark and vacant. She made no effort to cover herself. On the bedside table was a jug of water and an array of medicine bottles. A scattering of large white pills had fallen across the pale yellow Aubusson carpet.

He couldn't remember anything else, or exactly how long he had stood there before Beria came panting back up the stairs, all fired up by his conversation with Malenkov, throwing the girl's clothes at her, shouting at her to *get out, get out,* ordering Rapava to bring round the car.

Rapava asked who else he wanted. (He had in mind Nadaraya, the head of the bodyguard, who normally went everywhere with the Boss. And maybe Sarsikov, who at that moment was deep in a vodka stupor, snoring in the guard house at the side of the building.) At this, Beria, who had his back to Rapava and was beginning to shrug off his dressing gown, stopped for a moment, and glanced over his fleshy shoulder – thinking, thinking – you could see his little eyes flickering behind their rimless pince-nez.

'No,' he said at last. 'Just you.'

The car was American – a Packard, twelve cylinders, dark green bodywork, running-board a half-metre wide – a beauty. Rapava backed it out of the garage and reversed it down Vspolnyi Street until he was directly outside the front entrance. He left the engine running to try to get the heater going, jumped out and took up the standard NKVD position beside the rear passenger door: left hand on hip, coat and jacket pulled slightly open, shoulder holster exposed, right hand on the butt of his Makarov pistol, checking the street up and down. Beso Dumbadze, another of the Mingrelian boys, came running round the corner to see what was going on, just as the Boss stepped out of the house and on to the pavement.

'WHAT was he wearing?'

'What the hell do I know what he was wearing, boy?' said the old man, irritably. 'What the hell does it matter what he was wearing?'

ACTUALLY, now he stopped to think of it, the Boss was wearing grey – grey coat, grey suit, grey pullover, no tie – and what with this, and his pince-nez, and his sloping shoulders, and his big, domed head, he looked like nothing so much as an owl – an old, malevolent grey owl. Rapava opened the door and Beria got in the back, and Dumbadze – who was about ten yards away – made a little *what the fuck do I do?* gesture with his hands, to which Rapava gave a shrug – what the fuck did *he* know? He ran round the car to the driver's seat, slid behind the wheel, jammed the gear stick in to first, and they were off.

He had driven the fifteen miles out to Kuntsevo a dozen times before, always at night and always as part of the General Secretary's convoy – and *that* was some performance, boy, I can tell you. Fifteen cars with curtained rear windows, half the Politburo – Beria, Malenkov, Molotov, Bulganin, Khrushchev – plus bodyguards: out of the Kremlin, through the Borovitskiy Gate, down the ramp, accelerating to 75 miles an hour, the militia holding back the traffic at every intersection, two thousand plainclothes NKVD men lining the government route. And you never knew which car the GenSec was in until, at the last minute, just as they turned off the highway into the woods, one of the big ZiLs would pull out and accelerate to the front of the cortège, and the rest of them would all slow down to let the Rightful Heir of Lenin go in first.

But there was nothing like that tonight. The wide road was empty and once they were across the river Rapava was able to let the big Yankee car have its head, the speedo flickering up to nearly 90, while Beria sat in the back as still as a rock. After twelve minutes, the city was behind them. After fifteen, at the end of the highway from Poklonnaya Gora, they slowed for the hidden turning. The tall white strips of the silver birches strobed in the headlights.

How quiet the forest was, how dark, how limitless – like a gently rustling sea. Rapava felt that it might stretch all the way to the Ukraine. A half-mile of track took them to the first perimeter fence where a red-and-white pole lay waist-high across the road. Two NKVD specials in capes and caps carrying sub-machine guns strolled out of the sentry box, saw Beria's stone face, saluted smartly and raised the barrier. The road curved for another hundred yards, past the hunched shadows of big shrubs, and then the Packard's powerful lights picked out the second fence, a fifteen foot high wall with gun-slits. Iron gates were swung open from the inside by unseen hands.

And then the dacha.

Rapava had been expecting something unusual – he wasn't sure what – cars, men, uniforms, the bustle of a crisis. But the two-storey house was in darkness, save for one yellow lantern above the entrance. In this light, a figure waited – the unmistakable plump and dark-haired form of the Deputy Chairman of the Council of Ministers, Georgiy Maksimilanovich Malenkov. And here was an odd thing, boy: he had taken off his shiny new shoes and had them wedged under one fat arm.

Beria was out of the car almost before it had stopped and in a flash he had Malenkov by the elbow and was listening to him, nodding, talking quietly, looking this way and that. Rapava heard him say, 'Moved him? Have you moved him?' And then Beria snapped his fingers in Rapava's direction, and Rapava realised he was being summoned to follow them inside.

Always before on his visits to the dacha he had either waited in the car for the Boss to emerge, or had gone to the guardhouse for a drink and a smoke with the other drivers. You have to understand that *inside* was forbidden territory. Nobody except the GenSec's staff and invited guests ever went *inside*. Now, moving into the hall, Rapava suddenly felt almost suffocated by panic – physically choked, as if someone had their hands around his windpipe.

Malenkov was walking ahead in his stockinged feet and even the Boss was on tiptoe, so Rapava played follow-my-leader and tried not to make a sound. Nobody else was about. The house seemed empty. The three of them crept down a passage, past an upright piano, and into a dining room with chairs for eight. The light was on. The curtains were drawn. There were some papers on the table, and a rack of Dunhill pipes. A wind-up gramophone was in one corner. Above the fireplace was a blown up black and white photograph in a cheap wooden frame: the GenSec as a younger man, sitting in a garden somewhere on a sunny day with Comrade Lenin. At the far end of the room was a door. Malenkov turned to them and put a pudgy finger to his lips, then opened it very slowly.

THE old man closed his eyes and held out his empty glass for a refill. He sighed.

'You know, boy, people criticise Stalin, but you've got to say this for him: he lived like a worker. Not like Beria – *he* thought he was a prince. But Comrade Stalin's room was a plain man's room. You've got to say that for Stalin. He was always one of us.'

CAUGHT in the draught of the opening door, a red candle flickered in the corner beneath a small icon of Lenin. The only other source of light was a shaded reading lamp on a desk. In the centre of the room was a large sofa that had been made up as a bed. A coarse brown army blanket trailed off it on to a tiger-skin rug. On the rug, on his back, breathing heavily and apparently asleep, was a short, fat, elderly, ruddy-faced man in a dirty white vest and long woollen underpants. He had soiled himself. The room was hot and stank of human waste.

Malenkov put his podgy hand to his mouth and stayed close to the door. Beria went quickly over to the rug, unbuttoned his overcoat and fell to his knees. He put his hands on Stalin's forehead and pulled back both eyelids with his thumbs, revealing sightless, bloodshot yolks.

'Josef Vissarionovich,' he said softly, 'it's Lavrenty. Dear comrade, if you can hear me, move your eyes. Comrade?' Then to Malenkov, but all the while looking at Stalin: 'And you say he could have been like this for *twenty hours?*'

Behind his palm, Malenkov made a gagging sound. There were tears on his smooth cheeks.

'Dear comrade, move your eyes ... Your eyes, dear comrade ... Comrade? Ah, fuck it.' Beria pulled his hands away and stood up, wiping his fingers on his coat. 'It's a stroke right enough. He's meat. Where are Starostin and the boys? And Butusova?'

10

Malenkov was blubbing by now and Beria had to stand between him and the body – literally had to block his view to get his attention. He grasped Malenkov by the shoulders and began talking very quietly and very fast to him, as one would to a child – told him to forget Stalin, that Stalin was history, Stalin was meat, that the important thing was what they did next, that they had to stand together. Now: where were the boys? Were they still in the guard room?

Malenkov nodded and wiped his nose on his sleeve.

'All right,' said Beria. 'This is what you do.'

Malenkov was to put on his shoes and go tell the guards that Comrade Stalin was sleeping, that he was drunk and why the fuck had he and Comrade Beria been dragged out of their beds for nothing? He was to tell them not to touch the telephone, and not to call any doctors. ('You listening, Georgiy?') Especially no doctors, because the GenSec thought all doctors were Jewish poisoners – remember? Now, what was the time? Three? All right. At eight – no, better, seven-thirty – Malenkov was to start calling the leadership. He was to say that he and Beria wanted a full Politburo meeting here, at Blizhny, at nine. He was to say they were worried about Josef Vissarionovich's health and that a collective decision on treatment was necessary.

Beria rubbed his hands. 'That should start them shitting themselves. Now let's get him up on the couch. You,' he said to Rapava. 'Get hold of his legs.'

THE old man had been sinking deeper into his chair as he talked, his feet sprawled, his eyes shut, his voice a monotone. Suddenly he let out a long breath and hauled himself upright again. He looked around the hotel bedroom in a panic. 'Need to have a piss, boy. Gotta piss.'

'In there.'

He rose with a drunk's careful dignity. Through the flimsy wall, Kelso heard the sound of his urine drilling into the back of the toilet bowl. Fair enough, he thought. There was a lot to unload. He had been lubricating Rapava's memory for the best part of four hours by now: Baltika beer first, in the Ukraina's lobby bar, then Zubrovka in a café across the street, and finally single-malt Scotch in the cramped intimacy of his room. It was like playing a fish: playing a fish through a river of booze. He noticed the book of matches lying on the floor where Rapava had thrown it and he reached down and picked it up. On the back flap was the name of a bar or a nightclub – ROBOTNIK – and an address near the Dinamo Stadium. The lavatory flushed and Kelso quickly slipped the matches into his pocket, then Rapava reappeared, leaning against the door jamb, buttoning his flies.

'What's the time, boy?'

'Nearly one.'

'Gotta go. They'll think I'm your fucking boyfriend.' Rapava made an obscene gesture with his hand.

Kelso pretended to laugh. Sure, he'd call down for a taxi in a minute. Sure. But let's just finish this bottle first – he reached over for the Scotch and surreptitiously checked that the tape was still running – finish the bottle, comrade, *and finish the story.*

The old man scowled and looked at the floor. The story was finished already. There was nothing more to say. They got Stalin up on to the couch – so, what of it? Malenkov went off to talk to the guards. Rapava drove Beria home. Everyone knows the rest. A day or two later, Stalin was dead. And not long after that, Beria was dead. Malenkov – well, Malenkov hung around for years after his disgrace (Rapava saw him once, in the seventies, shuffling through the Arbat) but now even Malenkov was dead. Nadaraya, Sarsikov, Dumbadze, Starostin, Butusova – dead, dead. The Party was dead. The whole fucking country was dead, come to that.

'But there's more to your story, surely,' said Kelso. 'Please sit down Papu Gerasimovich, and let us finish the bottle.'

He spoke politely and hesitantly, for he sensed that the anaesthetic of alcohol and vanity might be wearing off, and that Rapava, on coming round, might suddenly realise he was talking far too much. He felt another spasm of irritation. Christ, they were always so bloody *difficult*, these old NKVD men – difficult and maybe even still *dangerous*. Kelso was a historian, in his middle forties, thirty years younger than Papu Rapava. But he was out of condition – to be truthful, he had never really been *in* condition – and he wouldn't have fancied his chances if the old man turned rough. Rapava, after all, was a survivor of the Arctic Circle camps. He wouldn't have forgotten how to hurt someone – hurt someone very quickly, guessed Kelso, and probably very badly.

He filled Rapava's glass, topped up his own, and forced himself to keep on talking.

'I mean, here you are, twenty-five years old, in the General Secretary's bedroom. You couldn't get any closer to the centre than that – that was the inner sanctum, that was *sacred*. So what was Beria up to, taking you in there?'

'You deaf, boy? I said. He needed me to move the body.'

'But why you? Why not one of Stalin's regular guards? It was they who'd found him, after all, and alerted Malenkov in the first place. Or why didn't Beria take one of his more senior boys out to Blizhny? Why did he specifically take *you*?'

Rapava was swaying, staring now at the glass of Scotch,

and afterwards Kelso decided that the whole night really turned upon this one thing: that Rapava needed another drink, and he needed it at that precise instant, and he needed these two things in combination more than he needed to leave. He came back and sat down heavily, drained the glass in one, then held it out to be filled again.

'Papu Rapava,' continued Kelso, pouring another three fingers of scotch. 'Nephew of Avksenty Rapava, Beria's oldest crony in the Georgian NKVD. Younger than the others on the staff. A new boy in the city. Maybe a little more naïve than the rest? Am I right? Precisely the sort of eager young fellow the Boss might have looked at and thought: *yes, I could use him, I could use Rapava's boy, he would keep a secret.*'

The silence lengthened and deepened until it was almost tangible, as if someone had come into the room and joined them. Rapava's head began to rock from side to side, then he leaned forward and clasped the back of his scrawny neck with his hands, staring at the worn carpet. His grey hair was cropped close to his skull. An old, puckered scar ran from his crown almost to his temple. It looked as if it had been stitched up by a blind man using string. And those fingers: blackened yellow tips and not a nail on one of them.

'Turn off your machine, boy,' he said, quietly. He nodded towards the table. 'Turn it off. Now take out the tape – that's it – and leave it where I can see it.'

COMRADE Stalin was only a short man – five foot four – but he was heavy. Holy Mother, he was heavy! It was as if he wasn't made of fat and bone, but of some denser stuff. They dragged him across the wooden floor, his head lolling and banging on the polished blocks, and then they had to lever him up, legs first. Rapava noticed – couldn't help noticing, as they were almost in his face – that the second and third toes of the GenSec's left foot were webbed – the Devil's mark – and when the others weren't looking, he crossed himself.

'Now, young comrade,' said Beria, when Malenkov had gone, 'do you like standing on the ground, or would you prefer to be under it?'

At first, Rapava couldn't believe he had heard properly. That was when he knew his life would never be the same again, and that he'd be lucky to survive this night. He whispered, 'I like standing on it, Boss.'

'Good lad.' Beria made a pincer of his thumb and forefinger. 'We need to find a key. About so big. Looks like the sort of key you might use to wind a clock. He keeps it on a brass ring with a piece of string attached. Check his clothes.'

The familiar grey tunic was hanging off the back of a chair. Grey pants were neatly folded over it. Beside them was a pair of high black cavalry boots, their heels built up an inch or so. Rapava's limbs moved jerkily. What kind of dream was this? The Father and Teacher of the Soviet People, the Inspirer and Organiser of the Victory of Communism, the Leader of All Progressive Humanity, with half his iron brain destroyed, lying filthy on the sofa, while the two of them went through his room like a pair of thieves? Nevertheless, he did as he was ordered and started on the tunic while Beria attacked the desk with an old Chekist's skill – pulling out drawers, upending them, scavenging through their contents, sweeping back the detritus and replacing them on their runners.

There was nothing in the tunic and nothing in the trousers, either, apart from a soiled handkerchief, brittle with dried phlegm. By now, Rapava's eyes had grown used to the gloom, and he was better able to see his surroundings. On one wall was a large Chinese print of a tiger. On another – and this was the strangest thing of all – Stalin had stuck up photographs of children. Toddlers, mostly. Not proper prints, but pictures roughly torn out of magazines and newspapers. There must have been a couple of dozen of them.

'Anything?'

'No, Boss.'

'Try the couch.'

They had put Stalin on his back, with his hands folded on his paunch, and you'd have thought the old fellow was merely asleep. His breathing was heavy. He was almost snoring. Close up, he didn't look much like his pictures. His face was mottled red and fleshy, pitted with shallow cratered scars. His moustache and eyebrows were whitish grey. You could see his scalp through his thin hair. Rapava leaned over him – ah! the smell: it was as if he were already rotting – and slid his hand down into the gap between the cushions and the sofa's back. He worked his fingers all the way down, leaning left towards the GenSec's feet then moving right again, up towards the head until, at last, the tip of his forefinger touched something hard and he had to stretch to retrieve it, his arm pressing gently against Stalin's chest.

And then – an awful thing: the most horrible, terrible thing. As he withdrew the key and called in a whisper to the Boss, the GenSec gave a grunt and his eyes jerked open – an animal's yellow eyes, full of rage and fear. Even Beria faltered when he saw them. No other part of the body moved, but a kind of straining growl came from the throat. Hesitantly, Beria came closer and peered down at him, then passed his hand in front of Stalin's eyes. That seemed to give him an idea. He took the key from Rapava and let it dangle at the end of its cord a few inches above Stalin's face. The yellow eyes locked on to it at once, and followed it, never left it, through all the points of the compass. Beria, smiling now, let it circle slowly for at least half a minute, then abruptly snatched it away and caught it in his palm. He closed his fingers around it and offered his clenched fist to Stalin.

Such a sound, boy! More animal than human! It pursued Rapava out of that room and along the passage and down all the years, from that night to this.

THE bottle of Scotch was drained and Kelso was on his knees now before the mini-bar like a priest before his altar. He wondered how his hosts at the historical symposium would feel when they got the bar bill, but that was less important right now than the task of keeping the old man fuelled and talking. He pulled out handfuls of miniatures – vodka, more Scotch, gin, brandy, something German made of cherries – and cradled them across the room to the table. As he sat down and released them a couple of bottles rolled on to the floor but Rapava paid them no heed. He wasn't an old man in the Ukraina any more; he was back in fifty-three – a frightened twenty-five-year-old at the wheel of a dark green Packard, the highway to Moscow shining white in the headlights before him, Lavrenty Beria rocklike in the rear.

THE big car flew along the Kutuzovskiy Prospekt and through the silent sweep of the western suburbs. At three-thirty it crossed the Moskva at the Borodinskiy Bridge and headed at speed towards the Kremlin, entering through the south-western gate on the opposite side to Red Square.

Once they had been waved inside, Beria leaned forward

and gave Rapava directions – left past the Armoury, then sharp right through a narrow entrance into an inner courtyard. There were no windows, just half a dozen small doors. The icy cobbles in the darkness glowed crimson like wet blood. Looking up, Rapava saw they were beneath a giant red neon star.

Beria was quickly through one of the doors and Rapava had to scramble to follow him. A little flagstoned passage took them to a cage-lift that was older than the Revolution. A rattle of iron and the drone of an engine accompanied their slow ascent through two silent, unlit floors. They jolted to a stop and Beria wrenched back the gate. Then he was off again, down the corridor, walking fast, swinging the key on the end of its length of string.

Don't ask me where we went, boy, because I can't tell you. There was a long, carpeted corridor lined with fancy busts on marble pedestals, then an iron spiral staircase which had to be climbed down, and then a huge ballroom, as vast as an ocean liner, with giant mirrors ten yards high, and fancy gilt chairs set around the walls. Finally, not long after the ballroom, came a wide corridor with lime-green, shiny plaster, a floor that smelt of wood-polish and a big, heavy door that Beria unlocked with a key he kept in a bunch on a chain.

Rapava followed him in. The door, on an old imperial pneumatic hinge, closed slowly behind them.

It wasn't much of an office. Eight yards by six. It might have done for some factory director at the arse-end of Vologda or Magnitogorsk – a desk with a couple of telephones, a bit of carpet on the floor, a table and a few chairs, a heavily-curtained window. On the wall was one of those big, pink, roll-up maps of the USSR – this was back in the days when there *was* a USSR – and next to the map was another, smaller door, to which Beria immediately headed. Again, he had a key. The door opened into a kind of walk-in cupboard in which there was a blackened samovar, a bottle of Armenian brandy and some stuff for making herbal teas. There was also a wall-safe, with a sturdy brass front on which was a manufacturer's label – not in Russian Cyrillic but in some western language. The safe wasn't very big – a foot across, if that. Square. Well fashioned. Straight handle, also brass.

Beria noticed Rapava staring at it and told him roughly to clear off back outside.

NEARLY an hour passed.

Standing in the corridor, Rapava tried to keep himself alert, practising drawing his pistol, imagining every little creak of the great building was a footstep, every moan of wind a voice. He tried to picture the GenSec striding down this wide, polished corridor in his cavalry boots, and then he tried to reconcile that image with the ruined figure lying imprisoned in his own rancid flesh out at Blizhny.

And you know something, boy? I cried. I might have cried a bit for myself as well – I can't deny it, I was scared – I was shitless – but really I cried for Comrade Stalin. I cried more over Stalin than I did when my own father died. And that goes for most of the boys I knew.

A distant bell chimed four.

At around half-past, Beria at last emerged. He was carrying a small leather satchel stuffed with something – papers, certainly, but there might have been other objects: Rapava couldn't tell. The contents, presumably, had come from the safe, and the satchel might have come from there, too. Or it might have come from the office. Or it might – Rapava couldn't swear to this, but it was possible – it might have been in Beria's hand right from the moment he got out of the car. At any rate, he had what he wanted, and he was smiling.

Smiling?

Like I say, boy. Yes – smiling. Not a smile of pleasure, mark you. More a kind of –

Rueful?

– That's it, a rueful kind of smile. A would-you-fucking-believe-it? kind of a smile. Like he'd just been beaten at cards.

They went back the way they had come, only this time in the bust-lined passage they ran into a guard. He practically dropped to his knees when he saw the Boss. But Beria just dead-eyed the man and kept on walking – the coolest piece of thievery you ever saw. In the car he said, 'Vspolnyi Street.'

By now it was nearly five, still dark, but the trams had started running and there were people on the streets – babushkas, mostly, who had cleaned the government offices under the Tsar and under Lenin, and who, after tomorrow, would be cleaning them under somebody else. Outside the Lenin Library a vast poster of Stalin, in red, white and black, gazed down upon a line of workers queuing outside the metro station. Beria had the satchel open on his lap. His head was bent. The interior light was on. He was reading something, tapping his fingers with anxiety.

'Is there a shovel in the back?' he asked, suddenly.

Rapava said there was. For snowdrifts.

'And a toolbox?'

'Yes, Boss.' A big one: car jack, wheel wrench, wheel nuts, spare starting handle, spark plugs . . .

Beria grunted and returned his attention to his reading.

*

BACK at the house, the surface of the ground was diamond-hard, set with glittering points of ice, much too hard for the shovel, and Rapava had to hunt around the outbuildings at the bottom of the garden for a pick-axe. He took off his coat and wielded the axe like he used to when he worked his father's patch of Georgian dirt, bringing it down in a great smooth arc over his head, letting the weight and the velocity of the tool do the job, the edge of the blade burying itself in the frozen earth almost to the shaft. He wrestled it back and forth and pulled it free, adjusted his stance, then brought it down again.

He worked in the little cherry orchard by the light of a hurricane lamp suspended from a nearby branch, and he worked at a frantic pace, conscious that in the darkness behind him, invisible on the far side of the light, Beria was sitting on a stone bench watching him. Soon he was sweating so heavily that despite the March cold he had to stop and take off his jacket and roll up his sleeves. A large patch of his shirt was stuck to his back and he had an involuntary memory of other men doing this while he nursed his rifle and watched – other men on a much hotter day, hacking away at the ground in a forest, then lying obediently on their faces in the freshly dug earth. He remembered the smell of moist soil and the hot drowsy silence of the wood and he wondered how cold it would be if Beria made him lie down now.

A voice came out of the darkness. 'Don't make it so wide. It's not a grave. You're making work for yourself.'

After a while, he began alternating between the axe and the shovel, hacking off chunks of earth and jumping into the hole to clear the debris. At first the ground came up to his knees, and then it lapped his waist, and finally it was at his chest – at which point Beria's moon face appeared above him and told him to stop, that he had done well, it was enough. The Boss was actually smiling and held out his hand to pull Rapava from the hole, and Rapava at that moment, as he grasped that soft palm, was filled with such love – such a surge of gratitude and devotion: he would never feel anything like it again.

It was as comrades, in Rapava's memory, that they each took hold of one end of the long metal toolbox and lowered it into the ground. They kicked the earth in after it, stamped it tight, and then Rapava hammered the mound flat with the back of the shovel and scattered dead leaves over the site. By the time they turned to walk across the lawn to the house, the faintest gleams of grey were beginning to infiltrate the eastern sky.

BETWEEN them, Kelso and Rapava had drained the miniatures and had moved on to a kind of home-made pepper vodka, which the old man had produced from a battered tin flask. God alone knew what he had made it from. It could have been shampoo. He sniffed it, sneezed, then winked and poured a brimming, oily glass for Kelso. It was the colour of a pigeon's breast and Kelso felt his stomach lurch.

'And Stalin died,' he said, trying to avoid taking a sip. His words slurred into one another. His jaw was numb.

'And Stalin died.' Rapava shook his head in sorrow. He suddenly leaned forward and clinked glasses. 'To Comrade Stalin!'

'To Comrade Stalin!'

They drank.

AND Stalin died. And everyone went mad with grief. Everyone, that is, except Comrade Beria, who delivered his eulogy to the thousands of hysterical mourners in Red Square like he was reading a railway announcement, and had a good laugh about it afterwards with the boys.

Word of this got around.

Now Beria was a clever man, much cleverer even than you are, boy – he'd have eaten you for breakfast. But clever people all make one mistake. They all think everyone else is stupid. And everyone isn't stupid. They just take a bit more time, that's all.

The Boss thought he was going to be in power for twenty years. He lasted three months.

It was late one morning in June and Rapava was on duty with the usual team – Nadaraya, Sarsikov, Dumbadze – when word came through that there was a special meeting of the Presidium in Malenkov's office in the Kremlin. And because it was at Malenkov's place, the Boss thought nothing of it. Who was fat Malenkov? Fat Malenkov was nothing. He was just a dumb brown bear. The Boss had Malenkov on the end of a rope.

So when he got in to the car to go to the meeting, he wasn't even wearing a tie, just an open-necked shirt and a worn-out old suit. Why should he wear a tie? It was a hot day and Stalin was dead and Moscow was full of girls and he was going to be in power for twenty years.

The cherry orchard at the bottom of the garden had not long finished flowering.

They arrived at Malenkov's building and the Boss went upstairs to see him, while the rest of them sat around in the ante-room by the entrance. And one by one the big guys arrived, all the comrades Beria used to laugh about behind their backs – old 'Stone Arse' Molotov and that fat peasant Khrushchev and the ninny Voroshilov, and finally Marshal Zhukov, the puffed-up peacock, with his boards of tin and ribbon. They all went upstairs and Nadaraya rubbed his hands and said to Rapava: 'Now then, Papu Gerasimovich, why don't you go to the canteen and get us some coffee?'

The day passed and from time to time Nadaraya would wander upstairs to see what was happening, and always he came back with the same message: meeting still in progress. And again: so what? It wasn't unusual for the Presidium to sit for hours. But by eight o'clock, the chief of the bodyguard was starting to look worried and, at ten, with the summer darkness gathering, he told them all to follow him upstairs.

They crashed straight past Malenkov's protesting secretaries and into the big room. It was empty. Sarsikov tried the phones and they were dead. One of the chairs had been tipped back and on the floor around it were some folded scraps of paper, on each of which, in red ink, in Beria's writing, was the single word 'Alarm!'

THEY could have made a fight of it, perhaps, but what would have been the point? The whole thing was an ambush, a Red Army operation. Zhukov had even brought up tanks – stationed twenty T34s at the back of the Boss's house (Rapava heard this later). There were armoured cars inside the Kremlin. It was hopeless. They wouldn't have lasted five minutes.

The boys were split up there and then. Rapava was taken to a military prison in the northern suburbs where they proceeded to beat ten kinds of shit out of him, accused him of procuring little girls, showed him witness statements and photographs of the victims and finally a list of thirty names that Sarsikov (great big swaggering Sarsikov – some tough guy *he* turned out to be) had written down for them on the second day.

Rapava said nothing. The whole thing made him sick.

And then, one night, about ten days after the coup – for a coup was how Rapava would always think of it – he was patched up and given a wash and a clean prison uniform and taken up in handcuffs to the director's office to meet some big shot from the Ministry of State Security. He was a tough-looking, miserable bastard, aged between forty and fifty – said he was a Deputy Minister – and he wanted to talk about Comrade Stalin's private papers.

Rapava was handcuffed to the chair. The guards were sent out of the room. The Deputy Minister sat behind the director's desk. There was a picture of Stalin on the wall behind him.

It seems, said the Deputy Minister – after looking at Rapava for a while – that Comrade Stalin, in recent years, to assist him in his mighty tasks, had got into the habit of making notes. Sometimes these notes were confided to ordinary sheets of writing paper and sometimes to an exercise book with a black oilskin cover. The existence of these notes was known only to certain members of the Presidium, and to Comrade Poskrebyshev, Comrade Stalin's long-standing secretary, whom the traitor Beria recently had falsely imprisoned on fraudulent charges. All witnesses agree that Comrade Stalin kept these papers in a personal safe in his private office, to which he alone had the key.

The Deputy Minister leaned forwards. His dark eyes searched Rapava's face.

Following Comrade Stalin's tragic death, attempts were made to locate this key. It could not be found. It was therefore agreed by the Presidium to have this safe broken into, in the presence of them all, to see if Comrade Stalin had left behind material that might be of historical value, or which might assist the Central Committee in its stupendous responsibility of appointing Comrade Stalin's successor.

The safe was duly broken open, under the supervision of the Presidium, and found to be empty, apart from a few minor items, such as Comrade Stalin's party card.

'And now,' said the Deputy Minister, getting slowly to his feet, 'we come to the crux of the matter.'

He walked around and sat on the edge of the desk directly in front of Rapava. Oh, he was a big bastard, boy, a fleshy tank.

We know, he said, from Comrade Malenkov that in the early hours of the second of March, you went to the Kuntsevo dacha in the company of the traitor, Beria, and that you were both left alone with Comrade Stalin for several minutes. Was anything removed from the room?

No, comrade.

Nothing at all?

No, comrade.

And where did you go when you left Kuntsevo?

I drove Comrade Beria back to his house, comrade.

Directly back to his house?

Yes, comrade.

You are lying.

No, comrade.

You are lying. We have a witness who saw you both inside the Kremlin shortly before dawn. A sentry who met you in a corridor.

Yes, comrade. I remember now. Comrade Beria said he needed to collect something from his office –

Something from Comrade Stalin's office!

No, comrade.

You are lying! You are a traitor! You and the English spy Beria broke into Stalin's office and stole his papers! Where are those papers?

No, comrade –

Traitor! Thief! Spy!

Each word accompanied by a punch in the face.

And so on.

I'LL tell you something, boy. Nobody knows the full truth of what happened to the Boss, even now – even after Gorbachev and Yeltsin have sold off our whole fucking birthright to the capitalists and let the CIA go picnicking in our files. The papers on the Boss are still closed. They smuggled him out of the Kremlin on the floor of a car, rolled up in a carpet, and some say Zhukov shot him that very night. Others say they shot him the following week. Most say they kept him alive for five months – *five months!* – sweated him in a bunker underneath the Moscow Military District – and shot him after a secret trial.

Either way, they shot him. He was dead by Christmas Day.

And this is what they did to me.

Rapava held up his mutilated fingers and wiggled them. Then he clumsily unbuttoned his shirt, pulled it from the waistband of his pants, and twisted his scrawny torso to show his back. His vertebrae were criss-crossed with shiny roughened panes of scar-tissue – translucent windows on to the flesh beneath. His stomach and chest were whorls of blue-black tattoos.

Kelso didn't speak. Rapava sat back leaving his shirt unbuttoned. His scars and his tattoos were the medals of his lifetime. He was proud to wear them.

NOT a word, boy. You listening? They did not get. One. Single. Word.

Throughout it all, he didn't know if the Boss was still alive, or if the Boss was talking. But it didn't matter: Papu Gerasimovich Rapava, at least, would hold his silence.

Why? Was it loyalty? A bit, perhaps – the memory of that reprieving hand. But he wasn't such a young fool that he didn't also realise that silence was his only hope. How long do you think they'd have let him live if he'd led them to that place? It was his own death warrant he'd buried under that tree. So, softly, softly: not a word.

He lay shivering on the floor of his unheated cell as the winter came and dreamed of cherry trees, the leaves dying and falling now, the branches dark against the sky, the howling of the wolves.

And then, around Christmas, like bored children, they suddenly seemed to lose interest in the whole business. The beating went on for a while – by now it was a matter of honour on both sides, you must understand – but the questions stopped, and finally, after one prolonged and imaginative session, the beating stopped as well. The Deputy Minister never came again and Rapava guessed that Beria must be dead. He also guessed that someone had decided that Stalin's papers, if they did exist, were better left unread.

Rapava expected to get his seven grams of lead at any moment. It never occurred to him that he wouldn't, not after Beria had been liquidated. So of his journey, in a snowstorm, to the Red Army building on Kommissariat Street, and of the makeshift courtroom, with its high, barred windows and its troika of judges, he remembered nothing. He blanked his mind with snow. He watched it through the window, advancing in waves up the Moskva and along the embankment, smothering the afternoon lights on the opposite side of the river – high white columns of snow on a death march from the east. Voices droned around him. Later, when it was dark and he was being taken outside, he assumed to be shot, he asked if he could stop for a minute on the steps and bury his hands in the drifts. A guard asked why, and Rapava said: 'To feel snow between my fingers one last time, comrade.'

They laughed a lot at that. But when they found out he was serious they laughed a whole lot more. 'If there's one thing you'll never go hungry for, Georgian,' they told him, as they pushed him into the back of the van, 'it's snow.' That was how he learned he had been sentenced to fifteen years' hard labour in the Kolyma territory.

KHRUSHCHEV amnestied a whole bunch of Gulag prisoners in fifty-six, but nobody amnestied Papu Rapava. Papu Rapava was forgotten. Papu Rapava alternately rotted and froze in the forests of Siberia for the next decade and a half – rotted in the short summer, when each man worked in his own private fever-cloud of mosquitoes, and froze in the long winter when the ice made rock of the swamps.

They say that people who survive the camps all look alike because, once a man's skeleton has been exposed, it doesn't matter how well-padded his flesh subsequently becomes, or how carefully he dresses – the bones will always poke through. Kelso had interviewed enough Gulag survivors in his time to recognise the camp skeleton in Rapava's face even now, as he talked, in the sockets of his eyes and in the crack of his jaw. He could see it in the hinges of his wrists and ankles, and the flat blade of his sternum.

He wasn't amnestied, Rapava was saying, because he killed

a man, a Chechen, who tried to sodomise him – gutted him with a shank he'd made from a piece of saw.

And what happened to your head? said Kelso.

Rapava fingered the scar. He couldn't remember. Sometimes, when it was especially cold, the scar ached and gave him dreams.

What kind of dreams?

Rapava showed the dark glint of his mouth. He wouldn't say.

Fifteen years . . .

They returned him to Moscow in the summer of sixty-nine, on the day the Yankees put a man on the moon. Rapava left the ex-prisoners' hostel and wandered round the hot and crowded streets and couldn't make sense of anything. Where was Stalin? That was what amazed him. Where were the statues and the pictures? Where was the respect? The boys all looked like girls and the girls all looked like whores. Clearly, the country was already halfway in the shit. But still – you have to say – at least in those days there were jobs for everyone, even for old *zeki* like him. They sent him to the engine sheds at the Leningrad Station, to work as a labourer. He was only forty-one and as strong as a bear. Everything he had in the world was in a cardboard suitcase.

Did he ever marry?

Rapava shrugged. Sure, he married. That was the way you got an apartment. He married and got himself fixed up with a place.

And what happened? Where was she?

She died. It was a decent block in those days, boy, before the drugs and the crime.

Where was his place?

Fucking criminals . . .

And children?

A son. He died as well. In Afghanistan. And a daughter.

His daughter was dead?

No. She was a whore.

And Stalin's papers?

Drunk as he was, there was no way Kelso could make *that* question casual and the old man shot him a crafty look; a peasant's look.

Rapava said softly, 'Go on, boy. Yes? And Stalin's papers? What about Stalin's papers?'

Kelso hesitated.

'Only that if they still existed – if there was a chance – a possibility –'

'You'd want to see them?'

'Of course.'

Rapava laughed.

'And why should I help you, boy? Fifteen years in Kolyma, and for what? To help you spin more lies? For love?'

'No. Not for love. For history.'

'For history? Do me a favour, boy!'

'All right – for money, then.'

'What?'

'For money. A share in the profits. A lot of money.'

The peasant Rapava stroked the side of his nose.

'How much money?'

'A lot. If this is true. If we could find them. Believe me: a lot of money.'

THE momentary silence was broken by the sound of voices in the corridor, voices talking in English, and Kelso guessed who this would be: his fellow historians – Adelman, Duberstein and the rest – coming back late from dinner, wondering where he'd got to. It suddenly seemed overwhelmingly important to him that no one else – least of all his colleagues – should know anything at all about Papu Rapava.

Someone tapped softly on the door and he held up a warning hand to the old man. Very quietly he reached over and turned off the bedside lamp.

They sat together and listened to the whispers, magnified by the darkness but still muffled and indistinct. There was another knock, and then a splutter of laughter, hushed by the others. Maybe they had seen the light go out. Perhaps they thought he was with a woman – such was his reputation.

After a few more seconds, the voices faded and the corridor was silent again. Kelso turned on the light. He smiled and patted his heart. The old man's face was a mask, but then he smiled and began to sing – he had a quavering, unexpectedly melodious voice –

> *Kolyma, Kolyma,*
> *What a wonderful place!*
> *Twelve months of winter*
> *Summer all the rest . . .*

AFTER his release, he was this and no more: Papu Rapava, railway worker, who had done a spell in the camps, and if anyone wanted to take it further – well? yes? come on, then, comrade! – he was always ready with his fists or an iron spike.

Two men watched him from the start. Antipin, who was a foreman in the Lenin No. 1 shed, and a cripple in the downstairs flat called Senka. And they were as pretty a pair of canaries as you could ever hope to meet. You could practically hear them singing to the KGB before you were out of the room. The others came and went – the men on foot, the men in parked cars, the men asking 'routine questions, comrade' – but Antipin and Senka were the faithful watchers, though they never got a thing, neither of them. Rapava had buried his past in a hole far deeper than the one he'd dug for Beria.

Senka died five years ago. He never knew what became of Antipin. The Lenin No. 1 shed was now the property of a private collective, importing French wine.

Stalin's papers, boy? Who gives a shit? He wasn't afraid of anything any more.

A lot of money, you say? Well, well –

He leaned over and spat into the ashtray, then seemed to fall asleep. After a while, he muttered, My lad died. Did I tell you that?

Yes.

He died in a night ambush on the road to Mazar-i-Sharif. One of the last to be sent. Killed by stone-age devils with blackened faces and Yankee missiles. Could anyone imagine Stalin letting the country be humiliated by such savages? Think of it! He'd have crushed them into dust and scattered the powder in Siberia! After the lad was gone, Rapava took to walking. Great long hikes that could last a day and a night. He criss-crossed the city, from Perovo to the lakes, from Bittsevskiy Park to the Television Tower. And on one of these walks – it must have been six or seven years ago, around the time of the coup – he found himself walking into one of his own dreams. Couldn't figure it out at first. Then he realised he was on Vspolnyi Street. He got out of there fast. His lad was a radio man in a tank unit. Liked fiddling with radios. No fighter.

And the house? said Kelso. Was the house still standing?

He was nineteen.

And the house? What had happened to the house?

Rapava's head drooped.

The *house,* comrade –

There was a red sickle moon, and a single red star. And the place was guarded by devils with blackened faces –

KELSO could get no more sense out of him after that. The old man's eyelids fluttered and closed. His mouth slackened. Yellow saliva leaked across his cheek.

Kelso watched him for a minute or two, feeling the pressure build in his stomach, then rose suddenly from his chair and moved as quickly as he could to the lavatory, where he was violently and copiously sick. He rested his hot forehead against the cold enamel bowl and licked his lips. His tongue felt huge to him, and bitter, like a swollen piece of black fruit. There was something stuck in his throat. He tried to clear it by coughing but that didn't work so he tried swallowing and was promptly sick again. When he pulled his head back, the bathroom fixtures seemed to have detached themselves from their moorings and to be revolving around him in a slow tribal dance. A line of silver mucus extended in a shimmering arc from his nose to the toilet seat.

Endure, he told himself. This, too, will pass.

He clutched again at the cool white bowl, a drowning man, as the horizon tilted and the room darkened, slid –

A RUSTLE in the blackness of his dreams. A pair of yellow eyes.

'Who are you,' said Stalin, 'to steal my private papers?'

He sprang from his couch like a wolf.

KELSO jerked awake and cracked his head on the protruding lip of the bath. He groaned and rolled on to his back, dabbing at his skull for signs of blood. He was sure he felt some tacky liquid, but when he brought his fingers up close to his eyes and squinted at them they were clean.

As always, even now, even as he lay sprawled on the floor of a Moscow bathroom, there was a part of him that remained mercilessly sober, like the wounded captain on the bridge of a stricken ship, calling calmly through the smoke of battle for damage assessments. This was the part of him which concluded that, bad as he felt, he had – amazingly – sometimes felt worse. And this was the part of him that also heard, beyond the dusty thump of his pulse, the creak of a footstep and the click of a door being quietly closed.

Kelso set his jaw and rose, by force of will, through all the stages of human evolution – from the slime of the floor, to his hands and knees, to a kind of shuffling, simian crouch – and propelled himself into the empty bedroom. Grey light seeped through thin orange curtains and lit the detritus of the night. The sour reek of spilled booze and stale smoke made his stomach coil. Still – and there was heroism as well as desperation in the effort – he headed for the door.

'Papu Gerasimovich! Wait!'

The corridor was dim and deserted. From the end of it, around the corner, came the ping of an arriving elevator. Wincing, Kelso loped towards it, arriving just in time to see the doors close. He tried to prise them open with his fingers, shouting into the crevice for Rapava to come back. He punched the call button with the heel of his hand a few times, but nothing happened so he took the stairs. He got as far as the twenty-first floor before he acknowledged he was beaten. He stopped on the landing and summoned the express elevator, and stood there waiting for it, leaning against the wall, breathless, nauseous, with a knife behind his eyes. The car was a long time coming and when, at last, it did arrive, it promptly took him back up the two floors he had just run down. The doors slid open mockingly on to the empty passage.

By the time Kelso reached ground level, his ears popping from the speed of his descent, Rapava was gone. In the marble vault of the Ukraina's reception there was nobody about except for a babushka, hoovering ash from the red carpet, and a platinum-blonde hooker with a fake sable curled over her shoulders, arguing with a security man. As he made for the entrance he was aware that all three had stopped what they were doing and were staring at him. He put his hand to his forehead. He was dripping with sweat.

It was cold outside and barely light. A sharp October morning. A damp chill rising off the river. Yet already the rush-hour traffic was beginning to build along the Kutuzovskiy Prospekt, backing up from the Kalininskiy Bridge. He walked on for a while until he came to the main road, and there he stood for a minute or two, shivering in his shirtsleeves. There was no sign of Rapava. Along the sidewalk to his right, an old grey dog, big and half-starved, went slouching past the heavy buildings, heading east, towards the waking city.

Part One

Moscow

'To choose one's victims, to prepare one's plans minutely,
to slake an implacable vengeance, and then to go to bed . . .
there is nothing sweeter in the world.'

J. V. Stalin
in conversation with Kamenev and Dzerzhinsky

Chapter One

OLGA KOMAROVA OF the Russian Archive Service, Rosarkhiv, wielding a collapsible pink umbrella, prodded and shooed her distinguished charges across the Ukraina's lobby towards the revolving door. It was an old door, of heavy wood and glass, too narrow to cope with more than one body at a time, so the scholars formed a line in the dim light, like parachutists over a target zone, and as they passed her, Olga touched each one lightly on the shoulder with her umbrella, counting them off one by one as they were propelled into the freezing Moscow air.

Franklin Adelman of Yale went first, as befitted his age and status, then Moldenhauer of the Bundesarchiv in Koblenz, with his absurd double-doctorate – Doctor Doctor Karl-bloody-Moldenhauer – then the neo-Marxists, Enrico Banfi of Milan and Eric Chambers of the LSE, then the great cold warrior, Phil Duberstein of NYU, then Ivo Godelier of the Ecole Normale Superieure, followed by glum Dave Richards of St Antony's, Oxford – another Sovietologist whose world was rubble – then Velma Byrd of the US National Archive, then Alastair Findlay of Edinburgh's Department of War Studies, who still thought the sun shone out of Comrade Stalin's arse, then Arthur Saunders of Stanford, and finally – the man whose lateness had kept them waiting in the lobby for an extra five minutes – Dr C. R. A. Kelso, commonly known as Fluke.

The door banged hard against his heels. Outside the weather had worsened. It was trying to snow. Tiny flakes, as hard as grit, came whipping across the wide grey concourse and spattered his face and hair. At the bottom of the flight of steps, shuddering in a cloud of its own white fumes, was a dilapidated bus, waiting to take them to the symposium. Kelso stopped to light a cigarette.

'Jesus, Fluke,' called Adelman, cheerfully, 'you look just *awful*.'

Kelso raised a fragile hand in acknowledgement. He could see a huddle of taxi drivers in quilted jackets stamping their feet against the cold. Workmen were struggling to lift a roll of tin off the back of a lorry. One Korean businessman in a fur hat was photographing a group of twenty others, similarly dressed. But of Papu Rapava: no sign.

'Doctor Kelso, please, we are waiting again.' The umbrella wagged at him in reproof. He transferred the cigarette to the corner of his mouth, hitched his bag up on to his shoulder and moved towards the bus.

'A battered Byron' was how one Sunday newspaper had described him when he had resigned his Oxford lectureship and moved to New York, and the description wasn't a bad one – curly black hair too long and thick for neatness, a moist, expressive mouth, pale cheeks and the glow of a certain reputation – if Byron hadn't died on Missolonghi but had spent the next ten years drinking whisky, smoking, staying indoors and resolutely avoiding all exercise, he, too, might have come to look a little like Fluke Kelso.

He was wearing what he always wore: a faded dark blue shirt of heavy cotton with the top button undone, a loosely knotted and vaguely stained dark tie, a black corduroy suit with a black leather belt over which his stomach bulged slightly, red cotton handkerchief in his breast pocket, scuffed boots of brown suede, an old blue raincoat. This was Kelso's uniform, unvaried for twenty years.

'Boy,' Rapava had called him, and the word was both absurd for a middle-aged man and yet oddly accurate. *Boy*.

The heater was going full blast. Nobody was saying much. He sat on his own near the back of the bus and rubbed at the wet glass as they jolted up the slip-road to join the traffic on the bridge. Across the aisle, Saunders made an ostentatious display of batting Kelso's smoke away. Beneath them, in the filthy waters of the Moskva, a dredger with a crane mounted on its aft deck beat sluggishly upstream.

He nearly hadn't come to Russia. That was the joke of it. He knew well enough what it would be like: the bad food, the stale gossip, the sheer bloody tedium of academic life – of more and more being said about less and less – that was one reason why he had chucked in Oxford and gone to live in New York. But somehow the books he was supposed to write had not quite materialised. And besides, he never could resist the lure of Moscow. Even now, sitting on a stale bus in the Wednesday rush-hour, he could feel the charge of history beyond the muddy glass: in the dark and renamed streets, the vast apartment blocks, the toppled statues. It was stronger here than anywhere he knew; stronger even than in Berlin. That was what always drew him back to Moscow – the way history hung in the air between the blackened buildings like sulphur after a lightning-strike.

'*You think you know it all about Comrade Stalin, don't you boy? Well, let me tell you: you don't know fuck.*'

Kelso had already delivered his short paper, on Stalin and the archives, at the end of the previous day: delivered it in his trademark style – without notes, with one hand in his pocket, extempore, provocative. His Russian hosts had looked gratifyingly shifty. A couple of people had even walked out. So, all in all, a triumph.

Afterwards, finding himself predictably alone, he had decided to walk back to the Ukraina. It was a long walk, and it was getting dark, but he needed the air. And at some point – he couldn't remember where: maybe it was in one of the back streets behind the Institute, or maybe it was later, along the Noviy Arbat – but at some point he had realised he was being followed. It was nothing tangible, just a fleeting impression of something seen too often – the flash of a coat, perhaps, or the shape of a head – but Kelso had been in Moscow often enough in the bad old days to know that you were seldom wrong about these things. You always knew if a film was out of synch, however fractionally; you always knew if someone fancied you, however improbably; and you always knew when someone was on your tail.

He had just stepped into his hotel room and was contemplating some primary research in the mini-bar when the front desk had called up to say there was a man in the lobby who wanted to see him. Who? He wouldn't give his name, sir. But he was most insistent and he wouldn't leave. So Kelso had gone down, reluctantly, and found Papu Rapava sitting on one of the Ukraina's imitation leather sofas, staring straight ahead, in his papery blue suit, his wrists and ankles sticking out as thin as broomsticks.

'*You think you know it all about Comrade Stalin, don't you, boy . . .?*' Those had been his opening words.

And that was the moment that Kelso had realised where he had first seen the old man: at the symposium, in the front row of the public seats, listening intently to the simultaneous translation over his headphones, muttering in violent disagreement at any hostile mention of J. V. Stalin.

Who are you? thought Kelso, staring out of the grimy window. Fantasist? Con man? The answer to a prayer?

*

THE symposium was only scheduled to last one more day – for which relief, in Kelso's view, much thanks. It was being held in the Institute of Marxism–Leninism, an orthodox temple of grey concrete, consecrated in the Brezhnev years, with Marx, Engels and Lenin in gigantic bas-relief above the pillared entrance. The ground floor had been leased to a private bank, since gone bust, which added to the air of dereliction.

On the opposite side of the street, watched by a couple of bored-looking militia men, a small demonstration was in progress – maybe a hundred people, mostly elderly, but with a few youths in black berets and leather jackets. It was the usual mixture of fanatics and grudge-holders – Marxists, nationalists, anti-semites. Crimson flags bearing the hammer and sickle hung beside black flags embroidered with the tsarist eagle. One old lady carried a picture of Stalin; another sold cassettes of SS marching songs. An elderly man with an umbrella held over him was addressing the crowd through a bullhorn, his voice a distorted, metallic rant. Stewards were handing out a free newspaper called *Aurora*.

'Take no notice,' instructed Olga Komarova, standing up beside the driver. She tapped the side of her head. 'These are crazy people. Red fascists.'

'What's he saying?' demanded Duberstein, who was considered a world authority on Soviet communism even though he had never quite got round to learning Russian.

'He's talking about how the Hoover Institution tried to buy the Party archive for five million bucks,' said Adelman. 'He says we're trying to steal their history.'

Duberstein sniggered. 'Who'd want to steal *their* goddamned history?' He tapped on the window with his signet ring. 'Say, isn't that a TV crew?'

The sight of a camera caused a predictable, wistful stir among the academics.

'I believe so . . . '

'How very flattering . . .'

'What's the name,' said Adelman, 'of the fellow who runs *Aurora*? Is it still the same one?' He twisted round in his seat and called up the aisle. 'Fluke – you should know. What's his name? Old KGB –'

'Mamantov,' said Kelso. The driver braked hard and he had to swallow to stop himself being sick. 'Vladimir Mamantov.'

'Crazy people,' repeated Olga, bracing herself as they came to a stop. 'I apologise on behalf of Rosarkhiv. They are not representative. Follow me, please. Ignore them.'

They filed off the bus and a television cameraman filmed them as they trudged across the asphalt forecourt, past a couple of drooping, silvery fir trees, pursued by jeers.

Fluke Kelso moved delicately at the rear of the column, nursing his hangover, holding his head at a careful angle, as if he was balancing a pitcher of water. A pimply youth in wire spectacles thrust a copy of *Aurora* at him and Kelso got a quick glimpse of the front page – a cartoon caricature of Zionist conspirators and a weird cabalistic symbol that was something between a swastika and a red cross – before he rammed it back in the young man's chest. The demonstrators jeered.

A thermometer on the wall outside the entrance read minus one. The old nameplate had been taken down and a new one had been screwed in its place, but it didn't quite fit so you could tell that the building had been renamed. It now proclaimed itself 'The Russian Centre for the Preservation and Study of Documents Relating to Modern History'.

Once again, Kelso lingered behind after the others had gone in, squinting at the hate-filled faces across the street. There were a lot of old men of a similar age, pinched and raw-cheeked in the cold, but Rapava wasn't among them. He turned away and moved inside, into the shadowy lobby, where he gave his coat and bag to the cloakroom attendant, before passing beneath the familiar statue of Lenin towards the lecture hall.

Another day began.

There were ninety-one delegates at the symposium and almost all of them seemed to be crowded into the small ante-room where coffee was being served. He collected his cup and lit another cigarette.

'Who's up first?' said a voice behind him. It was Adelman.

'Askenov, I think. On the microfilm project.'

Adelman groaned. He was a Bostonian, in his seventies, at that twilight stage in his career when most of life seemed to be spent in airplanes or foreign hotels: symposia, conferences, honorary degrees – Duberstein maintained that Adelman had given up pursuing history in favour of collecting air miles. But Kelso didn't begrudge him his honours. He was good. And brave. It had taken courage to write his kind of books, thirty years ago, on the Famine and the Terror, when every other useful idiot in academia was screeching for détente.

'Listen, Frank,' he said, 'I'm sorry about dinner.'

'Forget it. You got a better offer?'

'Kind of.'

The refreshment room was at the back of the Institute and looked out on to an inner courtyard, in the centre of which, dumped on their sides amid the weeds, were a pair of statues, of Marx and Engels – a couple of Victorian gentlemen taking time off from the long march of history for a morning doze.

'They don't mind taking down those two,' said Adelman. 'That's easy. They're foreigners. And one of them's a Jew. It's when they take down Lenin – that's when you'll know the place has really changed.'

Kelso took another sip of coffee. 'A man came to see me last night.'

'A man? I'm disappointed.'

'Could I ask your advice, Frank?'

Adelman shrugged. 'Go ahead.'

'In private?'

ADELMAN stroked his chin. 'You got his name, this guy?'

'Of course I got his name.'

'His real name?'

'How do I know if it's his real name?'

'His address, then? You got his address?'

'No, Frank, I didn't get his address. But he did leave these.'

Adelman took off his glasses and peered closely at the book of matches. 'It's a set-up,' he said at last, handing them back. 'I wouldn't touch it. Whoever heard of a bar called "Robotnik", anyhow? "Worker"? Sounds phoney to me.'

'But if it was a set-up,' said Kelso, weighing the match-book in his palm, 'why would he run away?'

'Obviously, because he doesn't want it to *look* like a set-up. He wants you to have to work at it – track him down, persuade him to help you. That's the psychology of a clever fraud – the victims wind up doing so much chasing around, they start *wanting* to believe it's true. Remember the Hitler diaries. Either that or he's a lunatic.'

'He was very convincing.'

'Lunatics often are. Or it's a practical joke. Someone wants to make you look a fool. Have you thought of that? You're not exactly the most popular kid in the school.'

Kelso glanced up the corridor towards the lecture hall. It wasn't a bad theory. There were plenty in there who didn't like him. He had appeared on too many television programmes, knocked out too many newspaper columns, reviewed too many of their useless books. Saunders was loitering at the corner, pretending to talk to Moldenhauer, both men obviously straining to overhear what he was saying to Adelman. (Saunders had complained bitterly after Kelso's paper about his 'subjectivity': 'Why was he even invited, that's what one wants to know. One had been given to understand this was a symposium for *serious* scholars . . .')

'They don't have the wit,' he said. He gave them a wave and was pleased to see them duck out of sight. 'Or the imagination.'

'You sure have a genius for making enemies.'

'Ah well. You know what they say: more enemies, more honour.'

Adelman smiled and opened his mouth to say something, but then seemed to think better of it. 'How's Margaret, dare one ask?'

'Who? Oh, you mean *poor* Margaret? She's fine, thank you. Fine and feisty. According to the lawyers.'

'And the boys?'

'Entering the springtime of their adolescence.'

'And the book? That's been a while. How much of this new book have you actually written?'

'I'm writing it.'

'Two hundred pages? A hundred?'

'What is this, Frank?'

'How many pages?'

'I don't know.' Kelso licked his dry lips. Almost unbelievably, he realised he could do with a drink. 'A hundred maybe.' He had a vision of a blank grey screen, a cursor flashing weakly, like a pulse on a life-support machine begging to be switched off. He hadn't written a word. 'Listen, Frank, there *could* be something in this, couldn't there? Stalin was a hoarder, don't forget. Didn't Khrushchev find some letter in a secret compartment in the old man's desk after he died?' He rubbed his aching head. 'That letter from Lenin, complaining about Stalin's treatment of his wife? And then there was that list of the Politburo, with crosses against everyone he was planning to purge. And his library – remember his library? He made notes in almost every book.'

'So what are you saying?'

'I'm just saying it's possible, that's all. That Stalin wasn't Hitler. That he wrote things down.'

'*Quod volimus credimus libenter*,' intoned Adelman. 'Which means –'

'I know what it means –'

' – which *means*, my dear Fluke, we always believe what we want to believe.' Adelman patted Kelso's arm. 'You don't want to hear this, do you? I'm sorry. I'll lie if you prefer it. I'll tell you he's the one guy in a million with a story like this who turns out not to be full of shit. I'll tell you he's going to lead you to Stalin's unpublished memoirs, that you'll rewrite history, millions of dollars will be yours, women will lie at your feet, Duberstein and Saunders will form a choir to sing your praises in the middle of Harvard Yard . . .'

'All right, Frank.' Kelso leaned the back of his head against the wall. 'You've made your point. I don't know. It's just – Maybe you had to be there with him –' He pressed on, reluctant to admit defeat. 'It's just it rings a bell with me somewhere. Does it ring a bell with you?'

'Oh sure. It rings a bell, okay. An alarm bell.' Adelman pulled out an old pocket watch. 'We ought to be getting back. D'you mind? Olga will be frantic.' He put his arm round Kelso's shoulders and led him down the corridor. 'In any case, there's nothing you can do. We're flying back to New York tomorrow. Let's talk when we get back. See if there's anything for you in the faculty. You were a great teacher.'

'I was a lousy teacher.'

'You were a great teacher, until you were lured from the path of scholarship and rectitude by the cheap sirens of journalism and publicity. Hello, Olga.'

'So here you are! The session is almost starting. Oh, Doctor Kelso – now this is not so good – no smoking, thank you.' She leaned over and removed the cigarette from his lips. She had a shiny face with plucked eyebrows and a very fine moustache, bleached white. She dropped the stub into the dregs of his coffee and took away his cup.

'Olga, Olga, why so bright?' groaned Kelso, putting his hand to his brow. The lecture hall exuded a tungsten glare.

'Television,' said Olga, with pride. 'They are making a programme of us.'

'Local?' Adelman was straightening his bow tie. 'Network?'

'Satellite, professor. *International.*'

'Say, now, where are our seats?' whispered Adelman, shielding his eyes from the lights.

'Doctor Kelso? Any chance of a word, sir?' An American accent. Kelso turned to find a large young man he vaguely recognised.

'I'm sorry?'

'R. J. O'Brian,' said the young man, holding out his hand. 'Moscow correspondent, Satellite News System. We're making a special report on the controversy –'

'I don't think so,' said Kelso. 'But Professor Adelman, here – I'm sure he'd be delighted –'

At the prospect of a television interview, Adelman seemed physically to swell in size, like an inflating doll. 'Well, as long as it's not in any *official* capacity . . .'

O'Brian ignored him. 'You sure I can't tempt you?' he said to Kelso. 'Nothing you want to say to the world? I read your book on the fall of communism. When was that? Three years ago?'

'Four,' said Kelso.

'Actually, I believe it was five,' said Adelman.

Actually, thought Kelso, it was nearer six: dear God, where were all the years going? 'No,' he said, 'thanks all the same, but I'm keeping off television these days.' He looked at Adelman. 'It's a cheap siren, apparently.'

'Later, please,' hissed Olga. 'Interviews are later. The director is talking. Please.' Kelso felt her umbrella in his back again as she steered him into the hall. 'Please. *Please –*'

BY the time the Russian delegates were added in, plus a few diplomatic observers, the press, and maybe fifty members of the public, the hall was impressively full. Kelso sank heavily into his place in the second row. Up on the platform, Professor Valentin Askenov of the Russian State Archives had launched into a long explanation of the microfilming of the Party records. O'Brian's cameraman walked backwards down the central aisle, filming the audience. The sharp amplification of Askenov's sonorous voice seemed to pierce some painful chamber of Kelso's inner ear. Already, a kind of metallic, neon torpor had descended over the hall. The day stretched ahead. He covered his face with his hands.

Twenty-five million sheets . . . recited Askenov, *twenty-five thousand reels of microfilm . . . seven million dollars . . .*

Kelso slid his hands down his cheeks until his fingers converged and covered his mouth. *Frauds!* he wanted to shout. *Liars!* Why were they all just sitting here? They knew as well as he did that nine-tenths of the best material was still locked up, and to see most of the rest required a bribe. He'd heard that the going rate for a captured Nazi file was $1,000 and a bottle of Scotch.

He whispered to Adelman, 'I'm getting out of here.'

'You can't.'

'Why not?'

'It's discourteous. Just sit there, for pete's sake, and pretend to be interested like everyone else.' Adelman said all this out of the side of his mouth, without taking his eyes off the platform. Kelso stuck it for another half minute.

'Tell them I'm ill.'

'I shall not.'

'Let me by, Frank. I'm going to be sick.'

'Jesus . . .'

Adelman swung his legs to one side and pressed himself back in his seat. Hunched in a vain effort to make himself less conspicuous, Kelso stumbled over the feet of his colleagues, kicking in the process the elegant black shin of Ms Velma Byrd.

'Aw, fuck, Kelso,' said Velma.

Professor Askenov looked up from his notes and paused in mid-drone. Kelso was conscious of an amplified, humming silence, and of a kind of collective movement in the audience, as if some great beast had turned in its field to watch his progress. This seemed to last a long time, for at least as long as it took him to walk to the back of the hall. Not until he had passed beneath the marble gaze of Lenin and into the deserted corridor did the droning begin again.

KELSO sat behind the bolted door of a lavatory cubicle on the ground floor of the former Institute of Marxism–Leninism and opened his canvas bag. Here were the tools of his trade: a yellow legal pad, pencils, an eraser, a small Swiss army knife, a welcome pack from the organisers of the symposium, a dictionary, a street map of Moscow, his cassette recorder, and a Filofax that was a palimpsest of ancient numbers, lost contacts, old girlfriends, former lives.

There *was* something about the old man's story that was familiar to him, but he couldn't remember what it was. He picked up the cassette recorder, pressed REWIND, let it spool back for a while, then pressed PLAY. He held it to his ear and listened to the tinny ghost of Rapava's voice.

'. . . *Comrade Stalin's room was a plain man's room. You've got to say that for Stalin. He was always one of us . . .* '

REWIND. PLAY.

'. . . *and here was an odd thing, boy – he had taken off his shiny new shoes and had them wedged under one fat arm . . .*'

REWIND. PLAY.

'. . . *Know what I mean by Blizhny, boy? . . .* '

'. . . *by Blizhny, boy? . . .*'

'. . . *by Blizhny . . .* '

Chapter Two

THE MOSCOW AIR tasted of Asia – of dust and soot and eastern spices, cheap petrol, black tobacco, sweat. Kelso came out of the Institute and turned up the collar of his raincoat. He walked across the rutted concourse, skirting the frozen puddles, resisting the temptation to wave at the sullen crowd – that would have been 'a western provocation'.

The street sloped southwards, down towards the centre of the city. Every other building was encased in scaffolding. Beside him, debris hurtled down a metal chute and exploded into a fountain of dust. He passed a shady casino, anonymous except for a sign showing a pair of rolling dice. A fur boutique. A shop selling nothing but Italian shoes. A single pair of handmade loafers would have cost any one of the demonstrators a whole month's wages and he felt a stab of sympathy. He remembered a line of Evelyn Waugh's he had used before about Russia: 'The foundations of Empire are often occasions of woe; their dismemberment, always.'

At the bottom of the hill he turned right, into the wind. The snow had stopped but the cold blast was hard and unyielding. He could see tiny figures bent into it, across the road, beneath the red rock-face of the Kremlin wall, while the golden domes of the churches rose above the parapet like the globes of some vast meteorological machine.

His destination lay straight ahead. Like the Institute of Marxism–Leninism, the Lenin Library had been renamed. It was now the Central Library of the Russian Federation, but everyone still called it the Lenin. He stepped through the familiar triple doors, gave his bag and coat to the babushka behind the cloakroom counter, then showed his old reader's ticket to an armed guard in a glass booth.

He signed his name in the register and added the time. It was eleven minutes past ten.

They had yet to get around to computerising the Lenin, which meant forty million titles were still on index cards. At the top of a wide flight of stone steps, beneath the vaulted ceiling, was a sea of wooden cabinets, and Kelso moved among them as he had done years ago, sliding open one drawer after another, riffling through the familiar titles. Radzinsky he would need, and the second volume of Volkogonov, and Khrushchev and Alliluyeva. The cards for these last two were marked with the Cyrillic symbol '¢' which meant they had been held in the secret index until 1991. How many titles was he allowed? Five, wasn't it? Finally, he decided on Chuyev's series of interviews with the ancient Molotov. Then he took his request slips to the issuing desk and watched as they were fitted into a metal canister and fired down the pneumatic tube into the Lenin's lower depths.

'What's the wait today?'

The assistant shrugged. Who was she to say?

'An hour?'

She shrugged again.

He thought: nothing changes.

He wandered back across the landing into Reading Room No. 3, and trod softly down the path of worn green carpet that led to his old seat. And nothing had changed here, either – not the rich brownness of the wood-panelled, galleried hall, nor the dry smell of it, nor its sacrilegious hush. At one end was a statue of Lenin reading a book, at the other an astrological clock. Maybe two hundred people were bent over their desks. Through the window to his left he could see the dome and spire of St Nicholas's. He might never have left; the past eighteen years might have been a dream.

He sat down and laid out his things and in that instant he was a student of twenty-six again, living in a single room in Corpus V of Moscow University, paying 260 roubles a month for a desk, a bed, a chair and a cupboard, taking meals in the basement canteen that was overrun by cockroaches, spending his days in the Lenin and his nights with a girlfriend – with Nadya, or Katya, or Margarita, or Irina. *Irina.* Now there was a woman. He ran his hand over the scratched surface of the desk and wondered what had become of Irina. Perhaps he should have stuck with her – serious, beautiful Irina, with her *samizdat* magazines and her basement meetings, making love to the accompaniment of a rattling Gestetner duplicator and afterwards vowing that they would be different, that they would change the world.

Irina. He wondered what she would make of the new Russia. The last he had heard she was a dental assistant in South Wales.

He glanced around the reading room and closed his eyes, trying to keep hold of the past for a minute longer, a fattening and hungover middle-aged historian in a black corduroy suit.

HIS books arrived at the issuing stack just after eleven, or at any rate four of them did: they had fetched up volume one of Volkogonov rather than volume two and he had to send it back. Still, he had enough. He carried the books back to his desk and gradually he became absorbed in his task, reading, noting and cross-referencing the various eyewitness accounts of Stalin's death. He found, as usual, an aesthetic pleasure in the sheer detective work of research. Secondhand sources and speculation he discarded. He was only interested in those people who had actually been in the same room as the GenSec and had left behind a description he could match against Rapava's.

By his reckoning there were seven: the Politburo members, Khrushchev and Molotov; Stalin's daughter, Svetlana Alliluyeva; two of Stalin's bodyguards, Rybin and Lozgachev; and two of his medical staff: the physician, Myasnikov, and the recuscitator, a woman named Chesnokova. The other eyewitnesses had either killed themselves (like the bodyguard, Khrustalev, who drank himself to death after watching the autopsy), or had died soon afterwards, or had disappeared.

The accounts all differed in detail but were in essence the same. Stalin had suffered a catastrophic haemorrhage in the left cerebral hemisphere some time when he was alone in his room between 4 a.m. and 10 p.m. on Sunday March 1 1953. Academician Vinogradov, who examined the brain after death, found serious hardening of the cerebral arteries which suggested Stalin had probably been half-crazy for a long while, maybe even years. Nobody could tell what time the stroke had hit. His door had stayed closed all day and his staff had been too scared to enter his room. The bodyguard Lozgachev told the writer Radzinsky that he had been the first to pluck up the courage:

I opened the door . . . and there was the Boss lying on the floor holding up his right hand like this. I was petrified. My hands and legs wouldn't obey me. He had probably not yet lost consciousness but he couldn't speak. He had good hearing, he'd obviously heard me coming, and probably raised his hand slightly to call me in to help him. I hurried up to him and said 'Comrade Stalin, what's wrong?' He'd – you know – wet himself while he was lying there, and was trying to straighten something with his left hand. I said, 'Shall I call the doctor, maybe?' He made some incoherent noise – like 'Dz – dz . . . ,' all he could do was keep on 'dz'-ing.

It was immediately after this that the guards had called in Malenkov. Malenkov had called in Beria. And Beria's order, tantamount to murder by negligence, had been that Stalin was drunk and should be left to sleep it off.

Kelso made a careful note of the passage. Nothing here contradicted Rapava. That didn't prove Rapava was telling the truth, of course – he could have got hold of Lozgachev's testimony for himself, and tailored his story to fit. But it didn't suggest he was lying, either, and certainly the details tallied – the time frame, the order not to call for medical help, the way Stalin had wet himself, the way he would regain consciousness but be unable to speak. This happened at least twice over the three days it took Stalin to die. Once, according to Khrushchev, when the doctors at last brought in by the Politburo were spoon-feeding him soup and weak tea, he had raised his hand and pointed at one of the pictures of children on the wall. The second return to consciousness occurred just before the end and was noted by everyone, especially his daughter, Svetlana:

At what seemed like the very last moment he suddenly opened his eyes and cast a glance over everyone in the room. It was a terrible glance, insane or perhaps angry and full of fear of death and the unfamiliar faces of the doctors bent over him. The glance swept over everyone in a second. Then something incomprehensible and terrible happened that to this day I can't forget and don't understand. He suddenly lifted his left hand as though he were pointing to something up above and bringing down a curse on us all. The gesture was incomprehensible and full of menace, and no one could say to whom or what it might be directed. The next moment, after a final effort, the spirit wrenched itself free of the flesh.

That had been written in 1967. After his heart had stopped, the doctors had ordered the resuscitator, Chesnokova – a strong young woman – to pound at Stalin's chest and blow into his mouth, until Khrushchev had heard the old man's ribs snap and had told her to pack it in. '. . . *no one could say to whom or what it might be directed* . . .' Kelso underlined the words lightly with his pencil. If Rapava was telling the truth, it was fairly obvious whom Stalin must have been cursing: the man who had stolen the key to his private safe – Lavrenty Beria. Why he should have pointed at a picture of a child was less clear.

Kelso tapped the pencil against his teeth. It was all very circumstantial. He could imagine Adelman's reaction if he tried to offer it as any sort of supporting evidence. The thought of Adelman made him look at his watch. If he set off now he could be back at the symposium comfortably in time for lunch and there was a good chance they wouldn't even have missed him. He gathered up the books and took them back to the issuing desk, where the second volume of Volkogonov had just arrived.

'Well,' said the librarian, her thin lips crimped with irritation, 'do you want it or not?'

Kelso hesitated, almost said no, then decided he might as well finish what he'd started. He handed over the other books and carried the Volkogonov back into the reading room.

It lay before him on his desk like a dull brown brick. *Triyumf i Tragediya: politicheskii portret I. V. Stalina,* Novosti publishers, Moscow 1989. He had read it when it first came out and hadn't felt the need to look at it since. He regarded it now without enthusiasm, then flicked the cover open with his finger. Volkogonov was a three-star Red Army general with powerful contacts inside the Kremlin, granted special access to the archives under Gorbachev and Yeltsin which he had used to produce a trio of tombstone lives – Stalin, Trotsky, Lenin – each one more revisionist than the last. Kelso picked it up and leafed through it to the index, looked up the relevant entries for Stalin's death – and a moment later there it was, the memory that had been niggling at the back of his mind ever since Papu Rapava disappeared into the Moscow dawn:

A. A. Yepishev, who was at one time deputy Minister of State Security, told me that Stalin kept a black oilskin exercise book in which he would make occasional notes, and that for some time Stalin kept letters from Zinoviev, Kamenev, Bukharin and even Trotsky. All efforts to discover either the notebook or these letters have failed, and Yepishev did not reveal his source.

Yepishev did not reveal his source but he did, according to Volkogonov, have a theory. He believed that Stalin's private papers had been removed from his Kremlin safe by Lavrenty Beria, while the General Secretary lay paralysed by his stroke.

Beria made a dash for the Kremlin where it is reasonable to assume he cleaned out the safe, removing the Boss's personal papers and with them, one assumes, the black notebook . . . Having destroyed Stalin's notebook, if indeed it was there, Beria would have cleared the path to his own ascendancy. Perhaps the truth will never be known, but Yepishev was convinced that Beria cleaned out the safe before the others could get to it.

*

Now calm yourself, and don't get excited, because this proves nothing, you understand? Nothing whatever.

But it does make it a thousand times more likely.

Back outside the entrance to the reading room, Kelso yanked open the narrow wooden drawer and searched through it quickly until he found the index cards to Yepishev, A. A. (1908–85). The old man had written a score of books, of uniform dullness and hackery: *History Teaches: The Lessons of the Twentieth Anniversary of Victory in the Great Patriotic War* (1965), *Ideological Warfare and Military Problems* (1974), *We Are True to the Ideas of the Party* (1981) . . .

Kelso's hangover had gone, to be replaced by that familiar phase of post-alcoholic euphoria – always, in the past, his most productive time of day – a feeling that alone was enough to make getting drunk worthwhile. He ran down the flight of steps and along the wide and gloomy corridor that led to the Lenin's military section. This was a small and self-contained area, neon-lit, with a subterranean feel to it. A young man in a grey pullover was leaning against the counter, reading a 1970s *MAD* comic.

'What do you have on an army man named Yepishev?' asked Kelso. 'A. A. Yepishev?'

'Who wants to know?'

Kelso handed over his reader's card and the young man examined it with interest.

'Hey, are you the Kelso who wrote that book a few years back on the end of the Party?'

Kelso hesitated – this could go either way – but finally he admitted he was. The young man put down the comic and shook his hand. 'Andrei Efanov. Great book. You really stuffed the bastards. I'll see what we have.'

THERE were two reference books with entries for Yepishev: the *Military Encyclopaedia of the USSR* and the *Directory of Heroes of the Soviet Union*, and both told pretty much the same story, if you knew how to read between the lines, which was that Aleksey Alekseevich Yepishev had been an armour-plated, ocean-going Stalinist of the old school: Komsomol and Party instructor in the twenties and thirties; Red Army Military Academy, 1938; Commissar of the Komintern Factory in Kharkov, 1942; Military Council of the Thirty-Eighth Army of the 1st Ukrainian Front, 1943; Deputy People's Commissar for Medium Machine Building, also 1943 –

'What's a "medium machine",' asked Efanov, who was peering at the books over Kelso's shoulder. Efanov turned out to have done his military service in Lithuania – two years of hell – and to have been refused admittance to Moscow University in the communist time on the grounds he was a Jew. Now he was taking a huge delight in poking over the dust and ashes of Yepishev's career.

'Cover-name for the Soviet atomic bomb programme,' said Kelso. 'Beria's pet project.' *Beria*. He made a note.

– Secretary of the Central Committee of the Ukrainian Communist Party, 1946 –

'That was when they purged the Ukraine of collaborators, after the war,' said Efanov. 'A bloody time.'

– First Secretary of the Odessa Regional Party Committee, 1950; Deputy Minister of State Security, 1951 –

Deputy Minister . . .

Each entry was illustrated with the same official photograph of Yepishev. Kelso looked again at the the square jaw, the thick brow, the grim face set above the boxer's neck.

'Oh, he was a big bastard, boy. A fleshy tank . . . '

'Gotcha,' whispered Kelso to himself.

After Stalin's death, Yepishev's career had taken a dive. First he had been sent back to Odessa, then he had been packed off abroad. Ambassador to Romania, 1955-61. Ambassador to Yugoslavia, 1961-62. And then, at last, the long-awaited summons back to Moscow, as Head of the Central Political Department of the Soviet Armed Forces – its ideological commissar – a position he held for the next twenty-three years. And who had served as his deputy? None other than Dmitri Volkogonov, three-star general and future biographer of Josef Stalin.

To extract these small plums of information it was necessary to dig through a great pudding of cliché and jargon, praising Yepishev for his 'important role in shaping the necessary political attitudes and enforcing Marxist–Leninist orthodoxy in the Armed Forces, in strengthening military discipline and fostering ideological readiness'. He had died aged seventy-seven. Volkogonov, Kelso knew, had died ten years later.

The list of Yepishev's honours and medals took up the rest of his entry: Hero of the Soviet Union, winner of the Lenin Prize, holder of four Orders of Lenin, the October Revolution Order, four Orders of the Red Banner, two

Orders of the Great Patriotic War (1st class), the Order of the Red Banner, three Orders of the Red Star, the Order of Service to the Motherland . . .

'It's a wonder he could stand up.'

'And I'll bet you he never shot anyone,' sneered Efanov, 'except on his own side. So what's so interesting about Yepishev, if you don't mind me asking?'

'What's this?' said Kelso suddenly. He pointed to a line at the foot of the column: 'V. P. Mamantov.'

'He's the author of the entry.'

'Yepishev's entry was written by Mamantov? *Vladimir* Mamantov? The KGB man?'

'That's him. So what? The entries are usually written by friends. Why? D'you know him?'

'I don't *know* him. I've *met* him.' He frowned at the name. 'His people were demonstrating – this morning –'

'Oh, them? They're always demonstrating. When did you meet Mamantov?'

Kelso reached for his notebook and began skimming back through the pages. 'About five years ago, I suppose. When I was researching my book on the Party.'

Vladimir Mamantov. My God, he hadn't thought about Vladimir Mamantov in half a decade, and suddenly here he was, crossing his path twice in a morning. The years fluttered through his fingers – *ninety-five, ninety-four* . . . Some details of the meeting were starting to come back to him now: a morning in late spring, a dead dog revealed in the thawing snow outside an apartment block in the suburbs, a gorgon of a wife. Mamantov had just finished serving fourteen months in Lefortovo for his part in the attempted coup against Gorbachev, and Kelso had been the first to interview him when he came out of jail. It had taken an age to fix the appointment and then it had proved, as so often in these cases, not worth the effort. Mamantov had refused point-blank to talk about himself, or the coup, and had simply spouted Party slogans straight out of the pages of *Pravda*.

He found Mamantov's home telephone number from 1991, next to an office address for a lowly Party functionary, Gennady Zyuganov.

'You're going to try to see him?' asked Efanov, anxiously. 'You know he hates all Westerners? Almost as much as he hates the Jews.'

'You're right,' said Kelso, staring at the seven digits. Mamantov had been a formidable man even in defeat, his Soviet suit hanging loose off his wide shoulders, the grey pallor of prison still dull on his cheeks, murder in his eyes. Kelso's book had not been flattering about Vladimir Mamantov, to put it mildly. And it had been translated into Russian – Mamantov must have seen it.

'You're right,' he repeated. 'It would be stupid even to try.'

FLUKE Kelso walked out of the Lenin Library a little after two that afternoon, pausing briefly at a stall in the lobby to buy a couple of bread rolls and a bottle of warm and salty mineral water.

He remembered passing a row of public telephones opposite the Kremlin, close to the Intourist office, and he ate his lunch as he walked – first down into the gloom of the metro station to buy some plastic tokens for the phone, and then back along Mokhavaya Street towards the high red wall and the golden domes.

He was not alone, it seemed to him. His younger self was ambling alongside him now – floppy-haired, chain-smoking, forever in a hurry, forever optimistic, a writer on the rise.

('Dr Kelso brings to the study of contemporary Soviet history the skills of a first-rate scholar and the energy of a good reporter' – *The New York Times*.) This younger Kelso wouldn't have hesitated to call up Vladimir Mamantov, that was for sure – by God, he would have battered his bloody door down by now if necessary.

Think about it: if Yepishev had told Volkogonov about Stalin's notebook, might he not also have told Mamantov? Might he not have left behind papers? Might he not have a family?

It had to be worth a try.

He wiped his mouth and fingers on the little paper napkin and as he picked up the receiver and inserted the tokens he felt a familiar tightening of his stomach muscles, a butteriness around his heart. Was this sensible? No. But who cared about that? Adelman – he was sensible. And Saunders – he was *very* sensible.

Go for it.

He dialled the number.

The first call was an anti-climax. The Mamantovs had moved and the man who now lived at their old address was reluctant to give out their new number. Only after he had held a whispered consultation with someone at his end did he pass it on. Kelso hung up and dialled again. This time the phone rang for a long time before it was answered. The tokens dropped and an old woman with a trembling voice said, 'Who is this?'

He gave his name. 'Could I speak with Comrade Mamantov?' He was careful to say 'comrade': 'mister' would never do.

'Yes? Who is this?'

Kelso was patient. 'As I said, my name is Kelso. I'm using a public telephone. It's urgent.'

'Yes, but who is this?'

He was about to repeat his name for a third time when he heard what sounded like a scuffle at the other end of the line and a harsh male voice cut in. 'All right. This is Mamantov. Who are you?'

'It's Kelso.' There was a silence. 'Doctor Kelso? You may remember me?'

'I remember you. What do you want?'

'To see you.'

'Why should I see you after that shit you wrote?'

'I wanted to ask you some questions.'

'About?'

'A black oilskin notebook that used to belong to Josef Stalin.'

'Shut up,' said Mamantov.

'What?' Kelso frowned at the receiver.

'I said shut up. I'm thinking it over. Where are you?'

'Near the Intourist building, on Mokhavaya Street.'

There was another silence.

Mamantov said, 'You're close.'

And then he said, 'You'd better come.'

He gave his address. The line went dead.

THE line went dead and Major Feliks Suvorin of the Russian intelligence service, the SVR, sitting in his office in the south-eastern suburb of Yasenevo, carefully slipped off his headphones and wiped his neat pink ears with a clean white handkerchief. On the notepad in front of him he had written: *A black oilskin notebook that used to belong to Josef Stalin . . .*

Chapter Three

'Confronting the Past'
An International Symposium on the
Archives of the Russian Federation

Tuesday 27 October,
final afternoon session

DR KELSO: *Ladies and gentlemen, whenever I think of Josef Stalin, I find myself thinking of one image in particular. I think of Stalin, as an old man, standing beside his gramophone.*

He would finish working late, usually at nine or ten, and then he would go to the Kremlin movie theatre to watch a film. Often, it was one of the Tarzan series – for some reason Stalin loved the idea of a young man growing up and living among wild animals – then he and his cronies in the Politburo would drive out to his dacha at Kuntsevo for dinner, and, after dinner, he would go over to his gramophone and put on a record. His particular favourite, according to Milovan Djilas, was a song in which howling dogs replaced the sound of human voices. And then Stalin would make the Politburo dance.

Some of them were quite good dancers. Mikoyan, for example: he was a lovely dancer. And Bulganin wasn't bad; he could follow a beat. Khrushchev, though, was a lousy dancer – 'like a cow on ice' – and so was Malenkov and so was Kaganovich, for that matter.

Anyway, one evening – drawn, we might speculate, by the peculiar noise of grown men dancing to the baying of hounds – Stalin's daughter, Svetlana, put her head round the door, and

Stalin made her start dancing, too. Well, after a time, she grew tired, and her feet were hardly moving, and this made Stalin angry. He shouted at her, 'Dance!' And she said, 'But I've already danced, papa, I'm tired.' At which Stalin – and here I quote Khrushchev's description – 'grabbed her like this, by the hair, a whole fistful, I mean by her forelock, as it were, and pulled, you understand, very hard . . . pulled, jerked and jerked.'

Now keep that image in your mind for a moment, and let us consider the fate of Stalin's family. His first wife died. His oldest son, Yakov, tried to shoot himself when he was twenty-one, but only succeeded in inflicting severe wounds. (When Stalin saw him, according to Svetlana, he laughed. 'Ha!' he said. 'Missed! Couldn't even shoot straight!') Yakov was captured by the Germans during the war and, after Stalin refused a prisoner exchange, he tried suicide again – successfully this time, by hurling himself at the electrified fence of his prison camp.

Stalin had one other child, a son, Vasily, an alcoholic, who died aged forty-one.

Stalin's second wife, Nadezhda, refused to bear her husband any more children – according to Svetlana, she had a couple of abortions – and late one night, aged thirty-one, she shot herself through the heart. (Or perhaps it would be more accurate to say that someone shot her: no suicide note has ever been found.)

Nadezhda was one of four children. Her older brother, Pavel, was murdered by Stalin during the purges; the death certificate recorded a heart attack. Her younger brother, Fyodor, was driven insane when a friend of Stalin's, an Armenian bank robber named Kamo, handed him a gouged-out human heart. Her sister, Anna, was arrested on Stalin's orders and sentenced to ten years in solitary confinement. By the time she came out she was no longer capable of recognising her own children. So that was one set of Stalin's relatives.

And what of the other set? Well, there was Aleksandr Svanidze, the brother of Stalin's first wife – he was arrested in thirty-seven and shot in forty-one. And there was Svanidze's wife, Maria, who was also arrested; she was shot in forty-two. Their surviving child, Ivan – Stalin's nephew – was sent into exile, to a ghastly state orphanage for the children of 'enemies of the state', and when he emerged, nearly twenty years later, he was profoundly psychologically damaged. And finally there was Stalin's sister-in-law, Maria – she was also arrested in thirty-seven and died mysteriously in prison.

Now let us go back to that image of Svetlana. Her mother is dead. Her half-brother is dead. Her other brother is an alcoholic. Two uncles are dead and one is insane. Two aunts are dead and one is in prison. She is being dragged around by her hair, by her father, in front of a roomful of the most powerful men in Russia, all of whom are being forced to dance, maybe to the sound of howling dogs.

Colleagues, whenever I sit in an archive or, more rarely these days, attend a symposium like this one, I always try to remember that scene, because it reminds me to be wary of imposing a rational structure on the past. There is nothing in the archives here to show us that the Deputy Chairman of the Council of Ministers, or the Commissar for Foreign Affairs, when they made their decisions, were shattered by exhaustion, and very probably terrified – that they had been up until three a.m. dancing for their lives, and knew they might well be dancing again that evening.

Not that I am saying that Stalin was crazy. On the contrary. One could argue that the man who worked the gramophone was the sanest person in the room. When Svetlana asked him why her Aunt Anna was being held in solitary confinement, he answered, 'Because she talks too much.' With Stalin, there was usually a logic to his actions. He didn't need a sixteenth-century English philosopher to tell him that 'knowledge is power'. That realisation is the absolute essence of Stalinism. Among other things, it explains why Stalin murdered so many of his own family and close colleagues – he wanted to destroy anyone who had any first-hand knowledge of him.

And this policy, we must concede, was remarkably successful. Here we are, gathered in Moscow, forty-five years after Stalin's death, to discuss the newly-opened archives of the Soviet era. Above our heads, in fire-proofed strong-rooms, maintained at a constant temperature of eighteen degrees celsius and sixty per cent humidity, are one and a half million files – the entire archive of the Central Committee of the Communist Party of the Soviet Union.

Yet how much does this archive really tell us about Stalin? What can we see today that we couldn't see when the communists were in power? Stalin's letters to Molotov – we can see those – and they are not without interest. But clearly they have been heavily censored. And not just that: they end in thirty-six, at precisely the point when the real killing started.

We can also see the death lists that Stalin signed. And we have his appointments book. So we know that on the eighth of December, nineteen thirty-eight, Stalin signed thirty death lists containing five thousand names, many of them of his so-called friends. And we also know, thanks to his appointments book, that on that very same evening he went to the Kremlin movie theatre and watched, not Tarzan this time, but a comedy called Happy Guys.

But between these two events, between the killing and the laughter, there lies – what? who? We do not know. And why? Because Stalin made it his business to murder almost everyone who might have been in a position to tell us what he was like . . .

Chapter Four

MAMANTOV'S NEW PLACE turned out to be just across the river, in the big apartment complex on Serafimovich Street known as the House on the Embankment. This was the building to which Comrade Stalin, with typical generosity, had insisted that leading Party members go to live with their families. There were ten floors with twenty-five different entrances at ground level, at each of which the GenSec had thoughtfully posted an NKVD guard – purely for your security, comrades.

By the time the purges were finished, six hundred of the building's tenants had been liquidated. Now the flats were privately owned and the good ones, with a view across the Moskva to the Kremlin, sold for upwards of half a million dollars. Kelso wondered how Mamantov could afford it.

He came down the steps from the bridge and crossed the road. Parked outside the entrance to Mamantov's staircase was a boxy white Lada, its windows open, two men in the front seat, chewing gum. One had a livid scar running almost from the corner of his eye to the edge of his mouth. They watched Kelso with undisguised interest as he walked past them towards the entrance.

Inside the apartment block, next to the elevator, someone had written, neatly, in English, in capitals and lower case, 'Fuck Off'. A tribute to the Russian education system, thought Kelso. He whistled nervously, a made-up tune. The lift rose smoothly and he got out at the ninth floor to be met by the distant thump of western rock music.

Mamantov's apartment had an outer door of steel plate. A

red aerosol swastika had been sprayed on to the metal. The paint was old and faded but no attempt had been made to clean it off. Set in the wall above it was a small remote TV camera.

There was already plenty about this set-up that Kelso didn't like – the heavy security, the guys in the car downstairs – and for a moment he could almost smell the terror from sixty years ago, as if the sweat had seeped into the brickwork: the clattering footsteps, the heavy knocking, the hurried goodbyes, the sobs, silence. His hand paused over the buzzer. What a place to choose to live.

He pressed the button.

After a long wait, the door was opened by an elderly woman. Madame Mamantov was as he remembered her – tall and broad, not fat, but heavily built. She was draped in a shapeless, flowery smock and looked as though she had just finished crying. Her red eyes rested on him briefly, distractedly, but before he could even open his mouth she had wandered off and suddenly there was Vladimir Mamantov, looming down the dark passage, dressed as if he still had an office to go to – white shirt, blue tie, black suit with a small red star pinned in his lapel.

He didn't say anything, but he offered his hand. He had a crushing handshake, perfected, it was said, by squeezing balls of vulcanized rubber during KGB meetings. (A lot of things were said about Mamantov: for example – and Kelso had put it in his book – that at the famous meeting in the Lubyanka on the night of 20 August 1991, when the plotters of the coup had realised the game was up, Mamantov had offered to fly down to Gorbachev's dacha at Foros on the Black Sea and shoot the Soviet President personally; Mamantov had dismissed the story as 'a provocation'.)

A young man in a black shirt with a shoulder holster appeared in the gloom behind Mamantov, and Mamantov said, without looking round, 'It's all right, Viktor. I'm dealing with the situation.' Mamantov had a bureaucrat's face – steel-coloured hair, steel-framed glasses and pouched cheeks, like a suspicious hound's. You could pass it in the street a hundred times and never notice it. But his eyes were bright: a fanatic's eyes, thought Kelso; he could imagine Eichmann or some other Nazi desk-murderer having eyes like these. The old woman had started making a curious howling noise from the other end of the flat, and Mamantov told Viktor to go and sort her out.

'So you're part of the gathering of thieves,' he said to Kelso.

'What?'

'The symposium. *Pravda* published a list of the foreign historians they invited to speak. Your name was on it.'

'Historians are hardly thieves, Comrade Mamantov. Even foreign historians.'

'No? Nothing is more important to a nation than its history. It is the earth upon which any society stands. Ours has been stolen from us – gouged and blackened by the libels of our enemies until the people have become lost.'

Kelso smiled. Mamantov hadn't changed at all. 'You can't seriously believe that.'

'You're not Russian. Imagine if your country offered to sell its national archive to a foreign power for a miserable few million dollars.'

'You're not selling your archive. The plan is to microfilm the records and make them available to scholars.'

'To scholars *in California*,' said Mamantov, as if this settled the argument. 'But this is tedious. I have an urgent appointment.' He looked at his watch. 'I can only give you five minutes, so get to the point. What's all this about Stalin's notebook?'

'It comes into some research I'm doing.'

'Research? Research into what?'

Kelso hesitated. 'The events surrounding Stalin's death.'

'Go on.'

'If I could just ask you a couple of questions, then perhaps I could explain the relevance –'

'No,' said Mamantov. 'Let us do this the other way round. You tell me about this notebook and then I might answer your questions.'

'You *might* answer my questions?'

Mamantov consulted his watch again. 'Four minutes.'

'All right,' said Kelso, quickly. 'You remember the official biography of Stalin, by Dmitri Volkogonov?'

'The traitor Volkogonov? You're wasting my time. That book is a piece of shit.'

'You've read it?'

'Of course not. There's enough filth in this world without my volunteering to go jump in it.'

'Volkogonov claimed that Stalin kept certain papers – private papers, including a black oilskin exercise book – in his safe at the Kremlin, and that these papers were stolen by Beria. His source for this story was a man you're familiar with, I think. Aleksey Alekseevich Yepishev.'

There was a slight movement – a flicker, no more – in Mamantov's hard grey eyes. He's heard of it, thought Kelso, he knows about the notebook –

'And?'

'And I wondered if you'd come across this story while you were writing your entry on Yepishev for the biographical guide. He was a friend of yours, I assume?'

'What's it to you?' Mamantov glanced at Kelso's bag. 'Have you found the notebook?'

'No.'

'But you know someone who may know where it is?'

'Someone came to see me,' began Kelso, then stopped. The apartment was very quiet now. The old woman had finished wailing, but the bodyguard hadn't reappeared. On the hall table was a copy of *Aurora*.

Nobody in Moscow knew where he was, he realised. He had dropped off the map.

'I'm wasting your time,' he said. 'Perhaps I might come back when I've –'

'That's unnecessary,' said Mamantov, softening his tone. His sharp eyes were checking Kelso up and down – flickering across his face, his hands, gauging the potential strength of his arms and chest, darting up to his face again. His conversational technique was pure Leninism, thought Kelso: *'Push out a bayonet. If it strikes fat, push deeper. If it strikes iron, pull back for another day.'*

'I'll tell you what, Doctor Kelso,' said Mamantov. 'I'll show you something. It will interest you. And then I'll tell you something. And then you'll tell me something.' He waved his fingers back and forth between them. 'We'll trade. Is it a deal?'

AFTERWARDS, Kelso tried to make a list of it all, but there was too much of it for him to remember: the immense oil painting, by Gerasimov, of Stalin on the ramparts of the Kremlin, and the neon-lit glass cabinet with its miniatures of Stalin – its Stalin dishes and its Stalin boxes, its Stalin stamps and Stalin medals – and the case of books by Stalin, and the books about Stalin, and the photographs of Stalin – signed and unsigned – and the scrap of Stalin's handwriting – blue pencil, lined paper, quarto-sized and framed – that hung above the bust of Stalin by Vuchetich ('. . . don't spare individuals, no matter what position they occupy, spare only the cause, the interests of the cause . . .').

He moved among the collection while Mamantov watched him closely.

The handwriting sample, said Kelso – that . . . that was a note for a speech, was it not? Correct, said Mamantov: October 1920, address to the Worker–Peasant Inspection. And the Gerasimov? Wasn't it similar to the artist's 1938 study of Stalin and Voroshilov on the Kremlin Wall? Mamantov nodded again, apparently pleased to share these moments with a fellow connoisseur: yes, the GenSec had ordered Gerasimov to paint a second version, leaving out Voroshilov – it was Stalin's way of reminding Voroshilov that life (how to put it?) could always be *rearranged* to imitate art. A collector in Maryland and another in Dusseldorf had each offered Mamantov $100,000 for the picture but he would never permit it to leave Russian soil. Never. One day, he hoped to exhibit it in Moscow, along with the rest of his collection – 'when the political situation is more favourable'.

'And you think one day the situation will be favourable?'

'Oh yes. Objectively, history will record that Stalin was right. That is how it is with Stalin. From the subjective perspective, he may seem cruel, even wicked. But the glory of the man is to be found in the objective perspective. There he is a towering figure. It is my unshakeable belief that when the proper perspective is restored, statues will be raised again to Stalin.'

'Goering said the same of Hitler during the Nuremberg trial. I don't see any statues –'

'Hitler lost.'

'But surely Stalin lost? In the end? From the "objective perspective"?'

'Stalin inherited a nation with wooden ploughs and bequeathed us an empire armed with atomic weapons. How can you say he lost? The men who came after him – they lost. Not Stalin. Stalin foresaw what would happen, of course. Khrushchev, Molotov, Beria, Malenkov – they thought they were hard, but he saw through them. "After I've gone, the capitalists will drown you like blind kittens." His analysis was correct, as always.'

'So you think that if Stalin had lived –'

'We would still be a superpower? Absolutely. But men of Stalin's genius are only given to a country perhaps once in a century. And even Stalin could not devise a strategy to defeat death. Tell me, did you see the survey of opinion to mark the forty-fifth anniversary of his passing?'

'I did.'

'And what did you think of the results?'

'I thought they were –' Kelso tried to find a neutral word ' – remarkable.'

(Remarkable? Christ. They were horrifying. One third of Russians said they thought Stalin was a great war leader. One in six thought he was the greatest ruler the country had ever had. Stalin was seven times more popular than Boris Yeltsin, while poor old Gorbachev hadn't even scored enough votes to register. This was in March. Kelso had been so appalled he had tried to sell an op-ed piece to the *New York Times* but they weren't interested.)

'Remarkable,' agreed Mamantov. 'I should even say astounding, considering his vilification by so-called "historians".'

There was an awkward silence.

'Such a collection,' said Kelso, 'it must have taken years to assemble.' And cost a fortune, he almost added.

'I have a few business interests,' said Mamantov, dismissively. 'And a considerable amount of spare time, since my retirement.' He put out his hand to touch the bust, but then hesitated and drew it back. 'The difficulty, of course, for any collector, is that he left so little behind in the way of personal possessions. He had no interest in private property, not like these corrupt swine we have in the Kremlin nowadays. A few sticks of government-issue furniture was all he had. That and the clothes he stood up in. And his private notebook, of course.' He gave Kelso a crafty look. 'Now that would be something. Something – what is the American phrase? – *to die for?*'

'So you have heard of it?'

Mamantov smiled – an unheard-of occurrence – a narrow, thin, rapid smile, like a sudden crack in ice. 'You're interested in Yepishev?'

'Anything you can tell me.'

Mamantov crossed the room to the bookshelf and pulled down a large, leather-bound album. On a higher shelf Kelso could see the two volumes of Volkogonov – of course Mamantov had read them.

'I first met Aleksey Alekseevich,' he said, 'in fifty-seven, when he was ambassador in Bucharest. I was on my way back from Hungary, after we'd sorted things out there. Nine months work, without a break. I needed a rest, I can tell you. We went shooting together in the Azuga region.'

He carefully peeled back a layer of tissue paper and offered the heavy album to Kelso. It was open at a small photograph, taken by an amateur camera, and Kelso had to stare at it closely to make out what was happening. In the background, a forest. In the foreground, two men in leather hunting caps with fleece-lined jackets, smiling, holding rifles, dead birds piled at their booted feet. Yepishev was on the left, Mamantov next to him – still hard-faced but leaner then, a cold war caricature of a KGB man.

'And somewhere there's another.' Mamantov leaned over Kelso's shoulder and turned a couple of pages. Close up, he smelled elderly, of mothballs and carbolic, and he had shaved badly, as old men do, leaving grey stubble in the shadow of his nose and in the cleft of his broad chin. 'There.'

This was a much bigger, professional picture, showing maybe two hundred men, arranged in four ranks, as if at a graduation. Some were in uniform, some in civilian suits. A caption underneath said 'Sverdlovsk, 1980'.

'This was an ideological collegium, organised by the Central Committee Secretariat. On the final day, Comrade Suslov himself addressed us. This is me.' He pointed to a grim face in the third row, then moved his finger to the front, to a relaxed, uniformed figure sitting cross-legged on the ground. 'And this – would you believe? – is Volkogonov. And here again is Aleksey Alekseevich.'

It was like looking at a picture of Imperial officers in the tsarist time, thought Kelso – such confidence, such order, such masculine arrogance! Yet within ten years, their world had been atomised: Yepishev was dead, Volkogonov had renounced the Party, Mamantov was in jail.

Yepishev had died in 1985, said Mamantov. He had passed on just as Gorbachev came to power. And that was a good time for a decent communist to die, in Mamantov's opinion: Aleksey Alekseevich had been *spared*. Here was a man whose whole life had been devoted to Marxism–Leninism, who had helped plan the fraternal assistance to Czechoslovakia and Afghanistan. What a mercy he hadn't lived to see the whole lot thrown away. Writing Yepishev's entry for the *Book of Heroes* had been a privilege, and if nobody ever read it nowadays – well, that was what he meant. The country had been robbed of its history.

'And did Yepishev tell you the same story about Stalin's papers as he told Volkogonov?'

'He did. He talked more freely towards the end. He was often ill. I visited him in the leadership clinic. Brezhnev and he were treated together by the parapsychic healer, Davitashvili.'

'I don't suppose he left any papers.'

'Papers? Men like Yepishev didn't keep papers.'

'Any relatives?'

'None that I knew of. We never discussed *families.*' Mamantov pronounced the word as if it was absurd. 'Did you know that one of the things Aleksey had to do was interrogate Beria? Night after night. Can you imagine what that must have been like? But Beria never cracked, not once in nearly half a year, until right at the very end, after his trial, when they were strapping him to the board to shoot him. He hadn't believed they'd dare to kill him.'

'How do you mean, he cracked?'

'He was squealing like a pig – that's what Yepishev said. Shouting something about Stalin and something about an archangel. Can you imagine that? Beria, of all people, getting religious! But then they put a scarf in his mouth and shot him. I don't know any more.' Mamantov closed the albums tenderly and placed them back on the shelf. 'So,' he said, turning to face Kelso with a look of menacing innocence, 'someone came to see you. When was this?'

Kelso was on his guard at once. 'I'd prefer not to say.'

'And he told you about Stalin's papers? He *was* a man, I assume? An eyewitness, from that time?'

Kelso hesitated.

'Named?'

Kelso smiled and shook his head. Mamantov seemed to think he was back in the Lubyanka.

'His profession, then?'

'I can't tell you that, either.'

'Does he know where these papers are?'

'Perhaps.'

'He offered to show you?'

'No.'

'But you *asked* him to show you?'

'No.'

'You're a very disappointing historian, Dr Kelso. I thought you were famous for your diligence –'

'If you must know, he disappeared before I had the chance.'

He regretted the words the instant they were out of his mouth.

'What do you mean, he "disappeared"?'

'We were drinking,' muttered Kelso. 'I left him alone for a minute. When I came back he'd run away.'

It sounded implausible, even to his own ears.

'Run away?' Mamantov's eyes were as grey as winter. 'I don't believe you.'

'Vladimir Pavlovich,' said Kelso, meeting his gaze and holding it, 'I can assure you this is the truth.'

'You're lying. Why? *Why?*' Mamantov rubbed his chin. 'I think it must be because you have the notebook.'

'If I had the notebook, ask yourself: Would I be here?

Wouldn't I be on the first flight back to New York? Isn't that what thieves are supposed to do?'

Mamantov continued to stare at him for a few more seconds, then looked away. 'Clearly we need to find this man.'

We . . .

'I don't think he wants to be found.'

'He will contact you again.'

'I doubt it.' Kelso badly wanted to get out of here now. He felt compromised, somehow; complicit. 'Besides, I'm flying back to America tomorrow. Which, now I come to think of it, really means I ought –'

He made a move towards the door but Mamantov barred it. 'Are you excited, Dr Kelso? Do you feel the force of Comrade Stalin, even from the grave?'

Kelso laughed unhappily. 'I don't think I quite share your . . . obsession.'

'Go fuck your mother! I've read your work. Does that surprise you? I'll pass no comment on its quality. But I'll tell you this: you're as obsessed as I am.'

'Perhaps. But in a different way.'

'Power,' said Mamantov, savouring the word in his mouth like wine, 'the absolute mastery and understanding of *power*. No man ever matched him for it. Do this, do that. Think this, think that. Now I say you live, and now I say you die, and all you say is, "Thank you for your kindness, Comrade Stalin." *That's* the obsession.'

'Yes, but then there's the difference, if you'll permit me, which is you want him back.'

'And you just like to watch, is that it? I like fucking and you like pornography?' Mamantov jerked his thumb at the room. 'You should have seen yourself just now. "Isn't this a

note for a speech?" "Isn't that a copy of an earlier painting?"
Eyes wide, tongue out – the western liberal, getting his safe
thrill. Of course, *he* understood that, too. And now you tell
me you're going to give up trying to find his private notebook
and just run away back to America?'

'May I get by?'

Kelso stepped to his left but Mamantov moved smartly to
block him.

'This could be one of the greatest historical discoveries of
the age. And you want to run away? It *must* be found. We
must find it *together*. And then you must present it to the
world. I want no credit – I promise you: I prefer the shadows
– the honour will be yours alone.'

'So, what's all this then, Comrade Mamantov?' said Kelso,
with forced cheerfulness. 'Am I a prisoner?'

Between him and the outside world there were, he
calculated, one fit and obviously crazy ex-KGB man, one
armed bodyguard, and two doors, one of them armour-
plated. And for a moment, he thought that Mamantov might
indeed be intending to keep him: that he had everything else
connected with Stalin, so why not a Stalin historian, pickled
in formaldehyde and laid out in a glass case, like V. I. Lenin?
But then Madame Mamantov shouted from the passage –
'What's going on in there?' – and the spell was broken.

'Nothing,' called Mamantov. 'Stop listening. Go back to
your room. Viktor!'

'But who is everyone?' wailed the woman. 'That's what I
want to know. And why is it always so dark?' She started to
cry. They heard the shuffle of her feet and the sound of a door
closing.

'I'm sorry,' said Kelso.

'Keep your pity,' said Mamantov. He stood aside. 'Go on,

then. Get out of here. Go.' But when Kelso was halfway down the passage he shouted after him: 'We'll talk again about this matter. One way or another.'

THERE were three men now in the car downstairs, although Kelso was too preoccupied to pay them much attention. He paused in the gloomy portal of the House on the Embankment, to hoist his canvas bag more firmly on to his shoulder, then set off in the direction of the Bolshoy Kamenniy bridge.

'That's him, major,' said the man with the scar, and Feliks Suvorin leaned forward in his seat to get a better look. Suvorin was young to be a full major in the SVR – he was only in his thirties – a dapper figure, with blond hair and cornflower blue eyes. And he wore a western aftershave, that was the other thing that was very noticeable at this moment: the little car was fragrant with the smell of Eau Sauvage.

'He had that bag with him when he went in?'

'Yes, major.'

Suvorin glanced up at the Mamantovs' ninth-floor apartment. What was needed here was better coverage. The SVR had managed to get a bug into the flat at the start of the operation, but it had lasted just three hours before Mamantov's people had found it and ripped it out.

Kelso had begun climbing the flight of stairs that led up to the bridge.

'Off you go, Bunin,' said Suvorin, tapping the man in front of him lightly on the shoulder. 'Nothing too obvious, mind you. Just try to keep him in view. We don't want a diplomatic protest.'

Grumbling under his breath, Bunin levered himself out of the car.

Kelso was moving rapidly now, had almost reached road-level, and the Russian had to jog across to the bottom of the steps to make up part of the distance.

Well, well, thought Suvorin, he's certainly in a hurry to get somewhere. Or is it just that he wants to get away from here?

He watched the blurred pink faces of the two men above the stone parapet as they headed north across the river into the grey afternoon and then were lost from view.

Chapter Five

KELSO PAID HIS two-rouble fare at the Borovitskaya metro station, collected his plastic token, and descended gratefully into the Moscow earth. At the entrance to the northbound platform something made him glance back up the moving staircase to see if Mamantov was following, but there was no sign of him among the tiers of exhausted faces.

It was a stupid thought – he tried to smile at himself for his paranoia – and he turned away, towards the welcoming dimness and the warm gusts of oil and electricity. Almost at once, a yellow headlight danced around a bend in the track and the rush of the train sucked him forwards. Kelso let the crowd jostle him into a carriage. There was an odd comfort in this dowdy, silent multitude. He hung on to the metal handrail and pitched and swayed with the rest as they plunged back into the tunnel.

They hadn't gone far when the train suddenly slowed and stopped – a bomb scare, it turned out, at the next station: the militia had to check it out – and so they sat there in the semi-darkness, nobody speaking, just the occasional cough, the tension rising by imperceptible degrees.

Kelso stared at his reflection in the dark glass. He was jumpy, he had to admit it. He couldn't help feeling he had just put himself into some kind of danger, that telling Mamantov about the notebook had been a reckless mistake. What had the Russian called it? Something *to die for?*

It was a relief to his nerves when the lights eventually flickered back on and the train jolted forwards. The soothing rhythm of normality resumed.

By the time Kelso emerged above ground it was after four. Low in the western sky, barely clearing the tops of the dark trees that fringed the Zoopark, was a lemony crack in the clouds. A winter sunset was little more than an hour away. He would have to hurry. He folded the map into a small square and twisted it so that the metro station was to his right. Across the road was the entrance to the zoo – red rocks, a waterfall, a fairy tower – and, a little further along, a beer garden, closed for the season, its plastic tables stacked, its striped umbrellas down and flapping. He could hear the roar of the traffic on the Garden Ring road, about two hundred yards straight ahead. Across that, sharp left, then right, and there it ought to be. He stuffed the map into his pocket, picked up his bag and climbed the cobbled slope that led to the big intersection.

Ten lanes of traffic formed an immense, slow-moving river of light and steel. He crossed it in a dog-leg and suddenly he was into diplomatic Moscow: wide streets, grand houses, old birch trees weeping dead leaves on to sleek black cars. There wasn't much life. He passed a silvery-headed man walking a poodle and a woman in green rubber boots that poked incongruously from beneath her Muslim robe. Behind the thick gauze of the curtained windows, he could see the occasional yellow constellation of a chandelier. He stopped at the corner of Vspolnyi Street and peered along it. A militia car drove towards him very slowly and passed away to his right. The road was deserted.

He located the house at once, but he wanted to get his bearings and to check if anyone was about, so he made himself walk past it, right to the end of the street before returning along the opposite side. *'There was a red sickle moon, and a single red star. And the place was guarded by devils with blackened faces . . .'* Suddenly he saw what the old man must have meant. A red sickle moon and a single red star – that would be a flag: a Muslim flag. And black faces? The place must have been an embassy – it was too big for anything else – an embassy of a Muslim country, perhaps in North Africa. He was certain he was right. It was a big building, that was for sure, forbidding and ugly, built of sandy-coloured stone which made it look like a bunker. It ran for at least forty yards along the western side of the road. He counted thirteen sets of windows. Above the massive entrance was an iron balcony with double doors leading on to it. There was no nameplate and no flag. If it had been an embassy it was abandoned now; it was lifeless.

He crossed the street and went up close to it, patting the coarse stone with his palm. He stood on tiptoe and tried to see through the windows. But they were set too high and besides were blanked off by the ubiquitous grey netting. He gave up and followed the façade around the corner. The house went on down this street, too. Thirteen windows again, no door, thirty or forty yards of heavy masonry – immense, impregnable. Where this elevation of the house eventually ended there was a wall made of the same stone, about eight feet high, with a locked, iron-studded wooden door set into it. The wall ran on – down this street, along the side of the ring-road, and finally back up the narrow alley which formed the fourth side of the property. Walking round it, Kelso could see why Beria had chosen it, and why his rivals had decided the only place to capture him was inside the Kremlin. Holed up in this fortress he could have withstood a siege.

In the neighbouring houses, the lights were becoming sharper as the afternoon faded into dusk. But Beria's place remained a square of darkness. It seemed to be gathering the shadows into itself. He heard a car door slam and he walked back up to the corner of Vspolnyi Street. While he had been at the back of the property, a small van had arrived at the front.

He hesitated, then began to move towards it.

The van was a Russian model – white, unmarked, unoccupied. Its engine had just been switched off and it was making a slight ticking noise as it cooled. As he came level with it, he glanced towards the door of the house and saw that it was slightly open. Again he hesitated, looking up and down the quiet street. He went over and put his head into the gap and shouted a greeting.

His words echoed in the empty hall. The light inside was weak and bluish, but even without taking another step he could see that the floor was of black and white tiles. To his left was the start of a wide staircase. The house smelled strongly of sour dust and old carpets, and there was an immense stillness to it, as though it had been shut up for months. He pushed the door wide open and took a step inside.

He called out again.

He had two options now. He could stay by the door, or he could go further inside. He went further inside and immediately, like a laboratory rat in a maze, he found his options multiplied. He could stay where he was, or he could take the door to his left, or the stairs, or the passage that led off into the darkness beyond the stairs, or one of the three doors to his right. For a moment, the weight of choice paralysed him. But the stairs were straight ahead and seemed the obvious course – and perhaps, subconsciously, he also wanted to get the advantage of height, to get above whoever might be on the ground floor, or at least to get on equal terms with them if they were already above.

The stairs were stone. He was wearing brown suede boots with leather soles he'd bought in Oxford years ago and no matter how quietly he tried to walk his steps seemed to ring like gunshots. But that was good. He wasn't a thief, and to emphasise the point he called out again. *Pree-vyet! Kto tam?* Hello? Is anybody there? The stairs curled round to his right and he had a good, high view now, looking down into the dark blue well of the hall, pierced by the softer shaft of blue that shone from the open door. He reached the top of the stairs and came out into a wide corridor that stretched to right and left, vanishing at either end into Rembrandt gloom. Ahead of him was a door. He tried to take his bearings. That must lead to the room above the front entrance, the one with the iron balcony. What was it? A ballroom? The master bedroom? The corridor floor was parquet and he remembered Rapava's description of Beria's damp footprints on the polished wood as he hurried off to take the call from Malenkov.

Kelso opened the heavy door and the stale air hit him like a wall. He had to clamp a hand to his mouth and nose to keep from gagging. The smell that pervaded the whole house seemed to have its source in here. It was a big room, bare, lit from the opposite wall by three tall, net-curtained windows, high oblongs of translucent grey. He moved towards them. The floor seemed to be strewn with pools of tiny black husks. His idea was that if he pulled back the curtain, he could throw light on the room, and see what he was treading on. But as his hand touched the rough nylon net, the material seemed to split and ripple downwards and a shower of black granules went pattering across his hand and brushed the back of his neck. He twitched the curtain again and the shower became a cascade, a waterfall of dead, winged insects. Millions of them must have hatched and died in here over the summer, trapped in the airless room. They had a papery, acid smell. They were in his hair. He could feel them rustling under his feet. He stepped backwards, furiously brushing at himself and shaking his head.

Down in the lobby, a man shouted. *Kto idyot?* Is somebody up there?

Kelso knew he should have shouted back. What greater proof could he have offered of his blameless intentions – of his innocence – than to have stepped at once out on to the landing, identified himself and apologised? He was very sorry. The door was open. This was an interesting old house. He was a historian. Curiosity had got the better of him. And obviously, there was nothing here to steal. Really, he was truly sorry –

That was Kelso's alternative history. He didn't take it. He didn't *choose* not to take it. He merely did nothing, which was a form of choice. He stood there, in Lavrenty Beria's old bedroom, frozen, half bent, as if the creaking of his bones might give him away, and listened. With each second that passed, his chances of talking his way out of the building dwindled. The man began to climb the staircase. He came up seven steps – Kelso counted them – then stopped and stayed very still for perhaps a minute.

Then he walked down again and crossed the lobby and the front door closed.

Kelso moved now. He went to the window. Without touching the curtain he found it was possible, by pressing his cheek to the wall, to peer around the edge of the dusty nylon mesh, down into the street. From this oblique angle, he could see a man in a black uniform, standing on the pavement next to the van, holding a flashlight. The man stepped off the kerb and into the gutter and squinted up at the house. He was squat and simian. His arms seemed too long for his thick trunk. Suddenly, he was looking directly at Kelso – a brutal, stupid face – and Kelso drew back. When he next dared to risk a look, the man was bending to open the door on the driver's side. He threw in the flashlight and climbed in after it. The engine started. The van drove off.

Kelso gave him thirty seconds then hurried downstairs. He was locked in. He couldn't believe it. The absurdity of his predicament almost made him smile. He was locked inside Beria's house! The front door was huge, with a big iron ball for a handle and a lock the size of a telephone directory. He tried it hopelessly, then looked around. What if there was an intruder alarm? In the gloom, he couldn't see anything attached to the walls, but maybe it was an old-fashioned system – that would be more likely, wouldn't it? – something triggered by pressure-pads rather than beams? The idea froze him.

What set him moving again was the gathering darkness and the realisation that if he didn't find an escape route now he might be trapped by his blindness all night. There was a light switch by the door but he didn't dare try it – the guard was obviously suspicious: he might drive by for a second look. In any case, something about the silence of the place, its utter deadness, made him sure all forms of life-support had been disconnected, that the house had been left to rot. He tried to recall Rapava's description of the lay-out when he came in to answer Malenkov's call. Something about coming in off a verandah, through a duty room, past a kitchen and into the hall.

He headed into the blackness of the passage beyond the stairs, feeling his way along the left-hand wall. The plaster was cool and smooth. The first door he encountered was locked. The second wasn't – he felt a draught of cold air, but sensed a drop, into a cellar, presumably – and closed it quickly. The third opened on to the dull blue gleam of metal surfaces and a faint smell of old food. The fourth was at the end, facing him, and revealed the room where he guessed that Beria's guards must once have sat.

Unlike the rest of the house, which seemed to have been stripped bare, there was furniture here – a plain wooden table and a chair, and an old sideboard – and some signs of life. A copy of *Pravda* – he could just make out the familiar masthead – a kitchen knife, an ashtray. He touched the table and felt crumbs. Pale light leaked through a pair of small windows. Between them was a door. It was locked. There was no key. He looked again at the windows. Too narrow for him to squeeze through. He took a breath. Some habits, surely, are international? He ran his hand along the sill to the right of the door and it was there and it turned easily in the lock.

When the door was opened he removed the key, and – a nice touch this, he remembered thinking – replaced it on the sill.

HE emerged on to a narrow verandah, about two yards wide, with weathered floorboards and a broken handrail. He could hear traffic at the bottom of the garden and the laborious whine of a big jet, dropping towards Sheremetevo Airport. The breeze was cold, scented by the smoke of a bonfire. There was a last pale flush of daylight in the sky.

He guessed the garden must have been abandoned at the same time as the house. Nobody could have worked in it for months. To his left was an ornate greenhouse with an iron chimney, partially overgrown by Russian vines. To his right, a ragged thicket of dark green shrubs. Ahead were trees. He stepped down off the verandah on to the carpet of leaves that covered the lawn. The wind stirred and lofted some of them, sent a detachment cartwheeling towards the house. He kicked through the drifts towards the orchard – a cherry orchard he could see now as he came closer: big old trees, maybe twenty feet high, at least a hundred of them, a Chekhovian scene. Suddenly he stopped. The ground beneath the trees was flat and level except in one place. At the base of one tree, close to a stone bench, was a patch of blackness, darker than the surrounding shadows. He frowned. Was he sure he wasn't imagining it?

He went over, knelt and slowly sank his hands into the leaves. On the surface they were dry but the lower levels were damp and mulchy. He brushed them back, releasing a rich smell of moist soil – the black and fragrant earth of Mother Russia.

'Don't make it so wide. It's not a grave. You're making work for yourself . . . '

He cleared away the leaves from an area about a yard square, and although he couldn't see much, he could see enough, and he could feel it. The grass had been removed and a hole had been dug. And then it had been filled in again and an attempt had been made to jam the turfs back into their original positions. But some parts had crumbled and others overlapped the lip of the hole and the result was a mess, like a broken, muddy jigsaw. It had been done in a hurry, thought Kelso, and it had been done recently, possibly even today. He stood and brushed the wet leaves from his coat.

'Do you feel the force of Comrade Stalin, even from the grave . . .?'

Beyond the high wall he could hear the traffic on the wide highway. Normality seemed close enough to touch. He used the side of his foot to scrape a covering of leaves back across the scarred surface, grabbed his bag and stumbled through the orchard towards the end of the garden, towards the sounds of life. He had to get out now. He didn't mind admitting it. He was rattled. The cherry trees stretched almost to the wall which rose up blank and sheer before him, like the perimeter of a Victorian gaol. There was no way he could scale it.

A narrow cinder path followed the line of the wall. He headed left. The path turned the corner and took him back in the direction of the house. About halfway along, he could see a darkened oblong – the garden door he had noticed from the street – but even this was overgrown and he had to pull back the trailing branches of a bush to get at it. It was locked, maybe even rusted shut. The big iron ring of the handle wouldn't turn. He flicked his cigarette lighter and held it close to get a better view. The door was solid but the frame looked weak. He stood back and aimed a kick at it, but nothing happened. He tried again. Hopeless.

He stepped back on to the path. He was now about thirty yards from the house. Its low roof was clearly silhouetted. He could see an aerial and the bulk of a tall chimney with a satellite dish attached to it. It was too big to be an ordinary domestic receiver.

It was while he was staring distractedly at the dish that his eye was caught by a glimmer of light in an upstairs window. It vanished so quickly he thought he might have imagined it and he told himself to keep his nerve, just find a tool, get out of here. But then it flashed again, like the beam of a lighthouse – pale, then bright, then pale again – as someone holding a powerful torch swivelled anti-clockwise towards the window then back towards the blackness of the room.

The suspicious security guard was back.

'God.' Kelso's lips were so tightly drawn he could barely shape his breath into the syllable. 'God, God, God.'

He ran up the path towards the greenhouse. A rickety door slid back just far enough for him to slip through. The vines made it darker inside than out. Trestle tables, an old trug, empty trays for seedlings, terracotta pots – nothing, nothing. He blundered down a narrow aisle, a frond of something brushed his face and then he collided with an object immense and metal. An old bulbous, cast-iron stove. And next to it, a heap of discarded implements – shovel, scuttle, riddling iron, poker. *Poker.*

He squeezed back on to the path, holding his prize, and jammed the poker into the gap between the garden door and the frame, just above the lock. He heaved and heard a crack. The poker came loose. He jammed it back and pulled again. Another crack. He worked it downwards. The frame was splintering.

He took a few paces back and ran at the door, rammed it with his shoulder, and some force that seemed to him beyond the physical – some fusion of will and fear and imagination – carried him through the door and out of the garden and into the quiet emptiness of the street.

Chapter Six

AT SIX O'CLOCK that evening, Major Feliks Suvorin, accompanied by his assistant, Lieutenant Vissari Netto, presented an account of the day's developments to their immediate boss, the chief of the RT Directorate, Colonel Yuri Arsenyev.

The atmosphere was informal, as usual. Arsenyev sprawled sleepily behind his desk, on which had been placed a map of Moscow and a cassette player. Suvorin reclined on the sofa next to the window, smoking his pipe. Netto worked the tape machine.

'The first voice you'll hear, colonel,' Netto was saying to Arsenyev, 'is that of Madame Mamantov.'

He pressed PLAY.

'*Who is this?*'

'*Christopher Kelso. Could I speak with Comrade Mamantov?*'

'*Yes? Who is this?*'

'*As I said, my name is Kelso. I'm using a public telephone. It's urgent.*'

'*Yes, but who is this?*'

Netto pressed PAUSE.

'Poor Ludmilla Fedorova,' said Arsenyev, sadly. 'Did you know her, Feliks? I knew her when she was at the Lubyanka. Oh, she was a piece of work! A body like a pagoda, a mind like a razor and a tongue to match.'

'Not any more,' said Suvorin. 'Not the mind, anyway.'

Netto said, 'The next voice will be even more familiar, colonel.'

PLAY.

'All right, this is Mamantov. Who are you?'

'It's Kelso. Doctor Kelso? You may remember me?'

'I remember you. What do you want?'

'To see you.'

'Why should I see you after that shit you wrote?'

'I wanted to ask you some questions.'

'About?'

'A black oilskin notebook that used to belong to Josef Stalin.'

'Shut up.'

'What?'

'I said shut up. I'm thinking it over. Where are you?'

'Near the Intourist building, on Mohavaja Street.'

'You're close. You'd better come.'

STOP.

'Play it again,' said Arsenyev. 'Not Ludmilla. The latter part.'

Through the armoured glass at Arsenyev's back Suvorin could see the ripple of the office lights reflected in Yasenevo's ornamental lake, and the massive floodlit head of Lenin, and beyond these, almost invisible now, the dark line of the forest, its edge serrated against the evening sky. A pair of headlights winked through the trees and disappeared. A security patrol, thought Suvorin, suppressing a yawn. He was happy to let Netto do the talking. Give the lad a chance.

'A black oilskin notebook that used to belong to Josef Stalin . . .'

'Fuck me,' said Arsenyev, softly, and his flabby face tautened.

'The call was initiated this afternoon, at fourteen-fourteen, by this man,' continued Netto, handing out two flimsy buff-coloured folders. 'Christopher Richard Andrew Kelso, commonly known as "Fluke".'

'Now this is nice,' said Suvorin, who hadn't seen the photograph before. It was still glistening from the darkroom, and reeked of sodium thiosulphate. 'Where are we?'

'Third floor, inner courtyard, opposite the entrance to Mamantov's staircase.'

'So now we can afford an apartment in the House on the Embankment?' grumbled Arsenyev.

'It's empty. Doesn't cost us a rouble.'

'How long did he stay?'

'Arrived at fourteen-thirty-two, colonel. Left at fifteen-seven. One of our operatives, Lieutenant Bunin, was then detailed to follow him. Kelso caught the metro at Borovitskaya, here, changed once, got out at Krasno-presnenskaya, and walked to a house here –' Netto again put his finger on the map ' – in Vspolnyi Street. A deserted property. He made an illegal entry and spent approximately forty-five minutes inside. He was last reported here, heading south on foot along the Garden Ring. That was ten minutes ago.'

'What does that mean exactly? "Fluke"?'

'"A lucky stroke", colonel,' said Netto, smartly. '"An unexpected success."'

'Sergo? Where's that damned coffee?' Arsenyev, immensely fat, had a habit of falling asleep if he didn't have caffeine every hour.

'It's coming, Yuri Semonovich,' said a voice from the intercom.

'Kelso's parents were both in their forties, sir, when he was born.'

Arsenyev turned a tiny and astonished eye towards Vissari Netto. 'Why do we care about his parents?'

'Well –' The young man wilted, stalled, appealed to Suvorin.

'Kelso was a fluke,' said Suvorin. 'The joke. It's a joke.'

'And that is funny?'

They were spared by the arrival of the coffee, borne in by Arsenyev's male assistant. The blue mug said 'I LOVE NEW YORK' and Arsenyev raised it towards them, as if drinking their health. 'So tell me,' he said, blinking through the steam over the rim, 'about Mister Fluke.'

'Born Wimbledon, England, nineteen fifty-four,' said Netto, reading from the file (he had done well, thought Suvorin, to get all this together in the space of an afternoon – the lad was keen, you couldn't fault him on ambition). 'Father, a typical petit-bourgeois, a clerk in legal chambers; three sisters, all older; standard education; nineteen seventy-three, scholarship to study history at the college of St John, Cambridge; starred first class honours degree, nineteen seventy-six –'

Suvorin had already skimmed through all of this – the personal file dredged up from the Registry, a few newspaper cuttings, the entry in *Who's Who* – and now he tried to reconcile the biography with this snatched picture of a figure in a raincoat leaving an apartment. The graininess of the picture had a pleasing, fifties feel: the man, glancing across the street, a cigarette in his mouth, had the appearance of a slightly seedy French actor playing a dodgy cop. *Fluke*. Does a name stick because it suits a man or does the man, unconsciously, evolve into his name? Fluke, the spoiled and lazy teenager, doted on by all these family women, who astonishes his teachers by winning a scholarship to Cambridge – the first in the history of his minor grammar school. Fluke, the carousing student who, after three years of no apparent effort, walks away with the best history degree of his year. Fluke, who just happens to turn up on the doorstep of one of the most dangerous men in Moscow – although, naturally, as a foreigner he would have felt invulnerable. Yes, one would have to be wary of this *Fluke* –

' – scholarship to Harvard, nineteen seventy-eight; admitted to Moscow University, under the "Students for Peace" scheme, nineteen eighty; dissident contacts – see annex "A" – led to recategorisation from "bourgeois-liberal" to "conservative and reactionary"; doctoral thesis published eighty-four, *Power in the Land: The Peasantry of the Volga Region, 1917–22*; lecturer in modern history, Oxford University, eighty-three to ninety-four; now resident in New York City; author of the *Oxford History of Eastern Europe, 1945–87; Vortex: The Collapse of the Soviet Empire*, published ninety-three; numerous articles –'

'All right, Netto,' said Arsenyev, holding up a hand. 'It's getting late. Did we ever make a pass at him?' This question was addressed to Suvorin.

'Twice,' said Suvorin. 'Once at the University, obviously, in nineteen eighty. Again in Moscow in ninety-one, when we tried to sell him on democracy and the New Russia.'

'And?'

'And? Looking at the reports? I should say he laughed in our faces.'

'He's a western asset, do we think?'

'Unlikely. He wrote an article in the *New Yorker* – it's in the file – describing how the Agency and SIS both tried to sign him. Rather a funny piece, in fact.'

Arsenyev frowned. He disapproved of publicity, on either side. 'Wife? Kids?'

Netto jumped in again: 'Married three times.' He glanced at Suvorin, and Suvorin made a little 'go ahead' gesture with his hand: he was happy to take a back seat. 'First, as a student, Katherine Jane Owen, marriage dissolved, seventy-nine. Second, Irina Mikhailovna Pugacheva, married eighty-one –'

'He married a Russian?'

'Ukrainian. Almost certainly a marriage of convenience. She was expelled from the University for anti-state activity. This is the beginning of Kelso's dissident contact. She was granted a visa in eighty-four.'

'So we blocked her entry into Britain for three years?'

'No, colonel, the British did. By the time they let her in, Kelso was living with one of his students, an American, a Rhodes Scholar. Marriage to Pugacheva dissolved in eighty-five. She is now married to an orthodontist in Glamorgan. There is a file but I'm afraid I haven't –'

'Forget it,' said Arsenyev. 'We'll drown in paper. And the third marriage?' He winked at Suvorin. 'A real romeo!'

'Margaret Madeline Lodge, an American student –'

'This is the Rhodes Scholar?'

'No, this is a different Rhodes Scholar. He married this one in eighty-six. The marriage was dissolved last year.'

'Kids?'

'Two sons. Resident with their mother in New York City.'

'One cannot help but admire this fellow,' said Arsenyev, who, despite his bulk, had a mistress of his own in Technical Support. He contemplated the photograph, the corners of his mouth turned down in admiration. 'What's he doing in Moscow?'

'Rosarkhiv are holding a conference,' said Netto, 'for foreign scholars.'

'Feliks?'

Major Suvorin had his right ankle swung up on to his left knee, his elbows resting casually on the sofa back, his sports jacket unbuttoned – easy, confident, Americanized: his style. He took a pull on his pipe before he spoke.

'The words used on the telephone are ambiguous, obviously. The implication could be that Mamantov has this notebook, and the historian wishes to see it. Or the historian himself has the notebook, or has heard of it, and wishes to check some detail with Mamantov. Whichever is the case, Mamantov is clearly aware of our surveillance, which is why he cuts the conversation short. When is Kelso due to leave the Federation, Vissari, do we know yet?'

'Tomorrow lunchtime,' said Netto. 'Delta flight to JFK, leaves Sheremetevo-2 at thirteen-thirty. Seat booked and confirmed.'

'I recommend we arrange for Kelso to be stopped and searched,' said Suvorin. 'Strip-searched, it had better be – delay the flight if necessary – on suspicion of exporting material of historical or cultural interest. If he's taken anything from this house in Vspolnyi Street, we can get it off him. In the meantime, we maintain our coverage of Mamantov.'

A buzzer sounded on Arsenyev's desk; Sergo's voice.

'There's a call for Vissari Petrovich.'

'All right, Netto,' said Arsenyev. 'Take it in the outer office.' When the door was closed, he scowled at Suvorin, 'Efficient little bastard, isn't he?'

'He's harmless enough, Yuri. He's just keen.

Arsenyev grunted, took two long squirts from his inhaler, unhitched his belt a notch, let his flesh sag towards his desk. The colonel's fat was a kind of camouflage: a blubbery, dimpled netting thrown over an acute mind, so that while other, sleeker men had fallen, Arsenyev had safely waddled on – through the cold war (KGB chief resident in Canberra and Ottawa), through glasnost and the failed coup and the break-up of the service, on and on, beneath the armoured soft protective shell of his flesh, until now, at last, he was into the final stretch: retirement in one year, dacha, mistress, pension, and the rest of the world could go fuck its collective mother. Suvorin rather liked him.

'All right, Feliks. What do you think?'

'The purpose of the Mamantov operation,' said Suvorin, carefully, 'is to discover how five hundred million roubles were siphoned out of KGB funds, where Mamantov hid them, and how this money is being used to fund the anti-democratic opposition. We already know he bankrolls that red fascist mucksheet –'

'*Aurora* –'

' – *Aurora* – if it now turns out he's spending it on guns as well, I'm interested. If he's buying Stalin memorabilia, or selling it, for that matter – well, it's sick, but –'

'This isn't just *memorabilia*, Feliks. This – this is famous – there was a file on this notebook – it was one of "the legends of Lubyanka".'

Suvorin's first reaction was to laugh. The old man couldn't be serious, surely? Stalin's *notebook?* But then he saw the expression on Arsenyev's face and hastily turned his laughter into a cough. 'I'm sorry, Yuri Semonovich – forgive me – if you take it seriously, then, of course, I take it seriously.'

'Run the tape again, Feliks, would you be so good? I never could work these damned machines.'

He slid it across the desk with a hairy, pudgy forefinger. Suvorin came over from the sofa and they listened to it together, Arsenyev breathing heavily, tugging at the thick flesh of his fat neck, which was what he always did when he scented trouble.

'. . . *a black oilskin notebook that used to belong to Josef Stalin . . .*'

They were still bent over the tape when Netto crept back in, his complexion three shades paler than usual, to announce he had bad news.

FELIKS Stepanovich Suvorin, with Netto at his heels, walked back, grim-faced, to his office. It was a long trek from the leadership suites in the west of the building to the operational block in the east, and in the course of it at least a dozen people must have nodded and smiled at him, for in the Finnish-designed, wood and white-tile corridors of Yasenevo, the major was the golden boy, the coming man. He spoke English with an American accent, subscribed to the leading American magazines and had a collection of modern American jazz, which he listened to with his wife, the daughter of one of the President's most liberal economic advisers. Even Suvorin's clothes were American – the button-down shirt, the striped tie, the brown sports jacket – each one a legacy of his years as the KGB resident in Washington.

Look at Feliks Stepanovich!, you could see them thinking, as they struggled into their winter coats and hurried past to catch the buses home. Put in as number two to that fat old timer, Arsenyev, primed to take over an entire directorate at the age of thirty-eight. And not just any directorate, either, but RT – one of the most secret of them all! – licensed to conduct foreign intelligence operations on Russian soil. Look at him, the coming man, hurrying back to his office to work, while we go off home for the night . . .

'Good evening to you, Feliks Stepanovich!'

'So long, Feliks! Cheer up!'

'Working late again, I see, comrade major!'

Suvorin half-smiled, nodded, gestured vaguely with his pipe, preoccupied.

The details, as Netto had relayed them, were sparse but eloquent. Fluke Kelso had left the Mamantovs' apartment at fifteen-seven. Suvorin had also left the scene a few minutes later. At fifteen-twenty-two, Ludmilla Fedorova Mamantova, in the company of the bodyguard, Viktor Bubka, was also observed to leave the apartment for her customary afternoon stroll to the Bolotnaya Park (given her confused condition, she had always to be accompanied). Since there was only one man on duty, they were not followed.

They did not return.

Shortly after seventeen hundred, a neighbour in the apartment beneath the Mamantovs' reported hearing prolonged, hysterical screams. The porter had been summoned, the apartment – with difficulty – opened and Madame Mamantov had been discovered alone, in her undergarments, locked inside a cupboard, through the door of which she had nevertheless managed to kick a hole using her bare feet. She had been taken to the Diplomatic Policlinic in a state of extreme distress. Both her ankles were broken.

'This must be an emergency escape plan,' said Suvorin, as they reached his office. 'He's clearly had this up his sleeve for quite a while, even down to establishing a routine for his wife. The question is: what's the emergency?'

He pressed the light switch. Neon panels stuttered into life. The leadership's side of the building had the view of the lake and the trees while Suvorin's office looked north, towards the Moscow ring road and the squat and crowded tower blocks of a housing estate. Suvorin threw himself into his chair, grabbed his tobacco pouch and swung his feet up on to the window sill. He saw Netto, reflected, coming in and closing the door. Arsenyev had given him a blasting, which wasn't really fair. If anyone was to blame, it was Suvorin, for sending Bunin after Kelso.

'How many men do we have at Mamantov's apartment right now?'

'Two, major.'

'Split them. One to the Policlinic to keep an eye on the wife, one to stay in place. Bunin's to stick with Kelso. What's his hotel?'

'The Ukraina.'

'Right. If he's heading south down the Garden Ring he's probably on his way back. Call Gromov at the Sixteenth and tell him we want a full communications intercept on Kelso. He'll tell you he hasn't the resources. Refer him to Arsenyev. Have the authorisation papers on my desk within fifteen minutes.'

'Yes, major.'

'Leave the Tenth to me.'

'The Tenth, major?' The Tenth was the archives branch.

'According to the colonel, there should be a file on this Stalin notebook.' Legend of the Lubyanka, indeed! 'I'll need to dream up some excuse to see it. Check on this place in Vspolnyi Street: what is it exactly? God, we need more men!' Suvorin banged his desk in frustration. 'Where's Kolosov?'

'He left for Switzerland yesterday.'

'Anybody else around? Barsukov?'

'Barsukov's in Ivanovo with his Germans.'

Suvorin groaned. This operation was running on paraffin and thin air, that was the trouble with it. It didn't have a name, a budget. Technically, it wasn't even legal.

Netto was writing rapidly. 'What do you want to do with Kelso?'

'Just continue to keep an eye on him.'

'Not pick him up?'

'For what exactly? And where do we take him? We have no cells. We have no legal basis to make arrests. How long's Mamantov been loose?'

'Three hours, major. I'm sorry, I –' Netto looked close to tears.

'Forget it, Vissi. It's not your fault.' He smiled at the young man's reflection. 'Mamantov was pulling stunts like that while we were in the womb. We'll find him,' he added, with a confidence he did not feel, 'sooner or later. Now off you go. I've got to call my wife.'

After Netto had gone, Suvorin removed the photograph of Kelso from its folder and pinned it to the noticeboard beside his desk. Here he was, with so much else to do, on issues which really mattered – economic intelligence, bio-technology, fibre optics – reduced to worrying about whether and why Vladimir Mamantov was after Stalin's notebook. It was absurd. It was worse than absurd. It was shaming. What kind of a country was this? Slowly, he tamped the tobacco in his pipe and lit it. And then he stood there for a full minute, his hands clasped behind his back, his pipe between his teeth, regarding the historian with an expression of pure loathing.

Chapter Seven

FLUKE KELSO LAY on his back, on his bed, in his room on the twenty-third floor of the Ukraina Hotel, smoking a cigarette and staring at the ceiling, the fingers of his left hand curled around the comforting and familiar shape of a quarter-bottle of Scotch.

He hadn't bothered to take off his coat, nor had he turned on the bedside lamp. Not that he needed to. The brilliant white floodlights that lit the Stalinist–Gothic skyscraper shone into his room and provided a feverish illumination. Through the closed window he could hear the sound of the early evening traffic on the wet road far below.

A melancholy hour this, he always thought, for a stranger in a foreign city – nightfall, the brittle lights, the temperature dropping, the office workers hurrying home, the business-men trying to look cheerful in the hotel bars.

He took another swig of Scotch, then reached over for the ashtray and balanced it on his chest, tapping the end of his cigarette into it. The bowl hadn't been cleaned properly. Still stuck to its dusty bottom, like a small green egg, nested a gobbet of Papu Rapava's phlegm.

It had taken Kelso only a few minutes – the length of one short visit to the Ukraina's business centre and the time it took to flick through an old Moscow telephone directory – to establish that the house on Vspolnyi Street had indeed once been an African embassy. It was listed under the Republic of Tunisia.

And it had taken him only slightly longer to extract the rest of the information he needed – sitting on the edge of his hard and narrow bed, talking earnestly on the telephone to the press attaché at the new Tunisian Embassy, pretending an intense interest in the booming Moscow property market and the precise design of the Tunisian flag.

According to the press attaché, the Tunisians had been offered the mansion on Vspolnyi Street by the Soviet government in 1956, on a short-term lease, renewable every seven years. In January, the ambassador had been notified that the lease would not be extended when it came up for renegotiation, and in August they had moved out. And in truth, sir, they had not been too sorry to go, no indeed, not after that unfortunate business in 1993 when workmen had dug up twelve human skeletons, victims of the Stalinist repression, buried beneath the pavement outside. No explanation for the eviction had been offered, but, as everyone knew, great swathes of state property were now being privatised in central Moscow and sold on to foreign investors; fortunes were being made.

And the flag? The flag of the Tunisian Republic, honourable sir, was a red crescent and a red star in a white orb, all on a red ground.

'. . . there was a red sickle moon and a single red star . . . '

The blue shaving of cigarette smoke curled and broke against the dusty plaster.

Oh, he thought, how prettily it all hung together – Rapava's story and Yepishev's story and the convenient emptiness of the Beria mansion and the freshly turned earth and the bar named 'Robotnik'.

He finished the Scotch and stubbed out his cigarette and lay there for a while, turning the book of matches over and over, anti-clockwise in his fingers.

*

STILL unsure of what he should do, Kelso went down to the front desk and changed the last of his travellers' cheques into roubles. He would need to have cash, whatever happened. He would need ready money. His credit card was not entirely reliable these days – witness that unfortunate incident at the hotel shop, when he had tried to use it to buy his Scotch.

He thought he saw someone he recognised – from the symposium, presumably – and he raised his hand but they had already turned away.

On the counter of the reception was a sign – *Any guest requiring to make an international telephone call must please to leave a cash deposit* – and seeing it gave him a second stab of homesickness. So much happening, nobody to tell. On impulse he handed over $50 and made his way back through the crowded lobby towards the elevators.

Three marriages. He contemplated this extraordinary feat as the elevator shot him skywards. Three divorces in ascending order of bitterness.

Kate – well, Kate, that hardly counted, they were students, it was doomed from the start. She had even sent him Christmas cards until he moved to New York. And Irina – she at least had got her passport, which was always, he suspected, the main point of the exercise. But Margaret – poor Margaret – she was pregnant when he married her, which was why he married her, and no sooner had one boy arrived than the next was coming, and suddenly they were stuck in four cramped rooms off the Woodstock Road: the history teacher and the history student who between them had no history. It had lasted twelve years – 'as long as the Third Reich,' Fluke, drunk, had told an inquiring gossip columnist on the day that Margaret's petition for divorce had been published. He had never been forgiven.

Still, she was the mother of his children. Maggie. Margaret. He would call poor Margaret.

The line sounded strange from the moment the operator got on to the international circuit, and his first reaction was, *Russian phones!* He shook it hard as the New York number began to ring.

'Hello.' The familiar voice, sounding unfamiliarly bright.

'It's me.'

'Oh.' Flat, suddenly; dead. Not even hostile.

'Sorry to ruin your day.' It was meant to be a joke, but it came out badly, bitter and self-pitying. He tried again. 'I'm calling from Moscow.'

'Why?'

'Why am I calling or why am I calling from Moscow?'

'Are you drinking?'

He glanced at the empty bottle. He had forgotten her capacity to smell breath at four thousand miles. 'How are the boys? Can I talk to them?'

'It's eleven o'clock on a Tuesday morning. Where do you think they are?'

'School?'

'Well done, *dad*.' She laughed, despite herself.

'Listen,' he said, 'I'm sorry.'

'For what in particular?'

'For last month's money.'

'*Three* months' money.'

'It was some cock-up at the bank.'

'Get a job, Fluke.'

'Like you, you mean?'

'Fuck you.'

'All right. Withdrawn.' He tried again. 'I spoke to Adelman this morning. He might have something for me.'

'Because things can't go on like this, you know?'

'I know. Listen. I may be on to something here –'

'What's Adelman offering?'

'Adelman? Oh, teaching. But that's not what I mean. I'm on to something here. In Moscow. It could be nothing. It could be huge.'

'What is it?'

There was definitely something odd about the line. Kelso could hear his own voice playing back in his ear, too late to be an echo. *'It could be huge,'* he heard himself say.

'I don't want to talk about it on the phone.'

'You don't want to talk about it on the phone –'

'I don't want to talk about it on the phone.'

' – no, sure you don't. You know why? Because it's just more of the same old shit –'

'Hold on, Maggie. Are you hearing me twice?'

' – and here's Adelman offering you a proper job, but of course you don't want that, because that means facing up –'

'Are you hearing me twice?'

' – to your responsibilities –'

Quietly, Kelso replaced the receiver. He looked at it for a moment, and chewed his lip, then lay back on the bed and lit another cigarette.

STALIN, as you know, was dismissive of women.

Indeed, he believed the very notion of an intelligent woman was an oxymoron: he called them 'herrings with ideas'. Of Lenin's wife, Nadezhda Krupskaya, he once observed to Molotov: 'She may use the same lavatory as Lenin, but that doesn't mean she knows anything about Leninism.' After Lenin's death, Krupskaya believed her status as the great man's widow would protect her from Stalin's purges, but Stalin quickly disabused her. 'If you don't shut your mouth,' he told her, 'we'll get the Party a new Lenin's widow.'

However, this is not the whole story. And here we come to one of those strange reversals of the accepted wisdom which occasionally make our profession so rewarding. For while the common view of Stalin has always been that he was largely indifferent to sex – the classic case of the politician who channels all his carnal appetites into the pursuit of power – the truth appears to have been the opposite. Stalin was a womaniser.

The recognition of this facet of his character is recent. It was Molotov, in 1988, who coyly told Chuyev (Sto sorok besed s Molotovym, Moscow) *that Stalin had 'always been attractive to women'. In 1990, Khrushchev, with the posthumous publication of his last set of interviews* (The Glasnost Tapes, Boston) *lifted the curtain a little further. And now the archives have added still more valuable detail.*

Who were these women, whose favours Stalin enjoyed both before and after the suicide of his second wife? Some we know of. There was the wife of A. I. Yegorov, First Deputy People's Commissar of Defence, who was notorious in Party circles for her numerous affairs. And then there was the wife of another military man – Gusev – a lady who was allegedly in bed with Stalin on the night Nadezhda shot herself. There was Rosa Kaganovich, whom Stalin, as a widower, seems for a time to have thought of marrying. Most interesting of all, perhaps, there was Zhenya Alliluyeva, the wife of Stalin's brother-in-law, Pavel. Her relationship with Stalin is described in a diary which was kept by his sister-in-law, Maria. It was seized on Maria's arrest and only recently declassified (F45 O1 D1).

These, of course, are only the women we know something about. Others are mere shadows in history, like the young maidservant, Valechka Istomina, who joined Stalin's personal staff in 1935 ('whether or not she was Stalin's wife is nobody else's business,' Molotov told Chuyev), or the 'beautiful young woman with dark skin' Khrushchev once saw at Stalin's dacha. 'I was told later she was a tutor for Stalin's children,' he said, 'but she was not there for long. Later she vanished. She was there on Beria's recommendation. Beria knew how to pick tutors . . .'

'Later she vanished . . .'

Once again, the familiar pattern asserts itself: it was never very wise to know too much about Comrade Stalin's private life. One of the men he cuckolded, Yegorov, was shot; another, Pavel Alliluyev, was poisoned. And Zhenya herself, his mistress and his sister-in-law by marriage – 'the rose of the Novgorod fields' – was arrested on Stalin's orders and spent so long in solitary confinement that when eventually she was released, after his death, she could no longer talk – her vocal cords had atrophied . . .

HE must have fallen asleep because the next he knew the telephone was ringing.

The room was still in semi-darkness. He switched on the lamp and looked at his watch. Nearly eight.

He swung his legs off the bed and took a couple of stiff paces across the room to the little desk next to the window.

He hesitated, then picked up the receiver.

But it was only Adelman, wanting to know if he was coming down to dinner.

'Dinner?'

'My dear fellow, it's the great symposium farewell supper, not to be missed. Olga's going to come out of a cake.'

'Christ. Do I have a choice?'

'Nope. The story, by the way, is that you had a hangover of such epic proportions this morning you had to go back to your room and sleep it off.'

'Oh, that's lovely, Frank. Thank you.'

Adelman paused. 'So what happened? You find your man?'

'Of course not.'

'It's all balls?'

'Absolutely. Nothing in it.'

'Only – you know – you were gone all day –'

'I looked up an old friend.'

'Oh, I *get* you,' said Adelman, with heavy emphasis. 'Same old Fluke. Say, are you looking at this view?'

A glittering nightscape spread out at Kelso's feet, neon banners hoisted across the city like the standards of an invading army. Philips, Marlboro, Sony, Mercedes-Benz . . . There was a time when Moscow after sunset was as gloomy as any capital in Africa. Not any more.

There wasn't a Russian word in sight.

'Never thought I'd live to see this, did you?' Adelman's voice crackled down the receiver. 'This is victory we're looking at, my friend. You realise that? Total victory.'

'Is it really, Frank? It just looks like a lot of lights to me.'

'Oh no. It's more than that, believe me. They ain't coming back from this.'

'You'll be telling me next it's "the end of history".'

'Maybe it is. But not the end of historians, thank God.' Adelman laughed. 'Okay, I'll see you in the lobby. Say twenty minutes?' He hung up.

The searchlight on the opposite side of the Moskva, next to the White House, shone fiercely into the room. Kelso reached across and opened the wooden frame of the inner window and then of the outer, admitting a particulate breath of yellow mist and the white noise of the distant traffic. A few snowflakes fluttered across the sill and melted.

The end of history, my arse, he thought. This was

History's town. This was History's bloody *country*.

He stuck his head into the cold, leaning out to see as much of the city as he could across the river, before it was lost in the murk of the horizon.

If one Russian in six believed that Stalin was their greatest ruler, that meant he had about twenty million supporters. (The sainted Lenin, of course, had many more.) And even if you halved that figure, just to get down to the hard core, that still left ten million. Ten million Stalinists in the Russian Federation, after forty years of denigration?

Mamantov was right. It was an astounding figure. Christ, if one in six Germans had said they thought Hitler was the greatest leader they'd ever had, the *New York Times* wouldn't just have wanted an op-ed piece. They'd have put it on the front page.

He closed the window and began gathering together what he would need for the evening: his last two packets of duty free cigarettes, his passport and visa (in case he was picked up), his lighter, his bulging wallet, the book of matches with Robotnik's address.

It was no use pretending he was happy about this, especially after that business at the embassy, and if it hadn't been for Mamantov, he might have been tempted to leave matters as they stood – to play it safe, the Adelman way, and to come back to find Rapava in a week or two, perhaps after wangling a commission in New York from some sympathetic publisher (assuming such a mythical creature still existed).

But if Mamantov was on the trail, he couldn't afford to wait. That was his conclusion. Mamantov had resources at his disposal Kelso couldn't hope to beat. Mamantov was a collector, a fanatic.

And it was the thought of what Mamantov might do with

this notebook, if he found it first, that was also beginning to nag at him. Because the more Kelso turned matters over in his mind, the more obvious it became that whatever Stalin had written was important. It couldn't be some mere compendium of senile jottings, not if Beria wanted it enough to steal it and then, having stolen it, was willing to risk hiding it, rather than destroying it.

'He was squealing like a pig . . . shouting something about Stalin and something about an archangel . . . Then they put a scarf in his mouth and shot him . . .'

Kelso took a last look around the bedroom and turned out the light.

IT wasn't until he got down to the restaurant that he realised how hungry he was. He hadn't had a proper meal for a day and a half. He ate cabbage soup, then pickled fish, then mutton in a cream cheese sauce, with the Georgian red wine, Mukuzani, and sulphurous Narzan mineral water. The wine was dark and heavy and after a couple of glasses on top of the whisky he could feel himself becoming dangerously relaxed. There were more than a hundred diners at four big tables and the noise of the conversation and the clink and chime of glass and cutlery were soporific. Ukrainian folk music was being played over loudspeakers. He started to dilute his wine.

Someone – a Japanese historian, whose name he didn't know – leaned across and asked if this was Stalin's favourite drink and Kelso said no, that Stalin preferred the sweeter Georgian wines, Kindzmarauli and Hvanchkara. Stalin liked sweet wines and syrupy brandies, sugared herbal teas and strong tobacco –

'And Tarzan movies . . .' said someone.

'And the sound of dogs singing . . .'

Kelso joined in the laughter. What else could he do? He clinked glasses with the Japanese across the table, bowed and sat back, sipping his watery wine.

'Who's paying for all this?' someone asked.

'The sponsor who paid for the symposium, I guess.'

'Who's that?'

'American?'

'Swiss, I heard . . .'

The conversation resumed around him. After about an hour, when he thought no one was looking, he folded his napkin and pushed back his chair.

Adelman looked up and said, 'Not again? You can't run out on them again?'

'A call of nature,' said Kelso, and then, as he passed behind Adelman, he bent down and whispered, 'What's the plan for tomorrow?'

'The bus leaves for the airport after breakfast,' said Adelman. 'Check-in at Sheremetevo at eleven-fifteen.' He grabbed Kelso's arm. 'I thought you said this was all balls?'

'I did. I just want to find out what kind of balls.'

Adelman shook his head. 'This just isn't history, Fluke –'

Kelso gestured across the room. 'And this is?' Suddenly there was the sound of a knife being rapped against a glass, and Askenov pushed himself heavily to his feet. Hands banged the table in approval.

'Colleagues,' began Askenov.

'I'd sooner take my chances, Frank. I'll see you.'

He detached himself gently from Adelman's grip and headed towards the exit.

The cloakroom was by the toilets, next door to the dining room. He handed over his token, put down a tip and collected his coat, and he was just shrugging it on when he saw, at the end of the passage leading to the hotel lobby, a man. The man wasn't looking in his direction. He was pacing backwards and forwards across the corridor, talking into a mobile phone. If Kelso had seen him full-face he probably wouldn't have recognised him, and then everything would have turned out differently. But in profile the scar on the side of his face was unmistakable. He was one of the men who had been parked outside Mamantov's apartment.

Through the closed door behind him, Kelso could hear laughter and applause. He backed towards it, until he could feel the doorhandle – all this time keeping his eyes on the man – then he turned and quickly re-entered the restaurant.

Askenov was still on his feet and talking. He stopped when he saw Kelso. 'Doctor Kelso,' he said, 'seems to have a deep aversion to the sound of my voice.'

Saunders called out, 'He has an aversion to the sound of everyone's voice, except his own.'

There was more laughter. Kelso strode on.

Through the swing doors the kitchen was in pandemonium. He had an overpowering impression of heat and steam and of noise and the hot stink of cabbage and boiled fish. Waiters were lining up with trays of cups and coffee pots, being screamed at by a red-faced man in a stained tuxedo. Nobody paid Kelso any attention. He walked quickly across the huge room to the far end, where a woman in a green apron was unloading trays of dirty crockery off a trolley.

'The way out?' he said.

'*Tam*,' she said, gesturing with her chin. '*Tam*.' Over there.

The door had been wedged open to let in some cold air. He went down a dark flight of concrete steps and then he was outside, in the slushy snow, moving through a yard of overflowing trash bins and burst plastic sacks. A rat went scrabbling for safety in the shadows. It took him a minute or so to find his way out, and then he was in the big, enclosed courtyard at the rear of the hotel. Dark walls studded with lit windows rose on three sides of him. The low clouds above his head seemed to boil a yellowish-grey where they were struck by the beam of the searchlight.

He got out down a side-street on to Kutuzovskiy Prospekt and trudged through the wet snow beside the busy highway trying to find a taxi. A dirty, unmarked Volga swerved across two lanes of traffic and the driver tried to persuade him to get in, but Kelso waved him away and kept on walking until he came to the taxi rank at the front of the hotel. He couldn't be bothered to haggle. He climbed into the back of the first yellow cab in the queue and asked to be driven off, quickly.

Chapter Eight

THERE WAS A big football match in progress at the Dinamo stadium – an international, Russia playing someone-or-other, two-all, extra time. The taxi driver was listening to the commentary on the radio and as they came closer to the stadium, the cheers on the cheap plastic loudspeaker were subsumed into the roar of eighty thousand Muscovite throats less than two hundred yards away. The flurries of snow swelled and lifted like sails in the floodlights above the stands.

They had to go up Leningradskiy Prospekt, make a U-turn and come back down the other side to reach the stadium of the Young Pioneers. The taxi, an old Zhiguli that stank of sweat, turned off right, through a pair of iron gates, and bounced down a rutted track and into the sports ground. A few cars were drawn up in the snow in front of the grandstand, and there was a queue of people, mostly girls, outside an iron door with a peep-hole set into it. A sign above the entrance said 'Robotnik'.

Kelso paid the taxi driver a hundred roubles – a ludicrous amount, the price of not haggling before the journey started – and watched with some dismay as the red lights bucked across the rough surface, turned and disappeared. An immense noise, like a breaking wave, came from the phosphorescent sky above the trees and rolled across the white sweep of the pitch. 'Three–two,' said a man with an Australian accent. 'It's over.' He pulled out a tiny black earpiece and stuffed it into his pocket. Kelso said to the nearest person, a girl, 'What time does it open?' and she turned to look at him. She was startlingly beautiful: wide dark eyes and wide cheekbones. She must have been about twenty. Snow flecked her black hair.

'Ten,' she said, and slipped her arm through his, pressing her breast against his elbow. 'Can I have a cigarette?'

He gave one to her and took one himself and their heads brushed as they bent to share the flame. He inhaled her perfume with the smoke. They straightened. 'One minute,' he said, smiling, and moved away, and she smiled back, waving the cigarette at him. He walked along the edge of the pitch, smoking, looking at the girls. Were they *all* hookers? They didn't seem like hookers. What were they, then? Most of the men were foreigners. The Russians looked rich. The cars were big and German, apart from one Bentley and one Rolls. He could see men in the back of them. In the Bentley, a red tip the size of a burning coal glowed and faded as someone smoked an immense cigar.

At five past ten, the door opened – a yellow light, the silhouettes of the girls, the steamy glow of their perfumed breath – a festive sight, thought Kelso, in the snow. And from the cars now came the serious money. You could tell the seriousness not just by the weight of the coats and the jewellery, but by the way their owners carried themselves, straight to the head of the queue, and by the amount of protection they left hanging around at the door. Clearly, the only guns allowed on the premises belonged to the management, which Kelso found reassuring. He went through a metal detector, then his pockets were checked for explosives by a goon with a wand. The admission fee was three hundred roubles – fifty dollars, the average weekly wage, payable in either currency – and in return for this he got an ultra-violet stamp on his wrist and a voucher for one free drink.

A spiral staircase led down to darkness, smoke and laser beams, a wall of techno-music pitched to make the stomach shake. Some of the girls were dancing listlessly together, the men were standing, drinking, watching. The idea of Papu Rapava showing his scowling face in here was a joke, and Kelso would have turned round there and then, but he felt in need of another drink, and fifty dollars was fifty dollars. He gave his voucher to the barman and took a bottle of beer. Almost as an afterthought, he beckoned the bartender towards him.

'Rapava,' he said. The barman frowned and cupped his ear, and Kelso bent closer. 'Rapava,' he shouted.

The barman nodded slowly, and said in English, 'I know.'

'You know?'

He nodded again. He was a young man, with a wispy blond beard and a gold earring. He began to turn away, to serve another customer so Kelso pulled out his wallet and put a one-hundred rouble note on the bar. That got his attention. 'I want to find Rapava,' he shouted.

The money was carefully folded and tucked into the barman's breast pocket. 'Later,' said the young man. 'Okay? I tell you.'

'When?'

But the young man smirked and moved further up the bar.

'Bribing bartenders?' said an American voice at Kelso's elbow. 'That's smart. Never thought of that. Get served first? Impress the ladies? Hello, Dr Kelso. Remember me?'

In the half-light, the handsome face was patched with colour and it took Kelso a couple of seconds to work out who he was. 'Mr O'Brian.' A television reporter. Wonderful. This was all he needed.

They shook hands. The young man's palm was moist and

fleshy. He was wearing his off-duty uniform – pressed blue jeans, white T-shirt, leather jacket – and Kelso registered broad shoulders, pectorals, thick hair glistening with some aromatic gel.

O'Brian gestured across the dance floor with his bottle. 'The new Russia,' he shouted. 'Whatever you want, you buy, and someone's always selling. Where're you staying?'

'The Ukraina.'

O'Brian made a face. 'Save your bribe for later's my advice. You'll need it. They're strict on the door at the old Ukraina. And those beds. Boy.' O'Brian shook his head and drained his bottle, and Kelso smiled and drank as well.

'Any other advice?' he yelled.

'Plenty, since you ask.' O'Brian beckoned him in close. 'The good ones'll ask for six hundred. Offer two. Settle on three. And we're talking all-night rates, remember, so keep some money back. As an incentive, let's say. And be careful of the real, *real* babes, 'cause they may be spoken for. If the other fellow's Russian, just walk away. It's safer, and there's plenty more – we're not talking life partners here. Oh, and they don't do triples. As a rule. These are respectable girls.'

'I'm sure.'

O'Brian looked at him. 'You don't get it, do you, professor? This ain't a whorehouse. Anna here –' he curled his arm around the waist of a blonde girl standing next to him and used his beer bottle as a microphone ' – Anna, tell the professor here what you do for a living.'

Anna spoke solemnly into the bottle. 'I lease property to Scandinavian businesses.'

O'Brian nuzzled her cheek and licked her ear and released her. 'Galina over there – the skinny one in the blue dress? – she works at the Moscow stock exchange. Who else? Damnit, they all look alike, after you've been here a time. Nataliya, the one you spoke to outside – oh, yes, I was watchin' you, professor, you sly old dog – Anna, darlin', what does Nataliya do?'

'Comstar, R.J.,' said Anna. 'Nataliya works for Comstar, remember?'

'Sure, sure. And what was the name of that cute kid at Moscow U? The psychologist, you know the one –'

'Alissa.'

'Alissa, right. Alissa – she in tonight?'

'She got shot, R.J.'

'Boy! Did she? *Really?*'

'Why were you watching me outside?' asked Kelso.

'That's commerce, I guess. You wanna make money, you gotta take risks. Three hundred a night. Let's say three nights a week. Nine hundred dollars. Give three hundred for protection. Still leaves six hundred clear. Twenty thousand dollars a year – that's not hard. What's that – seven times the average annual wage? And no tax? Gotta pay a price for that. Gotta take a risk. Like working on an oil rig. Let me get you a beer, professor. Why shouldn't I watch you? I'm a reporter, goddamnit. Everyone comes here watches everyone else. There's half a billion dollars worth of custom here tonight. And that's just the Russians.'

'Mafia?'

'No, just business. Same as any place else.'

The dance floor was packed now, the noise louder, the smoke denser. A new kind of lightshow had been switched on – lights that made everything that was white stand out dazzlingly bright. Teeth and eyes and nails and banknotes flashed in the gloom like knives. Kelso felt disorientated and vaguely drunk. But not, he thought, as drunk as O'Brian was pretending to be. There was something about the reporter that gave him the creeps. How old was he? Thirty? A young man in a hurry, if ever he'd seen one.

He said to Anna, 'What time does this finish?'

She held up five fingers. 'You want to dance, Mister Professor?'

'Later,' said Kelso. 'Maybe.'

'It's the Weimar Republic,' said O'Brian, coming back with two bottles of beer and a can of Diet Coke for Anna. 'Isn't that what you wrote? Look at it. Christ. All we need is Marlene Dietrich in a tuxedo and we might as well be in Berlin. I liked your book, professor, by the way. Did I say that already?'

'You did. Thanks. Cheers.'

'Cheers.' O'Brian raised his bottle and took a swig, then he leaned over and shouted in Kelso's ear. 'Weimar Republic, that's how I see it. Like you see it. Six things the same, okay? One: you have a big country, proud country, lost its empire, really lost a war, but can't figure out *how* – figures it must've been stabbed in the back, so there's a lot of resentment, right? Two: democracy in a country with no tradition of democracy – Russia doesn't know democracy from a fuckin' hole in the ground, frankly – people don't like it, sick of all the arguing, they want a strong line, *any* line. Three: border trouble – lots of your own ethnic nationals suddenly stuck in other countries, saying they're getting picked on. Four: anti-semitism – you can buy SS marchin' songs on the street corners, for Christ's sake. That leaves two.'

'All right.' It was disconcerting, hearing your own views so crudely parroted; like an Oxford tutorial –

'Economic crash, and that's coming, don't you think?'

'And?'

'Isn't it obvious? *Hitler.* They haven't found their Hitler yet. But when they do, it's watch out, world, I reckon.' O'Brian put his left forefinger under his nose and raised his right arm in a Nazi salute. Across the bar, a group of Russian businessmen whooped and cheered.

AFTER that, the evening accelerated. Kelso danced with Anna, O'Brian danced with Nataliya, they had more drinks – the American stuck to beer while Kelso tried the cocktails: B-52s, Kamikazes – they swapped girls, danced some more and then it was after midnight. Nataliya was in a tight red dress that was slippery, like plastic, and her flesh beneath it, despite the heat, felt cold and hard. She had taken something. Her eyes were wide and poorly focused. She asked if he wanted to go somewhere – she liked him a lot, she whispered, she'd do it for five hundred – but he just gave her fifty, for the pleasure of the dance, and went back to the bar.

Depression stalked him. He wasn't sure why. He could smell desperation, that was it: desperation stank as strongly as the perfume and the sweat. Desperation to buy. Desperation to sell. Desperation to pretend you were having a good time. A young man in a suit, so drunk he could barely walk, was being led away by his tie by a hard-faced girl with long blonde hair. Kelso decided he would have a smoke at the bar and then go – no, on second thoughts, forget the cigarette – he stuffed it back into the pack – he would go.

'Rapava,' yelled the barman.

'What?' Kelso cupped his hand to his ear.

'That's her. She's here.'

'What?'

Kelso looked to where the barman was pointing and saw her at once. *Her.* He let his gaze travel past her and then come back. She was older than the others: close-cropped black hair, black eyeshadow like bruises, black lipstick, a dead white face at once broad and thin, with cheekbones as sharp as a skull. Asiatic-looking. Mingrelian.

Papu Rapava: released from the camps in 1969. Married, say 1970, 1971. A son just old enough to fight in Afghanistan. And a daughter?

'My daughter's a whore . . .'

'Night night, professor –' O'Brian swept past with a wink over his shoulder, Nataliya on one arm, Anna on the other. The rest of his words were lost in the noise. Nataliya turned, giggled, blew Kelso a kiss. Kelso smiled vaguely, waved, put down his drink and moved along the bar.

A black cocktail dress – fabric shiny, knee-length, sleeveless – bare white throat and arms (not even a wrist watch), black stockings, black shoes. And something not quite right about her, some disturbance in the atmosphere around her, so that even at the crowded bar she was in a space, alone. No one was talking to her. She was drinking a bottle of mineral water without a glass and looking at nothing, her dark eyes were blank, and when he said hello she turned to face him, without interest. He asked if she wanted a drink.

No.

A dance, then?

She looked him over, thought about it, shrugged.

Okay.

She drained the bottle, set it on the bar, and pushed past him on to the dance floor, turned, waited for him. He followed her.

She didn't make much of a pretence and he rather liked her for that. The dance was merely a polite prelude to business, like a broker and a client spending ten seconds inquiring after each other's health. For about a minute she moved idly, at the edge of the pack, then she leaned over and said, 'Four hundred?'

No trace of perfume, just a vague scent of soap.

Kelso said, 'Two hundred.'

'Okay.'

She walked straight off the floor without looking back and he was so surprised by her failure to haggle that for a moment he was left alone. Then he went after her, up the spiral staircase. Her hips were full in the tight black dress, her waist thick, and it occurred to him that she didn't have long to go at this end of the game, that it was a mistake to invite immediate comparison with women eight, ten, maybe even twelve years her junior.

They collected their coats in silence. Hers was cheap, thin, too short for the season.

They went out into the cold. She took his arm. That was when he kissed her. He was slightly drunk and the situation was so surreal that he actually thought for a moment that he might combine business and pleasure. And he was curious, he had to admit it. She responded immediately, and with more passion than he'd expected. Her lips parted. His tongue touched her teeth. She tasted unexpectedly of something sweet and he remembered thinking that maybe her lipstick was flavoured with liquorice: was that possible?

She pulled away from him.

'What's your name?' he said.

'What name do you like?'

He had to smile at that. His luck: to find the first post-modern whore in Moscow. When she saw him smiling, she frowned.

'What's your wife's name?'

130

'I don't have a wife.'

'Girlfriend?'

'No girlfriend, either.'

She shivered and thrust her hands deep into her pockets. It had stopped snowing, and now that the metal door had closed behind them the night was silent.

She said, 'What's your hotel?'

'The Ukraina.'

She rolled her eyes.

'Listen,' he began, but he had no name to ease the conversation. 'Listen, I don't want to sleep with you. Or rather,' he corrected himself, 'I do, but that isn't what I had in mind.'

Was that clear?

'Ah,' she said, and looked knowing – looked like a whore for the first time, in fact. 'Whatever you want, it's still two hundred.'

'Do you have a car?'

'Yes.' She paused. 'Why?'

'The truth is,' he said, wincing at the lie, 'I'm a friend of your father's. I want you to take me to see him –'

That shocked her. She reeled back, laughing, panicky. 'You don't know my *father*.'

'Rapava. His name's Papu Rapava.'

She stared at him, slack mouthed, then slapped his face – hard, the heel of her hand connecting with the edge of his cheekbone – and started walking away, fast, stumbling a little: it couldn't have been easy in high heels on freezing snow. He let her go. He wiped his mouth with his fingers. They came away black with something. Not blood he realised: lipstick. Oh, but she packed a punch, though: he was hurting. Behind him, the door had opened. He was

131

aware of people watching, and a murmur of disapproval. He could guess what they were thinking: rich westerner gets honest Russian girl outside, tries to renegotiate the terms, or suggests something so disgusting she can only turn and run – *bastard*. He set off after her.

She had veered on to the virgin snow of the pitch and had stopped, somewhere near the halfway line, staring into the dark sky. He trod along the path of her small footprints, came up behind her and waited, a couple of yards away.

After a while, he said, 'I don't know who you are. And I don't want to know who you are. And I won't tell your father how I found him. I won't tell anyone. I give you my word. I just want you to take me to where he lives. Take me to where he lives and I'll give you two hundred dollars.'

She didn't turn. He couldn't see her face.

'Four hundred,' she said.

Chapter Nine

FELIKS SUVORIN, IN a dark blue Crombie overcoat from
Saks of Fifth Avenue, had arrived at the Lubyanka in the
snow a little after eight that evening, sweeping up the slushy
hill in the back of an official Volga.

His path had been eased by a call from Yuri Arsenyev to
his old buddy, Nikolai Oborin – hunting crony, vodka
partner and nowadays chief of the Tenth Directorate, or the
Special Federal Archive Resource Bureau, or whatever the
Squirrels had decided to call themselves that particular week.

'Now listen, Niki, I've got a young fellow in the office with
me, name of Suvorin, and we've come up with a ploy . . .
That's him . . . Now, listen, Niki, I can't say more than this:
there's a foreign diplomat – western, highly placed – he's got
a racket going, smuggling . . . No, not icons, this time, wait
for it – documents – and we thought we'd lay a trap . . .
That's it, that's it, you're way ahead of me, comrade –
something big, something irresistible . . . Yes, that's an idea,
but what about this: what about that notebook the old
NKVDers used to go on about, what was it? . . . That's it,
"Stalin's testament" . . . Well, this is why I'm calling now.
We've got a problem. He's meeting the target tomorrow . . .
Tonight? He can do tonight, Niki, I'm certain – I'm looking
at him now, he's nodding – he can do tonight . . .'

Suvorin hadn't even had to repeat the tale, let alone
elaborate upon it. Once inside the Lubyanka's marble hall,
his papers checked, he'd followed his instructions and called
a man named Blok, who was expecting him. He stood
around the empty lobby, watched by the silent, uncurious

guards and contemplated the big white bust of Andropov, and presently there were footsteps. Blok – an ageless creature, stooped and dusty, with a bunch of keys on his belt – led him into the depths of the building, then out into a dark, wet courtyard and across it and into what looked like a small fortress. Up the stairs to the second floor: a small room, a desk, a chair, a wood-block floor, barred windows –

'How much do you want to see?'

'Everything.'

'That's your decision,' said Blok, and left.

Suvorin had always preferred to look ahead rather than to live in the past: something else he admired about the Americans. What was the alternative for a modern Russian? Paralysis! The end of history struck him as an excellent idea. History couldn't end soon enough, as far as Feliks Suvorin was concerned.

But even he could not escape the ghosts in this place. After a minute he got to his feet and prowled around. Craning his head at the high window he found he could see up to the narrow strip of night sky, and then down to the tiny windows, level with the earth, that marked the old Lubyanka cells. He thought of Isaak Babel, down there somewhere, tortured into betraying his friends, then frantically retracting, and of Bukharin, and his final letter to Stalin (*'I feel, toward you, toward the Party, toward the cause as a whole nothing but great and boundless love: I embrace you in my thoughts, farewell forever . . .'*) and of Zinoviev, disbelieving, being dragged away by his guard to be shot (*'Please comrade, please, for God's sake call Josef Vissarionovich . . .'*)

He pulled out his mobile phone, tapped in the familiar number and spoke to his wife.

'Hi, you'll never guess where I am . . . Who's to say?' He

felt better immediately for hearing her voice. 'I'm sorry about tonight. Hey, kiss the babies for me, will you . . .? And one for you, too, Serafima Suvorina . . .'

The secret police was beyond the reach of time and history. It was protean. *That* was its secret. The Cheka had become the GPU, and then the OGPU, and then the NKVD, and then the NKGB, and then the MGB, and then the MVD, and finally the KGB: the highest stage of evolution. And then, lo and behold!, the mighty KGB itself had been obliged by the failed coup to mutate into two entirely new sets of initials: the SVR – the spies – stationed out at Yasenevo, and the FSB – internal security – still here, in the Lubyanka, amid the bones.

And the view in the Kremlin's highest reaches was that the FSB, at least, was really nothing more than the latest in the long tradition of rearranged letters – that, in the immortal words of Boris Nikolaevich himself, delivered to Arsenyev in the course of a steam bath at the Presidential dacha, 'those motherfuckers in the Lubyanka are still the same old motherfuckers they always were'. Which was why, when the President decreed that Vladimir Mamantov had to be investigated, the task could not be entrusted to the FSB, but had to be farmed out to the SVR – and never mind if they hadn't the resources.

Suvorin had four men to cover the city. He called Vissari Netto for an update. The situation hadn't changed: the primary target – No. 1 – had still not returned to his apartment, the target's wife – No. 2 – was still under sedation, the historian – No. 3 – was still at his hotel and now having dinner.

'Lucky for some,' muttered Suvorin. There was a clatter in the corridor. 'Keep me informed,' he added firmly, and pressed END. He thought it sounded like the right kind of thing to say.

He had been expecting one file, maybe two. Instead, Blok threw open the door and wheeled in a steel trolley stacked with folders – twenty or thirty of them – some so old that when he lost control of the heavy contraption and collided with the wall, they sent up protesting clouds of dust.

'That's your decision,' he repeated.

'Is this the lot?'

'This goes up to sixty-one. You want the rest?'

'Of course.'

HE couldn't read them all. It would have taken him a month. He confined himself to untying the ribbon from each bundle, riffling through the torn and brittle pages to see if they contained anything of interest, then tying them up again. It was filthy work. His hands turned black. The spores invaded the membrane of his nose and made his head ache.

Highly confidential

28 June 1953

To Central Committee, Comrade Malenkov

I hereby enclose the deposition of the cross-examination of prisoner A. N. Poskrebyshev, former assistant to J. V. Stalin, concerning his work as an anti-Soviet spy.

The investigation is continuing.

USSR Deputy Minister of State Security,

A. A. Yepishev

This had been the start of it – a couple of pages, in the middle of Poskrebyshev's interrogation, underscored in red ink almost half a century ago, by an agitated hand:

Interrogator: Describe the demeanour of the General Secretary in the four years, 1949-53.

Poskrebyshev: The General Secretary became increasingly withdrawn and secretive. After 1951, he never left the Moscow district. His health deteriorated sharply, I should say from his 70th birthday. On several occasions I witnessed cerebral disturbances leading to blackouts, from which he quickly recovered. I told him: "Let me call the doctors, Comrade Stalin. You need a doctor." The General Secretary refused, stating that the 4th Main Administration of the Ministry of Health was under the control of Beria, and that while he would trust Beria to shoot a man, he would not trust him to cure one. Instead I prepared for the General Secretary herbal infusions.

Interrogator: Describe the effect of these health problems upon the General Secretary's conduct of his duties.

Poskrebyshev: Before the blackouts commenced, the General Secretary would sustain a workload of approximately two hundred documents each day. Afterwards, this number declined sharply and he ceased to see many of his colleagues. He made numerous writings of his own, to which I was not permitted access.

Interrogator: Describe the form of these private writings.

Poskreybshev: These private writings took various forms. In his final year, for example, he acquired a notebook.

Interrogator: Describe this notebook.

Poskrebyshev: This notebook was of an ordinary sort,

which might be bought in any stationers, with a black oilskin cover.

Interrogator: Which other persons knew of the existence of this notebook?

Poskrebyshev: The chief of his bodyguard, General Vlasik, knew of it. Beria also knew of it and asked me on several occasions to obtain a copy of it. This was not possible, even for me, as the General Secretary confined it to an office safe to which he alone possessed the key.

Interrogator: Speculate as to the contents of this notebook.

Poskrebyshev: I cannot speculate. I do not know.

Highly Confidential
30 June 1953
To USSR Deputy Minister of State Security, A. A. Yepishev
You are instructed to investigate the whereabouts of the personal writings of J. V. Stalin referred to by A. N. Poskrebyshev as a matter of supreme urgency and using all appropriate measures.
Central Committee,
Malenkov

Cross-examination of prisoner Lieutenant-General N. S. Vlasik
1 July 1953 [Extract]
Interrogator: Describe the black notebook belonging to J. V. Stalin.
Vlasik: I do not remember such a notebook.
Interrogator: Describe the black notebook belonging to J. V. Stalin.

Vlasik: I remember now. I first became aware of this in December 1952. One day I saw this notebook on Comrade Stalin's desk. I asked Poskrebyshev what it contained, but Poskrebyshev could not tell me. Comrade Stalin saw me looking at it and asked me what I was doing. I replied that I was doing nothing, that my eye had merely fallen upon this notebook, but that I had not touched it. Comrade Stalin said: "You as well, Vlasik, after more than thirty years?" I was arrested the following morning and brought to the Lubyanka.

Interrogator: Describe the circumstances of your arrest.

Vlasik: I was arrested by Beria, and subjected to numberless cruelties at his hands. Beria questioned me repeatedly about the notebook of Comrade Stalin. I was unable to tell him details. I know nothing further of this matter.

Statement of Lieutenant A. P. Titov, Kremlin Guard
6 July 1953 [Extract]

I was on duty in the leadership area of the Kremlin from 22:00 on 1 March 1953 until 06:00 the following day. At approximately 04:40, I encountered in the Passage of Heroes Comrade L. P. Beria and a second comrade whose identity is not known to me. Comrade Beria was carrying a small case or bag.

Interrogation of Lieutenant P. G. Rapava, NKVD
7 July 1953 [Extract]

Interrogator: Describe what happened following your departure from J. V. Stalin's dacha with the traitor Beria.

Rapava: I drove Comrade Beria to his home.

Interrogator: Describe what happened following your departure from J. V. Stalin's dacha with the traitor Beria.

Rapava: I remember now. I drove Comrade Beria to the Kremlin to enable him to collect material from his office.

Interrogator: Describe what happened following your departure from J. V. Stalin's dacha with the traitor Beria.

Rapava: I have nothing to add to my previous statement.

Interrogator: Describe what happened following your departure from J. V. Stalin's dacha with the traitor Beria.

Rapava: I have nothing to add to my previous statement.

Interrogation of L. P. Beria

8 July 1953 [Extract]

Interrogator: When did you first become aware of the personal notebook belonging to J. V. Stalin?

Beria: I refuse to answer any questions until I have been allowed to express myself before a full meeting of the Central Committee.

Interrogator: Both Vlasik and Poskrebyshev have confirmed your interest in this notebook.

Beria: The Central Committee is the proper forum in which all these matters should be addressed.

Interrogator: You do not deny your interest in this notebook.

Beria: The Central Committee is the proper forum.

Highly Confidential
30 November 1953
To USSR Deputy Minister of State Security, A. A. Yepishev
You are instructed to bring the investigation into the anti-Party criminal and traitor Beria to a rapid conclusion, and to move this matter to trial.
Central Committee,
Malenkov
Khrushchev

Interrogation of L. P. Beria
2 December 1953 [Extract]
Interrogator: We know that you took possession of the notebook of J. V. Stalin, yet you continue to deny this matter. What was your interest in this notebook?
Beria: End it.
Interrogator: What was your interest in this notebook?
Beria: [The accused indicated by gesture his refusal to co-operate]

Highly confidential
23 December 1953
To Central Committee, Comrades Malenkov, Khrushchev
I beg to report that the sentence of death by shooting imposed on L. P. Beria was carried out today at 01:50.
T. R. Falin,
Procurator General

27 December 1953
Judgement of the People's Special Court in the case of

Lieutenant P. G. Rapava: 15 years' penal servitude.

SUVORIN couldn't bear the filth of his hands any longer. He wandered the empty corridor until he found a toilet with a sink where he could wash himself down. He was still in there, trying to get the last of the dust out from under his fingernails, when his mobile phone rang. In the silence of the Lubyanka it made him jump.

'Suvorin.'

'It's Netto. We've lost him. No. 3.'

'Who? What're you talking about?'

'No. 3. The historian. He went in to eat with the others. He never came out. It looks as though he left through the kitchens.'

Suvorin groaned, turned, leaned against the wall. This whole business was spinning out of control.

'How long ago?'

'About an hour. In defence of Bunin, he has been on duty for eighteen hours.' A pause. 'Major?'

Suvorin had the phone wedged between his chin and shoulder. He was drying his hands, thinking. He didn't blame Bunin, actually. To mount a decent surveillance took at least four watchers; six for safety.

'I'm still here. Stand him down.'

'Do you want me to tell the chief?'

'I think not, don't you? Not twice in one day. He might begin to think we're incompetent.' He licked his lips, tasting dust. 'Why don't you go home yourself, Vissari? We'll meet in my office, eight tomorrow.'

'Have you discovered anything?'

'Only that when people go on about "the good old days" they're talking shit.'

He rinsed his mouth, spat, went back to work.

BERIA was shot, Poskrebyshev released, Vlasik got a sentence of ten years, Rapava was sent to Kolyma, Yepishev was taken off the case, the investigation meandered on.

Beria's house was searched from attic to cellar and yielded no further evidence, apart from some pieces of human remains (female) that had been partially dissolved by acid and bricked up. He had his own private network of cells in the basement. The property was sealed. In 1956, the Ministry for Foreign Affairs asked the KGB if it had any suitable premises which might be offered as an embassy to the new Republic of Tunisia, and, after a final brief investigation, Vspolnyi Street was handed over.

Vlasik was interrogated twice more about the notebook, but added nothing new. Poskrebyshev was watched, bugged, encouraged to write his memoirs and, when he had finished, the manuscript was seized 'for permanent retention'. An extract, a single page, had been clipped to the file:

What went through the mind of this incomparable genius in that final year, as he confronted the obvious fact of his own mortality, I do not know. Josef Vissarionovich may have confided his most private thoughts to a notebook, which rarely left his side during his final months of unstinting toil for his people and the cause of progressive humanity. Containing, as it may do, the distillation of his wisdom as the leading theoretician of Marxism–Leninism, it must be hoped that this remarkable document will one day be discovered and published for the benefit . . .

Suvorin yawned, closed the bundle and put it to one side, grabbed another. This turned out to be the weekly reports of a Gulag stool-pigeon named Abidov, assigned to keep an eye on the prisoner Rapava during his time at the Butugychag uranium mine. There was nothing of interest in the smudged carbons, which ended abruptly with a laconic note from the camp KGB officer, recording Abidov's death from a stab wound, and Rapava's transfer to a forestry labour detail.

More files, more stoolies, more of nothing. Papers authorising Rapava's release at the conclusion of his sentence, reviewed by a special commission of the Second Chief Directorate – passed, stamped, authorised. Appropriate work selected for the returning prisoner at the Leningrad Station engine sheds; KGB informer-in-place: Antipin, foreman. Appropriate housing selected for the returning prisoner at the newly built Victory of the Revolution complex; KGB informer-in-place: Senka, building supervisor. More reports. Nothing. Case reviewed and classified as 'diversion of resources', 1975. Nothing on file until 1983, when Rapava was briefly re-examined at the request of the deputy chief of the Fifth Directorate (Ideology and Dissidents).

Well, well . . .

Suvorin pulled out his pipe and sucked at it, scratched his forehead with the stem, then went searching back through the files. How old was this fellow? Rapava, Rapava, Rapava – here it was, Papu Gerasimovich Rapava, born 9.9.27.

Old, then – in his seventies. But not *that* old. Not so old that even in a country where the average male life expectancy was fifty-eight and falling – worse than it had been in Stalin's time – not so old that he need necessarily be *dead*.

He flipped back to the 1983 report, and scanned it. It told him nothing he didn't know already. Oh, he was a tight one, this Rapava – not a word in thirty years. Only when he reached the bottom, and saw the recommendation to take no further action, and the name of the officer accepting this recommendation did he jolt up in his chair.

He swore and fumbled for his mobile, tapped out the number of the SVR's night duty officer and asked to be patched through to the home of Vissari Netto.

Chapter Ten

THEY SETTLED ON three hundred, and for that he insisted on two things: first, that she drove him there herself and, secondly, that she waited an hour. An address on its own would be useless at this time of night, and if Rapava's neighbourhood was as rough as the old man had implied it was *('it was a decent block in those days, boy, before the drugs and the crime . . .')* then no foreigner in his right mind would go stumbling around there alone.

Her car was a battered, ancient Lada, sand-coloured, parked in the dark street that led to the stadium, and they walked to it in silence. She opened her door first and then reached across to let him in. There was a pile of books on the passenger seat – legal textbooks, he noticed – and she moved them quickly into the back.

He said, 'Are you a lawyer? Are you studying the law?'

'Three hundred dollars,' she said, and held out her hand. 'US.'

'Later.'

'Now.'

'Half now,' he said, cunningly, 'half later.'

'I can get another fuck, mister. Can you get another ride?'

It was her longest speech of the night.

'Okay, okay.' He pulled out his wallet. 'You'll make a good lawyer.' Jesus. Three hundred to her, after more than a hundred at the club – it just about cleaned him out. He had thought he might try offering the old man some cash, this evening, as a downpayment for the notebook, but that wouldn't be possible now.

She re-counted the notes, folded them carefully and put them away in her coat pocket. The little car rattled down to the Leningradskiy Prospekt. She made a right into the quiet traffic, then did a U-turn, and now they were heading out of the city, back past the deserted Dinamo stadium, north-west, towards the airport.

She drove fast. He guessed she wanted to be rid of him. Who was she? The Lada's interior offered him no clues. It was fastidiously clean, almost empty. He gave her profile a surreptitious look. Her face was tilted downwards slightly. She was scowling at the road. The black lips, the white cheeks, the small and delicately pointed ears below the lick of short black hair – she had a vampirish look: disturbing, he thought again. Disturbed. He still had the taste of her in his mouth and he couldn't help wondering what the sex would have been like – she was so utterly out of reach now, yet fifteen minutes earlier she would have done whatever he asked.

She glanced up at the mirror and caught him looking at her. 'Cut that out.'

He continued to stare anyway – more frankly now: he was making a point, he had paid for the ride – but then he felt cheap and turned away.

The streets beyond the glass had become much darker. He didn't know where they were. They had passed the Park of Friendship, he knew that, and passed a power station, a railway junction. Thick pipes carrying communal hot water ran beside the road, across the road, along the other side, steam leaking from their joints. Occasionally, in the patches of blackness, he could see the flames of bonfires and people moving around them. After another ten minutes, they turned off left into a street as wide and rough as a field, with scruffy birch trees on either side. They hit a pothole and the chassis cracked, scraped rock. She spun the wheel and they hit another. Orange lights beyond the trees dimly lit the gantries and stairwells of a giant housing complex.

She had slowed the car now almost to walking pace. She stopped beside a broken-down wooden bus shelter.

'That's his place,' she said. 'Block number nine.'

It was about a hundred yards away, across a snowy strip of waste ground.

'You'll wait here?'

'Entrance D. Fifth floor. Apartment twelve.'

'But you'll wait?'

'If you want.'

'We did agree.'

Kelso looked at his watch. It was twenty-five past one. Then he looked again at the apartment block, trying to think what he would say to Rapava, wondering what reception he would get.

'So this is where you grew up?'

She didn't answer. She switched off the engine and turned up her collar, put her hands in her pockets, stared ahead. He sighed and got out of the car, walked around it. The powdery snow creaked as it compacted under his feet. He shivered and began to pick his way over the rough ground.

He was about halfway across when he heard the grating of an ignition and an engine firing up. He swung round to see the Lada moving off slowly, lights doused. She hadn't even bothered to wait until he was out of sight. *Bitch*. He began running towards her. He shouted – not loudly, and not in anger really: it was more a groan at his own stupidity. The little car was shuddering, stalling, and for a moment he thought he might catch up with it, but then it coughed, lurched, the lights came on and it accelerated away from him. He stood and watched it helplessly as it vanished into the labyrinth of concrete.

He was alone. Not a soul in view.

He turned and began quickly retracing his steps, crunching across the snow towards the building. He felt vulnerable in the open and panic sharpened his senses. Somewhere to his left, he could hear the bark of a dog and a baby's cry, and ahead of him there was music – it was faint, there was scarcely more than a thread of it, but it was coming from Block Nine and it was getting louder with each step. His eyes were making out details now – the ribbed concrete, the shadowed doorways, the stacked balconies crammed with junk: bed frames, bike frames, old tyres, dead plants; three windows were lit, the rest in darkness.

At Entrance D something crunched beneath his foot and he bent to pick it up, then dropped it, fast. A hypodermic syringe.

The stairwell was a sump of piss and vomit, stained newsprint, limp condoms, dead leaves. He covered his nose with the back of his hand. There was an elevator, and it might have been working – a Moscow miracle that would have been – but he didn't propose to try. He climbed the stairs, and by the time he reached the third floor he could hear the music much more clearly. Someone was playing the old Soviet national anthem – the *old* old anthem, that was – the one they used to sing before Khrushchev had it censored. 'Party of Lenin!' shouted the chorus. 'Party of Stalin!' Kelso took the last two flights more quickly, with a sudden rush of hope. She hadn't entirely tricked him, then, for who else but Papu Rapava would be playing the greatest hits of Josef Stalin at half-past one in the morning?

He came out on to the fifth floor and followed the noise along the dingy passage to number twelve. The block was largely derelict. Most of the doors were boarded over, but not Rapava's. Oh no, boy. Rapava's door wasn't boarded over. Rapava's door was open and outside it, for reasons Kelso couldn't begin to fathom, there were feathers on the floor.

The music stopped.

COME on then, boy. What're you waiting for? What's up? Don't tell me you haven't the balls –

For several seconds, Kelso stood on the threshold, listening.

Suddenly there was a drumroll.

The anthem began again.

Cautiously, he pushed at the door. It was partially open, but it wouldn't go back any further. There was something behind it, blocking it.

He squeezed around the edge. The lights were on.

Dear God –

Thought you'd be impressed, boy! Thought you'd be surprised! If you're going to get fucked over, you might as well get fucked over by professionals, eh?

At Kelso's feet were more feathers, leaking from a cushion that had been disemboweled. These feathers could not be said to be on the floor, however, because there was no floor. The boards were all prised up and stacked around the edges of the room. Strewn across the rib-cage of the joists were the remains of Rapava's few possessions – books with splayed and shattered spines, punched-through pictures, the skeletons of chairs, an exploded television, a table with its legs in the air, bits of crockery, shards of glass, shredded fabric. The interior walls had been skinned to expose the cavities. The exterior walls were bruised and dented, apparently by a sledgehammer. Much of the ceiling was hanging down. Plaster dust frosted the room.

Balanced in the centre of this chaos, amid a black and jagged pool of broken records, was a bulky 1970s Telefunken record player, set to automatic replay.

Party of Lenin!

Party of Stalin!

Kelso stepped carefully from rib to rib and lifted the needle.

In the silence: the dripping of a broken tap.

The extent of the destruction was so overwhelming, so utterly beyond anything he had ever seen, that once he was satisfied the apartment was empty, it barely occurred to him that he ought to be scared. Not at first. He peered around him, baffled.

So where am I, boy? That's the question. What have they done with poor old Papu? Come on then, come and get me. Chop, chop, comrade – we haven't got all night!

Kelso, wobbling, tightrope-walked along a joist, into the kitchen alcove: slashed packets, upended ice-box, wrenched-down cupboards . . .

He edged backwards and round the corner into a little passage, scrabbling at the broken wall to stop himself from slipping.

Two doors here, boy – right and left. You take your pick.

He swayed, indecisive, then reached out a hand.

The first – a bedroom.

Now you're getting warm, boy. By the way: did you want to fuck my daughter?

Slashed mattress. Slashed pillow. Overturned bed. Empty drawers. Small and tatty nylon carpet, rolled and stacked. Clumps of plaster everywhere. Floor up. Ceiling down.

Kelso back in the passage, breathing hard, balanced on a rib, summoning the nerve.

The second door –

Very warm now, boy!

– the second door: the bathroom. Cistern lid off, propped against the toilet. Sink dragged away from the wall. A white plastic tub brimming with pinkish water that made Kelso think of diluted Georgian wine. He dipped his finger in and pulled it out sharply, shocked at the coldness, his fingertip sheathed in red.

Floating on the surface: a ring of hair still attached to a small flap of skin.

Let's go, boy.

Rib to rib, plaster dust in his hair, on his hands, all over his coat, his shoes –

He stumbled in his panic, lost his footing on the beam, and his left shoe punched a hole into the ceiling of the flat beneath. A piece of debris detached itself. He heard it fall into the darkness of the empty apartment. It took him half a minute and both hands to pull his foot free, and then he was out of there.

He squashed himself around the door and into the corridor and moved quickly back along the passage, past the abandoned apartments, towards the stairs. He heard a thump.

He stopped and listened.

Thump.

Oh, you're hot, now, boy, you're very, very hot . . .

It was the elevator. It was someone inside the elevator.

Thump.

*

THE Lubyanka, the still of night, the long black car with the engine running, two agents in overcoats charging down the steps – *was there no escaping the past?* thought Suvorin, bitterly, as they accelerated away. He was surprised there were no tourists on hand to record this traditional scene of life in Mother Russia. *Why not put it in the album, darling, between St Basil's Cathedral and a troika in the snow?*

They thumped into a dip at the bottom of the hill near the Metropol Hotel, and his head connected with the cushioned roof. In the front seat, next to the driver, Netto was unfolding a large-scale map of the Moscow streets of a detail that no tourist would ever see because it was still officially secret. Suvorin snapped on the interior light and leaned forward for a better look. The apartment blocks of the Victory of the Revolution complex were scattered like postage stamps across the Tagansko–Krasno metro line, in the north-west outer suburb.

'How long do you reckon? Twenty minutes?'

'Fifteen,' said the driver, showing off. He gunned the engine, shot the lights, swung right, and Suvorin was pitched the other way, against the door. He had a brief impression of the Lenin Library flashing past.

'Relax,' he said, 'for pity's sake. We don't want to get a ticket.'

They sped on. Once they were clear of the centre, Netto unlocked the glove compartment and handed Suvorin a well-oiled Makarov and a clip of ammunition. Suvorin took it reluctantly, felt the unfamiliar weight in his hand, checked the mechanism and sighted briefly at a passing birch tree. He hadn't joined the service because he enjoyed this kind of thing. He had joined because his father was a diplomat who had taught him early on that the best thing to do if you lived in the Soviet Union was to get a posting abroad. Guns? Suvorin hadn't set foot on the Yasenevo range inside a year. He gave the weapon back to Netto who shrugged and stuffed it in his own pocket.

A blue dot grew noisily in the road behind them, swelled and flashed past like an angry fly – a patrol car of the Moscow militia. It dwindled into the distance.

'Asshole,' said their driver.

A few minutes later they turned off the main road and headed into the wilderness of concrete and wasteland that was the Victory of the Revolution. Fifteen years in Kolyma, thought Suvorin, then welcome home to this. And the joke was, it must have seemed like paradise.

Netto said, 'According to the map, Block Nine should be just round this corner.'

'Slow down,' ordered Suvorin, suddenly, putting his hand on the driver's shoulder. 'Can you hear something?'

He wound down his window. Another siren, off to the left. It faded for a moment, muffled by a building, then became very loud, and colours burst ahead – a blue and yellow light-show, rather pretty, moving fast. For a couple of seconds the patrol car seemed to be coming straight at them but then it swung off the road and bounced over the rough ground, and a moment later they were level with it and could see the entrance to the block themselves, lit up like a fairyland – three cars, an ambulance, people moving, shadowed tracks in the snow.

They cruised round the building a couple of times, a trio of ghouls, unnoticed, as the stretcher men brought out the body and then Kelso was driven away.

Chapter Eleven

SIMONOV TELLS THE *following story.*

At meetings of the Council of People's Commissars, it was Comrade Stalin's habit to rise from his place at the head of the long table and to pace behind the backs of the participants. Nobody dared to look round at him: they could establish where he was only by the soft squeak of his leather boots or by the passing fragrance of his Dunhill pipe. On this particular occasion, the conversation concerned the large number of recent plane crashes. The head of the air force, Rychagov, was drunk. 'There will continue to be a high level of accidents,' he blurted out, 'as long as we're compelled by you to go up in flying coffins.' There was a long silence, at the end of which Stalin murmured, 'You really shouldn't have said that.' A few days later, Rychagov was shot.

One could quote any number of such stories. His favourite technique, according to Khrushchev, was suddenly to look at a man and say: 'Why is your face so shifty today? Why can't you look Comrade Stalin directly in the eyes?' That was the moment when one's life hung in the balance.

Stalin's use of terror seems to have been partly instinctive (he was naturally physically violent: he sometimes struck his subordinates in the face) and partly calculated. 'The people,' he told Maria Svanidze, 'need a tsar.' And the tsar upon whom he modelled himself was Ivan the Terrible. We have written confirmation of that here in this archive, in Stalin's personal library, which contains a copy of A. M. Tolstoy's 1942 play, Ivan Grozny *(F558 O3 D350). Not only has Stalin corrected the speeches of Ivan to make them sound more clipped and laconic –*

to sound more like himself, in fact – but he has also scrawled repeatedly over the title page 'Teacher'.

Indeed, he had only one criticism of his role model: that he was too weak. As he told the director, Sergei Eisenstein: 'Ivan the Terrible would execute someone and then spend a long time repenting and praying. God got in his way in this matter. He ought to have been still more decisive!' (Moskovskie novosti, no. 32, 1988).

Stalin was nothing if not decisive.

Professor I. A. Kuganov estimates that some sixty-six million people were killed in the USSR between 1917 and 1953 – shot, tortured, starved mostly, frozen or worked to death. Others say the true figure is a mere forty-five million. Who knows?

Neither estimate, by the way, includes the thirty million now known to have been killed in the Second World War.

To put this loss in context: the Russian Federation today has a population of roughly 150 million. Assuming the ravages inflicted by communism had never occurred, and assuming normal demographic trends, the actual population should be about 300 million.

And yet – and this is surely one of the most astounding phenomena of the age – Stalin continues to enjoy a wide measure of popular support in this half-empty land. His statues have been taken down, true. The street names have been changed. But there have been no Nuremberg Trials, as there were in Germany. There has been no process here equivalent to de-Nazification. There has been no Truth Commission, of the sort established in South Africa.

And the opening of the archives? 'Confronting the past'? Come, ladies and gentlemen, let us say frankly what we all know to be the case. That the Russian government today is scared, and that it is actually harder to gain access to the archives now than *it was six or seven years ago. You all know the facts as well as I do. Beria's files: closed. The Politburo's files: closed. Stalin's files – the real files, I mean, not the window dressing on offer here: closed.*

I can see my remarks are not being well received by one or two colleagues –

All right, I shall draw them to a conclusion, with this observation: that there can now be no doubt that it is Stalin rather than Hitler who is the most alarming figure of the twentieth century.

I say this –

I say this not merely because Stalin killed more people than Hitler – although clearly he did – and not even because Stalin was more of a psychopath than Hitler – although clearly he was. I say it because Stalin, unlike Hitler, has not yet been exorcised. And also because Stalin was not a one-off like Hitler, an eruption from nowhere. Stalin stands in a historical tradition of rule by terror which existed before him, which he refined, and which could exist again. His, not Hitler's, is the spectre that should worry us.

Because, you know, you think about it. You hail a taxi in Munich – you don't find the driver displaying Hitler's portrait in his cab, do you? Hitler's birthplace isn't a shrine. Hitler's grave isn't piled with fresh flowers every day. You can't buy tapes of Hitler's speeches on the streets of Berlin. Hitler isn't routinely praised as 'a great patriot' by leading German politicians. Hitler's old party didn't receive more than forty per cent of the votes in the last German election –

But all these things are true of Stalin in Russia today, which is what makes the words of Yevtushenko, in 'The Heirs of Stalin', more relevant now than ever:

'So I ask our government
To double
To treble
The guard
Over this tomb.'

FLUKE Kelso was escorted into the headquarters of the central division of the Moscow City Militia shortly before three a.m. And there he was left, washed up with the rest of the night's detritus – half a dozen hookers, a Chechen pimp, two white-faced Belgian bankers, a troupe of transsexual dancers from Turkestan and the usual midnight chorus of outraged lunatics, tramps and bloodied addicts. High-corniced ceilings and half-blown chandeliers gave proceedings a Revolutionary epic look.

He sat alone on a hard wooden bench, his head leaning back on the peeling plaster, staring ahead, unseeing. So that – *that* was what it looked like? Oh, you could spend half a lifetime *writing* about it all, about the millions – about Marshal Tukhachevsky, say, beaten to a pulp by the NKVD: there was his confession in the archives, still sprinkled with his dried blood: you even held it in your hands – and you thought for a moment you had a sense of what it must have been like, but then you confronted the reality and you realised you hadn't understood it at all, you hadn't even *begun* to know what it was like.

After a while two militia men wandered up and stood at the metal drinking fountain next to him, discussing the case of the Uzbeki bandit, Tsexer, apparently machine-gunned earlier that evening in the cloakroom of the Babylon.

'Is anyone dealing with my case?' interrupted Kelso. 'It is a murder.'

'Ah, a murder!' One of the men rolled his eyes in mock surprise. The other laughed. They dropped their paper cones in the trash can and moved off.

'Wait!' shouted Kelso.

Across the corridor, an elderly woman with a bandaged hand started screaming.

He sank back on to the bench.

Presently, a third officer, powerfully built, with a Gorky moustache, came wearily downstairs and introduced himself as Investigator Belenky, a homicide detective. He was holding a piece of grubby paper.

'You're the witness in the business involving the old man, Rapazin?'

'Rapava,' corrected Kelso.

'Right. That's it.' Belenky squinted at the top and bottom of the paper. Perhaps it was the walrus moustache or maybe it was his watery eyes but he seemed immensely sad. He sighed. 'Okay. We'd better have a statement.'

Belenky led him up a grand staircase to the second floor, to a room with flaking green walls and an uneven, shiny woodblock floor. He gestured to Kelso to sit, and put a pad of lined forms in front of him.

'The old man had Stalin's papers,' began Kelso, lighting a cigarette. He exhaled quickly. 'You ought to know that. Almost certainly he had them hidden in his apartment. That's why –'

But Belenky wasn't listening. 'Everything you can remember.' He slapped a blue biro down on the table.

'But you hear what I'm saying? Stalin's papers –'

'Right, right.' The Russian still wasn't listening. 'We'll sort out the details later. Need a statement first.'

'All of it?'

159

'Of course. Who you are. How you met the old man. What you were doing at the apartment. The whole story. Write it down. I'll be back.'

After he had gone, Kelso stared at the blank paper for a couple of minutes. Mechanically, he wrote his full name, his date of birth and his address in neat Cyrillic script. His mind was a fog. '*I arrived,*' he wrote, and paused. The plastic pen felt as heavy between his fingers as a crowbar. '*I arrived in Moscow on –*' He couldn't even remember the date. He who was normally so good at dates! (25 October 1917, the battle-cruiser *Aurora* shells the Winter Palace and begins the Revolution; 17 January 1927, Leon Trotsky is expelled from the Politburo; 23 August 1939: the Molotov–Ribbentrop pact is signed . . .) He bent his head to the desk. '*– I arrived in Moscow on the morning of Monday October 26 from New York at the invitation of the Russian Archive Service to deliver a short lecture on Josef Stalin . . .*'

He finished his statement in less than an hour. He did as he was told and left nothing out – the symposium, Rapava's visit, the Stalin notebook, the Lenin Library, Yepishev and the meeting with Mamantov, the house on Vspolnyi Street, the freshly dug earth, Robotnik and Rapava's daughter . . . He filled seven pages with his tiny scrawl, and took the final section even quicker, hurrying over the scene in the apartment, the discovery of the body, his desperate search for a working telephone in the next-door block, eventually rousing a young woman with a baby on her hip. It felt good to be writing again, to be imposing some kind of rational order on the chaos of the past.

Belenky put his head round the door just as Kelso added the final sentence.

'You can forget that now.'

'I've done.'

'No?' Belenky stared at the small pile of sheets and then at Kelso. There was a commotion in the corridor behind him. He frowned, then yelled over his shoulder, 'Tell him to wait.' He came into the room and closed the door.

Something had happened to Belenky, that much was obvious. His tunic was unbuttoned, his tie loose. Dark patches of sweat stained his khaki shirt. Without taking his eyes off Kelso's face, he held out his massive hand and Kelso gave him the statement. He sat down with a grunt on the opposite side of the table and took a plastic case from his breast pocket. From the case he withdrew a surprisingly delicate pair of gold-framed, half-moon glasses, shook them open, perched them on the end of his nose, and began to read.

His heavy chin jutted forwards. Occasionally, his eyes would flicker up from the page to Kelso, study him for a moment, then return to the text. He winced. His moustache sagged lower over his tightening lips. He chewed the knuckle of his right thumb.

When he laid the final page aside he gave a sigh.

'And this is true?'

'All of it.'

'Well, fuck your mother.' Belenky took off his glasses and rubbed his eyes with the side of his hand. 'Now what am I supposed to do?'

'Mamantov,' said Kelso. 'He must have been involved. I was careful not to give him any details but –'

The door opened and a small, thin man, a Laurel to Belenky's Hardy, said, in a frightened voice, 'Sima! Quick! They're here!'

Belenky gave Kelso a significant look, gathered the statement together and pushed back his chair. 'You'll have to go down to the cells for a bit. Don't be alarmed.'

At the mention of cells Kelso felt a spasm of panic. 'I'd like to speak to someone from the embassy.'

Belenky stood and slid his tie back up into a tight knot, fastened the buttons of his tunic, tugged the jacket down in a hopeless attempt to straighten it.

'Can I speak to someone from the embassy?' repeated Kelso. 'I'd like to know my rights.'

Belenky squared his shoulders and moved towards the door. 'Too late,' he said.

IN the cells beneath the headquarters of the Central Division of the Moscow City Militia, Kelso was roughly frisked and parted from his passport, wallet, watch, fountain pen, belt, tie and shoelaces. He watched them shovelled into a cardboard envelope, signed a form, was handed a receipt. Then, with his boots in one hand, his chit in the other and his coat over his arm, he followed the guard down a whitewashed passage lined on either side with steel doors. The guard was suffering from a plague of boils – his neck above his greasy brown collar looked like a plate of red dumplings – and at the sound of his footsteps, the inmates of some of the cells began a frantic shouting and banging. He took no notice.

The eighth cubicle on the left. Three yards by four. No window. A metal cot. No blanket. An enamel pail in the corner with a square of stained wood for a lid.

Kelso went slowly into the cell on his stockinged feet, threw his coat and boots down on the cot. Behind him, the door swung shut with a submarine clang.

Acceptance. That, he had learned in Russia many years ago, was the secret of survival. At the frontier, when your papers were being checked for the fifteenth time. At the road block, when you were pulled over for no reason and kept waiting for an hour and a half. At the ministry, when you went to get your visa stamped and no one had bothered to show up. Accept it. Wait. Let the system exhaust itself. Protest will only raise your blood pressure.

The spyhole in the centre of the door clicked open, stayed open for a moment, clicked shut. He listened to the guard's footsteps retreat.

He sat on the bed and closed his eyes and saw, at once, unbidden, like the after-image of a bright light imprinted on his retina, the white and naked body revolving in the down draught of the elevator shaft – shoulders, heels and trussed hands rebounding gently off the walls.

He sprang at the door and hammered on it with his empty boots and yelled for a while, until he'd got something out of himself. Then he turned and rested his back against the metal, confronting the narrow limits of his cell. Slowly he allowed himself to slide down until he was resting on his haunches, his arms clasped around his knees.

TIME. Now here is a peculiar commodity, boy. The measurement of time. Best accomplished, obviously, with a watch. But, lacking a watch, a man may use instead the ebb and flow of light and dark. Lacking, however, a window through which to see such movement, the reliance must be devolved upon some inner mechanism of the mind. But if the mind has received a shock, the mechanism is disturbed, and time becomes as the ground is to a drunkard, variable.

Thus Kelso, at some point indeterminate, transferred his body from the doorway to the cot and drew his coat across himself. His teeth were chattering.

His thoughts were random, disconnected. He thought of Mamantov, going back over their meeting again and again, trying to remember if he had said anything that could have led him to Rapava. And he thought about Rapava's daughter and the way he had broken his word in his statement. She had abandoned him. Now he had revealed her as a whore. So the world turns. Somewhere, presumably, the militia would have her address on file. Her name as well. The news about her father would be broken to her, and she would be – what? Dry-eyed, he was fairly sure. Yet vengeful.

In his dreams he moved to kiss her again but she evaded his embrace. She danced jerkily across the snow outside the apartment block while O'Brian paraded up and down pretending to be Hitler. Madame Mamantov raged against her madness. And behind a door somewhere, Papu Rapava went on knocking to be let out. In here, boy! Thump. Thump. *Thump.*

HE woke to find a cool blue eye regarding him through the spyhole. The metal eyelid drooped and closed, the lock rattled.

Behind the pustulous guard there stood a second man – blond-headed, well-dressed – and Kelso's first thought was a happy one: *The embassy, they've come to get me out.* But then blond-head said, in Russian, 'Dr Kelso, put your boots on, please,' and the guard shook the contents of the envelope out on to the cot.

Kelso bent to thread his laces. The stranger, he noticed, was wearing a smart pair of western brogues. He straightened and strapped on his watch and saw that it was only six-twenty. A mere two hours in the cells, but enough to last him a lifetime. He felt more human with his boots on. A man can face the world with something on his feet. They passed down the corridor, triggering the same desperate hammering and shouting.

He assumed he would be taken back upstairs for more questioning, but instead they came out into a rear courtyard where a car was waiting with two men in the front seats. Blond-head opened the rear passenger door for Kelso – 'Please,' he said, with cold politeness – then went round and got in the other side. The interior of the car was hot and fetid, as if at the end of a long journey, sweetened only by blond-head's delicate aftershave. They pulled away, out of militia headquarters and into the quiet street. Nobody spoke.

It was beginning to get light – light enough, at least, for Kelso to recognise roughly where they were heading. He had already marked this trio down as secret police, which meant the FSB, which meant the Lubyanka. But to his surprise he realised they were travelling east, not west. They came down the Noviy Arbat, past the deserted shops, and the Ukraina came into view. So they were taking him back to the hotel, he thought. But he was wrong again. Instead of crossing the bridge they turned right and followed the course of the Moskva. Dawn was coming on quickly now, like a chemical reaction, darkness dissolving across the river, first to grey and then to a dirty alkali blue. Streaks of smoke and steam from the factory chimneys on the opposite bank – a tannery, a brewery – turned a corrosive pink.

They drove on in silence for a few more minutes and then suddenly swung off the embankment and parked in a derelict patch of reclaimed land that jutted out into the water. A couple of big sea-birds flapped and rose, and span away, crying. Blond-head was out first and then, after a brief hesitation, Kelso followed him. It crossed his mind that they had brought him to the perfect spot for an accident: a simple push, a flurry of news reports, a long investigation for a London colour supplement, suspicions raised and then forgotten. But he put a brave face on it. What else could he do?

Blond-head was reading the statement Kelso had given to the militia. It flapped in the breeze that was coming off the river. Something about him was familiar.

'Your plane,' he said, without turning round, 'leaves Sheremetevo-2 at one-thirty. You will be on board it.'

'Who are you?'

'You'll be taken back to your hotel now, and then you'll catch the bus to the airport with your colleagues.'

'Why are you doing this?'

'You may try to re-enter the Russian Federation in the near future. In fact, I'm sure you will: you're a persistent fellow, anyone can see that. But I must tell you that your application for a visa will be rejected.'

'This is a bloody *outrage*.' It was stupid, of course, to lose his temper, but he was too tired and shaken-up to help himself. 'A complete bloody *disgrace*. Anyone would think that I was the killer.'

'But you *did* kill him.' The Russian turned round. 'You *are* the killer.'

'This is a joke, is it? I didn't have to come forward. I didn't have to call the militia. I could have run away.'

And don't think I didn't consider it –

'It's here in your own words.' Blond-head slapped the statement. 'You went to Mamantov yesterday afternoon and told him a "witness from the old time" had approached you with information about Stalin's papers. That was a death sentence.'

Kelso faltered. 'I never gave a name. I've been over that conversation in my mind a hundred times –'

'Mamantov didn't need a name. He already *had* the name.'

'You can't be certain –'

'Papu Rapava,' said the Russian, with exaggerated patience, 'was re-investigated by the KGB in nineteen eighty-three. The investigation was at the request of the deputy chief of the Fifth Directorate – Vladimir Pavlovich Mamantov. Do you see?'

Kelso closed his eyes.

'Mamantov knew precisely who you were talking about. There is no other "witness from the old time". Everyone else is dead. So: fifteen minutes after you left Mamantov's apartment, Mamantov also left. He even knew where the old man lived, from his file. He had seven, possibly eight hours to question Rapava. With the assistance of his friends. Believe me, a professional like Mamantov can do a lot of damage to a person in eight hours. Would you like me to give you some of the medical details? No? Then go back to New York, Dr Kelso, and play your games of history in somebody else's country, because this isn't England or America, the past isn't safely dead here. In Russia, the past carries razors and a pair of handcuffs. Ask Papu Rapava.'

A gust of wind swept the surface of the river, raised waves, set a nearby buoy clanking against its rusting chains.

'I can testify,' said Kelso after a while. 'To arrest Mamantov, you'll need my evidence.'

For the first time, the Russian smiled. 'How well do you know Mamantov?'

'Hardly at all.'

'You know him hardly at all. That is your good fortune. Some of us have come to know him well. And I can assure you that Comrade V. P. Mamantov will have no fewer than six witnesses – none of them below the rank of full colonel – who will swear that he spent the whole of last evening with them, discussing charity work, one hundred miles from Papu Rapava's apartment. So much for the value of your testimony.'

He tore Kelso's statement in half, then halved it again, and again – kept on until it couldn't be reduced further. He crumpled the pieces between his hands, cupped them and threw the fragments out across the water. The wind caught them. The seagulls swooped in the hope of food then wheeled away, shrieking with disappointment.

'Nothing is as it was,' he said. 'You ought to know that. The investigation begins again from scratch this morning. This statement was never taken. You were never detained by the militia. The officer who questioned you has been promoted and is being transferred, even as we speak, by military transport plane to Magadan.'

'Magadan?' Magadan was on the eastern rim of Siberia, four thousand miles away.

'Oh, we'll bring him back,' said the Russian, airily, 'when this is sorted out. What we don't want is the Moscow press corps trampling over everything. That really would be embarrassing. Now, I tell you all this, knowing there's nothing we can do to prevent you publishing your version of events abroad. But there will be no official corroboration from here, you understand? Rather the contrary. We reserve the right to make public *our* record of your day's activity, in which your motives will be made to look quite different. For example: you were arrested for indecent exposure to a couple of children in the Zoopark, the daughters of one of my men. Or you were picked up drunk on the Smolenskaya embankment, urinating into the river, and had to be locked up for violent and abusive behavior.'

'Nobody will believe it,' said Kelso, trying to summon a last vestige of outrage. But, of course, they would. He could make a list now of everyone who would believe it. He said, bitterly, 'So that's it then? Mamantov goes free? Or perhaps you'll try to find Stalin's papers yourselves, so you can bury them somewhere, like you people bury everything else that's "embarrassing"?'

'Oh, but you *irritate* me,' said the Russian, and now it was his turn to lose his temper. 'People like you. How much more is it you want of us? You've won, but is that enough? No, you have to rub our faces in it – Stalin, Lenin, Beria: I'm sick of hearing their damn names – make us turn out all our filthy closets, wallow in guilt, so you can feel superior –'

Kelso snorted, 'You sound like Mamantov.'

'I *despise* Mamantov,' said the Russian. 'Do you understand me? For the same reason I despise you. We want to put an end to Comrade Mamantov and his kind – what d'you suppose this is all about? But now you've come along – blundered into something much bigger – something you can't even begin to understand –'

He stopped – goaded, Kelso could tell, into saying more than he intended – and then Kelso realised where he must have seen him before.

'You were there, weren't you?' he said. 'When I went to see him. You were one of the men outside his apartment –'

But he was talking to himself. The Russian was striding back to the car.

'Take him to the Ukraina,' he said to the driver, 'then come back here and pick me up. I need some air.'

'Who *are* you?'

'Just go. And be grateful.'

Kelso hesitated but suddenly he was too tired to argue. He climbed, weary and defeated, into the back seat as the engine started. The Russian slammed the door on him, emphatically. He felt numb and shut his eyes again and there was Rapava's corpse swinging in the darkness. Thump. *Thump.* He opened his eyes and saw that it was the blond-headed man, knocking on the window. Kelso wound it down.

'A final thought.' He was making an effort to be polite again. He even smiled. 'We're working on the assumption, obviously, that Mamantov now has this notebook. But have you considered the alternative? Remember, Papu Rapava withstood six months of interrogation back in fifty-three, and then fifteen years in Kolyma. Suppose Mamantov and his friends didn't manage to break him in one evening. It's a possibility: it would explain the . . . ferocity of their behaviour: frustration. In that case, if you were Mamantov, who would you want to question next?' He banged on the roof. 'Sleep well in New York.'

SUVORIN watched the big car as it bounced over the rough ground and out of sight. He turned away, towards the river, and walked along the quayside, smoking his pipe, until he came to a big metal post set into the concrete, to which ships had moored in the communist time, before economics had accomplished what Hitler's bombers had never managed, and laid waste the docks. His performance had exhausted him. He wiped the surface with his handkerchief, sat down, and pulled out his photocopy of Kelso's statement. To have written so much – perhaps two thousand words – so quickly and with such clarity, after such an experience . . . Well, it proved his hunch: he was a clever one, this fellow, Fluke.

Troublesome. Persistent. *Clever.*

He went through the pages again with a gold propelling pencil and made a list of matters for Netto to check. They needed to visit the house on Vspolnyi Street – Beria's place, well, well. They ought to find this daughter of Rapava's. They should compile a list of every forensic document examiner in the Moscow region to whom Mamantov might take the notebook for authentication. And every handwriting expert. And they should find a couple of tame historians and ask them to make the best guess possible as to what this notebook might contain. *And and and . . .* He felt as though he was trying to stuff gas back into a cylinder with his hands.

He was still writing when Netto and the driver returned. He rose stiffly. To his dismay he found that the mooring-post had left a rust-coloured mark on the back of his beautiful coat, and he spent much of the journey to Yasenevo picking at it obsessively, trying to make it clean.

Chapter Twelve

KELSO'S HOTEL ROOM was in darkness, the curtains closed. He pulled aside the cheap nylon drapes. There was an odd smell of something – talcum powder? Aftershave? Someone had been in here. Blond-head, was it? Eau Sauvage? He lifted the telephone receiver. The line hummed. He felt breathless. His skin was crawling. He could have done with a whisky but the mini-bar was still empty after his night with Rapava; there was nothing in it apart from soda and orange juice. And he could have done with a bath but there wasn't a plug.

He guessed now who the blond-headed man was. He knew the species – smooth and sharply-dressed, westernised, *deracinated* – too sharp for the secret police. He had been meeting men like that at embassy receptions for more than twenty years, dodging their discreet invitations for lunch and drinks, listening to their carefully indiscreet jokes about life in Moscow. They used to be called the First Chief Directorate of the KGB. Now they called themselves the SVR. The name had changed but the job had not. Blond-head was a spy. And he was investigating Mamantov. They had set the spies on Mamantov, which was not much of a vote of confidence in the FSB.

At the thought of Mamantov, he stepped quickly over to the door and turned the heavy lock and set the chain. Through the spy-hole he took a fish-eyed squint down the empty corridor.

'But you did kill him . . . You are the killer.'

He was shaking now with delayed shock. He felt filthy,

somehow, defiled. The memory of the night was like grit against his skin.

He went into the little green-tiled bathroom, took off his clothes and turned on the shower, set the water as hot as he could bear, and soaped himself from head to foot. The suds turned grey with the Moscow grime. He stood under the steaming jet and let it scourge him for another ten minutes, thrashing his shoulders and his chest, then he stepped out of the tub, slopping water over the uneven lino. He lit a cigarette and smoked as he shaved, transferring it from one side of his mouth to the other, working his razor around it, standing in a puddle. Then he dried himself off, got into bed and pulled the cover up to his chin. But he didn't sleep.

A little after nine o'clock the telephone began to ring. The bell was shrill. It rang for a long while, stopped, then started again. This time, though, whoever it was hung up quickly.

A few minutes later, someone knocked softly on his bedroom door.

Kelso felt vulnerable now, naked. He waited ten minutes, threw off the sheet, dressed, packed – that didn't take long – then sat in one of the foam rubber chairs facing the door. The cover of the other chair was rucked, he noticed, the seat still slightly depressed from the imprint of poor Papu Rapava.

AT ten-fifteen, carrying his suitcase in one hand and with his raincoat over his arm, Kelso unlocked and unchained his door, checked the corridor and descended via the express elevator into the hubub of the ground floor.

He handed in his key at the reception desk and was in the act of turning away, towards the main entrance, when a man shouted 'Professor!'

It was O'Brian, hurrying over from the news-stand. He

was still wearing his clothes from the night before – jeans a little less pressed, T-shirt no longer as white – and he had a couple of newspapers tucked under his arm. He hadn't shaved. He seemed even bigger in the daylight. 'Morning, professor. So. What's new?'

Kelso made a groaning noise in the back of his throat but managed to hoist up a smile. 'Leaving, I'm afraid.' He displayed his suitcase, bag and coat.

'Now I'm sorry to hear that. Let me help you with those.'

'I'm fine.' He began to move around O'Brian. 'Really.'

'Aw, come on.' The reporter's arm flashed out, grabbing the handle, squeezing Kelso's fingers out of the way. In a second he had the suitcase. He quickly transferred it to his other hand, out of Kelso's reach. 'Where to, sir? Outside?'

'What the fuck are you playing at?' Kelso strode after him. People sitting in reception turned to watch. 'Give me back my case –'

'That was some night, though, wasn't it? That place? Those girls?' O'Brian shook his head and grinned as they walked. 'And then you go and find that body and all – must've been one hell of a shock. Look out, professor, here we go.'

He plunged through the revolving door and Kelso, after a hesitation, followed him. He came out the other side to find O'Brian looking serious.

'All right,' said O'Brian, 'don't let's embarrass one another. I know what's going on.'

'I will take my case now, thank you.'

'I decided to hang around outside Robotnik last night. Forgo the pleasures of the flesh.'

'My *case* –'

'Let's say I had a hunch. Saw you leave with the girl. Saw

you kiss her. Saw her *hit* you – what was that all about, by the way? Saw you get in her car. Saw you go into the apartment block. Saw you run out ten minutes later like all the hounds of hell were after you. And then I saw the cops arrive. Oh, professor, you are a character, you are a man of surprises.'

'And you're a creep.' Kelso began pulling on his raincoat, making an effort to seem unconcerned. 'What were you doing at Robotnik anyway? Don't tell me: it was a coincidence.'

'I go to Robotnik, sure,' said O'Brian. 'That's how I like my relationships: on a business footing. Why get a girl for free when you can pay for one, that's my philosophy.'

'God.' Kelso held out his hand. 'Just give me my case.'

'Okay, okay.' O'Brian glanced over his shoulder. The bus was in its usual place, waiting to ferry the historians to the airport. Moldenhauer was taking a picture of Saunders with the hotel in the background, Olga was watching them, fondly. 'If you want to know the truth, it was Adelman.'

Kelso drew his head back slowly. '*Adelman?*'

'Yeah, at the symposium yesterday, during the morning break, I asked Adelman where you were and he told me you were after some Stalin papers.'

'*Adelman* said that?'

'Oh, come on, don't tell me you trusted Adelman?' O'Brian grinned. 'One sniff of a scoop and you guys make the paparazzi look like choirboys. Adelman proposed a deal. Fifty-fifty. He said I should try to find the papers, see if there was anything in it, and if there was then he'd authenticate them. He told me everything you'd told him.'

'Including Robotnik?'

'Including Robotnik.'

'Bastard.'

Now Olga was taking a picture of Moldenhauer and Saunders. They stood shyly, side by side, and it struck Kelso for the first time that they were gay. Why hadn't he realised it before? This trip was nothing but surprises –

'Come on, professor. Don't get all shocked on me. And don't get shocked about Adelman, either. This is a story. This is a *hell* of a story. And it just keeps on getting better. Not only d'you find this poor bastard hanging in the elevator shaft with his pecker in his mouth, you also tell the militia that the guy who did it is none other than Vladimir Mamantov. And not only that – the whole investigation's now been canned on the orders of the Kremlin. Or so I hear. What's so funny?'

'Nothing.' Kelso couldn't help smiling, thinking of the blond-headed spy. (*'What we don't want is the Moscow press corps trampling over everything . . .'*) 'Well, I'll say this for you, Mr O'Brian: you have good contacts.'

O'Brian made a dismissive gesture. 'There's not a secret in this town that can't be bought for a bottle of Scotch and fifty bucks. And man, I tell you, they're in a *rage* down there, you know? They're leaking like a *nuclear reactor*. They don't like being told what to do.'

The driver of the bus sounded his horn. Saunders was on board now. Moldenhauer had taken out his handkerchief to wave goodbye. Kelso could see the faces of the other historians through the glass, like pale fish in an aquarium.

He said, 'You really had better give me my case now. I've got to go.'

'You can't just run out, professor.' But there was a defeated tone to his appeal and this time he let Kelso take the handle. 'Come on, Fluke, just one little interview? One brief comment?' He followed at Kelso's heels, an importunate beggar. 'I need an interview, to stand this thing up.'

'It would be irresponsible.'

'Irresponsible? Balls! You won't talk because you want to keep it all for yourself! Well, you're crazy. The cover-up isn't working. This story's going to blow – if not today, tomorrow.'

'And you want it today, naturally, ahead of everyone else?'

'That's my job. Oh, come on, professor. Stop being so goddamn snooty. We're not so very different –'

Kelso was at the door of the bus. It opened with a pneumatic sigh. From the interior came a ragged, ironic cheer.

'Goodbye, Mr O'Brian.'

Still O'Brian wouldn't give up. He climbed up on to the first step. 'Take a look at what's happening here.' He jammed his roll of newspapers into Kelso's coat pocket. 'Take a look. That's Russia. Nothing here keeps until *tomorrow*. This place might not be here *tomorrow*. You're – oh, shit –'

He had to jump to avoid the closing door. He gave a last, despairing thump on the bodywork from outside.

'Dr Kelso,' said Olga, stonily.

'Olga,' said Kelso.

He pushed his way down the aisle. When he came level with Adelman he stopped, and Adelman, who must have watched his whole encounter with O'Brian, glanced away. Beyond the muddy glass the reporter was trudging towards the hotel, his hands in his pockets. Moldenhauer's white handkerchief fluttered in farewell.

The bus lurched. Kelso turned, half-walking, half-tumbling, towards his usual place, alone and at the back.

*

For five minutes he did nothing except stare out of the window. He knew he ought to write this down, prepare another record while it was still clear in his mind. But he couldn't, not yet. For now, all roads of thought seemed to lead back to the same image of the figure in the elevator-shaft.

Like a side of beef in a butcher's shop –

He patted his pockets to find his cigarettes and pulled out O'Brian's newspapers. He threw them on the seat beside him and tried to ignore them. But after a couple of minutes he found himself reading the headlines upside down, then reluctantly he picked them up.

They were nothing special, just a couple of English-language freesheets, given away in every hotel lobby.

The *Moscow Times*. Domestic news: the President was ill again, or drunk again, or both. A serial cannibal in the Kemerovo region was believed to have killed and eaten eighty people. Interfax reported that 60,000 children were sleeping on the streets each night in Moscow. Gorbachev was recording another television commercial for Pizza Hut. A bomb had been planted at the Nagornaya metro station by a group opposed to plans to remove Lenin's mummified body from public display in Red Square.

Foreign news: The IMF was threatening to withold $700 million in aid unless Moscow cut its budget deficit.

Business news: interest rates had tripled, stock market prices halved.

Religious news: A nineteen-year-old nun with ten thousand followers was predicting the end of the world on Hallowe'en. A statue of the Virgin Mother was trundling around the Black Earth region, weeping real blood. There was a holy man from Tarko-Sele who spoke in tongues.

Archangel

There were fakirs and Pentecostalists, faith healers, shamans, workers of miracles, anchorites and marabouts and followers of the *skoptsy*, who believed themselves the Lords Incarnate . . . It was like Rasputin's time. The whole country was a tumult of bloody auguries and false prophets.

He picked up the other paper, *The eXile*, this one written for young westerners like O'Brian working in Moscow. No religion here, but a lot of crime:

> In the village of Kamenka, in the Smolenskaya Oblast, where the local collective farm is bankrupt and state employees haven't been paid all year, the big summer activity for kids is hanging around the Moscow–Minsk highway and sniffing gasoline, bought in half-litre jugs for a rouble. In August, two of the biggest gasoline addicts, Pavel Mikheenkov, 11, and Anton Malyarenko, 13, graduated from their favourite pastime – torturing cats – to tying a five year-old boy named Sasha Petrochenkov to a tree and burning him alive. Malyarenk was deported to his native Tashkent, but Mikheenkov has had to stay in Kamenka, unpunished: sending him to reform school would cost 15,000 roubles and the town doesn't have the money. The victim's mother, Svetlana Petrochenkova, has been told she can have her son's killer sent away if she digs up the money herself, but failing that must live with him in the village. According to police, Mikheenkov had been drinking vodka regularly with his parents since the age of four.

He turned the page quickly and found a guide to Moscow night life. Gay bars – Dyke, The Three Monkeys, Queer

179

Nation; strip clubs – Navada, Rasputin, The Intim Peep Show; nightclubs – the Buchenwald (where the staff wore Nazi uniforms), Bulgakov, Utopiya. He looked up Robotnik: *'No place could better exemplify the excesses of the New Russia than Robotnik: bitchin interior, ear-splitting techno, Babe-O-Litas and their flathead keepers, Die Hard security, black-eyed patrons sucking down Evians. Get laid and see someone get shot.'*

That sounded about right, he thought.

THE departure terminal at Sheremetevo-2 was crammed with people trying to get out of Russia. Queues formed like cells under a microscope – grew from nothing, wormed back on themselves, broke, re-formed, and merged into other queues: queues for customs, for tickets, for security, for passport controls. You finished one and joined the next. The hall was dark and cavernous, sour with the reek of aviation spirit and the thin acid of anxiety. Adelman, Duberstein, Byrd, Saunders and Kelso, plus a couple of Americans who had been staying at the Mir – Pete Maddox of Princeton and Vobster of Chicago – stood in a group at the end of the nearest line while Olga went off to see if she could speed things up.

After a couple of minutes, they still hadn't moved. Kelso ignored Adelman who sat on his suitcase reading a biography of Chekhov with extravagant intensity. Saunders sighed and flapped his arms with frustration. Maddox wandered away and came back to report that customs seemed to be opening every bag.

'Shit, and I bought an icon,' complained Duberstein. 'I knew I shouldn't've bought an icon. I'll never get it through.'

'Where'd you get it?'

'That big bookstore on the Noviy Arbat.'

'Give it to Olga. She'll get it out. How much d'you pay?'

'Five hundred bucks.'

'Five *hundred?*'

Kelso remembered he hadn't any money. There was a news-stand at the end of the terminal. He needed more cigarettes. If he asked for a seat in smoking he could keep clear of the others.

'Phil,' he said to Duberstein, 'you couldn't lend me ten dollars, could you?'

Duberstein started laughing. 'What're you going to do, Fluke? Buy Stalin's notebook?'

Saunders sniggered. Velma Byrd raised her hand to her mouth and looked away.

'You told them as well?' Kelso stared at Adelman in disbelief.

'And why not?' Adelman licked a finger and turned over a page without looking up. 'Is it a secret?'

'Tell you what,' said Duberstein, pulling out his wallet. 'Here's twenty. Buy one for me as well.'

They all laughed at that, and openly this time, watching Kelso to see what he would do. He took the money.

'All right, Phil,' he said, quietly. 'I'll tell you what. Let's make a deal. If Stalin's notebook turns up by the end of the year, I'll just keep this and then we're quits. But if it doesn't, I'll pay you back a thousand dollars.'

Maddox gave a low whistle.

'Fifty to one,' said Duberstein, swallowing. 'You're offering me fifty to one?'

'We've got a deal?'

'Well, you bet.' Duberstein laughed again, but nervously this time. He glanced around at the others. 'You hear that everyone?'

They'd heard. They were staring at Kelso. And for him, at that moment, it was worth a thousand dollars – worth it just for the way they looked: open-mouthed, stricken, panicked. Even Adelman had temporarily forgotten his book.

'Easiest twenty dollars I ever made,' said Kelso. He stuffed the bill into his pocket and picked up his suitcase. 'Save my place for me, will you?'

He moved off across the crowded terminal, quickly, quitting while he was still ahead, easing his way through the people and the piles of luggage. He felt a childish pleasure. A few fleeting victories here and there – what more could a man hope for in this life?

Over the loudspeaker, a woman with a harsh voice made a deafening announcement about the departure of an Aeroflot flight to Delhi.

At the news-stand he made a quick check to see if they had the paperback of his book. They did not. Naturally. He turned his attention to a rack of magazines. Last week's *Time* and *Newsweek*, and the current *Der Spiegel*. So. He would take *Der Spiegel*. It would do him good. It would certainly last him an eleven-hour plane ride. He fished in his pocket for Duberstein's $20 and turned towards the till. Through the plate glass window he could see the wet sweep of concrete, a jammed line of cars and taxis and buses, grey buildings, abandoned trolleys, a girl with cropped dark hair, a white face watching him. He looked away casually. Frowned. Checked himself.

He stuffed the magazine back into the rack and returned to the window. It was her, all right, standing alone, in jeans and a fleece-lined leather jacket. His breath misted on the cold glass. *Wait*, he mouthed at her. She stared at him blankly. He pointed at her feet. *Stay there.*

To get to her he had to walk away from her, following the line of the glass wall, trying to find an exit. The first set of doors was chained shut. The second opened. He came out into the cold and wet. She was standing about fifty yards away. He looked back at the crowded terminal – he couldn't see the others – and then at her, and now she was moving away from him, heading across a pedestrian crossing, heedless of the cars. He hesitated: what to do? A bus momentarily wiped her from view and that made his mind up for him. He hoisted his luggage and set off after her, breaking into a trot. She drew him on, always maintaining the same distance, until they were into the big outdoor car park, and then he lost her.

Grey light, snow and frozen slush. The stink of fuel much sharper here. Row upon row of boxy cars, some muffled white, others thinly wrapped in a film of mud and grit. He walked on. The air shook. A big old Tupolev jet swept directly over his head, so low he could see the lines of rust where the plates of the fuselage were welded together. Instinctively, he ducked, just as a sandy-coloured Lada emerged slowly from the end of the line and stopped, its engine running.

SHE didn't make it easy for him, even then. She didn't drive over to where he was; he had to walk to her. She didn't open the door; he had to do it. She didn't speak; it was left to him to break the silence. She didn't even tell him her name – not then, at least, although he discovered it later. She was called Zinaida. Zinaida Rapava.

She knew what had happened, that was obvious by the strain on her face, and he felt guiltily relieved at that, because at least he wouldn't have to break the news. He had always been a coward when it came to breaking bad news – that was one reason he'd been married three times. He sat in the front passenger seat, his suitcase wedged across his knees. The heater was running. The windscreen wiper flicked intermittently across the dirty glass. He knew he would have to say something soon. Delta to New York was the one event of the symposium he had no intention of missing.

'Tell me what I can do to help.'

'Who killed him?'

'A man named Vladimir Mamantov. Ex-KGB. He knew of your father from the old time.'

'The old time,' she said, bitterly.

Silence – long enough for the wiper to scrape back and forth, back and forth.

'How did you know where to find me?'

'Always, all my life: the *old time.*'

Another Tupolev rumbled low overhead.

'Listen,' he said, 'I've got to go in a minute. I've got to catch a plane to New York. When I get there, I'm going to write everything down – are you listening? I'll send you a copy. Tell me where to send it. You need anything, I'll help.'

It was hard to move with his case on his lap. He unbuttoned his coat and reached awkwardly into his inside pocket for his pen. She wasn't listening to him. She was staring straight ahead, talking almost to herself.

'It'd been years since I saw him. Why would I want to? I hadn't been near that dump in eight years till you asked me to take you.' She turned to him for the first time. She had washed off her makeup. She looked younger, more pretty. Her leather jacket was old, brown, zipped tight to the neck. 'After I left you, I went home. Then I went back to his place again. I had to find out – you know – what was going on.

Never saw so many cops in my life. You'd been taken away by then. I didn't say who I was. Not to the cops. I had to think things through. I –' She stopped. She seemed baffled, lost.

'What's your name?' he said. 'Where can I reach you?'

'Then, this morning, I went to the Ukraina. I rang you. Went up to your room. When they said you'd checked out I came here and waited.'

'Can't you just tell me your name?' He looked at his watch, hopelessly. 'Only I've got to catch this plane, you see.'

'I don't ask favours,' she said fiercely. 'I never ask favours.'

'Listen, don't worry. I want to help. I feel responsible.'

'Then help me. He said you'd help me'

'*He?*'

'The thing is, mister, he's left me something.' Her leather jacket creaked as she unzipped it. She felt around inside and brought out a scrap of paper. 'Something worth a lot? In a toolbox? He says that you can tell me what it is.'

Chapter Thirteen

THEY DROVE OUT of the airport perimeter onto the St Petersburg highway and turned south towards the city. A big truck overtook them, its wheels as high as their roof, rocking them in its wake, soaking them in a filthy spray.

Kelso had promised himself he wouldn't look back, but of course he did – looked back and saw the terminal building, like a great grey ocean liner, sink out of sight behind a line of birch trees until only a few watery lights were visible, and then they disappeared.

He winced and nearly asked the girl to take him back. He gave her a sideways glance. In her scuffed flying jacket she looked intrepid: an aviatrix at the controls of her battered plane.

He said, 'Who's Sergo?'

'My brother.' She glanced in the rear-view mirror. 'He's dead.'

He turned the note over and read it again. Rough paper. Pencil scrawl. Written quickly. Stuffed under the door of her apartment, or so she said: she had found it when she got back after dropping Kelso outside her father's block.

My little one, Greetings!
I have been a bad one, you're right. All you said was right.
So don't think I don't know it! But here is a chance to do
some good. You wouldn't let me tell you yesterday, so listen
now. Remember that place I used to have, when Mama
was alive? It's still there! And there's a toolbox with a present
for you that's worth a lot.

Are you listening, Zinaida?
Nothing will happen to me, but if it does – take the box and hide it safe. But it could be dangerous, so mind yourself. You'll see what I mean.
Destroy this note.
I kiss my little one,
Papa.
– There's a Britisher called Kelso, get him through the Ukraina, he knows the story. Remember your papa!
I kiss you again, Zinaida.
Remember Sergo!!

'So he came to see you – when was it? The day before yesterday?'

She nodded, without looking round at him, concentrating on the road. 'It was the first time I'd seen him in nearly ten years.'

'You didn't get on, then?'

'Oh, you're a smart one.' Her laugh was brief, sarcastic: a short expulsion of breath. 'No, we didn't get on.'

He ignored her aggression. She was entitled to it. 'What was he like, the last time you saw him?'

'Like?'

'His mood.'

'A bastard. Same as always.' She frowned at the oncoming traffic. 'He must have been waiting for me all night, outside my place. I got back about six. I'd been at the club, you know, been working. The moment he saw me he started shouting. Saw my clothes. Called me a whore.' She shook her head at the memory.

'Then what happened?'

'He followed me in. Into my place. I said to him, I said:

"You hit me, I'll take your fucking eye out, I'm not your little girl any more." That calmed him down.'

'What did he want?'

'To talk, he said. It was a shock after all that time. I didn't think he knew where I lived. I didn't even know he was still alive. Thought I'd got away from him for good. Oh, but he'd known, he said – known where I was for a long time. Said he used to come and watch me sometimes. He said, "You don't get away from the past that easily." Why did he come to see me?' She looked at Kelso for the first time since they'd left the airport. 'Can you tell me that?'

'What did he want to talk about?'

'I don't know. I wouldn't listen. I didn't want him in my place, looking at my things. I didn't want to hear his stories. He started going on about his time in the camps. I gave him some cigarettes to get rid of him and told him to go. I was tired and I'd got to go to work.'

'Work?'

'I work at GUM in the daytime. I learn law at college in the evenings. Some nights, I screw. Why? Is it a problem?'

'You lead a full life.'

'I have to.'

He tried to picture her behind the counter at GUM. 'What do you sell?'

'What?'

'At the store. What do you sell?'

'Nothing.' She checked the mirror again. 'I work the switchboard.'

Closer to the city, the road was clogged. They slowed to a crawl. There had been an accident up ahead. A rickety Skoda had run into the back of a big old Zhiguli. Broken glass and bits of metal were scattered across two lanes. The militia were on the scene. It looked as though one of the drivers had punched the other: he had splashes of blood on the front of his shirt. As they passed the policemen, Kelso turned his head away. The road cleared. They picked up speed.

He tried to fit all this together: Papu Rapava's last two days on earth. Tuesday 27 October: he goes to see his daughter for the first time in a decade, because, he says, he wants to talk. She throws him out, buys him off with a pack of cigarettes and a book of matches labelled 'Robotnik'. In the afternoon, he turns up, of all places, at the Institute of Marxism–Leninism and listens to Fluke Kelso deliver a paper on Josef Stalin. Then he follows Kelso back to the Ukraina and sits up all night drinking. And talking. He certainly talked. *Perhaps he told me what he would have told his daughter if she'd only listened.*

And then it's dawn and he leaves the Ukraina. This is now Wednesday 28 October. And what does he do after he's slipped away into the morning? Does he go to the deserted house on Vspolnyi Street and dig up the secret of his life? He must have done. And then he hides it, and he leaves a note for his daughter, telling her where to find it (*'remember that place I used to have when Mama was alive?'*) and then, late in the afternoon, his killers come for him. And either he had told them everything, or he hadn't, and if he hadn't, then it must have been partly out of love, surely? To make certain that the only thing he had in the world that might be worth anything should go not to them but to his daughter.

God, thought Kelso, what an ending. What a way to leave a life – and how in keeping with the rest of it.

'He must have cared for you,' said Kelso. He wondered if she knew how the old man had died. If she didn't, he couldn't bring himself to tell her. 'He must have cared for you, to have come to find you.'

'I don't think so. He used to hit me. And my mother. And my brother.' She glared at the oncoming traffic. 'He used to hit me when I was little. What does a child know?' She shook her head. 'I don't think so.'

Kelso tried to imagine the four of them in the one-bedroom apartment. Where would her parents have slept? On a mattress in the sitting-room? And Rapava, after a decade and a half in Kolyma – violent, unstable, confined. It didn't bear contemplating.

'When did your mother die?'

'Do you ever stop asking questions, mister?'

They came off the highway and down a slip road. Half of it had never been completed. One lane curved like a water-chute, ending abruptly in a row of dripping metal rods and a ten-yard drop to waste ground.

'When I was eighteen, if that makes any difference.'

The ugliness around them was heroic. In Russia it could afford to be – could afford to take its time, stretch out a bit. Minor roads ran as wide as motorways, with flooded potholes the size of ponds. Each concrete stack of apartments, each belching industrial plant had an entire wilderness to itself to pollute. Kelso remembered the night before – the endless run from Block Nine to Block Eight to raise the alarm: it had gone on and on, like a journey in a nightmare.

Rapava's place in the daylight looked even more derelict than it had seemed in the darkness. Scorch marks shot up the wall from a set of windows on the second floor where an apartment had been torched. There was a crowd outside and Zinaida slowed so they could take a look.

O'Brian was right. The word was out. That much was obvious. A solitary militia man blocked the doorway, holding at bay a dozen cameramen and reporters, who were themselves being watched by a straggling semi-circle of apathetic neighbours. Some kids kicked a ball on the waste ground. Others hung around the media's fancy western cars.

'What was he to them?' Zinaida said suddenly. 'What was he to any of you? You're all vultures.'

She gave a grimace of disgust, and for the third time Kelso noticed her adjusting the rear-view mirror.

'Is someone behind us?' He turned round sharply.

'Maybe. A car from the airport. But not any more.'

'What sort of a car?' He tried to keep his voice calm.

'A BMW. Seven series.'

'You know about cars?'

'More questions?' She shot him another look. 'Cars were my father's interest. Cars and Comrade Stalin. He was a driver, wasn't he, for some big shot in the old days? You'll see.'

She put her foot down.

She knows nothing, thought Kelso. She has no idea of the risks. He began making promises to himself of what he would do: you take a quick look now to see if this toolbox is here (it wouldn't be) then ask her to take you back to the airport and see if you can talk your way on to the next flight out –

Two minutes from Rapava's apartment they turned off the main street and on to a muddy track that led through a scrappy copse of birch to a field that had been divided into small-holdings. A pig snuffled in the earth in an enclosure made of old car doors tied together with wire. There were a few scrawny chickens, some frost-blasted vegetables. Children had made a snowman out of yesterday's fall. It had melted in the light rain and looked grotesque in the dirt, like a lump of white fat.

Facing this rural scene was a row of lock-up garages. On the long flat roof sat the remains of half a dozen small cars – rusted red skeletons picked bare of windows, engines, tyres, upholstery. Zinaida switched off the engine and they climbed out into the mud. An old man leaned on his shovel and watched them. Zinaida stared him down, her hands on her hips. Eventually, he spat on the ground and returned to his digging.

She had a key. Kelso looked back along the deserted track. His hands felt numb. He stuffed them into his coat pockets. She was the calm one. She was wearing a pair of knee-length leather boots and to avoid getting them dirty she stepped carefully across the lumpy ground. He looked around again. He didn't like it: the encroaching trees, the derelict cars, this bewildering woman with her kaleidoscope of roles – GUM telephonist, would-be lawyer, part-time hooker and now griefless daughter.

He said, 'Where did you get the key?'

'It was with the note.'

'I don't understand why you didn't come here on your own straight away. Why do you need me?'

'Because I don't know what I'm looking for, do I? Are you coming or not?' She was fitting the key into a big padlock on the nearest lock-up. 'What are we looking for, anyway?'

'A notebook.'

'What?' She stopped fiddling with the key and stared at him.

'A black oilskin notebook that used to belong to Josef Stalin.' He repeated the familiar phrase. It was becoming his mantra. (It wouldn't be here, he told himself again. It was the Holy Grail. The quest was all that mattered. It wasn't supposed to be found.)

'Stalin's notebook? And what's that worth?'

'Worth?' He tried to make it sound as if the question had never occurred to him. 'Worth?' he repeated. 'It's hard to put an exact figure on it. There are some rich collectors. It depends what's in it.' He spread his hands. 'Half a million, maybe.'

'Roubles?'

'Dollars.'

'Dollars? Shit. *Shit.*' She resumed her efforts to undo the padlock, clumsy now with her eagerness.

And suddenly, watching her, he caught her mood and then of course he knew why he had come. Because it was everything, really, wasn't it? It was much more than mere money. It was vindication. Vindication for twenty years of freezing his arse off in basement archives, and dragging himself to lectures in the winter dark – first to listen, then to give them – twenty years of teaching and faculty politics and trying to write books that mostly didn't sell and all the while hoping that one day he would produce something worthwhile – something true and big and definitive – a piece of history that would explain *why things had happened as they did.*

'Here,' he said, almost pushing her out of the way, 'let me try.'

He jiggled the key in the lock. At last it turned and the arm sprang open. He pulled the chain through the heavy eye-bolts.

COLD, oily darkness. No window. No electricity. An ancient paraffin lamp hanging on a nail by the door.

He took down the lamp and shook it – it was full – and she said she knew how to light it. She knelt on the earth floor and struck a match, applied it to the wick. A blue flame, then yellow. She held it up while he dragged the door shut behind them.

The garage was a bone-yard of old spare parts, stacked around the walls. At the far end in the shadows was a row of car seats arranged to form a bed, with a sleeping bag and a blanket, neatly folded. Suspended from a beam in the roof was a block and tackle, a chain, a hook. Beneath the hook were floorboards forming a rectangle a yard and a half wide by two yards long.

She said, 'He's had this place for as long as I've been alive. He used to sleep here, when things were bad.'

'How bad did they get?'

'Bad.'

He took the lamp and walked around, shining it into the corners. There was nothing like a toolbox that he could see. On a work bench was a tin tray with a metal brush, some rods, a cylinder, a small coil of copper wire: what was all that? Fluke Kelso's ignorance of mechanics was deep and carefully maintained.

'Did he have a car of his own?'

'I don't know. He fixed them up for people. People gave him things.'

He stopped next to the makeshift bed. Something glinted above it. He called to her, 'Look at this,' and raised the light to the wall. Stalin's sombre face gazed down at them from an old poster. There were a dozen more pictures of the General Secretary, torn from magazines. Stalin looking thoughtful behind a desk. Stalin in a fur hat. Stalin shaking hands with a general. Stalin, dead, lying in state.

'And who's this? This is you?'

It was a photograph of Zinaida, aged about twelve, in

school uniform. She stepped closer to it, surprised.

'Who'd have thought it?' She laughed uneasily. 'Me up there with Stalin.'

She stared at it a while longer.

'Let's find this thing,' she said, turning away. 'I want to get out of here.'

Kelso was prodding one of the floorboards with his foot. It rested loosely on a wooden frame set into the earth. This was it, he thought. This had to be the place.

They worked together, watched by Stalin, stacking the short planks against the wall, uncovering a mechanic's pit. It was deep. In the weak light it looked like a grave. He held the lamp over it. The floor was sand, stamped smooth and hard, stained black with oil. The sides were shored up with old timber, into which Rapava had let alcoves for tools. He gave her the lamp and wiped his palms on his coat. Why was he so damned nervous? He sat on the edge for a moment, legs dangling, before cautiously lowering himself. He knelt on the floor of the pit, his bones cracking, and felt around in the damp gloom. His hands touched sacking.

He called up to her, 'Shine the light here.'

The rough cloth pulled away easily. Next came something solid, wrapped in newspaper. He passed it up to Zinaida. She set down the lamp and unwrapped a gun. She was surprisingly deft with it, he noticed, sliding out the clip of ammunition, checking it – eight rounds loaded – sliding it back again, pushing the safety catch down then up.

'You know how it works?'

'Of course. It's his. A Makarov. When we were little, he taught us how to strip it, clean it, fire it. He always kept it by him. He said he'd kill if he had to.'

'That's a nice memory.' He thought he heard a sound

outside. 'Did you hear that?'

But she shook her head, preoccupied with the gun.

He sank back down to his knees.

And here, jammed into the aperture, was the square end of a metal box, flaking with rust and dried mud. If you didn't know what you were looking for, you would never have bothered with it. Rapava had hidden well. He put his hands on either side of it and tugged.

Well, *something* was heavy. Either the box or what was in it. The handles had rusted flat. It was hard to get a grip. He dragged it into the centre of the pit and hoisted it up to the edge. His cheek was close to it. He could taste the smell of rusted steel, like blood in his mouth. Zinaida bent to help. And this was peculiar: for an instant he thought that the box was exuding an unearthly, blue-grey light. There was a rush of cold air. But then he saw that the garage door was open and that framed in it was the silhouette of a man, watching them.

AFTERWARDS, Kelso was to recognise this as the decisive moment: as the point at which he lost control of events. If he didn't see it at the time it was because his main concern was simply to stop her blowing a hole in R. J. O'Brian's chest.

The reporter stood against the garage wall, his hands above his head. Kelso could tell he didn't quite believe she would shoot. But a gun was a gun. They could go off accidentally. And this one was old.

'Professor, do me a favour, would you, and tell her to put that thing down?'

But Zinaida jabbed it again towards his chest and O'Brian, groaning, raised his hands still further.

Okay, okay, he said. He was sorry. He had followed them

from the airport. It hadn't been hard, for Christ's sake. He was only doing his job. *Sorry.*

His eyes flickered to the toolbox. 'Is that it?'

Kelso's immediate reaction on seeing the American had been relief: thank God it was only O'Brian who had followed them from Sheremetevo and not Mamantov. But Zinaida had grabbed the gun and had backed him against the wall.

She said, 'Shut up.'

'Look, professor, I've seen these suckers go off. And I have to tell you: they really make a mess.'

Kelso said to her, in Russian, 'Put it away, Zinaida.' It was the first time he had used her name. 'Put it away and let's sort this out.'

'I don't trust him.'

'Neither do I. But what can we do? Put it away.'

'Zinaida? Who is she? Don't I know her from someplace?'

'She goes to the Robotnik.' Kelso spoke through his teeth. 'Will you let me handle this?'

'Does she, by God?' O'Brian passed his tongue across his thick lips. In the yellow lamplight his broad and well-fed face looked like a Hallowe'en pumpkin. 'That's right. Of course she does. She's the babe you were with last night. I thought I knew her.'

'Shut up,' she said again.

O'Brian grinned. 'Listen, Zinaida, we don't have to be in competition. We can share, can't we? Split this three ways? I just want a story. Tell her, Fluke. Tell her I can keep her name out of it. She knows me. She'll understand. She's a business-minded kind of a girl, aren't you, darlin'?'

'What's he saying?'

He told her.

'*Nyet,*' she said. And then, in English, to O'Brian, 'No way.'

'You two,' said O'Brian. 'You make me laugh. The historian and the whore. Okay, tell her this. Tell her she can either deal with me or we can stand around like this for an hour or two and you'll have half the Moscow press pack on your back. And the militia. And maybe the guys who killed the old man. Tell her that.'

But Kelso didn't need to translate. She understood.

She stood there for another quarter of a minute, frowning, then clicked on the safety catch and slowly lowered the gun. O'Brian let out a breath.

'What's she doing in all this anyway?'

'She's Papu Rapava's daughter.'

'Ah.' O'Brian nodded. Now he got the picture.

THE toolbox lay on the earth floor. O'Brian wouldn't let them open it, not right away. He wanted to capture the great moment, he said – 'for posterity and the evening news'. He went off to get his camera.

Once he'd gone, Kelso shook a cigarette out of his half-empty pack and offered it to Zinaida. She took it and leaned towards him, looking at him steadily as he lit it for her, the flame reflected in her dark eyes. He thought: less than twelve hours ago you were going to go to bed with me for $200 – who the hell are you?

She said, 'What's on your mind?'

'Nothing. Are you all right?'

'I don't trust him,' she repeated. She threw back her head and blew smoke at the roof. 'What's he doing?'

'I'll tell him to hurry up.'

Outside, O'Brian was sitting in the front seat of a four-wheel drive Toyota Land Crusier, snapping a new battery on to the back of a tiny video camera. At the sight of the Toyota,

Kelso felt a fresh sweat of anxiety.

'You don't drive a BMW?'

'A BMW? I'm not a businessman. Why should I?'

The field was deserted. The old man who had been digging had gone.

'Zinaida thought we were followed from the airport by a BMW. Seven series.'

'Seven series? That's a mafia car.' O'Brian got out of the Toyota and put the camera to his eye. 'I wouldn't pay any attention to Zinaida. She's crazy.' The pig emerged from its sty and trotted over for a look at them, hopeful of some food. 'Here, piggy piggy.' He began filming it. 'Remember what the man said? "A dog looks up to you, a cat looks down on you, but a pig looks you straight in the eye"?' He swung round and pointed the camera at Kelso's face. 'Smile, professor. I'm going to make you famous.'

Kelso put his hand over the lens. 'Listen, Mr O'Brian –'

'R. J.'

'And what does that stand for?'

'Everybody calls me R. J.'

'All right, *R. J.* I'm going to do this. I'll let you film me. If you insist. But on three conditions.'

'Which are?'

'One, you stop calling me bloody *professor*. Two, you keep her name out of it. And three, none of this is shown – not a second, you hear? – until this notebook, or whatever it is, has been forensically verified.'

'Agreed.' O'Brian slipped the camera into his pocket. 'Actually, it may surprise you to hear this, but I've got a reputation of my own to consider. And from what I hear, *doctor*, it's one hell of a sight better than yours.'

He pointed a remote key at the Toyota. It bleeped and

locked. Kelso took a last look around and followed him into the garage.

O'BRIAN made Kelso put the toolbox back in its hiding place and drag it out again. He made him do this twice, filming him once from the front and then from the side. Zinaida watched them closely but was careful to keep out of shot. She smoked incessantly, one arm clasped defensively across her stomach. When O'Brian had what he needed, Kelso carried the box over to the workbench and brought the lamp up close to it. There wasn't a lock. There were two spring-loaded catches at either end of the lid. They had been cleaned up recently, and oiled. One was broken. The other opened.

Here we go, boy.

'What I want you to do,' said O'Brian, 'is describe what you see. Talk us through it.'

Kelso contemplated the box.

'D'you have any gloves?'

'Gloves?'

'If what's inside is genuine, Stalin's fingerprints should be on it. And Beria's. I don't want to contaminate the evidence.'

'Stalin's *fingerprints?*'

'Of course. Don't you know about Stalin's fingers? The Bolshevik poet, Demyan Bedny, once complained that he didn't like lending his books to Stalin because they always came back with such greasy finger marks on them. Osip Mandelstam – a much greater poet – got to hear about this, and put the image into a poem about Stalin: "His fingers are fat as grubs".'

'What did Stalin think of that?'

'Mandelstam died in a labour camp.'

'Right. I guess I should have figured that out.' O'Brian dug around in his pockets. 'Okay: gloves. There you go.'

Kelso pulled them on. They were dark blue leather, slightly too big, but they would do. He flexed his fingers – a surgeon before a transplant, a pianist before a concert. The thought made him smile. He glanced at Zinaida. Her face was clenched. O'Brian's expression was hidden by the camera.

'Okay. I'm running. In your own time.'

'Right. I'm opening the lid, which is . . . *stiff*, as you'd . . . *expect*.' Kelso winced with the effort. The top wrenched up a crack, just wide enough for him to jam his fingers into the gap, and then it took all his strength to break the two edges apart. It came open suddenly, like a broken jaw, with a scream of oxidised metal. 'There's only one object inside . . . a bag of some kind . . . leather, by the look of it . . . badly moulded.'

The satchel had grown a shroud of fungus – of different fungi – pale blues and greens and greys, vegetative filaments and white patches mottled black. It stank of decay. He lifted it clear of the box and turned it round in the light. He rubbed at the surface with his thumb. Very faintly, the ghost of an image began to appear. 'It's embossed here with the hammer and sickle . . . That suggests it's an official document pouch of some kind . . . Oil here on the buckle . . . Some of the rust has been cleaned off . . . ' He imagined Rapava's nail-less fingers, fumbling to discover what had cost him so much of his life.

The strap unthreaded through the pitted metal, leaving a floury residue. The satchel opened. The hyphae had spread inside, feeding off the dank skin, and as he lifted out the contents he knew, whatever else it was, that this was genuine, that no forger would have done all this, would have allowed so much damage to be inflicted on his work: it went against nature. What had once been a packet of papers had fused together, swollen, and was covered in the same destructive cancer of spores as the leather. The pages of the notebook had also warped, but less badly, protected as they were by a smooth outer layer of black oilskin.

The cover opened, the binding split.

On the first page: nothing.

On the second: a photograph, neatly cut out of a magazine, glued down in the centre of the page. A group of young women, in their late teens, dressed as athletes – shorts, singlets, sashes – marching in step, eyes right, carrying a picture of Stalin. Parading in Red Square by the look of it. Caption: *Komsomol Unit No. 2 from Archangel oblast display their paces! Front row, l. to r. I. Primakova, A. Safanova, D. Merkulova, K. Til, M. Arsenyeva* . . . Against the youthful face of A. Safanova there was a tiny red cross.

He picked up the notebook and blew, to separate the second page from the third. His hands were sweating inside the gloves. He felt absurdly clumsy, as if he were trying to thread a needle while wearing gauntlets.

On the third page: writing, in faint pencil.

O'Brian touched his shoulder, prompting him to say something.

'It's not Stalin's writing, I'm sure of that . . . It reads more like someone writing *about* Stalin . . .' He held it closer to the lamp. '"He stands apart from the others, high on the roof of Lenin's tomb. His hand is raised in greeting. He smiles. We pass beneath him. His glance falls across us like the rays of the sun. He looks directly into my eyes. I am pierced by his power. All around us, the crowd breaks into stormy

202

applause." The next part is smudged. And then it's written, "Great Stalin lived! Great Stalin lives! Great Stalin will live for ever! . . .'"

Chapter Fourteen

> *. . . Great Stalin lived!*
> *Great Stalin lives!*
> *Great Stalin will live for ever!*

12.5.51 Our picture is in Ogonyok! Maria runs in at the end of the first class to show me. I am displeased with my appearance and M. chides me for my vanity. (She always says I think too much of being pretty: it is not fitting for a candidate-member of the Party. Fine for her to say, who always looks like a tank!) All morning comrades hurry up to us to offer their congratulations. The usual trouble of this time is forgotten for once. We are so happy . . .

5.6.51 The day is hot and sunny. The Dvina is gold. I return home from the Institute. Papa is there, much earlier than usual, looking grave. Mama is strong, as ever. With them is a stranger, a comrade from the organs of the Central Committee in Moscow! I am not afraid of him. I know I have done nothing wrong. And the stranger is smiling. A little man – I like him. Despite the heat he is carrying a hat and wears a leather coat. This stranger is named, I think, Mekhlis. He explains that after a thorough investigation, I have been selected for special tasks relating to the high Party leadership. He cannot say more for reasons of security. If I accept, I must travel to Moscow and stay for one year, perhaps for two. Then I may return to Archangel and resume my studies. He offers to come back the next morning for my answer, but I give it now, with all my heart: Yes! But because I am nineteen, he needs the permission of my parents. Oh, please papa! Please,

please! Papa is deeply moved by the scene. He goes with Comrade Mekhlis into the garden, and when he returns his face is solemn. If it is my wish, and if it is the will of the Party, he will not prevent me. Mama is so proud.

To Moscow, then, for the second time in my life!

I know His hand is behind this.

I am so happy, I could die . . .

10.6.51 Mama brings me to the station. Papa stays behind. I kiss her dear cheeks. Farewell to her, farewell to childhood. The carriages are crowded. The train moves off. Others run along the platform, but mama stays still and is quickly lost. We cross the river. I am alone. Poor Anna! And this is the worst of days to travel. But I have my clothes, some food, a book or two, and this journal, in which I shall record my thoughts – this will be my friend. We plunge south through the forest, the tundra. A great red sunset blazes like a fire through the trees. Isakogorka. Obozerskiy. And now I have written down everything that has happened until this time and I can no longer see to write.

11.6.51 Monday morning. The town of Vozhega appears with the dawn. Passengers alight to stretch their legs, but I stay where I am. From the corridor comes a smell of smoke. A man watches me write from the opposite seat, pretending to be asleep. He is curious about me. If only he knew! And still there are eleven hours to Moscow. How can one man rule such a nation? How could such a nation exist without such a man to rule it?

Konosha. Kharovsk. Names on a map become real to me.

Vologda. Danilov. Yaroslavl.

A fear has come upon me. I am so far from home. Last time there were twenty of us, silly laughing girls. O, papa!

Alexandrov.

And now we reach the outskirts of Moscow. A tremor of excitement runs through the train. The blocks and factories stretch as far and wide as the tundra. A hot haze of metal and smoke. The June sun is much warmer than at home. I am excited again.

4.30! Yaroslavskaya station! And now what?

LATER. *The train halts, the man opposite, who had been watching me all journey, leans forward. 'Anna Mikhailovna Safanova?' For a moment I am too amazed to speak. Yes? 'Welcome to Moscow. Come with me, please.' He wears a leather coat, like Comrade Mekhlis. He carries my case along the platform to the station entrance on Komsomolskaya Square. A car is waiting, with a driver. We drive for a long while. An hour at least. I don't know where. Right across the city it seems to me, and out again. Along a highway that leads to a birch forest. There is a high fence and soldiers who check our papers. We drive some more. Another fence. And then a house, in a large garden.*

(And Mama, yes, it is a modest house! Two storeys only. Your good Bolshevik heart would rejoice at its simplicity!)

I am taken around the side of the house to the back. A servants' wing, connected to the main quarters by a long passageway. Here in the kitchen a woman is waiting. She is grey-haired, almost old. And kindly. She calls me 'child'. Her name is Valechka Istomina. A simple meal has been prepared – cold meat and bread, pickled herring, kvas. She watches me. (Everyone here watches everyone else: it is strange to look up and find a pair of eyes regarding you.) From time to time, guards come by to take a look at me. They don't talk much but when they do they sound like Georgians. One asks, 'Well, now, Valechka, and what was the Boss's humour this morning?' but Valechka hushes him and nods to me.

I am not such a young fool as to ask any questions. Not yet.

Valechka says: 'Tomorrow we shall talk. Now rest.'

I have a room to myself. The girl who had it before has gone away. Two plain black blouses and skirts have been left behind for me.

I have a view of a corner of the lawn, a tiny summer house, the woods. The birds sing in the early summer evening. It seems so peaceful. Yet every couple of minutes a guard goes past the window.

I lie on my little bed in the heat and try to sleep. I think of Archangel in the winter: the coloured lanterns strung out across the frozen river, skating on the Dvina, the sound of ice cracking at night, hunting for mushrooms in the forest. I wish I was at home. But these are foolish thoughts.

I must sleep.

Why did that man watch me on the train for all that time?

LATER: In the darkness, the sound of cars.

He is home.

12.6.51 This is a day! I can hardly set it down. My hand shakes so. (It did not at the time but now it does!) At seven I go to the kitchen. Valechka is already up, sorting through a great mess of broken crockery, glass, spilled food, which lies in a heap in the centre of a big tablecloth. She explains how the table is cleared every night: two guards each take two corners of the cloth and carry everything out! So our first task every morning is to rescue all that isn't broken, and wash it. As we work, Valechka explains the routine of the house. He rises quite late and sometimes likes to work in the garden. Then he goes to the Kremlin and his quarters are cleaned. He never returns before nine or ten in the evening, and then there is a dinner. At two or three He goes to bed. This happens seven days a week. The rules: when one approaches Him, do so openly, He hates it when people creep up on Him. If a door has to be knocked on, knock upon it loudly. Don't stand around. Don't speak unless you are spoken to. And if you do have to speak, always look Him in the eyes.

She prepares a simple breakfast of coffee, bread and meat, and takes it out. Later, she asks me to collect the tray. Before I go, she makes me tie up my hair and turn around while she examines me. I will do, she says. She says He is working at a table at the edge of the lawn on the south side of the house. Or was. He moves restlessly, from place to place. It is His way. The guards will know where to look.

What can I write of this moment? I am calm. You would have been proud of me. I remember what to do. I walk around the edge of the lawn and approach Him in plain view. He's sitting on a bench, alone, bent over some papers. The tray is on a table beside Him. He glances up at my approach, then returns to His work. But as I walk away across the grass — then, I swear, I feel His eyes upon my back, all the way, until I'm out of sight. Valechka laughs at my white face.

I don't see Him again after that.

Just now (it is after ten): the sound of cars.

14.6.51 Last night. Late. I'm in the kitchen with Valechka when Lozgachev (a guard) comes rushing in, all steamed up, to say the Boss is out of Ararat. Valechka fetches a bottle, but instead of giving it to Lozgachev, she gives it to me: 'Let Anna take it in.' She wants to help me — dear Valechka! So Lozgachev takes me down the passage to the main part of the house. I can hear male voices. Laughter. He knocks hard on the door and stands aside. I go in. The room is hot, stuffy. Seven or eight men around a table — familiar faces, all of them. One — Comrade Khrushchev,

I think – is on his feet, proposing a toast. His face is flushed, sweating. He stops. There is food all over the place, as if they have been throwing it. All look at me. Comrade Stalin is at the head of the table. I set the brandy next to him. His voice is soft and kindly. He says, 'And what is your name, young comrade?' 'Anna Safanova, Comrade Stalin.' I remember to look into his eyes. They are very deep. The man next to him says, 'She's from Archangel, Boss.' And Comrade Khrushchev says, 'Trust Lavrenty to know where she's from!' More laughter. 'Ignore these rough fellows,' says Comrade Stalin. 'Thank you, Anna Safanova.' As I close the door, their talk resumes. Valechka is waiting for me at the end of the passage. She puts her arm around me and we go back in to the kitchen. I am shaking, it must be with joy.

16.6.51 Comrade Stalin has said that from now on I am to bring him breakfast.

21.6.51 He is in the garden as usual this morning. How I wish the people could see him here! He likes to listen to the birdsong, to prune the flowers. But his hands shake. As I am setting down the tray, I hear him curse. He has cut himself. I pick up the napkin and take it over to him. At first, he looks at me suspiciously. Then he holds out his hand. I wrap it in the white linen. Bright spots of blood soak through. 'You are not afraid of Comrade Stalin, Anna Safanova?' 'Why should I be afraid of you, Comrade Stalin?' 'The doctors are afraid of Comrade Stalin. When they come to change a dressing on Comrade Stalin, their hands shake so much, he has to do it himself. Ah, but if their hands didn't shake – well then, what would that mean? Thank you, Anna Safanova.'

O, mama and papa, he is so lonely! Your hearts would go out to him. He is only flesh and blood, after all, like us. And close-up he is old. Much older than he appears in his pictures. His moustache is grey, the underside stained yellow by his pipe smoke. His teeth are almost all gone. His chest rattles when he breathes. I fear for him. For all of us.

30.6.51 Three a.m. A knock at my door. Valechka is outside, in her nightdress, with a pocket torch. He has been in the garden, pruning by moonlight, and he has cut himself again! He is calling for me! I dress quickly and follow her along the passage. The night is warm. We pass through the dining room and in to his private quarters. He has three rooms and he moves between them, one night in this one, one night in another. Nobody is ever sure where. He sleeps beneath a blanket on a couch. Valechka leaves us. He is sitting on the couch, his hand outstretched. It is only a graze. It takes me half a minute to bind it with my handkerchief. 'The fearless Anna Safanova . . .'

I sense he wants me to stay. He asks me about my home and parents, my Party work, my plans for the future. I tell him of my interest in the law. He snorts: he doesn't think much of lawyers! He wants to know of life in Archangel in the winter. Have I seen the lights of the Northern Aurora? (Of course!) When do the first snows come? At the end of September, I tell him, and by the end of October, the city is snowbound and only the trains can get through. He is hungry for details. How the Dvina freezes and wooden tracks are laid across it and there is light for only four hours a day. How the temperature drops to 35 below and people go into the forests for ice-fishing . . .

He listens most intently. 'Comrade Stalin believes the soul of Russia lies in the ice and solitude of the far north. When Comrade Stalin was in exile – this was before the Revolution, in Kureika, within the Arctic Circle – it was his happiest time. It *was here Comrade Stalin learned how to hunt and fish. That swine Trotsky maintained that Comrade Stalin used only traps. A filthy lie! Comrade Stalin set traps, yes, but he also set lines in the ice holes, and such was his success in the detection of fish that the local people credited him with supernatural powers. In one day, Comrade Stalin travelled forty-five versts on skis and killed twelve brace of partridge with twenty-four shots. Could Trotsky claim as much?'*

I wish I could remember all he said. Perhaps this should be my destiny: to record his words for History?

By the time I leave him to return to my bed, it is light.

8.7.51 The same performance as last time. Valechka at my door at 3 a.m.: he has cut himself, he wants me. But when I get there, I can see no wound. He laughs at my face – his joke! – and tells me to bind his hand in any case. He strokes my cheek, then pinches it. 'You see, fearless Anna Safanova, how you make a prisoner of me?!'

He is in a different room from the last time. On the walls are pictures of children, torn from magazines. Children playing in a cherry orchard. A boy on skis. A girl drinking goat's milk from a horn. Many pictures. He notices me staring at them and this prompts him to talk frankly of his own children. One son dead. One a drunkard. His daughter married twice, the first time to a Jew: he never even allowed him in to the house! What has Comrade Stalin done to deserve this? Other men produce normal children. Was it bad blood or bad upbringing? Was there something wrong with the mothers? (He thinks so, to judge from their families, who have been a constant plague to him.) Or was it impossible for the children of Comrade Stalin ever to develop normally, given his high position in the State and Party? Here is the age-old conflict, older even than the struggle between the classes.

He asks if I have heard of Comrade Trofim Lysenko's 1948 speech to the Lenin All-Union Academy of Agricultural Sciences? I say that I have. My answer pleases him.

'But Comrade Stalin wrote this speech! It was Comrade Stalin's insight, after a lifetime of study and struggle, that acquired characteristics are inheritable. Though naturally these discoveries must be put into the mouths of others, just as it is for others to turn the principle into a practical science.'

'Remember Comrade Stalin's historic words to Gorky: "It is the task of the proletarian state to produce engineers of human souls."'

'Are you a good Bolshevik, Anna Safanova?'

I swear to him that I am.

'Will you prove it? Will you dance for Comrade Stalin?'

There is a gramophone in the corner of the room. He goes to it. I —

Chapter Fifteen

'AND THAT'S HOW it ends?' said O'Brian. His voice was heavy with disappointment. 'Just like that?'

'See for yourself.' Kelso turned the book round and showed it to the other two. 'The next twenty pages have been removed. And here – look – you can see the way it's been done. The torn edges attached to the spine are all different lengths.'

'What's so significant about that?'

'It means they weren't torn out all at once, but one by one. Methodically.' Kelso resumed his examination. 'There are some pages left at the back, about fifty, but they've not been written on. They've been drawn on – doodled on, I should say – in red pencil. The same image again and again, d'you see?'

'What are they?' O'Brian moved in closer with the camera running. 'They look like wolves.'

'They are wolves. The heads of wolves. Stalin often drew wolves in the margins of official documents when he was thinking.'

'Jesus. So it's genuine, you think?'

'Until it's been forensically tested, I'm not prepared to say. I'm sorry. Not officially.'

'Unofficially, then – not for attribution until later – what d'you think?'

'Oh, it's genuine,' said Kelso, without hesitation. 'I'd stake my life on it.'

O'Brian switched the camera off.

*

THEY had left the lock-up by this time and were sitting in the Moscow bureau of the Satellite News System which occupied the top floor of a ten-storey office block just south of the Olympic Stadium. A glass partition separated O'Brian's room from the main production office, where a secretary sat listlessly before a computer screen. Next to her, a mute television, tuned to SNS, was showing clips of the previous night's baseball games. Through a skylight Kelso could see a big satellite dish, raised like an offertory plate to the bulging Moscow clouds.

O'Brian said, 'And how long is it going to take us to get this stuff tested?'

'A couple of weeks, perhaps,' said Kelso. 'A month.'

'No way,' said O'Brian. 'No way can we wait that long.'

'Well, think about it. First of all this material technically belongs to the Russian government. Or Stalin's heirs. Or someone. Anyway, it isn't ours – Zinaida's, I mean.'

Zinaida was standing at the window, staring out through a gap she had made with her fingers in the slatted blinds. At the mention of her name she glanced briefly in Kelso's direction. She had barely said a word in the last hour – not when they were still in the garage, not even on their cautious drive across Moscow, following O'Brian.

'So it isn't safe to keep it here,' continued Kelso. 'We've got to get it out of the country. That's the first priority. God knows who's after it now. Just being in the same *room* is bloody dangerous as far as I'm concerned. The tests themselves – well, we can have those done anywhere. I know some people in Oxford who can check the ink and paper. There are document examiners in Germany, Switzerland –'

O'Brian didn't seem to be listening. He had his feet up on his desk, his long body lolling back in his chair, his hands clasped behind his head. 'You know what we've really got to do?' he mused. 'We've got to find the girl.'

Kelso stared at him for a moment. 'Find the girl? What are you talking about? There isn't going to be a girl. The girl's going to be dead.'

'You can't be sure of that. She'd only be – what? – sixty-something?'

'She'd be sixty-six. But that's hardly the point. It's not *old age* she'll have died of. Who d'you think she was getting mixed up with here? Prince Charming? She won't have lived happily ever after.'

'Maybe not, but we still need to find out what happened to her. What happened to her folks. Human interest. *That's* the story.'

The wall behind O'Brian's head was plastered with photographs: O'Brian with Yasser Arafat, O'Brian with Gerry Adams, O'Brian in a flak jacket next to a mass grave in the Balkans somewhere and another of him, in protective gear, stepping through a minefield with the Princess of Wales. O'Brian in a tuxedo, collecting an award – for the sheer genius of simply being O'Brian, perhaps? Citations for O'Brian. Reviews of O'Brian. A herogram from the Chief Executive of SNS, praising O'Brian for his 'relentless dedication to triumphing over our competitors'. For the first time, and far too late, Kelso began to get a measure of the man's ambition.

'Nothing,' said Kelso very deliberately, so there was no room for misunderstanding, '*nothing* is to be made public until this material is out of the country and has been forensically verified. Do you hear me? That's what we agreed.'

O'Brian clicked his fingers. 'Yeah, yeah, yeah. All right.

But in the meantime we should find out what happened to the girl. We've got to do that anyway. If we go on air with the notebook before we find out what happened to Anna, someone else'll come along and get the best part of the story.' He lifted his feet off the desk and spun around in his chair to a set of bookshelves beside his desk. 'Now where the hell is Archangel, anyway?'

IT happened with a kind of inexorable logic so that later, when Kelso had the time to review his actions, he still could never identify a precise moment when he could have stopped it, when he could have diverted events on to a different course –

'"Archangel,"' said O'Brian, reading aloud from a guidebook. '"Northern Russian port city. Population: four hundred thousand. Situated on the River Dvina, thirty miles upstream from the White Sea. Principal industries: timber, shipbuilding and fishing. From the end of October until the beginning of April, Archangel is snowbound." Shit. What's the date?'

'October the twenty-ninth.'

O'Brian picked up the telephone and jabbed out a number. From his position on the sofa Kelso watched through the thick glass wall as the secretary reached silently for the receiver.

'Sweetheart,' said O'Brian, 'do me a favour will you? Get on to the System's weather centre in Florida and get the latest weather prediction for Archangel.' He spelt it out for her. 'That's it. Quick as you can.'

Kelso closed his eyes.

The point was – he knew it in his heart – that O'Brian was right. The story *was* the girl. And the story couldn't be pursued in Moscow. If the trail could be picked up anywhere, it could only be in the north, on her home territory, where it was possible there might still be some family or friends who would remember her: remember the Komsomol girl of nineteen and the dramatic summons to Moscow in the summer of 1951 –

'"Archangel,"' resumed O'Brian, '"was founded by Peter the Great and named after Archangel Michael, the Warrior-Angel. See the Book of Revelation, chapter twelve, verses seven to eight: 'And there was war in heaven: Michael and his angels fought against the dragon; and the dragon fought and his angels,/And prevailed not.' In the nineteen-thirties – "'

'Do we really have to listen to this?'

But O'Brian held up his finger.

'" – in the nineteen-thirties, Stalin exiled two million Ukrainian kulaks into the Archangel oblast, a region of forest and tundra larger than the whole of France. After the war, this vast area was used for testing nuclear weapons. Archangel's outpost is Severodvinsk, centre of Russia's nuclear submarine construction programme. Until the fall of communism, Archangel was a closed city, forbidden to all outside visitors.

'"Traveller's tip,"' concluded O'Brian. '"When arriving at the Archangel Railway Station, always be sure to check the digital radiation meter – if it shows 15 microRads per hour or below, it's safe."' He closed the book with a cheerful snap. 'Sounds like a fun place. What d'you think? You up for this?'

I am trapped, thought Kelso. *I am a victim of historical inevitability. Comrade Stalin would have approved.*

'You know I've no money – ?'

'I'll lend you money.'

'No winter clothes –'

'We've got clothes.'

'No *visa* –'

'A detail.'

'A *detail?*'

'Come on, Fluke. You're the Stalin expert. I need you.'

'Well that's touching. And if I say no, presumably you'll go anyway?'

O'Brian grinned. The telephone rang. He picked it up, listened, made a few notes. When he put it down, he was frowning and Kelso entertained a brief hope of reprieve. But no.

The weather in Archangel at 11:00 GMT that day (3 p.m. local time) was being reported as partly cloudy, minus four degrees, with light winds and snow flurries. However, a deep depression was rolling westwards from Siberia and that was promising snow heavy enough to close the city within a day or two.

In other words, said O'Brian, they would have to hurry.

HE fetched an atlas and opened it on his desk.

The fastest way into Archangel, obviously, was by air, but the Aeroflot flight didn't leave until the following morning and the airline would require Kelso to show his visa which would expire at midnight. So that was out. The train took more than twenty hours, and even O'Brian could see the risks in that – trapped on board a slow-moving sleeper for the best part of a day.

Which left the road – specifically, the M8 – which ran nearly 700 miles, more or less direct, according to the map, swerving slightly to take in the city of Yaroslavl, then following the river plateaux of the Vaga and the Dvina, across the taiga and the tundra and the great virgin forests of northern

Russia, directly into Archangel itself, where the road ended.

Kelso said, 'It's not a freeway, you know. There are no motels.'

'It's nothing, man. It'll be a breeze, I promise. What've we got now – let's see – couple of hours of daylight left? That should get us well clear of Moscow. You drive, don't you?'

'Yes.'

'There you go. We'll take turns. These journeys, I tell you, they always look worse on paper. Once we're in the groove, we'll eat those miles. You'll see.' He was making a calculation on a pad. 'I figure we could hit Archangel about nine or ten tomorrow morning.'

'So we drive through the night?'

'Sure. Or we can stop if you'd sooner. The thing is to quit talking and start moving. Quicker we hit the road, quicker we get there. We need to pack that book in something –'

He came round from behind his desk and headed towards the notebook that was lying on the coffee table, next to the congealed mass of papers. But before he could reach it, Zinaida grabbed it.

'This,' she said in English, 'mine.'

'What?'

'Mine.'

Kelso said, 'That's right. Her father left it for her.'

'I only want to borrow it.'

'*Nyet!*'

O'Brian appealed to Kelso. 'Is she crazy? Supposing we find Anna Safanova?'

'Supposing we do? What do you have in mind exactly? Stalin's grey-haired old lover in a rocking chair, reading aloud for the viewers?'

'Oh, funny guy. Listen: people are a whole lot more likely

to talk to us if we're carrying proof. I say that book should come with us. Why's it hers, anyhow? It's no more hers than mine. Or anybody else's.'

'Because that was the deal, remember?'

'Deal? Seems to me it's you two've got the only *deal* going round here.' He slipped back into his wheedling mode. 'Come on, Fluke, it's not safe for her in Moscow. Where's she gonna keep it? What if Mamantov comes after her?'

Kelso had to concede this point. 'Then why doesn't she come with us?' He turned to Zinaida, 'Come with us to Archangel –'

'With him?' she said in Russian. 'No way. He'll kill us all.'

Kelso was beginning to lose patience. 'Then let's postpone Archangel,' he said irritably to O'Brian, 'until we can get the material copied.'

'But you heard the forecast. In a day or two we won't be able to move up there. Besides, this is a story. Stories don't keep.' He raised his hands in disgust. 'Shit, I can't stand around here bitching all afternoon. Need to get some equipment together. Need supplies. Need to get going. Talk some sense into her, man, for God's sake.'

'I told you,' said Zinaida, after O'Brian had stamped out of the office, banging the glass door behind him. 'I told you we couldn't trust him.'

Kelso sank back into the sofa. He rubbed his face with both hands. This was starting to get dangerous, he thought. Not physically – in a curious way that was still unreal to him – but professionally. It was professional danger he scented now. Because Adelman was right: these big frauds did usually follow a pattern. And part of it involved being rushed to judgement. Here he was – a trained scholar, supposedly – and what had he done? He'd read through the notebook once. *Once.* He hadn't even done the most basic check to see whether the dates in the journal tallied with Stalin's known movements in the summer of 1951. He could just imagine the reaction of his former colleagues, probably leaving Russian airspace right now. If they could see how he was handling this –

The thought bothered him more than he cared to admit.

And then there was the other bundle of papers, lying on the table, mouldering and congealed. Those he hadn't even begun to look at.

He pulled on O'Brian's gloves and leaned forwards. He ran his forefinger experimentally through the grey spores on the top sheet. There was writing underneath. He rubbed again and the letters NKVD appeared.

'Zinaida,' he said.

She was sitting behind O'Brian's desk, turning the pages of the notebook, *her* notebook. At the sound of her name she looked up.

KELSO borrowed her tweezers to peel away the outer layer of paper. It came off like dead skin, flaking here and there, but cleanly enough for him to make out some of the words on the page underneath. It was a typed document, a surveillance report of some kind by the look of it, dated 24 May 1951, signed by Major I. T. Mekhlis of the NKVD.

'... *summary of finding to the 23rd instant ... Anna Mikhailovna Safanova, born Archangel 27.2.32 ... Maxim Gorky Academy ... reputation (see attached). Health: good ... diptheria, aged 8 yrs. 3 mths ... Rubella, 10yrs. 1 mth ... No family history of genetic disorder. Party work: outstanding ... Pioneers ... Komsomol ...'*

Kelso peeled back more layers. Sometimes they came away

singly, sometimes fused in twos or threes. It was painstaking work. Through the glass partition he caught occasional glimpses of O'Brian, lugging suitcases across the outer office to the elevator doors, but he was too absorbed to pay much attention. What he was reading was as full a record of a nineteen-year-old girl's life as it was possible for a secret police force to compile. There was something almost pornographic about it. Here was an account of every childhood ailment, details of her blood group (O), the state of her teeth (excellent), her height and weight and hair-colour (light auburn), her physical aptitude ('in gymnastics she displays a particularly high aptitude . . .'), mental abilities ('overall, in the 90th percentile . . . '), ideological correctness ('the firmest grasp of Marxist theory . . . '), interviews with her doctor, coach, teachers, Komsomol group leader, schoolfriends.

The worst that could be said about her was that she had, perhaps 'a slightly dreamy temperament' (Comrade Oborin) and 'a certain tendency to subjectivity and bourgeois sentimentalism rather than objectivity in all her personal relations' (Elena Satsanova). Against a further criticism from the same Comrade Satsanova, that she was 'naïve,' a marginal comment had been appended, in red pencil: 'Good!' and, later, 'Who is this old bitch?' There were numerous other underlinings, exclamation marks, queries and marginalia: 'Ha ha ha', 'And so?', 'Acceptable!'

Kelso had spent enough time in the archives to recognise this hand and style. The jagged scrawl was Stalin's. There was no question of it.

After half an hour he put the papers back in their original order and took off his gloves. His hands felt claw-like, raw and sweaty. He was suddenly overcome with self-disgust.

Zinaida was watching him.

'What do you think happened to her?'

'Nothing good.'

'He brought her down from the north to screw her?'

'That's one way of putting it.'

'Poor kid.'

'Poor kid,' he agreed.

'So why did he keep her book?'

'Obsession? Infatuation?' He shrugged. 'Who's to say. He was a sick man by then. He only had twenty months to live. Maybe she described what happened to her, then thought better of it, and tore out the pages. Or, more likely, he got hold of her book and ripped them out himself. He didn't like people knowing too much about him.'

'Well, I can tell you one thing: he didn't screw her that night.'

Kelso laughed. 'And how do you know that?'

'Easy. Look.' She opened the notebook. 'Here on the twelfth of May, she's got "the usual trouble of this time", right? On the tenth of June, on the train, it's "the worst of days to travel". Well, you can work it out for yourself, can't you? There's exactly twenty-eight days between the two. And twenty-eight days after the tenth of June is July the eighth. Which is the last entry.'

Kelso stood slowly and went over to the desk. He peered over her shoulder at the childish writing.

'What are you talking about?'

'She was a regular girl. A regular little Komsomol girl.'

Kelso absorbed this information, put the gloves back on, took the book from her, flicked between the two pages. Well, now, this was crazy, wasn't it? This was *sick*. He could barely bring himself to acknowledge the suspicion that was forming in the back of his mind. But why else would Stalin have been so interested in whether or not she had had *rubella*, of all things? Or whether her family had any history of congenital disorders?

'Tell me,' he said, quietly, 'when would she have been fertile?'

'Fourteen days later. On the twenty-second.'

AND suddenly she couldn't get out of there fast enough.

She pushed her chair back from the desk and stared at the notebook with revulsion.

'Take the damned thing,' she said. 'Take it. Keep it.'

She didn't want to touch it again. She didn't even want to *see* it.

It was *cursed*.

In a couple of seconds she had her bag over her shoulder and was flinging open the door and Kelso had to scramble to catch up with her as she strode across the office towards the elevators. O'Brian came out of an editing suite to see what was going on. He was in a heavy waterproof jacket with two pairs of binoculars slung around his thick neck. He started to follow them but Kelso waved him back.

'I'll handle this.'

She was standing in the corridor, her back to him.

'Listen Zinaida,' he said. The lift door opened and he stepped in after her. 'Listen. It's not safe for you out there –'

Almost immediately the car stopped and a man got in – heavy-set, middle-aged, black leather coat and a black leather cap. He stood between them, glanced at Zinaida, then at Kelso, sensing the edge to their silence. He looked straight ahead and stuck out his chin, smiling slightly. Kelso could tell what he was thinking: *a lovers' tiff – well, that was life, they'd get over it.*

When they reached the ground floor he stood back politely to let them out first and Zinaida clattered quickly across the marble in her knee-length boots. A security guard pressed a switch to unlock the doors.

'You,' she said, zipping up her jacket, 'should worry about yourself.'

It was just after four. People were beginning to leave from work. In the offices across the road Kelso could see the green glow of computer screens. A woman had shrunk herself into a doorway and was talking into a mobile phone. A motorcyclist went past, slowly.

'Zinaida, listen.' He grabbed her arm, stopping her from walking away. She wouldn't look at him. He pulled her close to the wall. 'Your father died badly, do you understand what I'm saying? The people who did it – Mamantov and his people – they're after this notebook. They know there's something important about it – don't ask me how. If they realise your father had a daughter – and they're bound to because Mamantov used to have access to his file – well, think about it. They're going to come after you.'

'And they killed him for *that*?'

'They killed him because he wouldn't tell them where it was. And he wouldn't tell them where it was because he wanted you to have it.'

'But it wasn't worth *dying* for. The stupid old fool.' She glared at him. Her eyes were wet for the first time that day. 'Stupid *stubborn* old fool.'

'Is there someone you can stay with? Family?'

'My family are dead.'

'A friend maybe?'

'Friend? I've got this, remember?' She lifted the flap of her bag, showing him her father's pistol.

Kelso said, as calmly as he could, 'At least give me your address, Zinaida. Your phone number –'

She looked at him suspiciously. 'Why?'

'Because I feel responsible.' He glanced around. This was madness, talking in the street. He felt in his pocket for a pen, couldn't find any paper, tore the side off a pack of cigarettes. 'Come on, write it for me. Quickly.'

He thought she wouldn't do it. She turned to go. But then, abruptly, she swung back and scribbled something down. She had a place near Izmaylovo Park, he saw, where the big flea market was.

She didn't say goodbye. She set off up the street, dodging the pedestrians, walking fast. He watched her, waiting to see if she might look back. But of course she didn't. He knew she wouldn't. She wasn't the looking-back kind.

Part Two

Archangel

'If you are afraid of wolves, keep out of the woods.'
J. V. Stalin, 1936

Chapter Sixteen

BEFORE THEY COULD get out of Moscow they had to take on fuel – because, as O'Brian said, you never knew what kind of rusty, watered-down *horse's piss* they might try to sell you once you got out of town. So they stopped at the new Nefto Agip on Prospekt Mira and O'Brian filled the Land Cruiser's tank and four big jerrycans with forty gallons of high-octane, lead-free gasoline. Then he checked the tyres and the oil, and by the time they were back on the road the evening rush was in full and sluggish spate.

It took them the best part of an hour to reach the outer ring, but there, at last, the traffic thinned, the monotonous apartment blocks and factory chimneys fell away, and suddenly they were out and free – into the flat open countryside, with its grey-green fields and giant pylons and a vast sky: a Kansas sky. It was more than ten years since Kelso had ventured north on the M8. Village churches, used as grain stores since the Revolution, were being restored, encased in web-works of wooden scaffolding. Near Dvoriki, a golden dome gathered the weak afternoon light and shone from the horizon like an autumn bonfire.

O'Brian was in his element. 'On the road,' he would say occasionally, 'and out of town – it's great, isn't it? Just great.' He drove at a steady sixty-five miles an hour, talking constantly, one hand on the wheel, the other beating time to a tape of thumping rock music.

'*Just great . . .* '

The satchel was on the back seat, wrapped in plastic. Heaped around it was an extravagant array of equipment and provisions: a couple of sleeping bags, thermal underwear ('Got any thermals, Fluke? Gotta have those thermals!'), two waterproof and fur-lined jackets, rubber boots and army boots, ordinary binoculars, binoculars with night-imaging, a shovel, a compass, water bottles, water purification tablets, two six-packs of Budweiser, a box of Hershey chocolate bars, two vacuum flasks filled with coffee, pot noodles, a torch, a short-wave transistor radio, spare batteries, a travelling kettle that could be plugged into the car's cigarette lighter – Kelso lost count after that.

In the rear section of the Toyota were the jerrycans and four rigid cases stamped SNS, whose contents O'Brian described with professional relish: a miniaturised, digital camcorder; an Inmarsat satellite telephone; a laptop-sized DVC-PRO video editing machine; and something he called a Toko Video Store and Forward Unit. Total value of these four items: $120,000.

'Ever hear of travelling light?' asked Kelso.

'Light?' O'Brian grinned. 'You can't get any lighter. Give me four suitcases and I can do what it used to take six guys and a truckful of equipment to do. If there's any excess baggage around here, my friend, it's you.'

'It wasn't my idea to come.'

But O'Brian wasn't listening. Thanks to these four cases, he said, his beat was the *world*. African famines. The genocide in Rwanda. The bomb in the village in Northern Ireland that he'd actually filmed go off (he'd won an award for that one). The mass graves in Bosnia. The cruise missiles in Baghdad, trundling down the streets at roof-top level – left, then right, then right again, and which way, please, for the presidential palace? And then of course there was Chechnya. Now, the trouble with Chechnya –

(You are a bird of ill-omen, thought Kelso. You circle the world and wherever you land there is famine and death and destruction: in an earlier and less credulous age, the local citizens would have gathered at the first sight of you and driven you off with stones –)

– the trouble with Chechnya, O'Brian was saying, was that the sucker had ended just as he arrived, so he had pitched up in Moscow for a while. Now *that* was a scary town: 'Give me Sarajevo any day.'

'How long are you planning to stay in Moscow?'

'Not long. Till the presidential elections. Should be fun, I reckon.'

Fun?

'And then where are you going?'

'Who knows? Why d'you ask?'

'I just want to make sure I'm nowhere around, that's all.'

O'Brian laughed and put his foot down. The speedometer flickered up towards seventy.

THEY maintained this pace as the afternoon turned to dusk, O'Brian still prattling on. (Jesus, did the man *never* shut up?) At Rostov the road ran beside a great lake. Boats, moored and tarpaulined for the winter, lined a jetty, close to a row of shut-tered, timbered buildings. Far out on the water Kelso could see a lone sailboat with a light at its stern. He watched it swing about in the wind and tack for the shore and he felt again the familiar depression of nightfall starting to creep over him.

He could sense Stalin's papers behind him now almost as a physical presence, as if the GenSec were in the car with them. He worried about Zinaida. He would have liked a drink, or a cigarette, come to that, but O'Brian had declared the Toyota a smoke-free zone.

'You're jumpy,' said O'Brian, interrupting himself. 'I can tell.'

'Do you blame me?'

'Why? Because of Mamantov?' The reporter flicked his hand. 'He doesn't scare me.'

'You didn't see what he did to the old man.'

'Yeah, well he wouldn't do that to us. Not to a Brit and a Yank. He's not completely nuts.'

'Maybe not. But he might do it to Zinaida.'

'I wouldn't worry about Zinaida. Besides, she hasn't got the stuff any more. We have.'

'You're a nice man, you know that? And what if they don't believe her?'

'I'm just saying you should quit bothering about Mamantov, that's all. I've interviewed him a couple of times and I can tell you, he's a busted flash. The man lives in the past. Like you.'

'And you? You don't live in the past, I suppose?'

'Me? No way. Can't afford to, in my job.'

'Now let's just analyse that,' said Kelso, pleasantly. In his mind he was opening a drawer, selecting the sharpest knife he could find. 'So all these places you've been boasting about for the past two hours – Africa, Bosnia, the Middle East, Northern Ireland – the past isn't important there, is that what you're saying? You think they're all living in the present? They all just woke up one morning, saw you were there with your four little suitcases, and decided to have a war? It wasn't happening till you arrived? "Gee, hey, look everyone, I'm R. J. O'Brian and I just discovered the fucking *Balkans* – "'

'Okay,' muttered O'Brian, 'there's no need to be offensive about it.'

'Oh but there is.' Kelso was warming up. 'This is the great

myth, you see, of our age. The great western myth. The arrogance of our time, personified – if you'll excuse me for saying so – in *you*. That just because a place has a McDonalds and MTV and takes American Express it's exactly the same as everywhere else – it doesn't have a past any more, it's Year Zero. But it's not true.'

'You think you're better than me, don't you?'

'No.'

'Smarter then?'

'Not even that. Look. You say Moscow is a scary town. It is. Why? I'll tell you. Because there's no tradition of private property in Russia. First of all there were workers and peasants who had nothing and the nobility owned the country. Then there were workers and peasants with nothing and the Party owned the country. Now there are still workers and peasants with nothing and the country's owned, as it's always been owned, by whoever has the biggest fists. Unless you understand that, you can't begin to understand Russia. You can't make sense of the present unless a part of you lives in the past.' Kelso sat back in his seat. 'End of lecture.'

And for half an hour, as O'Brian pondered this, there was blessed peace.

THEY reached the big town of Yaroslavl just after nine and crossed the Volga. Kelso poured them each a cup of coffee. It slopped across his lap as they hit a rough patch of road. O'Brian drank as he drove. They ate chocolate. The headlights that had blazed towards them around the city gradually dwindled to the occasional flash.

Kelso said, 'Do you want me to take over?'

O'Brian shook his head. 'I'm fine. Let's change at midnight. You should get some sleep.'

They listened on the radio to the news at ten o'clock. The communists and the nationalists in the lower senate, the Duma, were using their majority to block the President's latest measures: another political crisis threatened. The Moscow stock exchange was continuing its plunge. A secret report from the Interior Ministry to the President, warning of a danger of armed rebellion, had been leaked and printed in *Aurora*.

Of Rapava, Mamantov or Stalin's papers there was no mention.

'Shouldn't you be in Moscow, covering all this?'

O'Brian snorted. 'What? "New Political Crisis in Russia"? Give me a break. R. J. O'Brian won't be on the hour every hour with *that*.'

'But he will with this?'

'"Stalin's Secret Lover, Mystery Girl Revealed"? What do you think?'

O'Brian switched off the radio.

Kelso reached over to the back seat and dragged one of the sleeping bags into the front. He opened it out and wrapped it around him like a blanket, then pressed a button and his seat slowly reclined.

He closed his eyes but he couldn't sleep. Images of Stalin gradually invaded his mind. Stalin as an old man. Stalin as glimpsed by Milovan Djilas after the war, leaning forward in his limousine while he was being driven back to Blizhny, turning on a little light in the panel in front of him to see the time on a pocket watch hanging there – 'and I observed directly in front of me his already hunched back and the bony grey nape of his neck with its wrinkled skin above the stiff marshal's collar . . .' (Djilas thought Stalin was senile that night: cramming his mouth with food, losing the thread of his stories, making jokes about the Jews.)

And Stalin, less than six months before he died, delivering his last, rambling speech to the Central Committee, describing how Lenin faced the crises of 1918 and repeating the same word over and over – 'he thundered away in an incredibly difficult situation, he thundered on, fearing nothing, he just thundered away . . .' – while the delegates sat stunned, transfixed.

And Stalin, alone in his bedroom, at night, tearing pictures of children out of magazines and plastering them around his walls. And then Stalin making Anna Safanova dance for him –

It was curious, but whenever Kelso tried to picture Anna Safanova dancing, the face he always gave her was that of Zinaida Rapava.

Chapter Seventeen

ZINAIDA RAPAVA WAS sitting in her parked car in Moscow in the darkness with her bag on her lap and her hands in that bag, feeling the outline of her father's Makarov pistol.

She had discovered that she could still strip and load it without looking at it – like riding a bicycle, it seemed: one of those childish accomplishments you never forgot. Release the spring at the bottom of the grip, pull out the magazine, squeeze in the bullets (six, seven, *eight* of them, smooth and cold to the touch), push the magazine back up, click, slide, then press the safety catch down to fire. *There.*

Papa would have been proud of her. But then she always had been better at this game than Sergo. Guns made Sergo nervous. Which was a joke, seeing as he was the one who had to do military service.

Thinking of Sergo made her cry again, but she wouldn't let herself give in to it for long. She pulled her hands out of her bag and wiped each eye irritably – so then so – on either sleeve of her jacket, then went back to her task.

Push. Click. Slide. Press . . .

SHE was scared. So scared, in fact, that when she had walked away from the westerner that afternoon she had wanted to look back at him standing outside the office block – had wanted to *go* back to him – but if she'd done that he would have known she was afraid, and fear, she had been taught, was something you must never show. Another of her father's lessons.

So she had hurried on to her car and had driven around

for a while without thinking until presently she had found herself heading in the direction of Red Square. She had parked in Bolshaya Lubyanka and had walked uphill to the little white Church of the Icon of the Virgin of Vladimir, where a service was in progress.

The place was packed. The churches were always packed now, not like in the old days. The music washed over her. She lit a candle. She wasn't sure why she did this because she had no faith; it was the sort of thing her mother used to do. *'And what has your god ever done for us?'* – her father's sneering voice. She thought of him, and of the girl who wrote the journal, Anna Safanova. Silly bitch, she thought. Poor silly bitch. And she lit a candle for her, too, and much good might it do her, wherever she was.

She wished her memories were better but they weren't and there was nothing to be done. She could remember him drunk, mostly, his eyes like worm holes, his fists flying. Or tired from work at the engine sheds, as rank as an old dog, too weary to rise from his chair to go to bed, sitting on a sheet of *Pravda* to keep the oil off the cover. Or paranoid, up half the night, staring out of the window, prowling the corridors – who was that looking at him? who was that talking about him? – spreading yet more sheets from *Pravda* down on the floor and obsessively cleaning his Makarov. (*'I'll kill them if I have to . . .'*)

But sometimes, when he wasn't drunk or exhausted or mad – in the mellow hour, between mere inebriation and oblivion – he'd talk about life in Kolyma: how you survived, traded favours and scraps of tobacco for food, wangled the easier jobs, learned to smell a stoolie – and then he'd take her on his lap and sing to her, some of the Kolyma songs, in his fine Mingrelian tenor.

That was a better memory.

At fifty he had seemed so *old* to her. He always had been an old man. His youth had gone when Stalin died. Maybe that was why he went on about him so much? He even had a picture of Stalin on the wall – remember that? – Stalin with his glossy moustaches, like great black slugs? Well, she could never take her friends back *there*, could she? Never let them see the pig state in which they lived. Two rooms, and her in the only bedroom, sharing first with Sergo and then, when he was too big and too embarrassed to look at her, with mama. And mama a wraith even before the cancer got her, then turning to gossamer and finally melting to nothing.

She'd died in eighty-nine when Zinaida was eighteen. And six months later they were back at the Troekurovo cemetery putting Sergo in the earth beside her. Zinaida closed her eyes and remembered papa, drunk, at the funeral, in the rain, and a couple of Sergo's army comrades, and a nervous young lieutenant, just a kid himself, who had been Sergo's commanding officer, talking about how Sergo had died for the motherland whilst rendering fraternal assistance to the progressive forces of the People's Republic of –

– oh, fuck it, what did it matter? The lieutenant had cleared off as soon as he decently could, after about ten minutes, and Zinaida had moved her things out of the ghost-filled apartment that night. He had tried to stop her, hitting her, sweating vodka through his open pores, stinking even more like an old dog from his soaking in the rain, and she had never seen him again. Never seen him again until last Tuesday morning when he had turned up on her doorstep and called her a whore. And she had thrown him out like a beggar, sent him away with a couple of packs of cigarettes, and now he was dead and she really would never see him again.

She bent her head, lips moving, and anyone watching might have thought she was praying, but actually she was reading his note and talking to herself.

'I have been a bad one, you're right. All you said was right. So don't think I don't know it –'

Oh, papa, you were, you know that? You really were.

'But here is a chance to do some good –'

Good? Is that what you call it? Good? That's a joke. They killed you for it and now they're going to kill me.

'Remember that place I used to have, when mama was alive?'

Yes, yes, I remember.

'And remember what I used to tell you? Are you listening to me, girl? Rule number one? What's rule number one?'

She folded away the note and glanced around. This was stupid.

'Speak up, girl!'

She bowed her head meekly.

Never show them you're afraid, papa.

'Again!'

'Never show them you're afraid.'

'And rule number two? What's rule number two?'

You've only got one friend in this world.

'And that friend is?'

Yourself.

'And what else?'

This.

'Show me.'

This, papa. This.

In the concealed darkness of the bag her fingers began to work her rosary, clumsily at first but with increasing dexterity –

Push. Click. Slide. Press –

*

SHE had left the church when the service ended and hurried down into Red Square, knowing what she had to do, much calmer now.

The westerner was right. She didn't dare risk her apartment. There wasn't a friend she knew well enough to ask if she could stay. And in a hotel she would have to register, and if Mamantov had friends in the FSB –

That only left one option.

It was nearly six and the shadows were beginning to collect and deepen around the base of Lenin's tomb. But across the cobbles the lights of the GUM department store blazed brighter by the minute – a line of yellow beacons, it seemed to her, in the gloom of the late October afternoon.

She made her purchases quickly, starting with a knee-length black cocktail dress of raw silk. She also bought herself sheer black tights, short black gloves, a black purse, a pair of black high-heeled shoes and make-up.

She paid for it all in cash, in dollars. She never went out with less than $1,000 in cash. She refused to use a credit card: they left too many traces. And she didn't trust the banks, either: thieving alchemists, the lot of them, who would take your precious dollars and conjure them into roubles, turn gold into base metal.

At the cosmetic counter one of the salesgirls recognised her – Hi, Zina! – and she had to turn and flee.

She went back into the boutique and took off her jeans and shirt and tugged herself into her new dress. It was hard to fasten the zip – she had to twist her left arm half way up her back and push her right hand down between her shoulder blades until her fingers touched, but it fastened eventually, pinching her flesh, and she stepped back a pace to look at herself – her hand on her hip, her chin tilted, her profile turned to the mirror.

Good.

Well: *good enough*.

The make-up took another ten minutes. She stuffed her old warm clothes into the GUM carrier bag, slipped on her leather jacket, and headed back into Red Square, tottering on her high heels over the big stones.

She was careful not to look at the Lenin mausoleum, nor at the Kremlin wall behind it, where her father used to take her when she was a girl to file past Stalin's tomb. Instead she walked quickly through the gate in the northern edge of the square, turned right and headed towards the Metropol. She wanted to have a drink at the hotel bar but the security men wouldn't let her through.

'No way, darling. Sorry.'

She could hear them laughing as she walked away.

'Starting early tonight?' one of them called after her.

It was dark by the time she reached her car.

WHICH was where she now sat.

Strange, she thought, looking back, the deaths of mama and Sergo – these two little deaths. *Strange*. They were like two small pebbles at the start of an avalanche. Because not long after they went, everything went – all the old, familiar world slid after them into the wet ground.

Not that Zinaida took much notice of the politics of it all. The first couple of years after leaving papa were a haze in her memory. She lived in a squat out in the Krasnogorsk district. Got pregnant twice. Had two abortions. (And not many days had gone by since when she hadn't wondered what they might have been like, those two – they'd be nearly nine and seven now – and whether they could have been any more clamorous than the spaces they'd left behind.)

Still: if she didn't notice the politics, she did notice the money that was now beginning to appear around the rich hotels – the Metropol, the Kempinski and the rest. And the money noticed her, like it noticed all the Moscow girls. Zinaida wasn't one of the most beautiful, maybe, but she was *good enough*: sufficiently Mingrelian to have an almost Oriental sharpness to her face, sufficiently Russian to have a padding of voluptuousness despite her skinny frame.

And as no girl in Moscow could earn in a month what a western businessman might spend in a night on a bottle of wine, you didn't have to be a genius at economics – you didn't have to be one of the hard-faced management consultants drinking at the bar – to see there was a market in the making here. Which was why one night in December 1992, at the age of twenty-one, in the hotel suite of a German engineer from Ludwigshafen am Rhein, Zinaida Rapava became a whore, tottering down the corridor after ninety sweaty minutes with $125 hidden in her bra, which was more money than she had ever even *seen*.

And shall I tell you something else, papa, now that we're talking at last? It was fine. *I* was fine. Because what was I doing, really, that ten million other girls don't do every night, only they don't have the sense to get paid for it? *That* was decadent. *This* was business – *kapitalism* – and it was fine, and it was like you said, I only had one friend: myself.

After a time, the trade moved out of the hotels and into the clubs, and that was easier. The clubs paid protection to the mafia, collecting a percentage from the girls, and in return the mafia kept the pimps out of it, so it all looked nice and respectable and everyone could pretend it was pleasure, not business.

Tonight, almost six years after that first encounter, hidden in her apartment – which was bought and paid for, by the way – Zinaida Rapava had nearly $30,000 in cash. And she had plans. She was studying law. She was going to be a lawyer. She was going to give up Robotnik, and Moscow with it, and move to St Petersburg and become a proper legal whore – a lawyer.

She was going to do all this until, on Tuesday morning, Papu Rapava had turned up out of nowhere, wanting to talk, calling her filthy names, bringing with him from the street the familiar, stinking dog's breath stench of *the past*.

SHE listened to the ten o'clock news, then switched on the ignition and drove slowly out of Bolshaya Lubyanka, heading north-west across Moscow to the Stadium of the Young Pioneers, where she parked in her usual spot, just off the darkened track.

The night was cold. The wind whipped the thin dress tight around her legs. She held on to her bag as she stumbled towards the lights. She would be safer inside.

Outside Robotnik there was a good crowd for a Thursday night, a nice line of rich western sheep all waiting to be fleeced. Normally her eyes would have flashed as sharp across them as a pair of shears, but not tonight, and she had to force herself forwards.

She went round to the back entrance, as normal, and the barman, Aleksey, let her in. She checked her jacket into the cloakroom and hesitated over her bag but then gave that to the old woman attendant as well: the floor of the Robotnik was not the wisest place in Moscow to be caught carrying a gun.

She could always pretend to be someone else when she

came to the club, and apart from the money that was the other good thing about it. (*'What's your name?'* they would say, trying to make some human contact. *'What name do you like?'* she would always reply.) She could leave her history at the door of the Robotnik, and hide behind this other Zinaida: sexy, self-possessed, hard. But not tonight. Tonight, as she stood in the ladies' toilet, freshening her make-up, the trick didn't seem to be working, and the face that stared back at her was indisputably her own: raw-eyed, frightened Zinaida Rapava.

SHE sat in one of the shadowy booths for an hour or more, watching. What she needed was someone who would take her for the whole night. Someone decent and respectable, with an apartment of his own. But how could you ever judge what men were really like? It was the young ones with the swaggering walks and the loud mouths who ended up bursting into tears and showing you pictures of their girlfriends. It was the bespectacled bankers and lawyers who liked to knock you around.

Just after half-past eleven, when the place was at its busiest, she made her move.

She circled the dance floor, smoking, holding a bottle of mineral water. Holy Mother, she thought, there were girls in here tonight who barely looked fifteen. She was practically old enough to have given them birth.

She was coming to the end of this life.

A man with dark curly hair poking through the straining buttons of his shirt came over to her but he reminded her of O'Brian and she side-stepped him through a cloud of aftershave, in favour of a big south-east Asian in an Armani suit.

He drained his drink – vodka, neat, no ice, she noticed: noticed it too late – and he got her on the dance floor. He quickly grabbed her backside, a cheek in either hand, and began digging his fingers into her, almost lifting her out of her new shoes. She told him to cut it out but he didn't seem to understand. She tried to press her arms against him, push him back, but he only increased his grip and something gave in her then, or rather joined – a kind of merging of the two Zinaidas –

'Are you a good Bolshevik, Anna Safanova? Will you prove it? Will you dance for Comrade Stalin?'

– and suddenly she raked the fingers of her right hand down his smooth cheek, so deep she was sure she could feel the glossy flesh clogging beneath her nails.

He released her then all right – roared and doubled over, shaking his head, spraying beads of blood around him in a series of perfect arcs, like a wet dog shaking off water. Someone screamed and people rippled away to give him space.

This was what they had come to see!

Zinaida ran – across the bar, up the spiral staircase, past the metal detectors and out into the cold. Her legs splayed like a cow's and gave way on the ice. She was sure he was coming after her. She dragged herself back up on to her feet and somehow made it to her car.

THE Victory of the Revolution apartment complex. Block Nine. In darkness. The cops had gone. The little crowd had gone. And soon the place itself would be gone – it had been jerrybuilt even by Soviet standards; it was going to be pulled down in a month or two.

She parked across the street, in the spot where she had

brought the westerner the night before, and stared at it across the roughened, freezing snow.

Block Nine.

Home.

She was so tired.

She grasped the top of the steering wheel with both hands and laid her forehead on her bare arms. She was done with crying by then. She had a very strong sense of her father's presence, and that stupid song he used to sing.

> *Kolyma, Kolyma,*
> *What a wonderful place!*
> *Twelve months of winter*
> *Summer all the rest . . .*

And wasn't there another verse? Something about twenty-four hours of work each day and sleeping all the rest? And so on and on? She knocked her head against her arms in time to the imagined beat, then rested her cheek against the wheel, and that was the moment that she remembered that she had left her bag with her gun in it back at the club.

She remembered it because a car, a big car, had drawn alongside her, very close, preventing her from pulling out, and a man's face was staring at her – a white blur distorted through two panes of dirty wet glass.

Chapter Eighteen

Silence woke him.

'What time is it?'

'Midnight.' O'Brian yawned noisily. 'Your shift.'

They were parked beside the deserted highway with the engine off. Kelso could see nothing, apart from a few faint stars up ahead. After the noise of the journey the stillness was almost physical, a pressure in the ears.

He pulled himself upright. 'Where are we?'

'About a hundred, maybe a hundred and twenty miles north of Vologda.' O'Brian snapped on the interior light, making Kelso flinch. 'Should be about here, I figure.'

He leaned over with the map, his big fingernail pressed to a spot that looked entirely blank, a white space split by the red line of the highway, with a few symbols for marshland dotted on either side of it. Further north the map turned green for the forest.

'I need a piss,' said O'Brian. 'You coming?'

It was much colder than in Moscow, the sky even bigger. A great fleet of vast clouds, pale-edged by the moonlight, moved slowly southwards, occasionally unveiling patches of stars. O'Brian had a torch. They scrambled down a short bank and stood urinating, companionably, side by side, for half a minute, steam rising from the ground before them, then O'Brian zipped up his flies and shone his torch around. The powerful beam stretched for a couple of hundred yards into the darkness, then dissipated; it lit nothing. A freezing mist hung low to the ground.

'Can you hear anything?' said O'Brian. His breath

flickered in the cold.

'No.'

'Neither can I.'

He switched off the torch and they stood there for a while.

'Oh, daddy,' whispered O'Brian, in a little boy's voice, 'I'm so *scared.*'

He turned the light back on and they climbed the bank to the Toyota. Kelso poured them both more coffee while O'Brian lifted up the rear door and dragged out a couple of the jerrycans. He found a funnel and began filling the tank.

Kelso, nursing his coffee, moved away from the gasoline fumes and lit a cigarette. In the darkness, in the cold, under the immense Eurasian sky, he felt disconnected from reality, frightened yet strangely exhilarated, his senses sharpened. He heard a rumble far away and a yellow dot appeared far back on the straight highway. He watched it grow slowly, saw the gleam divide and become two big headlights, and for a moment he thought they were coming directly at him, and then a big truck, a sixteen-wheeler, rushed past, the driver merrily sounding his horn. The noise of the engine was still faintly audible in the distance long after the red tail lights had vanished in the dark.

'Hey, Fluke! Give us a hand here, will you?'

Kelso took a last draw on his cigarette and flicked it away, spinning orange sparks across the road.

O'Brian wanted help lifting down one of his precious pieces of equipment, a white polycarbonate case, about two feet long and eighteen inches wide, with a small pair of black wheels mounted on one end. Once they'd pulled it out of the Toyota, O'Brian trundled it round to the front passenger door.

'Now what?' said Kelso.

'Don't tell me you've never seen one of these before?'

O'Brian opened the lid of the box and removed what looked like four white plastic trays, of the kind that fold out of aircraft seats. He slotted these together, creating a flat square about a yard across, which he then attached to the side of the case. Into the centre of the square he screwed a long, telescopic prong. He ran a cable from the side of the box to the Toyota's cigarette lighter, came back, flicked a switch and a variety of small lights blinked on.

'Impressed?' He produced a compass from his jacket pocket and shone his torch on it. 'Now where the hell is the Indian Ocean?'

'What?'

O'Brian glanced back along the M8. 'Right the way down there, by the look of it. Directly down there. A satellite in stationary orbit twenty thousand miles above the Indian Ocean. Think of that. Oh, but the world's a small place, is it not, Fluke? I swear I can almost hold it in my hand.' He grinned and knelt by the box, moving it around by degrees until the antenna was pointing directly south. At once the machine began to emit a whine. 'There you go. She's locked on to the bird.' He pressed a switch and the whining stopped. 'Now, we plug in the handset – so. We dial zero-four for the ground station at Eik in Norway – so. And now we dial the number. Easy as that.'

He stood and held out the handset and Kelso cautiously put his ear to it. He could hear a number ringing in America, and then a man said, 'Newsroom.'

KELSO lit another cigarette and walked away from the Toyota. O'Brian was in the front seat with the light on and even with the windows closed his voice carried in the cold silence.

'Yeah, yeah, we're on the road . . . About halfway I guess . . . Yeah, he's with me . . . No, he's fine.' The door opened and O'Brian shouted, 'You're fine, aren't you, professor?'

Kelso raised his hand.

'Yeah,' resumed O'Brian, 'he's fine.' The door slammed and he must have lowered his voice because Kelso couldn't catch much after that. 'Be there about nine . . . sure . . . good stuff . . . looking good . . .'

Whatever it was, Kelso didn't like the sound of it. He walked back to the car and flung open the door.

'Whoops. Gotta go, Joe. Bye.' O'Brian hung up quickly and winked.

'What are you telling them exactly?'

'Nothing.' The reporter looked like a guilty boy.

'What d'you mean, nothing?'

'Come on, I had to give them the bones, Fluke. Give them the gist –'

'The *gist?*' Kelso was shouting now. 'This was supposed to be confidential –'

'Well, they're not going to tell anyone, are they? Come on, I can't just take off without giving them an idea of what I'm doing.'

'Christ.' Kelso slumped against the side of the Toyota and appealed to the sky. 'What am I *doing?*'

'Want to make a call, Fluke?' O'Brian waved the handset at him. 'Call a wife? On us?'

'No. There's no one I want to call right now. Thank you.'

'Zinaida?' said O'Brian craftily. 'Why don't you call Zinaida?' He climbed out of the seat and pressed the telephone into Kelso's hand. 'Go ahead. I can tell you're worried. It's *sweet.* Zero-four, then the number. Only don't take all night about it. A fellow could freeze his balls off out here.'

He wandered away, flapping his arms against the cold, and Kelso, after a second's hesitation, hunted through his pockets for the scrap of paper with her address on it.

As he waited for the number to connect he tried to visualise her apartment, but he couldn't do it, he didn't know enough about her. He stared southwards down the M8 at the shadowy mass of departing clouds, fleeing as if from some calamity, and he imagined the route his call was taking – from the middle of nowhere to a satellite above the Indian Ocean, down to Scandinavia, across the earth to Moscow. O'Brian was right: you could stand in a great wilderness and the world still felt small enough to hold in your hand.

He let the number ring for a long time, alternately willing her to answer it so that he'd know she was safe, and hoping that she wouldn't, because her apartment was the least safe place of all.

She didn't answer and after a couple of minutes he hung up.

AND then it was Kelso's turn to drive while O'Brian slept, and even then the reporter couldn't be quiet. The sleeping bag was drawn tight up to his chin. His seat was tilted back almost to the horizontal. 'Yeah,' he'd mutter, and then, almost immediately, and with greater emphasis, '*yeah.*' He grunted. He curled up and flopped around like a landed fish. He snorted. He scratched his groin.

Kelso gripped the steering wheel hard. 'Can you shut up, O'Brian?' he said into the windscreen. 'I mean, just for once, could you possibly, as a favour to humanity, and more particularly to me, put a sock in your great fat mouth?'

There was nothing to see except the shifting patch of road in the headlights. Occasionally a car appeared in the opposite carriageway, lights full beam, blinding him. After about an hour he overtook the big truck that had passed them earlier. The driver hooted cheerfully again, and Kelso hooted back.

'Yeah,' said O'Brian, turning over at the sound of the horn, 'oh *yeah* –'

The drumming of the tyres was hypnotic and Kelso's thoughts were random, disconnected. He wondered what O'Brian would have been like in a *real* war, one in which he actually had to fight rather than just take pictures. Then he wondered what *he* would have been like. Most of the men he knew asked themselves that question, as if never having fought somehow made them incomplete – left a hole in their lives where a war should have been.

Was it possible that this *absence* of war – marvellous though it was and so forth: that went without saying – was it possible that it had actually *trivialised* people? Because everything was so bloody trivial now, wasn't it? This was The Trivial Age. Politics was trivial. What people worried about was trivial – mortgages and pensions and the dangers of passive smoking. Jesus! – he shot a look at O'Brian – is this what we've been reduced to, worrying about passive smoking, when our parents and our grandparents had to worry about being shot or bombed?

And then he began to feel guilty, because what was he implying here? That he wanted a war? Or a cold war, come to that? But it was true, he thought: he *did* miss the cold war. He was glad it was over, of course, in a way – glad the right side had won and all that – but at least while it was on people like him had known where they stood, could point to something and say: well, we may not know what we do believe in, but we don't believe in *that*.

The fact was, almost nothing had gone right for him since

the cold war ended. Here was a good joke. He and Mamantov: twin career victims of the end of the USSR! Both bemoaning the trivia of the modern world, both preoccupied with the past, and both in search of the mystery of Comrade Stalin –

He frowned, remembering something Mamantov had said.

'I'll tell you this, you're as obsessed as I am.'

He had laughed it off at the time. But now that he thought of it again, the line struck him as unexpectedly shrewd – unsettling, even, in the quality of its insight – and he found himself returning to it again and again as the temperature dropped and the road uncoiled endlessly from the freezing darkness.

HE drove for more than four hours, until his legs were numb and at one point he actually fell asleep, jerking awake to find the Toyota veering across the centre of the highway, the white lines flashing up at them like spears in the headlights.

A few minutes later they passed a kind of truckers' lay-by. He braked hard, stopped, and reversed back into it. Beside him, O'Brian struggled blearily into consciousness.

'Why're we stopping?'

'The tank's empty. And I've got to rest.' Kelso turned off the ignition and massaged the back of his neck. 'Why don't we stop here for a bit?'

'No. We need to keep moving. Fix us some coffee, will you? I'll fill her up.'

They went through the same ritual as before, O'Brian stumbling out into the cold and hoisting a pair of jerrycans from the back of the Toyota, while Kelso wandered away for a cigarette. The wind had a sharper edge to it this far north.

He could hear it slicing through trees he couldn't see. Running water splashed somewhere, softly.

When he got back into the car, O'Brian was in the driver's seat with the interior light on, running an electric shaver over his big chin, studying the map. It was an unnatural time to be awake, thought Kelso. It meant nothing good. He associated it with emergency, bereavement, conspiracy, flight; the sad skulk away at the end of a one-night affair.

Neither man spoke. O'Brian put away his shaver and stuffed the map into the pocket beside him.

The reclined seat was warm and so was the sleeping bag and within five minutes, despite his anxieties, Kelso was asleep – a dreamless, falling sleep – and when he awoke a few hours later it was as if they had crossed a barrier and entered another world.

Chapter Nineteen

A LITTLE TIME before this, when Kelso was still at the wheel, Major Feliks Suvorin had bent to kiss his wife, Serafima.

She offered him merely her cheek at first but then seemed to think the better of it. A warm, soft arm snaked up from beneath the duvet, a hand cupped the back of his head and drew him down. He kissed her mouth. She was wearing Chanel. Her father had brought it back from the last G8 meeting.

She whispered, 'You won't be back tonight.'

'I will.'

'You won't.'

'I'll try not to wake you.'

'Wake me.'

'Sleep.'

He put his finger to her lips and turned off the bedside lamp. The light from the passage showed him the way out of the bedroom. He could hear the sound of the boys' breathing. An ormolu clock announced it was one-thirty-five. He had been home two hours. *Hell.* He sat down on a gilt chair beside the door and put his shoes on, then collected his coat from its carved wooden hanger. The decor was copied from some glossy western magazine and it all cost far more than he earned as a major in the SVR; in fact, on his salary, they could barely afford the magazine. His father-in-law had paid.

On his way out, Suvorin glimpsed himself in the hall mirror, framed against a Jackson Pollock print. The lines and shadows of his exhausted face seemed to merge with those of the picture. He was getting too old for this kind of game, he thought: the golden boy no longer.

THE news that the Delta flight had taken off without Fluke Kelso had reached Yasenevo shortly after two in the afternoon. Colonel Arsenyev had expressed in various colourful colloquialisms – and had no doubt minuted elsewhere, for the record, more discreetly – his amazement that Suvorin had not arranged for the historian to be escorted on to the aircraft. Suvorin had choked back his response, which would have been to inquire, acidly, how he was supposed to locate Mamantov, control the militia, find the notebook *and* nursemaid an independent-minded western academic through Sheremetevo-2, all with the assistance of four men.

Besides, by then this was of less pressing importance than the discovery that the Interfax news agency was putting out a story on Papu Rapava's death, quoting unnamed 'militia sources' to the effect that the old man had been murdered while trying to sell some secret papers of Josef Stalin to a western author. Three outraged communist deputies had already attempted to raise the matter in the Duma. The Office of the President of the Federation had been on the line to Arsenyev, demanding to know (a direct quote from Boris Nikolaevich, apparently) *what the fuck was going on?* Ditto the FSB. Half a dozen reporters were camped outside Rapava's apartment block, more were besieging militia HQ, while the militia's official position was to hold up their hands and whistle.

For the first time, Suvorin had begun to see the merit of the old ways, when news was what Tass was pleased to announce and everything else was a state secret.

He had made one last attempt to play devil's advocate.

Weren't they in danger of getting this out of proportion? Weren't they playing Mamantov's game? What could Stalin's notebook possibly contain that would have any modern relevance?

Arsenyev had smiled: always a dangerous sign.

'When were you born, Feliks?' he had asked, pleasantly. 'Fifty-eight? Fifty-nine?'

'Sixty.'

'Sixty. You see, I was born in thirty-seven. My grandfather . . . he was shot. Two uncles went to the camps . . . never came back. My father died in some crazy business at the start of the war, trying to stop a German tank outside Poltava with a bit of rag and a bottle, and all because Comrade Stalin said that any soldier who surrendered would be considered a traitor. So I don't underestimate Comrade Stalin.'

'I'm sorry –'

But Arsenyev had waved him away. His voice was rising, his face red. 'If that bastard kept a notebook in his safe, he kept it for a reason, I can tell you that. And if Beria stole it, he had a reason. And if Mamantov is willing to risk torturing an old man to death, then he has a damned good reason for wanting to get his hands on it, too. So find it, Feliks Stepanovich, please, if you would be so good. *Find it.*'

And Suvorin had done his best. Every forensic document examiner in Moscow had been contacted. Kelso's description had been circulated, discreetly, to all the capital's militia posts, as well as to the traffic cops, the GAI. Technically, the SVR was now 'liaising' with the militia's murder inquiry, which meant at least he now had some resources to draw on: he had worked out a common line with the militia which they could spin to the media. He had spoken to a friend of his father-in-law's – the owner of the biggest chain of newspapers in the Federation – to plead for a little restraint. He had sent Netto to poke around Vspolnyi Street. He had arranged for a watch to be put on the apartment of Rapava's daughter, Zinaida, who had disappeared, and when she still hadn't turned up by nightfall he had sent Bunin to hang around the club she worked in, Robotnik.

Shortly after eleven o'clock, Suvorin had gone home.

And at one twenty-five he got the call that told him she had been found.

'WHERE was she?'

'Sitting in her car,' said Bunin. 'Outside her father's place. We followed her from the club. Waited to see if she was meeting anyone, but nobody else showed, so we picked her up. She's been in a fight, I reckon.'

'Why?'

'Well, you'll see when you go up. Take a look at her hand.'

They were standing, talking quietly, in the downstairs lobby of her apartment block, in the Zayauze district, a drab hinterland of eastern Moscow. She had a place close to the park – privatised, to judge by the neatness of its common parts; respectable. Suvorin wondered what the neighbours would think if they knew the girl on the third floor was a tart.

'Anything else?'

'The apartment's clean, and so's her car,' said Bunin. 'There's a bag of clothes in the back – jeans, T-shirt, pair of boots, knickers. But she's got a lot of money stashed up there. She doesn't know I found it yet.'

'How much?'

'Twenty, maybe thirty thousand dollars. Bound up tight in polythene and hidden in the lavatory cistern.'

'Where is it now?'

'I've got it.'

'Let's have it.'

Bunin hesitated, then handed it over: a thick bundle, all hundreds. He looked at it hungrily. It would take him four or five years to make that much and Suvorin guessed he had probably been on the point of helping himself to a percentage. Maybe he already had. He stuffed it into his pocket. 'What's she like?'

'A hard bitch, major. You won't get a lot out of her.' He tapped the side of his head. 'She's cracked, I reckon.'

'Thank you, lieutenant, for that valuable psychological insight. You can wait down here.'

Suvorin climbed the stairs. On the landing of the second floor, a middle-aged woman with her hair in curlers stuck her head round her door.

'What's going on?'

'Nothing, madam. Routine inquiries. You're perfectly safe.'

He carried on climbing. He had to make something of this, he thought. He must. It was the only lead he had. Outside the girl's apartment he squared his shoulders, knocked politely on the open door and went inside. A militia man got to his feet.

'Thank you,' said Suvorin. 'Why don't you go down and keep the lieutenant company?'

He waited until the door had closed before he took a proper look at her. She had a grey woollen cardigan on over her dress and she was sitting in the only chair, her legs crossed, smoking. In a dish on the little table next to her were the stubbed remains of five cigarettes. The apartment consisted of only this one room but it was neat and nicely done, with plenty of evidence of money spent: a western-made television with a satellite decoder, a video, a CD-player, a rack of dresses, all black. A little kitchen was off in one corner. A door led to the bathroom. There was a couch that presumably folded into a bed. Bunin was right about her hand, he noticed. The fingers that held the cigarette had blood crusted under the nails. She saw him looking.

'I fell,' she said, and uncrossed her legs, displaying a scraped knee, torn tights. 'All right?'

'I'll sit down.' She didn't reply, so he sat down anyway, on the edge of the couch, moving a couple of toys out of the way, a soldier and a ballerina. 'You have children?' he asked.

No answer.

'I have children. Two boys.' He searched the room for some other point of contact, some way of opening, but there was no evidence of any personality anywhere: no photographs, no books apart from legal manuals, no ornaments or knick-knacks. There was a row of CDs, all western and all by artists he'd never heard of. It reminded him of one Yasenevo's safe houses – a place to spend a night in and then move on.

She said, 'Are you a cop? You don't look like a cop.'

'No.'

'What are you, then?'

'I'm sorry about your father, Zinaida.'

'Thanks.'

'Tell me about your father.'

'What's to tell?'

'Did you get on with him?'

She looked away.

'Only I'm wondering, you see, why you didn't come forward when his body was discovered. You went to his apartment last night, didn't you, when the militia were there? And then you just drove away.'

'I was upset.'

'Naturally.' Suvorin smiled at her. 'Where's Fluke Kelso?'

'Who?'

Not bad, he thought: she didn't even flicker. But then she didn't know he had Kelso's statement.

'The man you drove to your father's apartment last night.'

'Kelso? Was that his name?'

'Oh you're a sharp one, Zinaida, aren't you? Sharp as a knife. So where have you been all day?'

'Driving around. Thinking.'

'Thinking about Stalin's notebook?'

'I don't know what you –'

'You've been with Kelso, haven't you?'

'No.'

'Where's Kelso? Where's the notebook?'

'Don't know what you're talking about. What d'you mean, anyway – you're not a cop? You got some papers that tell me who you are?'

'You spent the day with Kelso –'

'You've no right to be in my place without the proper papers. It says so in there.' She pointed to her legal books.

'Studying the law, Zinaida?' She was beginning to irritate him. 'You'll make a good lawyer.'

She seemed to find that funny: perhaps she had heard it before? He pulled out the bundle of dollars and that stopped her laughing. He thought she was going to faint.

'So what's the Federation statute on prostitution, Zinaida Rapava?' Her eyes on the money were like a mother's on her baby. 'You're the lawyer: you tell me. How many men in this little pile? A hundred? A hundred and fifty?' He flicked through the notes. 'Must be a hundred and fifty, surely – you're not getting any younger. But the others are, aren't they? They're getting younger every day. You know, I think you might never make this much back.'

'Bastard –'

He weighed the dollars from hand to hand. 'Think about it. A hundred and fifty men in return for telling me where I can find one? A hundred and fifty for one. That's not such a bad deal.'

'Bastard,' she said again, but with less conviction this time.

He leaned forward, soft-voiced, coaxing. 'Come on Zinaida: where's Fluke Kelso? It's important.'

And for a moment he thought she was going to tell him. But then her face hardened. '*You*,' she said. 'I don't care who *you* are. There's more honesty in whoring.'

'Now that may be true,' conceded Suvorin. Suddenly, he threw her the money. It bounced off her lap and on to the floor between her legs. She didn't even bend to pick it up, just looked at him. And he felt a great sadness then: sad for himself, that it should have come to this, sitting on a tart's bed in the Zayauze district, trying to bribe her with her own money. And sad for her, because Bunin was right, she *was* cracked, and now he would have to break her.

Chapter Twenty

IT NEVER SEEMED to get properly light, even two hours after dawn. It was as if the day had given up on itself before it even started. The sky stayed grey and the long concrete ribbon of road that ran straight ahead of them dwindled into a damp murk. On either side of the highway lay a wrinkled dead land of rust-coloured swamps and sickly, yellowish plains – the sub-Arctic tundra – that turned in the middle distance to dense, dark green forests of pine and fir.

It started to snow.

There was a lot of military traffic on the road. They passed a long column of armoured cars with watery headlights and soon afterwards began to see evidence of human settlement – shacks, barns, bits of agricultural machinery – even a collective farm with a broken hammer and sickle over the gate, and an old slogan: PRODUCTION IS VITAL FOR THE VICTORY OF SOCIALISM.

After a couple of miles the road crossed a railway line and a row of big chimneys appeared up ahead in the murk, gushing black soot into the snowy sky.

'That must be it,' said Kelso, looking up from the map. 'The M8 ends here, in the southern outskirts.'

'Shit,' said O'Brian.

'What?'

The reporter gestured with his chin. 'Road block.'

A hundred yards ahead a couple of GAI cops with lighted sticks and guns were waving down every vehicle to check the occupants' papers. O'Brian looked quickly in his mirror, but he couldn't reverse – there was too much traffic slowing behind them. And concrete sleepers laid across the centre of the road made it impossible to perform a U-turn and join the southbound carriageway. They were being forced into a single-lane queue.

'What did you call it?' said Kelso. 'My visa? A *detail?*'

O'Brian tapped his fingers on the top of the steering wheel.

'Is this check permanent, do you think, or just for us?'

Kelso could see a glass booth with a GAI man in it, reading a newspaper.

'I'd say permanent.'

'Well, that's something.' O'Brian began rummaging in the glove compartment. 'Pull your hood up,' he said, 'and get that sleeping bag up over your face. Pretend to be asleep. I'll tell 'em you're my cameraman.' He hauled out a crumpled set of papers. 'You're Vukov, okay? Foma Vukov.'

'Foma Vukov? What kind of a name is that?'

'You want to go straight back to Moscow? Well, do you? I'd say you've got two seconds to make up your mind.'

'And how old is this Foma Vukov?'

'Twentysomething.' O'Brian reached behind him and grabbed the leather satchel. 'You got a better idea? Stick this under your seat.'

Kelso hesitated, then wedged the satchel behind his legs. He lay back, drew up the sleeping bag and closed his eyes. Travelling without a visa was one crime. Travelling without a visa and using someone else's papers – that, he suspected, was quite another.

The car edged forwards, braked. He heard the engine switch off and then the hum of the driver's window being lowered. A blast of cold air. A gruff male voice said in Russian, 'Get out of the car please.'

The Toyota rocked as O'Brian clambered out.

With his heel, Kelso gently pushed at the satchel, jamming it further out of sight.

There was a second rush of cold as the rear door was lifted.

The sound of boxes being swung out, of catches snapping. Footsteps. A quiet conversation.

The door next to Kelso opened. He could hear the pattering of snowflakes, a man breathing. And then the door was closed – closed softly, with consideration, so as not to wake a sleeping passenger, and Kelso knew that he was safe.

He heard O'Brian load up the back and come round to the driver's seat. The engine started.

'It is surely most amazing,' said O'Brian, 'the effect of a hundred bucks on a cop who ain't been paid for six months.' He pulled the sleeping bag away from Kelso. 'This is your wake-up call, professor. Welcome to Archangel.'

THEY thumped across an iron bridge above the Northern Dvina. The river was wide, stained yellow by the tundra. Swollen currents rolled and flexed like muscles beneath its dirty skin. A couple of big black cargo barges, chained together, steamed north towards the White Sea. On the opposite bank, through the filter of snow and the spars of the bridge, they could see factory chimneys, cranes, apartment blocks, a big television tower with a winking red light.

As the vista broadened, even O'Brian's spirits seemed to fall. He called it a dump. He declared it a hole. He said it was the worst goddamn place he had ever seen.

A goods train clanked along the railroad track beside them. At the end of the bridge they turned left, towards what seemed to be the main part of the city. Everything had decayed. The façades of the buildings were pitted and peeling. Parts of the road had subsided. An ancient tram, in a brown and mustard livery, went rattling by, making a sound like a chain being dragged over cobbles. Pedestrians tilted drunkenly into the snow.

O'Brian drove slowly, shaking his head, and Kelso wondered what more he had been expecting. A press centre? A media hotel? They came out into the wide open space of a bus station. On the far side of it, on the waterfront, four giant Red Army men, cast in bronze, stood back to back, facing the four points of the compass, their rifles raised in triumph. At their feet, a pack of wild dogs scavenged among the trash. Nearby was a long, low building of white concrete and plate glass with a big sign: 'Harbour Master of Archangel'. If the city had a centre, this was probably it.

'Let's pull up over there,' suggested Kelso.

They cruised around the edge of the square and parked with their front bumper up close to the bent railings, looking directly out across the water. A husky watched them with detached interest, then brought its hind paw up to its neck and vigorously scratched its fleas. In the distance, through the snow, it was just possible to make out the flat shape of a tanker.

'You do realise,' said Kelso quietly, staring straight ahead across the water, 'that we are at the edge of the world? That at this point we are one hundred miles south of the Arctic Circle and there is nothing between us and the North Pole but sea and ice? You are aware of that?'

He started to laugh.

'What's funny?'

'Nothing.' He glanced at O'Brian and tried to stop himself, but it was no good, there was something about the reporter's utter dejection that set him off again. His vision was blurred by tears. 'I'm sorry,' he gasped. 'Sorry –'

'Oh, go ahead, enjoy yourself,' said O'Brian, bitterly. 'This is my idea of a perfect fucking Friday. Drive eight hundred miles to some dump that looks like Pittsburgh after a nuclear strike to try to find Stalin's fucking *girlfriend* –'

He snorted and started to laugh as well.

'You know what we haven't done?' O'Brian managed to say after a while.

Kelso took a breath and swallowed. 'What?'

'We haven't been to the railway station and checked the radiation meter . . . We're probably . . . being . . . fucking . . . *irradiated!*'

They roared. They cried. The Toyota rocked with it. The snow fell and the husky watched them, its head cocked in surprise.

O'BRIAN locked the car and they hurried through the snow, across the treacherous expanse of subsiding concrete, into the port authority building.

Kelso carried the satchel.

They were both still slightly shaky and the advertised ferry sailings – to Murmansk and the Groaning Islands – briefly set them off again.

The Groaning Islands?

'Oh come on, man. Stop it. We've got to do some work here.'

The building was bigger than it looked from the outside. On the ground floor there were shops – little kiosks selling clothes and toiletries – plus a café and a ticket booth. Downstairs, beneath banks of fluorescent lights, most of which had blown, was a gloomy underground market – stalls offering seeds, books, pirated cassettes, shoes, shampoo, sausages and some immense, sturdy Russian brassières in black and beige: miracles of cantilevered engineering.

O'Brian bought a couple of maps, one of the city and the other of the region, then they both went back upstairs to the ticket office where Kelso, in return for offering a dollar bill to a suspicious man in a greasy uniform, was permitted a brief look at the Archangel telephone directory. The book was small, red-bound, with hard covers and it took him less than thirty seconds to establish that no Safanov or Safanova was listed.

'Now what?' said O'Brian.

'Food,' said Kelso.

The café was an old-style *stolovaya*, a self-service workers' canteen, its floor wet and filthy with melted snow. There was a warm fug of strong tobacco. At the next door table a couple of German seamen were playing cards. Kelso had a big bowl of *shchi* – cabbage soup with a dollop of sour cream bobbing in its centre – black bread, a couple of hard-boiled eggs, and the effect of all this on his empty stomach was immediate. He began to feel almost euphoric. This was going to be all right, he thought. They were safe up here. Nobody could find them. And if they played it properly, they could be in and out in a day.

He tipped half a miniature of cognac into his instant coffee, looked at it, thought, *Sod it, why not?* and added the rest. He lit a cigarette and glanced around. The people up here appeared shabbier than they did in Moscow. They stared at foreign strangers. But when you attempted to meet their eyes they looked away.

O'Brian pushed his plate to one side. 'I've been thinking about this college, whatever it was – this "Maxim Gorky Academy". They'll have old records, right? And there was this girl she knew – what was her name, the ugly kid?'

'Maria.'

'Maria. Right. Let's find her class yearbook and find Maria.'

Class yearbook? thought Kelso. Who did O'Brian think she was? The Maxim Gorky prom queen, 1950? But he was too full of goodwill to pick a fight. 'Or,' he said, diplomatically, '*or* we could try the local Party. She was in Komsomol, remember. They might still have the old files.'

'Okay. You're the expert. How d'we find 'em?'

'Easy. Give me the town plan.'

O'Brian pulled the map from his inside pocket and scraped his chair round until he was sitting next to Kelso. They spread out the city plan.

The bulk of Archangel was crammed into a wide headland, about four miles across, with ribbons of development running out along either bank of the Dvina.

Kelso put his finger on the map. 'There,' he said. 'That's where they are. Or were. On the ploshchad Lenina, in the biggest building on the square. That's where the bastards always were.'

'And you think they'll help?'

'No. Not willingly. But if you can provide a little financial lubrication . . . It's worth a try, anyway.'

On the map it looked like a five-minute walk.

'You're really getting into this, aren't you?' said O'Brian. He gave Kelso's arm an affectionate pat. 'We make a good team, you know that? We'll show 'em.' He folded away the map and put five roubles under his plate as a tip.

Kelso finished his coffee. The cognac gave him a warm glow. O'Brian really wasn't such a bad fellow, he thought. Sooner him than Adelman and the rest of those waxworks, no doubt safely stowed in New York by now.

History wasn't made without taking risks, that much he knew. So maybe sometimes you had to take risks to write it, too?

O'Brian was right.

He would show them.

Chapter Twenty-one

THEY WENT BACK out into the snow, past the Toyota and past the shuttered front of a decaying hospital: the Northern Basin Seamen's Policlinic. The wind was driving the snow inshore across the water, whining through the steel rigging of the boats on the wooden jetty, bending the stumpy trees that had been planted along the promenade to protect the buildings. The two men had to struggle to keep their feet.

A couple of the boats had sunk, and so had the wooden hut at the end of the jetty. Benches had been heaved by vandals over the railings into the river. There was graffiti on the walls: a Star of David, dripping blood, with a swastika daubed across it; SS flashes; KKK.

One thing was sure: there wouldn't be any Italian shoe boutiques up here.

They turned inland.

Every Russian town still had its statue of Lenin. Archangel's portrayed the Leader, fifteen yards high, rising out of a block of granite, his face determined, his overcoat flapping, a roll of papers in his outstretched hand. He looked as if he were trying to hail a taxi. The square that still carried his name was huge, and smooth with snow, and deserted; in one corner, a couple of tethered goats nibbled at a bush. Fronting it were a big museum, the city's central post office, and a huge office block with the hammer and sickle still attached to the balcony.

Kelso led the way towards it and they had almost made it when a sandy-coloured jeep with a searchlight mounted on its hood came round the corner: Interior Ministry troops, the

MVD. That sobered him up. He could be stopped at any minute, he realised, and forced to show his visa. The pale faces of the soldiers stared at them. He bowed his head and trotted up the steps, O'Brian close behind him, as the jeep completed its cautious circuit of the square and passed out of sight.

THE communists had not been forced entirely from the building; they had merely moved round to the back. Here they maintained a small reception area presided over by a big, middle-aged woman with a froth of dyed yellow hair. Beside her, along the window sill, was a row of straggling spider plants in old tin cans; opposite her, a big colour poster of Gennady Zyuganov, the Party's pudding-faced candidate in the last presidential election.

She studied O'Brian's business card intently, turning it over, holding it to the light, as if she suspected forgery. Then she picked up the telephone and spoke quietly into the receiver.

Outside, through the double glass, the snow was beginning to pile in the courtyard. A clock ticked. Beside the door Kelso noticed a bundle of the latest issue of *Aurora*, tied up with string, awaiting distribution. The headline was a quote from the Interior Ministry's report to the president: 'VIOLENCE IS INEVITABLE'.

After a couple of minutes, a man appeared. He must have been about sixty – an odd-looking figure. His head was too small for his heavy torso, his features too small for his face. His name was Tsarev, he said, holding out a hand stained black with ink. *Professor* Tsarev. Deputy First Secretary of the Regional Committee.

Kelso asked if they could have a word.

Yes. Perhaps. That would be possible.

Now? In private?

Tsarev hesitated, then shrugged. 'Very well.'

He led them down a dark corridor and into his office, a little time warp from the Soviet days, with its pictures of Brezhnev and Andropov. Kelso reckoned he must have visited a score of offices like this over the years. Wood block flooring, thick water pipes, a heavy radiator, a desk calendar, a big green Bakelite telephone, like something out of a 1950s science fiction movie, the smell of polish and stale air – every detail was familiar, right down to the model Sputnik and the clock in the shape of Zimbabwe left behind by some visiting Marxist delegation. On the shelf behind Tsarev's head were six copies of Mamantov's memoirs, *I Still Believe*.

'I see you have Vladimir Mamantov's book.' It was a stupid thing to say but Kelso couldn't help himself.

Tsarev turned round, as if noticing them for the first time. 'Yes. Comrade Mamantov came to Archangel and campaigned for us, during the presidential elections. Why? Do you know him?'

'Yes. I know him.'

There was a silence. Kelso was aware of O'Brian looking at him, and of Tsarev waiting for him to speak. Hesitantly, he began his rehearsed speech. First of all, he said, he and Mr O'Brian would like to thank Professor Tsarev for seeing them at such short notice. They were in Archangel for one day only, making a film about the residual strength of the Communist Party. They were visiting various towns in Russia. He was sorry they had not been in contact earlier to make a proper appointment, but they were working quickly –

'And Comrade Mamantov sent you?' interrupted Tsarev.

'Comrade Mamantov sent you *here*?'

'I can truthfully say we would not be here without Vladimir Mamantov.'

Tsarev began nodding. Well, this was a most excellent subject. This was a subject *wilfully ignored* in the west. How many people in the west knew, for example, that in the Duma elections, the communists had taken thirty per cent of the votes, and then, in 1996, in the presidential elections, forty per cent? Yes, they would be in power again soon. Sharing power to begin with, perhaps, but afterwards – who could say?

He became more animated.

Take the situation here in Archangel. They had millionaires, of course. Wonderful! Unfortunately, they also had organised crime, unemployment, AIDS, prostitution, drug addiction. Were his visitors aware that life expectancy and child-mortality in Russia had now reached African levels? Such progress! Such freedoms! Tsarev had been a professor of Marxist theory in Archangel for twenty years – the post was now abolished, naturally – so he had taught Marxism in a Marxist state, but it was only now, as they were literally tearing down Marx's statues, that he had come to appreciate the genius of the man's insight: that money robs the whole world, both the human world and nature, of their own proper value –

'Ask him about the girl,' whispered O'Brian. 'We haven't got time for all this bullshit. Ask him about Anna.'

Tsarev had halted in mid-speech and was looking from one man to the other.

'Professor Tsarev,' said Kelso, 'to illustrate our film we need to look at particular human stories –'

That was good. Yes. He understood. The human element.

There were many such stories in Archangel.

'Yes, I'm sure. But we have in mind one in particular. A girl. Now a woman in her sixties. She would be about the same age as you. Her unmarried name was Safanova. Anna Mikhailovna Safanova. She was in the Komsomol.'

Tsarev stroked the end of his squat nose. The name, he said, after a moment's thought, was not familiar. This would have been some time ago, presumably?

'Almost fifty years.'

Fifty years? It was not possible! Please! He would find them other persons –

'But you must have records?'

– he would show them females who fought the fascists in the Great Patriotic War, Heroes of Socialist Labour, Holders of the Order of the Red Banner. Magnificent people –

'Ask him how much he wants,' said O'Brian, not even bothering to whisper now. He was pulling out his wallet. 'To look in his files. What's his price?'

'Your colleague,' said Tsarev, 'is not happy?'

'My colleague was wondering,' said Kelso, delicately, 'if it would be possible for you to undertake some research work for us. For which we would be happy to pay you – to pay the Party, that is – a fee . . .'

IT would not be easy, said Tsarev.

Kelso said he was sure it would not be.

The membership of the Communist Party in the last years of the Soviet Union comprised seven per cent of the adult population. Apply those figures to Archangel and what did you get? Maybe 20,000 members in the city alone, and perhaps the same number again in the oblast. And to those figures you had to add the membership of Komsomol and of all the other Party outfits. And then, if you included all the people who had been members over the past eighty years – the people who had died or dropped out, been shot, imprisoned, exiled, purged – you had to be looking at a really large number. A huge number. Still –

Two hundred dollars was the sum they agreed on. Tsarev insisted on providing a receipt. He locked the money into a battered cash box which he then locked in a drawer, and Kelso realised, with a curious sense of admiration, that Tsarev probably did intend to give the money to Party funds. He wouldn't keep it for himself: he was a true believer.

The Russian conducted them back along the passage and into reception. The woman with the dyed blonde hair was watering her tinned plants. *Aurora* still proclaimed that violence was inevitable. Zyuganov's fat smile remained in place. Tsarev collected a key from a metal cupboard and they followed him down two flights of stairs into the basement. A big, blast-proof iron door, studded with bolts, thickly painted a battleship grey, swung open to show a cellar, lined with wooden shelving, piled with files.

Tsarev put on a pair of heavy-framed spectacles and began pulling down dusty folders of documents while Kelso looked around with wonder. This was not a storeroom, he thought. This was a catacomb, a necropolis. Busts of Lenin, and of Marx and Engels, crowded the shelves like perfect clones. There were boxes of photographs of forgotten Party apparatchiks and stacked canvases of socialist realism, depicting bosomy peasant girls and worker-heroes with granite muscles. There were sacks of decorations, diplomas, membership cards, leaflets, pamphlets, books. And then there were the flags – little red flags for children to wave, and swirling crimson banners for the likes of Anna Safanova to parade with.

It was as if a great world religion had been suddenly obliged to strip its temples and hide everything underground – to preserve its texts and icons out of sight, in the hope of better times, the Second Coming –

The Komsomol lists for 1950 and 1951 were missing.

'What?'

Kelso wheeled round to find Tsarev frowning over a pair of folders, one in either hand.

It was most curious, Tsarev was saying. This would need to be investigated further. They could see for themselves – he held out the files for their inspection – the lists were here for 1949 and here, also, for 1952. But in neither of those years was there an Anna Safanova listed.

'She was too young in forty-nine,' said Kelso, 'she wouldn't have qualified.' And by 1952 God alone knew what might have happened to her. 'When were they removed?'

'April, fifty-two,' said Tsarev, frowning. 'There's a note. "To be transferred to the archives of the Central Committee, Moscow."'

'Is there a signature?'

Tsarev showed it him: '"A. N. Poskrebyshev."'

O'Brian said, 'Who's Poskrebyshev?'

Kelso knew. And so, he could see, did Tsarev.

'General Poskrebyshev,' said Kelso, 'was Stalin's private secretary.'

'So,' said Tsarev, a little too quickly, 'a mystery.' He began putting the files back up on the shelf. Even after fifty years and all that had happened the signature of Stalin's secretary was still enough to unsettle a man of the right age. His hands shook. One of the folders slipped through his fingers and flopped to the floor. Pages spilled. 'Leave it, please. I'll attend to it.' But Kelso was already on his knees, gathering the loose sheets.

'There is one other thing you could do for us,' he said.

'I don't think so –'

'We believe that Anna Safanova's parents were probably both Party members.'

It was impossible, said Tsarev. He couldn't let them look. Those records were confidential.

'But you could look for us –'

No. He didn't think so.

He held out his inky hand for the missing pages and suddenly O'Brian was beside him, bending, and pressing into his outstretched palm another two hundred dollars.

'It really would help us very much,' said Kelso, desperately waving O'Brian away and nodding to emphasise each word, '*help us very much with our film*, if you could look them up.'

But Tsarev ignored him. He was staring at the two one-hundred dollar bills, and the face of Benjamin Franklin, shrewd and appraising, gazed back up at him.

'There isn't anything, is there,' he said slowly, 'that you people don't think you can buy with money?'

'No insult was intended,' said Kelso. He gave O'Brian a murderous look.

'Yeah,' muttered O'Brian, 'no offence.'

'You buy our industries. You buy our missiles. You try to buy our archives –'

His fingers contracted around the notes, screwing them tight, then he let the money fall.

'Keep your money. To hell with you and your money.'

He turned and bent his head, busied himself with putting all the records in the proper order. There was silence save for the rustling of dried paper.

Well done, mouthed Kelso at O'Brian. *Congratulations –*

A minute passed.

And then, unexpectedly, Tsarev spoke. 'What did you say their names were?' he said, without looking round. 'The parents?'

'Mikhail,' said Kelso quickly, 'and –' And, hell, what was the mother called? He tried to remember the NKVD report. Vera? Varushka? No, Vavara, that was it. 'Mikhail and Vavara Safanova.'

Tsarev hesitated. He turned to look at them, an expression on his narrow face that mingled dignity with contempt. 'Wait here,' he said. 'Don't touch anything.'

He disappeared to another part of the storeroom. They could hear him moving around.

O'Brian said, 'What's going on?'

'I think,' said Kelso, 'I *think* it's called making a point. He's gone to see if there are any records on Anna's parents. And no bloody thanks to you. Didn't I tell you: *leave the talking to me?*'

'Well, it worked didn't it?' O'Brian stooped and picked up the crumpled dollars, smoothed them out and replaced them in his wallet. 'Jesus, what a boneyard.' He picked up a nearby head of Lenin. 'Alas, poor Yorick ...' He stopped. He couldn't remember the rest of the quotation. 'Here you go, professor. Have a souvenir.' He tossed the bust to Kelso, who caught it and quickly set it down.

'Don't,' he said. His good mood had gone. He was sick of O'Brian, but it wasn't only that. There was something else – something about the atmosphere down here. He couldn't define it exactly.

O'Brian sneered. 'What's up with you?'

'I don't know. "God is not mocked."'

'And neither is Comrade Lenin? Is that it? Poor old Fluke. You know what? I think you're beginning to lose it.'

Kelso would have told him to go to hell, but Tsarev was on his way back, carrying another file and now he was looking triumphant.

Here was a subject who would be suitable for their filming. Here was a woman who had never been bought – he glared at O'Brian – a person who was a lesson to them all. Vavara Safanova had joined the Communist Party in 1935 and had stayed with it, through good times and bad. She had a list of citations bestowed by the Archangel Central Committee that took up half a page. Oh yes: here was the indomitable spirit of socialism that could never be conquered!

Kelso smiled at him. 'When did she die?'

Ah! That was the thing. She hadn't died.

'Vavara Safanova?' repeated Kelso. He couldn't believe it. He exchanged a look with O'Brian. 'Anna Safanova's *mother*? Still *alive*?'

Still alive last month, said Tsarev. Still alive at eighty-five! It was written here. They could take a look. More than sixty years a faithful member – she had just paid her Party dues.

Chapter Twenty-two

IT WAS MORNING in Moscow.

Suvorin was in the back of the car with Zinaida Rapava. Militia liaison was sitting up front with the driver. The doors were locked. The Volga was wedged in the stream of sluggish traffic on the road heading south towards Lytkarino.

The militia man was complaining. They should have come in a different car – to force their way through this lot needed revolving lights and sound effects.

And who do you think you are? thought Suvorin. The President?

Zinaida's eyes looked bruised and puffy from lack of sleep. She wore a raincoat over her dress and her knees were turned towards the door, putting as much seat leather as she could between herself and Suvorin. He wondered if she knew where they were going. He doubted it. She seemed to have gone off somewhere into the heart of herself and barely to be aware of what was happening.

Where was Kelso? What was in the notebook? The same two questions, over and over, first at her place, then upstairs in the front office that the SVR maintained in downtown Moscow – the place where visiting western journalists were entertained by the Service's smiling, Americanized public relations officer. (See, gentlemen, how democratic we are! Now what can we do to help?) No coffee for her and no cigarettes, either, once she had smoked the last of her own. Write a statement, Zinaida, then we tear it up and we write it again, and again, as the clock drags on till nine, which is when Suvorin can play his ace.

She was as stubborn as her father.

In the old days, in the Lubyanka, they had operated a system called The Conveyer Belt: the suspect was passed between three investigators working eight-hour shifts in rotation. And after thirty-six hours without sleep most people would sign anything, incriminate anyone. But Suvorin didn't have back-up and he didn't have thirty-six hours. He yawned. His eyes seemed full of grit. He guessed he was as tired as she was.

His mobile telephone rang.

'Go ahead.'

It was Netto.

'Good morning, Vissari. What do you have?'

A couple of things, said Netto. One: the house in Vspolnyi Street. He had established that it belonged to a medium-sized property company called Moskprop, who were trying to let it for $15,000 a month. No takers so far.

'At that price? I'm not surprised.'

Two: it looked as though something *had* been dug up in the garden in the past couple of days. There was loose soil in one spot to a depth of five feet, and forensics reported traces of ferrous oxide in the earth. Something had been rusting away down there for years.

'Anything else?'

'No. Nothing on Mamantov. He's evaporated. And the colonel's agitated. He's been asking for you.'

'Did you tell him where I was?'

'No, lieutenant.'

'Good man.' Suvorin rang off. Zinaida was watching him.

'You know what I think?' said Suvorin, 'I think your old papa went and dug up that toolbox just before he died. And then I think he gave it to you. And then I reckon you gave it to Kelso.'

It was only a theory, but he thought he saw something flicker in her eyes before she turned away.

'You see,' he said, 'we *will* get there in the end. And we'll get there without you, if necessary. It's just going to take us more time, that's all.'

He settled back in his seat.

Wherever Kelso was, he thought, the notebook would be. And wherever the notebook was, Vladimir Mamantov would be as well – if not now, then very soon. So the answer to one question – where was Kelso? – would provide the solution to all three problems.

He glanced at Zinaida. Her eyes were closed.

And *she* knew it, he was sure of it.

It was so infuriatingly simple.

He wondered if Kelso had any idea how physically close Mamantov might be to him at that moment, and how much danger he was in. But of course he wouldn't, would he? He was a westerner. He would think he was immune.

The journey dragged on.

'THAT'S it,' said the militia man, pointing a thick forefinger. 'Up there, on the right.'

It looked a grim place in the rain, a warehouse of dull red brick, with small windows set behind the usual cobweb of iron bars. There was no nameplate beside the dingy entrance.

'Let's drive round the back,' suggested Suvorin. 'See if you can park.'

They swung right and right again, through open wooden gates, into an asphalt courtyard glistening in the wet. There was an old green ambulance with its windows painted out parked in one corner, next to a large black van. Big drums of corrugated metal were piled with white plastic sacks, tied with tape and stamped SURGICAL WASTE in red letters. Some had toppled off and split open, or been torn open by dogs, more like. Sodden, bloodied linen soaked up the rain.

The girl was sitting erect now, staring about her, beginning to guess where she was. The militia man levered his big frame out of the front seat and came round to open her door. She didn't move. It was Suvorin who had to take her gently by her arm and coax her out of the car.

'They've had to convert this place. And there's another warehouse out in Elektrostal, apparently. But there you are. That's the crime-wave for you. Even the dead are obliged to sleep rough. Come on, Zinaida. It's a formality. It has to be done. Besides, I'm told it often helps. We must always look our terrors in the eye.'

She shook her arm free of him and gathered her coat around herself and he realised that actually he was more nervous than she was. He had never seen a corpse before. Imagine it: a major of the former First Chief Directorate of the KGB and he had never seen a dead man. This whole case was proving an education.

They picked their way through the refuse, past a goods lift, and into the back of the warehouse – the militia man in the lead, then Zinaida, then Suvorin. It had been a cold store originally, for fish trucked north from the Black Sea, and there was still a slight tang of brine to the air, despite the smell of chemicals.

The policeman knew the drill. He put his head into a glassed-in office and shared a brief joke with whoever was inside, then another man appeared, shrugging on a white coat. He held back a high curtain of thick black rubber strips and they passed into a long corridor, wide enough to take a fork-lift truck, with heavy refrigerated doors off to either side.

In America – Suvorin had seen this on a video of a cops-and-robbers programme Serafima liked to watch – the bereaved could view their loved ones on a monitor, comfortably screened from the physical reality of death. In Russia, no such delicacy attended the extinct. But, there again, in fairness to the authorities, it had to be said that they had done their best with limited resources. The viewing room – if approached from the street entrance – was out of sight of the refrigerators. Also, a couple of bowls of plastic flowers had been placed on a covered table, on either side of a brass cross. The trolley was in front of these, the outline of the body clear beneath the white sheet. *Small*, thought Suvorin. He had expected a larger man.

He made sure he stood next to Zinaida. The militia man was beside his friend, the morgue technician. Suvorin nodded and the technician folded back the top part of the sheet.

Papu Rapava's mottled face, his thin grey hair combed back and neatly parted, stared through blackened eyelids at the peeling roof.

The militia man intoned the formal words in a bored voice, 'Witness, is this Papu Gerasimovich Rapava?'

Zinaida, her hand to her mouth, nodded.

'Speak please.'

'It is.' They could hardly hear her. And then, more loudly: 'Yes. It is.'

She glanced sideways at Suvorin, defiantly.

The technician began to replace the sheet.

'Wait,' said Suvorin.

He reached out for the edge of the sheet that was closest to him and pulled, hard. The thin nylon whisked away, billowed clear of the body and settled on the floor.

A silence, and then her scream split the room.

'And is *this* Papu Gerasimovich Rapava? Take a look, Zinaida.' He didn't look himself – he had only a vague impression, thankfully – his eyes were fixed on her. 'Take a look at what they did to him. This is what they'll do to you. And to your friend Kelso, if they catch him.'

The technician was shouting something. Zinaida, yelling, reeled away, towards the corner of the room, and Suvorin went after her – this was his moment, his only moment: he had to strike. 'Now, tell me where he is. I'm sorry, but you've got to tell me. Tell me where he is. I'm sorry. Now.'

She turned and her arm flailed out at him, but the militia man had her by her coat and was pulling her backwards. 'Eh, eh,' he said, 'enough of that,' and he spun her round and on to her knees.

Suvorin got on to his knees as well and shuffled after her. He cupped her face between his hands. 'I'm so sorry,' he said. Her face seemed to be dissolving beneath his fingers, her eyes were liquid, blackness was trickling down her cheeks, her mouth a black smear. 'It's all right. I'm sorry.'

She went still. He thought she might have fainted but her eyes were still open.

She wouldn't break. He knew it at that moment. She was her father's daughter.

After maybe half a minute, he released her and sat back on his heels, head bowed, breathing hard. Behind him, he heard the noise of the trolley being wheeled away.

'You're a madman,' said the technician, incredulously. 'You're fucking mad, you are.'

Suvorin raised his arm in weary acknowledgement. The door slammed shut. He rested his palms on the cold stone floor. He hated this case, he realised, not simply because it was so damned impossible and freighted with risk, but because it made him realise just how much he hated his own country: hated all those old-timers turning out on Sunday mornings with their pictures of Marx and Lenin, and the hard-faced fanatics like Mamantov who just wouldn't give up, who just didn't get it, couldn't see that the world had changed.

The dead weight of the past lay across him like a toppled statue.

It took an effort, pressing hard on the smooth stone, to push himself up on to his feet.

'Come on,' he said. He offered her his hand.

'Archangel.'

'What?' He looked down at her. She was watching him from the floor. There was a frightening calmness about her. He moved closer to her. 'What was that?'

She said it again.

'Archangel.'

HE held on to the tails of his overcoat and carefully lowered himself back to the floor and sat close to her. They both had their backs propped up against the wall, like a couple of survivors after an accident.

She was staring straight ahead and was talking in an odd monotone. He had his notebook open and his pen was working fast, tearing across the page, filling one sheet then flicking it over to start another. Because she might stop, he thought, stop talking as suddenly as she'd started –

He had gone to Archangel, she said. Driving. Gone up north, him and the reporter from the television.

Fine, Zinaida, take your time. And when was this?

Yesterday afternoon.

287

When exactly?

Four, maybe. Five. She couldn't remember. Did it matter?

What reporter?

O'Brian. An American. He was on the television. She didn't trust him.

And the notebook?

Gone. Gone with them. It was hers but she didn't want it. She wouldn't touch it. Not after she had worked out what it was about. It was cursed. The thing was cursed. It killed everyone who touched it.

She paused, staring at the spot where her father's body had been. She covered her eyes.

Suvorin waited, then said, Why Archangel?

Because that was where the girl had lived.

Girl? Suvorin stopped writing. What was she talking about? What *girl?*

'LISTEN,' he said, a few minutes later, when he had put his notebook away, 'you're going to be all right. I'm going to see to that, personally, do you understand me? The Russian government *guarantees* it.'

(What was he talking about? The Russian government couldn't guarantee a damned thing. The Russian government couldn't guarantee its president wouldn't drop his pants at a diplomatic reception and try to set light to one of his farts –)

'Now what I'm going to do is this. Here's my office number: it's a direct line. I'm going to get one of my men to take you back to your apartment, okay? And you can get some sleep. And I'll make sure there's a guard outside on the landing and one in the street. So no one's going to be able to get at you and harm you in any way. Right?'

He rushed on, making more promises he couldn't keep. I

should go into politics, he thought. I'm a natural.

'We're going to make sure Kelso is safe. And we're going to find the people – the man – who did this terrible thing to your father, and we're going to lock him up. Are you listening, Zinaida?'

He was on his feet again, surreptitiously looking at his watch.

'I've got to set things moving now. I've got to go. All right? I'm going to call Lieutenant Bunin – you remember Bunin, from last night? – and I'll get him to take you home.'

Halfway out the door he looked back at her.

'My name is Suvorin, by the way. Feliks Suvorin.'

THE militia man and the morgue assistant were waiting in the corridor. 'Leave her alone,' he said. 'She'll be fine.' They were looking at him strangely. Was it contempt, he wondered, or a wary respect? He wasn't sure which he deserved and he didn't have time to decide. He turned his back on them and called Arsenyev's number at Yasenevo.

'Sergo? I need to speak to the colonel . . . Yes, it's urgent. And I need you to fix some transport for me . . . Yes – are you ready? – I need you to fix me a *plane*.'

Chapter Twenty-three

ACCORDING TO HER Party record, Vavara Safanova had lived at the same address for more than sixty years, a place in the old part of Archangel, about ten minutes' drive from the waterfront, in a neighbourhood built of wood. Wooden houses were reached by wooden steps from wooden pavements – ancient timber, weathered grey, that must have been floated down the Dvina from the forests upstream long before the Revolution. It looked picturesque in the winter weather, if you could close your eyes to the concrete apartment blocks towering in the background. There were stacks of cordwood beside some of the houses and here and there a curl of smoke rose to lick the falling snow.

The roads were broad and empty, guarded on either side by sentinels of silver birch, and the surface in the snow was deceptively smooth. But the roads weren't made. The Toyota plunged into potholes as deep as a man's shin, jarring and bouncing down the wide track, until Kelso suggested they pull over and continue the search on foot.

He stood shivering on the duckboards as O'Brian rummaged around in the back. Across the street were a dozen railroad freight cars. Suddenly a homemade door in the side of one of them opened and a young woman climbed out, followed by two small children so thickly bundled against the cold they were almost spherical. She set off across the snowy field, the children dawdling behind her and staring at Kelso with solemn curiosity, until she turned and shouted sharply for them to follow her.

O'Brian locked the car. He was carrying one of the

aluminium cases. Kelso still had the satchel.

'Did you see that?' said Kelso. 'There are people actually living over there in those freight cars. Did you see that?'

O'Brian grunted and pulled up his hood.

They trudged down the side of the road, past a row of patched and tumbledown houses, each tilted at its own mad angle to the ground. Every summer the land must thaw, thought Kelso, and shift, and the houses with it. And then fresh boards would have to be nailed over the new cracks, so that some of the walls had skins of repairs that must date back to the Tsars. He had a sense of time frozen. It wasn't hard to imagine Anna Safanova, fifty years ago, walking where they walked, with a pair of ice skates slung around her shoulders.

It took them another ten minutes to find the old woman's street – an alley, really, no more, running off the main road, behind a clump of birch trees, and leading to the back of the house. In the yard were some animal coops: chickens, a pig, a couple of goats. And looming over it all, ghostly in the snow, a slab-sided fourteen-storey tower block, with a few yellow lights visible on the lower floors.

O'Brian unlocked his case, took out his video camera and started filming. Kelso watched him, unhappily.

'Shouldn't we check she's in first? Shouldn't you get her permission?'

'You ask her. Go ahead.'

Kelso glanced at the sky. The flakes seemed to be getting bigger – thick and soft as a baby's hand. He could feel a knot of tension in his stomach the size of his fist. He picked his way across the yard, past the hot stink of the goats, and started to climb the half-dozen loose wooden steps that led to the back porch. On the third step he paused. The door was partially open and in the narrow gap he could see an old woman, bent forwards, two hands resting on a stick, watching him.

He said, 'Vavara Safanova?'

She didn't say anything for a moment. Then she muttered, 'Who wants her?'

He took this as an invitation to climb the remaining steps. He wasn't a tall man but when he reached the rickety porch he soared above her. She had osteoporosis, he could see now. The tops of her shoulders were on a level with her ears and it gave her a watchful look.

He tugged down his hood and for the second time that morning he launched into his carefully prepared lie – they were in town to make a film about the communists; they were looking for people with interesting memories; they had been given her name and address by the local Party – and all the time he was appraising her, trying to reconcile this hunched figure with the matriarch who featured briefly in the girl's journal.

'Mama is strong, as ever . . . Mama brings me to the station . . . I kiss her dear cheeks . . .'

She had opened the door a crack wider to get a better look at him, and he could see more of her. Apart from her shawl the clothes she wore were masculine – old clothes: her dead husband's clothes, perhaps – with a man's thick socks and boots. Her face was still handsome. She might have been stunning once – the evidence was there, in the sharpness of her jaw and cheekbones, in the keenness of her one good blue-green eye; the other was milky with a cataract. It didn't take much effort to imagine her as a young communist in the 1930s, pioneer builder of a new civilisation, a socialist heroine to warm the hearts of Shaw or Wells. He bet she would have worshipped Stalin.

'And Mama, yes, it is a modest house! Two storeys only. Your good Bolshevik heart would rejoice at its simplicity . . . '

' – so if it would be possible,' he concluded, 'for us to take up some of your time, we would be very grateful.'

He transferred the satchel uneasily, from hand to hand. He was conscious of the snow settling in a cold clump on his back, of water trickling from his scalp, and of O'Brian at the foot of the steps, filming them.

Oh God, throw us out, he thought suddenly. Tell us to go to hell, and take our lies with us: I would if I were you. You must know why we're here.

But all she did was turn and shuffle back into the room, leaving the door wide open behind her.

KELSO went in first, and then O'Brian, who had to duck to get through the low entrance. It was dark. The solitary window was thickly glazed with snow.

If they wanted tea, she said, setting herself down heavily in a hard-backed wooden chair, then they would have to make it themselves.

'Tea?' said Kelso softly to O'Brian. 'She's offering to let us make her tea. I think yes, don't you?'

'Sure. I'll do it.'

She issued a stream of irritated instructions. Her voice, emanating from her buckled frame, was unexpectedly deep and masculine.

'Well, get the water from the pail, then – no, not *that* jug: *that* one, the *black* one – use the ladle, that's it – no, no *no –*' she banged her stick on the floor ' – not that much, *that* much. Now put it on the stove. And you can put some wood on the fire, too, while you're about it.' Another two bangs of the stick. '*Wood? Fire?*'

O'Brian appealed helplessly to Kelso for a translation.

'She wants you to put some wood on the fire.'

'Tea in that jar. No, no. Yes. *That* jar. Yes. *There.*'

Kelso couldn't get a handle on any of this – on the town, on her, on this place, on the speed with which everything seemed to be happening. It was like a dream. He thought he ought to start taking some notes, so he pulled out his yellow pad and began making a discreet inventory of the room. On the floor: a large square of grey linoleum. On the linoleum: one table, one chair and a bed covered with a woollen blanket. On the table: a pair of spectacles, a collection of pill-bottles and a copy of the northern edition of *Pravda*, open at the third page. On the walls: nothing, except in one corner, where a flickering red candle on a small sideboard punctuated the gloom, lighting a wood-framed photograph of V. I. Lenin. Hanging next to it were two medals for Socialist Labour and a certificate commemorating her fiftieth anniversary in the Party in 1984; by the time of her sixtieth, presumably, they couldn't run to such extravagance. The bones of communism and of Vavara Safanova had crumbled together.

The two men sat awkwardly on the bed. They drank their tea. It had a peculiar, herbal flavour, not unpleasant – cloudberries in it somewhere: a taste of the forest. She seemed to find nothing surprising in the fact of two foreigners arriving in her yard with a Japanese video camera, claiming to be making a film about the history of the Archangel Communist Party. It was as if she had been expecting them. Kelso guessed she would find no surprise in anything any more. She had the resigned indifference of extreme old age. Buildings and empires rose and fell. It snowed. It stopped snowing. People came and went. One day death would come for her, and she would not find that surprising, either, and she would not care – not so long as He trod in the proper places: 'No, not *there*. *There . . .*'

WELL, yes, she remembered the past, she said, settling back. Nobody in Archangel remembered the past better than she did. She remembered *everything*.

She could remember the Reds in 1917 coming out on to the street, and her uncle wheeling her up in the air, and kissing her and telling her the Tsar had gone and Paradise was on the way. She could remember her uncle and her father running away into the forest to hide when the British came to stop the Revolution in 1918 – a great grey battleship moored in the Dvina and runty little English soldiers swarming ashore. She *played* to the sound of gunfire. And then she remembered early one morning walking down to the harbour and the ship had gone. And that afternoon her uncle came back – but not her father: her father had been taken by the Whites and he never came back.

She remembered all these things.

And the kulaks?

Yes, she remembered the kulaks. She was seventeen. They arrived at the railway station, thousands of them, in their strange national dress. Ukrainians: you never saw so many people – covered in sores and carrying their bundles – they were locked in the churches and the townspeople were forbidden to approach them. Not that they wished to. The kulaks carried contamination, they all knew that.

Their sores were contagious?

No. The *kulaks* were contagious. Their *souls* were contagious. They carried the spores of counter-revolution. Bloodsuckers, spiders and vampires: that was what Lenin called them.

And so what happened to the kulaks?

It was like the English battleship. You went to bed at night and they were there, and you got up in the morning and they were gone. The churches were all closed after that. But now the churches were open again – she had seen it with her own eyes. The kulaks had come back. They were *everywhere*. It was a *tragedy*.

And the Great Patriotic War, she remembered that – the Allied ships moored out beyond the mouth of the river, and the docks working all day and all night, under the heroic direction of the Party, and the fascist planes dropping fire-bombs over the old wooden town and burning it, burning so much of it down. Those were the hardest times – her husband away fighting at the front, herself working as an auxiliary nurse at the Seamen's Policlinic, no food in the town and not much fuel, the black-out, the bombs and a daughter to bring up on her own . . .

ALL of this, of course, took much longer to extract than the printed record would suggest. There was a lot of banging of her stick and doubling-back and repitition and meandering, and Kelso was acutely aware of O'Brian fidgeting beside him and of the snow piling up and muffling the sounds outside. But he let her talk. Indeed, he kicked O'Brian twice on the ankle to warn him to be patient. He wanted to let her come to things in her own time.

Fluke Kelso was an expert at this. This was how the whole business had started, after all.

He sipped his cold tea.

So you had a daughter, Comrade Safanova? That's interesting. Tell us about your daughter.

Vavara prodded the linoleum with her stick. Her mouth turned down.

That was of no consequence to the history of the Archangel Regional Party.

'But it was of consequence to you?'

Well, naturally it was of consequence to *her*. She was the child's *mother*. But what was a child when set against the forces of history? It was a matter of *subjectivity* and *objectivity*. Of *who* and *whom*. And of various other slogans of the Party she could no longer fully remember, but which she knew to be true and which had been a comfort to her at the time.

She sat back, hunched in her chair.

Kelso reached for the satchel.

'Actually, I know something of what happened to your daughter,' he began. 'We have found a book, a journal, that Anna kept. That was her name, wasn't it? Anna? I wonder – can I show it you?'

Her eyes followed the movement of his hands, warily, as he began to unfasten the straps.

HER fingers were spotted with age, like the book itself, but they didn't tremble as she opened the cover. When she saw the picture of Anna, she touched it hesitantly, then her knuckle went to her mouth. She sucked on it. Slowly she brought the page up level with her face and held it close.

'I ought to be getting this on camera,' whispered O'Brian.

'Don't you dare even move,' hissed Kelso.

He couldn't see her expression, but he could hear her laboured breathing and again he had the odd sensation that she had been waiting for them – for years, maybe.

Eventually, she said, 'Where did you get this?'

'It was dug up. In a garden in Moscow. It was with some papers belonging to Stalin.'

When she lowered the book, her eyes were dry. She closed it and held it out to him.

'No. Read it,' he said. 'Please. It's hers.'

But she shook her head. She didn't want to.

'But that *is* her writing?'

'Yes, it's hers. Take it away.'

She waved the book at him and wouldn't rest until it was safely put back in the satchel. Then she sat back, leaning to her right, one hand covering her good eye, stabbing at the floor with her stick.

ANNA, she said, after a time.

Well. Anna.

Where to begin?

Truth to tell, she had been pregnant with Anna when she married. But people didn't care about such things in those times – the Party had done away with *priests*, thank God.

She was eighteen. Mikhail Safanov was five years older – a metallurgist in the shipyards and a member of the Party's factory committee.

A good-looking man. Their daughter took after him. Oh yes, Anna was a pretty thing. *That* was her tragedy.

'Tragedy?'

Clever, too. And growing up a good young communist. She was following her parents into the Party. She had served her time as a Pioneer. She was in the Komsomol: she looked like something out of a poster in her uniform. So much so that she had been picked for the Archangel Komsomol delegation to pass through Red Square – oh, a great honour, this – picked to pass beneath the eyes of the *Vozhd* himself, on May Day 1951.

Anna's picture had been in *Ogonyok* afterwards and

questions had been asked. That had been the start of it. Nothing had been the same after that.

Some comrades had come up from the Central Committee in Moscow the following week and had started asking around about her. And about the Safanovs.

And once word of this got out, some of their neighbours had started to avoid them. After all, though the arch-fiend Trotsky was dead at last, his spies and saboteurs might not be. Perhaps the Safanovs were wreckers or deviationists?

But of course nothing could have been further from the truth.

Mikhail had come home early from the shipyard one afternoon in the company of a comrade from Moscow – Comrade Mekhlis: she would never forget his name – and it was this comrade who had given them the good news. The Safanovs had been thoroughly checked and found to be loyal communists. Their daughter was a particular credit to them. So much so that she had been selected for special Party work in Moscow, attending to the needs of the senior leadership. Domestic service, but still: the work required intelligence and discretion, and afterwards the girl could resume her studies with good words on her file.

Anna – well, once Anna got to hear of it – there was no stopping her. And Vavara was in favour of it, too. Only Mikhail had been opposed. Something had happened to Mikhail. It pained her to say it. Something during the war. He had never spoken of it, except once, when Anna was talking, full of wonder, about the genius of Comrade Stalin. Mikhail said he had seen a lot of comrades die at the front: could she tell him, then, if Comrade Stalin was such a genius, why so many millions had had to die?

Vavara had made him rise from this very table – she struck

it with her hand – and go outside into the yard for his foolishness. No. He was not the man he had been before the war. He wouldn't even go to the railway station to see his daughter off.

She fell silent.

Kelso said quietly, 'And you never saw her again?'

Oh yes, said Vavara, surprised at the question. They saw her again.

She made a curving motion with her hands, outwards from her belly.

They saw her again when she came home to have the baby.

SILENCE.

O'Brian coughed and bent forwards, head down, his hands clasped tight in front of him, his elbows on his knees. 'Did she just say what I thought she said?'

Kelso ignored him. With great effort, he managed to keep his voice neutral.

'And when was this?'

Vavara thought for a while, tapping her stick against her boot.

The spring of 1952, she said eventually. That was it. She got through on the train in March 1952, when it was starting to thaw a bit. They had had no warning, she had just turned up, with no explanation. Not that she needed to explain anything. You only had to look at her. She was seven months gone by then.

'And the father . . . ? Did she say . . . ?'

No.

A vigorous shake of the head.

But you guessed, didn't you? thought Kelso.

No, she didn't say anything about the father, or about

what had happened in Moscow, and after a while they gave up asking. She just sat in the corner and waited for her term to come. She was very silent, this new girl, not like their old Anna. She wouldn't see her friends, or step outside. The truth was, she was scared.

'Scared? What was she scared of?'

Of giving birth, of course. And why not? Men! she said – and some of her old fire returned – what did men know of life? Naturally she was scared. Anyone with eyes in their head and a mind to think would be *scared*. And that baby didn't give her an easy time, either, the little devil. It sucked the goodness out of her. Oh, a proper little devil – what a kick it had! They would sit here in the evening and watch her belly heave.

Mekhlis came by sometimes to keep an eye on her. Most weeks there was a car at the bottom of the street with a couple of his men it.

No, they didn't ask who the father was.

She started to bleed at the beginning of April. They took her to the clinic. And that was the last time they saw her. She had a haemorrhage in the delivery room. The doctor told them everything about it afterwards. There was nothing to be done. She died on the operating table two days later. She was twenty.

'And the baby?'

The baby lived. A boy.

THE arrangements were all made by Comrade Mekhlis.

It was the least he could do, he told them. He felt responsible.

It was Mekhlis who provided the doctor – an academician, no less, the country's leading expert, flown up specially from

Moscow – and Mekhlis who arranged the adoption. The Safanovs would have reared the child themselves, willingly – they asked to do so: they begged – but Mekhlis had a paper, signed by Anna, in which she said that if anything happened to her, she wanted the baby to be adopted. She named some relatives of the father, a couple named Chizhikov.

'Chizhikov?' said Kelso. 'You're sure of that name?'

Certain.

They never even saw the baby. They weren't allowed inside the hospital.

Now she was willing to accept all this, because Vavara Safanova believed in the discipline of the Party. She still did. She would believe in it until the day she died. The Party was her god, and sometimes, like a god, the Party moved in a mysterious way.

But Mikhail Safanov no longer accepted the doctrine of infallibility. He was set on finding these Chizhikovs, whatever Mekhlis said, and he still had enough friends in the regional Party to help him do it. And that was how he discovered that the Chizhikovs were not fancy Moscow folk at all – which was what he had expected – but were northerners, like them, and had gone to live in a village in the forest outside Archangel. The whisper in the town was that Chizhikov was not their real name. That they were NKVD.

By this time it was winter and there was nothing Mikhail could do. And then one morning in early spring, while he was still looking out each day for the first signs of a thaw, they woke to solemn music on the radio and the news that Comrade Stalin was dead.

She had wept, and he had, too. Did that surprise him? Oh, they had howled and clutched at one another! They had cried in a way they never had before, not even for Anna. The whole of Archangel was in grief. She could still remember the day of the funeral. The long silence, broken by a thirty-gun salute. The echo of the gunfire had rolled across the Dvina like a distant storm in the forest.

Two months later, in May, when the ice had gone, Mikhail had filled a backpack and had set off to find his grandson.

She had known nothing good could come of it.

One day passed, then two, then three. He was a fit man, strong and healthy – he was only forty-five.

On the fifth day some fishermen had found his body, about thirty *versts* upstream, rushing along in the yellow meltwater that was pouring out of the forest, not far from Novodvinsk.

KELSO unfolded O'Brian's map and laid it out on the table. She put on her spectacles and hunted up and down the blue line of the Dvina, her good eye held very close.

There, she said, after a while, and pointed. That was the place where her husband's body had been found. A wild spot! There were wolves here in the forest, and lynx and bear. In some places the trees were too dense for a man to move. In others, there were swamps that could eat you in a minute. And here and there the grey weathered bones of the old kulak settlements. Almost all of the kulaks had perished, of course. There was not much of a living to be scratched in such a place.

Mikhail knew the forest as well as any man. He had been roaming the taiga since he was a child.

It had been a heart attack, according to the militia. That was what they said. Maybe he had been trying to fill his water bottle? He had fallen into the cold yellow water and the shock had stopped his heart.

She had buried him in the Kuznecheskoye Cemetery, next to Anna.

'And what,' said Kelso, conscious again of O'Brian just behind them, filming them now with his wretched miniature camera, 'what was the name of the village where your husband said the Chizhikovs lived?'

Ah! This was crazy! How could she be expected to remember that? It was so long ago – nearly fifty years . . .

She brought her face down close to the map again.

Here somewhere – she placed a wavering finger on a spot just north of the river – somewhere around here: a place too small to be worth recording. Too small to have a name, even.

She had never tried to find it herself?

Oh no.

She looked at Kelso in horror.

Nothing good could come of it. Not then. And not now.

Chapter Twenty-four

THE BIG CAR braked hard and swerved off the south Moscow highway into the Zhukovsky military airbase shortly before noon, Feliks Suvorin hanging grimly to the strap in the rear. Beyond the checkpoint, a jeep waited. It pulled away as the barrier rose, its tail lights flashing, and they followed it around the side of the terminal building, through a wire fence and on to the concrete apron.

A small grey aircraft, as requested – six-seater, prop-driven – was being fuelled by a tanker. Beyond the plane was a line of dark green army helicopters with drooping rotors; parked next to it, a big ZiL limousine.

Well, well, thought Suvorin. Some things still work round here.

He stuffed his notes into his briefcase and darted through the wind and rain towards the limousine where Arsenyev's driver was already opening the rear door.

'And?' said Arsenyev from the warmth of the interior.

'And,' said Suvorin, sliding along the seat to join him, 'it's not what we thought it was. And thank you for fixing the plane.'

'Wait in the other car,' said Arsenyev to his chauffeur.

'Yes, colonel.'

'What's not as who thought it was?' said Arsenyev, when the door was shut. 'Good morning, by the way.'

'Good morning, Yuri Semonovich. The notebook. Everybody's always believed it was Stalin's. Actually it turns out to have been a journal kept by a girl servant of Stalin's, Anna Mikhailovna Safanova. He had her brought down from Archangel to work for him in the summer of '51, about eighteen months before he died.'

Arsenyev blinked at him.

'And that's it? That's what Beria stole?'

'That's it. That and some papers about her, apparently.'

Arsenyev stared at Suvorin for a second or two, then started laughing. He shook his head with relief. 'Go fuck your mother! The old bastard was screwing his maid? Is that what he was up to?'

'Apparently.'

'That is priceless. That is brilliant!' Arsenyev punched the seat in front of him. 'Oh, let me be there! Let me be there to see Mamantov's face when he finds out his great Stalin testament is nothing more than a maid's account of getting screwed by the mighty *Vozhd!*' He glanced at Suvorin, his fat cheeks flushed with mirth, diamonds glistening in his eyes. 'What's the matter, Feliks? Don't tell me you can't see the funny side?' He stopped laughing. 'What's the matter? You are sure this is true, aren't you?'

'Pretty well sure, colonel, yes. This is all according to the woman we picked up last night, Zinaida Rapava. She read the notebook yesterday afternoon – her father left it hidden for her. I can't think that she would invent such a story. It defies imagination.'

'Right, right. So cheer up, eh? And where's this notebook now?'

'Well, that's the first complication.' Suvorin spoke hesitantly. It seemed such a shame to spoil the old fellow's mood. 'That's why I needed to talk to you. It seems she showed it to the historian, Kelso. According to her, he's taken it with him.'

'With him?'

'To Archangel. He's trying to find the woman who wrote it, this Anna Safanova.'

Arsenyev tugged nervously at his thick neck. 'When did he leave?'

'Yesterday afternoon. Four or five. She can't remember exactly.'

'How?'

'Driving.'

'Driving? That's all right. You'll catch him easily. By the time you land, you'll only be a few hours behind him. He's a rat in a trap up there.'

'Unfortunately, it's not just him. He's got a journalist with him. O'Brian. You know him? That correspondent with the satellite television station.'

'Ah.' Arsenyev stuck out his lower lip and pulled at his neck some more. After a while he said, 'But even so, the chances of this woman still being alive are small. And if she is – well, so, so, it's no disaster. Let them write their books and make their fucking news reports. I can't see Stalin entrusting his *maid* with a message for future generations. Can you?'

'Well, this is my worry –'

'His *maid?* Come on, Feliks! He was a Georgian, after all, and an old one at that. Women were good for only three things, as far as Comrade Stalin was concerned. Cooking, cleaning and having kids. He –' Arsenyev stopped. 'No –'

'It's insane,' said Suvorin, holding up his hand. 'I know that. I've been telling myself all the way over that it's crazy. But then, he *was* crazy. And he was a Georgian. Think about it. Why would he go to so much trouble to check out one girl? He had her medical records, apparently. And he wanted her checked for congenital abnormalities. Also, why would he keep her diary in his safe? And then there's more, you see –'

'More?' Arsenyev was no longer punching the front seat. He was clutching it for support.

'According to Zinaida, there are references in the girl's journal to Trofim Lysenko. You know: "the inheritability of acquired characteristics" and all that rubbish. And apparently he also goes on about how useless his own children are, and how "the soul of Russia is in the north".'

'Stop it, Feliks. This is too much.'

'And then there's Mamantov. I've never understood why Mamantov should have taken such an insane risk – to murder Rapava, and in such a way. Why? This is what I tried to say to you yesterday: what could Stalin possibly have written that could have any effect upon Russia nearly fifty years later? But if Mamantov knew – had heard some rumour years ago, maybe, from some of the old timers at the Lubyanka – that Stalin might deliberately have left behind an heir –'

'An *heir*?'

' – well, that would explain everything, wouldn't it? He'd take the risk for that. Let's face it, Yuri, Mamantov's just about sick enough to – oh, I don't know –' he tried to think of something utterly absurd ' – to run Stalin's son for the Presidency, or something. He does have half a billion roubles, after all . . .'

'Wait a minute,' said Arsenyev. 'Let me think about this.' He looked across the airfield to the line of helicopters. Suvorin could see a muscle like a fish hook twitching deep in his fleshy jaw. 'And we still have no idea where Mamantov is?'

'He could be anywhere.'

'Archangel?'

'It's a possibility. It must be. If Zinaida Rapava had the brains to find Kelso at the airport, why not Mamantov? He could have been tailing them for twenty-four hours. They're not professionals; he is. I'm worried, Yuri. They'd never know a thing until he made his hit.'

Arsenyev groaned.

'You got a phone?'

'Sure.' Suvorin dug in his pocket and produced it.

'Secure?'

'Supposedly.'

'Call my office for me, will you?'

Suvorin began punching in the number. Arsenyev said, 'Where's the Rapava girl?'

'I got Bunin to take her back home. I've fixed up a guard, for her own protection. She's not in a good state.'

'You saw this, I suppose?' Arsenyev pulled a copy of the latest *Aurora* out of the seat pocket. Suvorin saw the headline: 'VIOLENCE IS INEVITABLE'.

'I heard it on the news.'

'Well, you can imagine how pleasantly *that's* gone down –'

'Here,' said Suvorin, giving him the phone. 'It's ringing.'

'Sergo?' said Arsenyev. 'It's me. Listen. Can you patch me through to the President's office . . . ? That's it. Use the second number.' He put his hand over the mouthpiece. 'You'd better go. No. Wait. Tell me what you need.'

Suvorin spread his hands. He barely knew where to begin. 'I could do with the militia or someone up in Archangel to check out every Safanov or Safanova and have the job finished by the time I arrive. That would be a start. I'll need a couple of men to meet me at the airfield. Transport I'll need. And some place to stay.'

'It's done. Go carefully, Feliks. I hope –' But Suvorin never did discover what the colonel hoped, because Arsenyev suddenly held up a warning finger. 'Yes . . . Yes, I'm ready.' He took a breath and forced a smile; if he could have stood up and saluted, he would have done so. 'And good day to you, Boris Nikolaevich –'

Suvorin climbed quietly out of the car.

The tanker had been unhooked from the little aircraft and the hose was being wound up. There were rainbows of oil in the puddles beneath the wings. Close up, the dented, rust-streaked Tupolev looked even older than he expected. Forty, at least. Older than he was, in fact. Holy Mother, what a bucket!

A couple of ground crew watched him without curiosity.

'Where's the pilot?'

One of the men gestured with his head to the plane. Suvorin pulled himself up the steps and into the fuselage. It was cold inside and smelled like an old bus that hadn't been driven for years. The door to the cockpit was open. He could see the pilot idly pressing switches on and off. He ducked his head and went forward and tapped him on the shoulder. The airman had a pouchy face, with the sandy, dull-eyed, bloodshot look of a heavy drinker. Great, thought Suvorin. They shook hands.

'What's the weather like in Archangel?'

The pilot laughed. Suvorin could smell the booze: it was not only on his breath – he was sweating it. 'I'll risk it if you will.'

'Shouldn't you have a navigator or someone?'

'There's nobody about.'

'Great. Terrific.'

Suvorin went aft and took his seat. One engine coughed and started with a spurt of black smoke, and then the other.

Arsenyev's limousine had already gone, he noticed. The Tupolev turned and taxied across the deserted apron, out towards the runway. They turned again, the sawing whine of the propellers falling then rising, rising, rising. The wind whipped the rain like dirty laundry, in horizontal sheets across the concrete. He could see the narrow trunks of silver birches on the airfield perimeter, grown close together like a white palisade. He closed his eyes – it was stupid to be scared of flying, but there it was: he always had been – and they were off, scuttling and swaying down the runway, the pressure pushing him back in his seat, and then there was a lurch and they were airborne.

He opened his eyes. The plane rose beyond the edge of the airfield and banked across the city. Objects seemed to rush into his field of vision, only to dwindle and tilt away – yellow headlights reflecting on the wet streets, flat grey roofs and the dark green patches of trees. So many trees! It always surprised him. He thought of all the people he knew down there – Serafima at home in the apartment they couldn't quite afford and the boys at school and Arsenyev trembling after his call to the President and Zinaida Rapava and her silence when he left her in the morgue –

They hit the sudden underside of the low cloud and he was permitted one, two, three last glimpses through the shreds of thickening gauze before Moscow was blanked from view.

Chapter Twenty-five

R. J. O'BRIAN stood on the street corner at the end of the alleyway leading to Vavara Safanova's yard, his metal case on the ground between his legs, his head bent over the map.

'How long d'you figure it'll take us to get there? A couple of hours?'

Kelso looked back at the tiny wooden house. The old woman was still standing at her open door, leaning on her stick, watching them. He raised his hand to wave goodbye and the door slowly closed.

'Get where?'

'The Chizhikov place,' said O'Brian. 'How long d'you figure?'

'In this?' Kelso raised his eyes to the heavy sky. 'You want to try to find it now?'

'There's only one road. See for yourself. She said it was a village, right? If it's a village, it'll be on the road.' He brushed a dusting of snowflakes off the map and gave it to Kelso. 'I'd say two hours.'

'That's not a road,' said Kelso. 'That's a dotted line. That's a track.' It wandered eastwards through the forest, parallel with the Dvina for perhaps fifty miles, then struck north and ended nowhere – just stopped in the middle of the taiga after about two hundred miles. 'Take a look around you, man. They haven't even made most of the roads in the city. What d'you think they'll be like out there?'

He thrust the map back at O'Brian and began walking in the direction of the Toyota. O'Brian came after him. 'We got four-wheel drive, Fluke. We got snow chains.'

'And what if we break down?'

'We got food. We got fuel for a fire and a whole damn forest to burn. We can always drink the snow. We've got the satellite phone.' He clapped Kelso on the shoulder. 'Tell you what, how about this: you get scared, you can call your mommy. How's that?'

'My mommy's dead.'

'Zinaida then. You can call Zinaida.'

'Tell me, *did* you screw her, O'Brian? As a matter of interest?'

'What's that got to do with anything?'

'I just want to know why she doesn't trust you. Whether she's right. Is it sex or is it something personal?'

'Oh-ho. Is that what all this is about?' O'Brian smirked. 'Come on, Fluke. You know the rules. A gentleman never talks.'

Kelso huddled further into his jacket and increased his pace.

'It's not a question of being scared.'

'Oh really?'

They were within sight of the car now. Kelso stopped and turned to face him. 'All right, I admit it. I am scared. And you know what scares me most? The fact you're *not* scared. That *really* scares me.'

'Bullshit. A bit of snow –'

'Forget the snow. I'm not bothered about the snow.' Kelso glanced around at the tumbling houses. The scene was entirely brown and white and grey. And silent, like an old movie. 'You just don't get it, do you?' he said. 'You don't understand. You've no history, that's your problem. It's like this name "Chizhikov". What's that to you?'

'Nothing. It's just a name.'

'But it's not, you see. "Chizhikov" was one of Stalin's aliases before the Revolution. Stalin was issued with a passport in the name of P. A. Chizhikov in 1911.'

(*Are you excited, Dr Kelso? Do you feel the force of Comrade Stalin, even from the grave?'* And he did. He did feel it. He felt as if a hand had reached out from the snow and touched his shoulder.)

O'Brian was quiet for a few seconds, but then he gave a dismissive sweep of his metal case. 'Well, you can stand here and *commune* with history if you want. I'm going to go and *find* it.' He set off across the street, turning as he walked. 'You coming or not? The train to Moscow leaves at ten past eight tonight. Or you can come with me. Make your choice.'

Kelso hesitated. He looked up again at the tumbling sky. It wasn't like any snowfall he had ever known in England or the States. It was as if something was disintegrating up there – flaking to pieces and crashing around them.

Choice? he thought. For a man with no visa and no money, no job, no book? For a man who had come this far? And what *choice* would that be, exactly?

Slowly, reluctantly, he began to walk towards the car.

THEY headed back out of the city, along a minor road, and northwards, so at least there was no GAI checkpoint to negotiate.

By now it must have been about one o'clock.

The road ran alongside an overgrown railroad track lined with ancient freight cars, and to start with it wasn't too bad. It could almost have been romantic, in the right company.

They overtook a gaily painted cart being pulled by a pony, its head down into the wind, and soon there were more wooden houses, also bright with paint – blue, green, red –

leaning in a picturesque way out in the marshland at the end of wooden jettys. In the snow it wasn't possible to tell where the solid ground ended and water began. Boats, cars, sheds, chicken coops and tethered goats were jumbled together. Even the big wood pulp mill across the wide Dvina, on the southern headland, had a kind of epic beauty, its cranes and smoking chimneys silhouetted against the concrete sky.

But then, abruptly, the houses disappeared and so did their view of the river. At the same time the hard surface gave way beneath their wheels and they began jolting along a rutted track. Birch and pine trees closed around them. In less than fifteen minutes they might have been a thousand miles from Archangel rather than a mere ten. The road wound on through the muffled forest. Sometimes the trees grew high and fine. But occasionally the woodland would thin and they would find themselves in a wilderness of blackened, blighted stumps, like a battlefield after heavy shelling. Or – and this was oddly more disconcerting – they would suddenly come across a small plantation of tall radio antennae.

Listening posts, O'Brian said, eavesdropping on Northern NATO.

He started to sing. *Walking in a Winter Wonderland.*

Kelso stood it for a couple of verses. 'Do you have to?'

O'Brian stopped.

'Gloomy sonofabitch,' he muttered under his breath.

The snow was still falling steadily. Occasional gunshots cracked and echoed in the distance – hunters in the woods – sending panicky birds flapping and crying across the track.

They went through several small villages, each smaller and more dilapidated than the last – a barracks in one with graffiti on its walls, and a satellite dish: a little chunk of Archangel dropped in the middle of nowhere. There was no one to be seen except a couple of gawping children and an old woman dressed entirely in black who stood at the roadside and tried to wave them down. When O'Brian didn't slow she shook her fist and cursed them.

'Hag.' O'Brian looked back at her in the mirror. 'What's eating her? Where are all the men, anyway? Drunk?' He meant it as a joke.

'Probably.'

'No? What? *All* of them?'

'Most of them, I should think. Home-made vodka. What else is there to do?'

'Jesus, what a country.'

After a while O'Brian began to sing again, but under his breath now and less confidently than before.

'We're walking in a winter wonderland . . .'

ONE hour passed, then another.

A couple of times the river came back briefly into view, and that, as O'Brian said, was a sight and a half – the swampy land, the wide and sluggish mass of water and, far beyond it, the flat, dark mass of trees picking up again, only to dissolve into the waves of snow. It was a primordial landscape. Kelso could imagine a dinosaur moving slowly across it.

From the map it was hard to tell exactly where they were. No habitations were recorded, no landmarks. He suggested they stop at the next village and try to regain their bearings.

'Whatever you want.'

But the next village was a long time coming, it never came, and Kelso noticed that the snow on the track was virgin: there hadn't been any traffic this far out for hours. They hit a drift for the first time – a pothole disguised by snow – and the Toyota slewed, its rear tyres flailing, until they bit on something solid. The car lurched. O'Brian spun the wheel and brought them back on course. He laughed – 'Whoa, that was fun!' – but Kelso could tell that even he was starting to feel unsettled now. The reporter slowed the engine, switched on the headlights and shifted forwards in his seat, peering into the swirling flakes.

'Fuel's low. I'd say we've got about fifteen minutes.'

'Then what?'

'Either we head back to Archangel, or we go on and try to find some place to stay the night.'

'Oh, what? You mean a Holiday Inn?'

'Fluke, Fluke –'

'Listen, if we try to stay the night here, we'll end up staying the winter.'

'Oh, come on, man, they have to send a snow plough, don't they? Surely? At some point?'

'*At some point?*' repeated Kelso. He shook his head. And there would have been another row if, just then, they hadn't rounded a curve and seen, above the snow-topped trees, a smudge of smoke.

O'BRIAN stood in the doorway of the Toyota, leaning on the roof, staring ahead through his binoculars. It looked as if there might be a settlement of some sort, he said, about half a mile off the road, along a rough track.

He slipped back behind the wheel. 'Let's take a look.'

The passage through the trees was like a tunnel, barely wide enough for a single vehicle, and O'Brian drove down it slowly. The branches clawed at them, slapping the windscreen, raking the sides of the car. The track worsened. They rocked sharply – hard left, hard right – and suddenly the Toyota plunged forwards and Kelso was thrown at the windscreen; only the seat belt saved him. The engine revved helplessly for a second, then stalled.

O'Brian turned the ignition, put the car into reverse and cautiously pressed the accelerator. The back wheels whined in the loose snow. He tried it again, harder. A howl like an animal trapped.

'Get out, could you, Fluke? Take a look.' He couldn't quite keep the edge of panic out of his voice.

Kelso had to push hard even to open the door. He jumped out and immediately sank up to his knees. The drift was axle-deep.

He banged on the back door and gestured to O'Brian to switch off the engine.

In the silence he could hear the snowflakes pattering in the trees. His knees were wet and cold. He trod awkwardly, bow-legged, through the deep drift round to the driver's door and had to dig away the snow with his gloved hands before he could drag it open. The Toyota was tilted forwards at an angle of at least twenty degrees. O'Brian struggled out.

'What'd we hit?' he demanded. He waded round to the front of the car. 'Jesus, it's like someone's dug a tank-trap. Will you look at this?'

It was indeed as if a trench had been laid across the track. A few paces further on the snow became more solid again.

'Maybe they were laying a cable or something,' said Kelso. But a cable for what? He cupped his hands above his eyes and stared through the snow towards the huddle of wooden huts about three hundred yards ahead. They didn't look as though they were connected to electricity, or to anything else. He noticed that the smoke had disappeared.

'Someone's put that fire out.'

'We're gonna need a tow.' O'Brian gave the side of the

Toyota a gloomy kick. 'Heap of junk.'

He held on to the car for support and edged round to the back, opened it up and pulled out a couple of pairs of boots, one of green rubber, the other of leather, high-sided, army-issue. He threw the rubber boots to Kelso. 'Get these on,' he said. 'Let's go parley with the natives.'

Five minutes later, their hoods up, the car locked, and each with a pair of binoculars hung round his neck, they set off down the track.

The settlement had been abandoned for at least a couple of years. The handful of wooden shacks had been ransacked. Rubbish poked through the snow – rusting sheets of corrugated tin roofing, shattered window frames, rotting planks, a torn fishing net, bottles, tin cans, a holed rowing boat, bits of machinery, ripped sacking and, bizarrely, a row of cinema seats. A timber-framed greenhouse fitted with polythene instead of glass had blown over on to its side.

Kelso ducked his head into one of the derelict buildings. It was roofless, freezing. It stank of animal excreta.

As he came out O'Brian caught his eye and shrugged.

Kelso stared towards the edge of the clearing. 'What's that over there?'

Both men raised their binoculars and trained them on what appeared to be a row of wooden crosses, half-hidden by the trees – Russian crosses, with three pairs of arms: short at the top, longer in the centre, and slanted downwards, left to right, at the bottom.

'Oh, that's marvellous,' said Kelso, trying to laugh. 'A cemetery. That's bloody perfect.'

'Let's take a look,' said O'Brian.

He set off eagerly with long, determined strides. Kelso, more reluctant, followed as best he could. Twenty years of cigarettes and Scotch seemed to have convened a protest meeting in his heart and lungs. He was sweating with the effort of moving through the snow. He had a pain in his side.

It was a cemetery right enough, sheltered by the trees, and as they came closer he could see six – or was it eight? – graves, arranged in twos, with a little wooden fence around each pair. The crosses were home-made but well done, with white enamel name-plates and small photographs covered in glass, in the traditional Russian manner. *A. I. Sumbatov*, read the first one, *22.1.20 – 9.8.81*. The picture showed a man, in middle age, in uniform. Next to him was *P. J. Sumbatova, 6.12.26 – 14.11.92*. She, too, was in uniform: a heavy-faced woman with a severe central parting. Next to them were the Yezhovs. And next to the Yezhovs, the Golubs. They were married couples, all about the same age. They were all in uniform. T. Y. Golub had been the first to die, in 1961. It was impossible to see his face. It had been scratched out.

'This must be the place,' said O'Brian, quietly. 'No question. This is it. Who are they all, Fluke? Army?'

'No.' Kelso shook his head slowly. 'The uniform is NKVD, I think. And here, look. Look at this.'

It was the final pair of graves, the ones furthest from the clearing, set slightly apart from the others. They had been the last survivors. *B. D. Chizhikov* – a major, by the look of his insignia – *19.2.19 – 9.3.96*. And next to him *M. G. Chizhikova, 16.4.24 – 16.3.96*. She had outlasted her husband by exactly one week. Her face was also obliterated.

They stood like mourners for a while: silent, their heads bowed.

'And then there were none,' murmured O'Brian.

'Or one.'

'I don't think so. No way. This place has been empty quite

a while. Shit,' he said suddenly, and took a kick at the snow, 'would you believe it, after all that? We *missed* him?'

The trees were thick here. It was impossible to see beyond a few dozen yards.

O'Brian said, 'I'd better get a shot of this while it's light. You wait here. I'll go back to the car.'

'Oh, great,' said Kelso. 'Thank you.'

'Scared, Fluke?'

'What do you think?'

'Whoo,' said O'Brian. He raised his arms and fluttered his fingers above his head.

'If you try playing any jokes, O'Brian, I'm warning you, I'll kill you.'

'Ho ho ho,' said O'Brian, moving away towards the track. 'Ho ho ho.' He disappeared beyond the trees. Kelso heard his stupid laugh for a few more seconds and then there was silence – just the rustle of the snow and the sound of his own breathing.

My God, what a set-up *this* was, just look at these dates: they were a story in themselves. He walked back to the first grave, pulled off his gloves, took out his notebook. Then he went down on one knee and began to copy the details from the crosses. An entire troop of bodyguards had been dispatched into the forest more than forty years earlier to protect one solitary baby boy, and all of them had stuck it out, had stayed at their posts, out of loyalty or habit or fear, until eventually they had dropped down dead, one after another. They were like those Japanese soldiers who stayed hidden in the jungle, unaware that the war was over.

He began to wonder how close Mikhail Safanov might have managed to get in the spring of 1953, and then he consciously abandoned this line of thought. It didn't bear contemplating – not yet; not *here*.

It was hard to hold the pencil between his cold fingers, and difficult to write as the snowflakes settled across the page. Still, he worked his way along to the final crosses.

'*B. D. Chizhikov,*' he wrote. '*Tough-looking, brutal face. Dark-skinned. A Georgian?? Died aged 77 . . .*'

He wondered what Comrades Golub and Chizhikova might have looked like, and who had blacked out their faces, and why. There was something infinitely sinister about their featureless silhouettes. He found himself writing, '*Could they have been purged?*'

Oh, where the hell was O'Brian?

His back was aching. His knees were wet. He stood and another thought occurred to him. He brushed the page clear of snow again and licked the end of his pencil.

'*The graves are all well kept,*' he wrote, '*plots appear to be weeded. If this place is abandoned, like the buildings, shouldn't they have grown over?*'

'O'Brian?' he called. 'R. J.?'

The snow deadened his shout.

He put away the notebook and began walking quickly away from the cemetery, pulling on his gloves. The wind stirred in the abandoned buildings ahead of him, catching the snow and lifting it here and there like the corner of a curtain. He picked his way across the ground, following O'Brian's large footprints until he came to the start of the track. The prints led off clearly in the direction of the Toyota. He raised the binoculars to his eyes and twisted the focus. The stricken car filled his vision, so still and distant it seemed unreal. There was no sign of anyone around it.

Odd.

He turned round very slowly, a complete 360 degrees,

scanning through the binoculars. Forest. Tumbled walls and wreckage. Forest. Graves. Forest. Track. Toyota. Forest again.

He lowered the binoculars, frowning, then began walking towards the car, still following O'Brian's trail. It took him a couple of minutes. Nobody else had been this way in the snow, that much was obvious: there were two pairs of tracks heading up to the clearing and one pair heading back. He approached the car and, by lengthening his stride and planting his feet in the prints of the bigger man, he was able to retrace O'Brian's movements exactly: so and so . . . and . . . *so* . . .

Kelso stopped, arms outstretched, wobbling. The American had definitely come this way, round to the back of the Toyota, had taken out the metal camera case – it was missing, he could see – and then it looked as though something had distracted him, because instead of heading back up the track to the settlement his footprints turned sharply and led directly away from the vehicle, at a right angle, straight into the forest.

He called O'Brian's name, softly. And then, in a spasm of panic, he cupped his hands and bellowed it as loud as he could.

Again, that same curious deadening effect, as if the trees were swallowing his words.

Cautiously, he stepped into the undergrowth.

Oh, but he had always hated forests, hadn't he? Hated even the woodland around Oxford, with its poetic shafts of dusty bloody sunlight, and its mossy vegetation, and the way things suddenly flew up at you or rustled away! And branches slapping back into your face . . . *Sorry, sorry* . . . Oh yes, give him a wide open space any day. Give him a hill. Give him a cliff-top. Give him the sparkling sea!

'R. J.?' What a damned silly name to have to yell, but he yelled it louder anyway: 'R. J.!'

There were no footprints visible here. The ground was rough. He could smell the decay of a swamp somewhere, as rank as dog's breath, and it was dark, too. He would have to watch himself, he thought, keep his back firmly to the road, because if he went too far, he would lose his bearings, and maybe end up walking further and further away from the car, until there would be nothing left to do but lie down in the darkness and freeze.

There was a sudden heavy crash off to his left, and then a succession of smaller bursts, like echoes. It sounded at first like someone running but then he realised it was only snow dislodging from the tops of some branches and plunging to the earth.

He cupped his hands.

'R. J . . . !'

And then he heard a human sound. A moan, was that it? A sob?

He tried to place where it was coming from. And then he heard it again. Nearer, and behind him now, it seemed to be. He pushed through a gap between a couple of close-growing trees into a tiny clearing, and there was O'Brian's camera case lying open on the ground and there, beyond it, was O'Brian himself, upside down and swinging gently, his fingertips barely brushing the surface of the snow, suspended by his left leg from a length of oily rope.

Chapter Twenty-six

THE ROPE WAS attached to the top of a tall birch sapling, bent almost double by O'Brian's weight. The reporter was groaning. He was barely conscious.

Kelso knelt by his head. At the sight of him, O'Brian began struggling feebly. He didn't seem able to form a sentence.

'It's all right,' said Kelso. He tried to sound calm. 'Don't worry. I'll get you down.'

Get him down. Kelso took off his gloves. Get him down. Right. Using what? He had a knife for sharpening pencils, but it was in the car. He patted his pockets and found his lighter. He flicked it on, showed the flame to O'Brian.

'We'll get you down. Look. You'll be all right.'

He stood and reached up, grabbing O'Brian by his booted ankle. A noose of thin rope had dug deep into the leather. It took all Kelso's weight to drag him down far enough for him to apply the flame to the taut rope just above his sole. O'Brian's shoulders rested in the snow.

'Asornim,' he was saying. 'Asornim.'

The rope was wet. It seemed to take an age for the lighter to have any effect. Kelso had to stop and shake it. The flame was beginning to turn blue and die before the first strands started to smoulder. But then under the strain they parted fast. The last of them snapped and the sapling whipped back and Kelso tried to support the legs with his free hand but he couldn't manage it and O'Brian's body crashed heavily into the snow.

The reporter struggled to sit up, managed to prop himself

on his elbows, then slumped back again. He was still mumbling something. Kelso knelt beside him.

'You're okay. You'll be fine. We'll get you out of here.'

'Asornim.'

I sore nim?

I saw him.

'Saw who? Who did you see?'

'Oh, Jesus. Oh, fuck.'

'Can you bend your leg? Is it broken?' Kelso shuffled on his knees through the snow and began digging with his fingernails at the knot of the noose, embedded in the side of O'Brian's boot.

'Fluke –' O'Brian held up his arm, desperately flexing his fingers. 'Give me a lift here, will you?'

Kelso took his hand and pulled until O'Brian was sitting upright. Then he put his arm round the reporter's broad chest and together they managed to get him up on to his feet. O'Brian stood, leaning heavily against Kelso, putting his weight on his right leg.

'Can you walk?'

'Not sure. Think so.' He hobbled a few steps. 'Just give me a minute.'

He stayed where he was, with his back to Kelso, staring into the trees. When he seemed to be breathing more normally, Kelso said, 'Saw *who?*'

SAW *him,* said O'Brian, turning round. His eyes were wild and fearful now, searching the forest behind Kelso's head. Saw *the man.* Saw him staring out of the fucking trees next to the car. *Jesus.* Just about jumped out of my fucking *skin.*

'What do you mean? What man?'

Took one step towards him – hands up, let's be friends,

white-man-he-come-in-peace – and presto! he was *gone*. I mean, he *vanished*. Never saw him properly again after that. Heard him, though, and kind of glimpsed him once – moving fast through the forest up ahead, away to the right – sort of a sawn-off figure, like a quarterback, built low to the ground. And *quick*. So quick you wouldn't believe it. Man, he seemed to move like an *ape*. Next thing I know, the world's turned upside down.

'He led me on, Fluke, you know that, don't you? Led me right into his fucking *trap*. He's probably out there now, *watching us*.'

He was getting his strength back, his recovery speeded by fear.

He hobbled a few steps. When he tried to put his left leg down properly he winced. But he could move it, that was something. It definitely wasn't broken.

'We gotta go. We gotta get out of here.' He bent awkwardly and closed the catches on the camera case.

Kelso needed no persuading. But they would have to go carefully, he said. They had to *think*. They had blundered into two of his traps already – one on the track and one here – and who could guess how many more there might be. In this snow it was so damned hard to see.

'Maybe,' said Kelso, 'if we try to follow my footprints –'

But his tracks were already beginning to be lost beneath the ceaseless soft downpour.

'Who is he, Fluke?' whispered O'Brian, as they went back into the trees. 'I mean, *what* is he? What is he so goddamned scared of?'

He's his father's son, thought Kelso, that's who he is. He's a forty-five-year-old paranoid psychopath, if such a thing is possible.

'Oh man,' said O'Brian, 'what was *that*?'

Kelso stopped.

It wasn't another avalanche of snow from the treetops, that was for sure. It went on too long. A heavy, sustained rustling, somewhere in front of them.

'It's him,' said O'Brian. 'He's moving again. He's trying to head us off.' The noise stopped abruptly and they stood, listening. 'Now what's he doing?'

'Watching us, at a guess.'

Again, Kelso strained his eyes into the gloom, but it was hopeless. Dense undergrowth, great patches of shadow, occasionally broken by torrents of snow – he couldn't get a fix on anything, it was so unlike any place he had ever seen. He was really sweating now, despite the cold. His skin was prickling.

That was when the howling started – a deafening, inhuman wail. It took Kelso a couple of seconds to realise it was the car alarm.

Then came two loud gunshots in rapid succession, a pause, and then a third.

Then silence.

AFTERWARDS, Kelso was never sure how long they stood there. He remembered only the immobilising sense of terror: the paralysis of thought and action that came from the realisation there was nothing they could do. He – whoever *he* was – knew where they were. He had shot up their car. He had booby-trapped the forest. He could come for them whenever he wanted. Or he could leave them where they were. There was no prospect of rescue from the outside world. He was their absolute master. Unseen. All-seeing. Omnipotent. *Mad.*

After a minute or two they risked a whispered conference. The telephone, said O'Brian, what if he had damaged the Inmarsat telephone? It was their only hope and it was in the back of the Toyota.

Maybe he wouldn't know what a satellite telephone looked like, said Kelso. Maybe if they stayed where they were until dark and then went to retrieve it –

Suddenly O'Brian grabbed him hard by the elbow.

A face was looking at them through the trees.

Kelso didn't see it at first, it was so perfectly still – so unnaturally, perfectly immobile, it took a moment for his mind to register it, to separate the pieces from the shapes of the forest, to assemble them and declare the composite human:

Dark impassive eyes that didn't blink. Black, arched brows. Coarse black hair hanging loose across a leathery forehead. A beard.

There was also a hood made of some kind of brown animal fur.

The apparition coughed. It grunted.

'Com-rades,' it said. The word was slurred, the voice harsh, like a tape being played at too slow a speed.

Kelso could feel the hair stirring on his scalp.

'Aw, Jesus,' said O'Brian, 'Jesusjesusjesus –'

There was another cough and a great gathering of phlegm. A gobbet of yellow spit was ejected into the undergrowth. 'Com-rades, I am a rude fell-ow. I cannot deny it. And I have been out of the way of hu-man com-pany. But there it is. Well then? D'yer want me to shoot yer? Yes?'

He stepped out in front of them – quickly, sharply: he barely disturbed a twig. He was wearing an old army greatcoat – patched, hacked off above the knees and belted with a length of rope – and cavalry boots into which his baggy trousers were stuffed. His hands were bare and huge. In one he carried an old rifle. In the other was the satchel with Anna Safanova's notebook and the papers.

Kelso felt O'Brian's grip tighten on his arm.

'This is the book of which it is spok-en? Yes? And the papers prove it!' The figure leaned towards them, rocking his head this way and that, studying them intently. 'You are the ones, then? You are truly the ones?'

He came closer, peering at them with his dark eyes, and Kelso could smell the stench of his body, sour with stale sweat.

'Or are you, perhaps, *spiders?*'

He took a pace back and swiftly raised the rifle, aiming it from his waist, his finger on the trigger.

'We are the ones,' said Kelso, quickly.

The man cocked an eyebrow in surprise. 'Imperialists?'

'I am an English comrade. The comrade here is American.'

'Well, well! England and America! And Engels was a Jew!' He laughed, showing black teeth, then spat. 'And yet you have not asked me for proof. Why so?'

'We trust you.'

'"We trust you."' He laughed again. 'Imperialists! Always sweet words. Sweet words and then they kill you for a kopek. For a kopek! If you *were* the ones, you would *demand* proof.'

'We demand proof.'

'I have *proof,*' he said defiantly. He glanced from one man to the other, then lowered the rifle, turned and began moving quickly back towards the trees.

'Now what?' whispered O'Brian.

'God knows.'

'Can we get that rifle off him? Two of us, one of him?'

Kelso stared at him in astonishment. 'Don't even *think* it.'

'Boy, but he's quick, though, isn't he? And completely fucking crazy.' O'Brian gave a nervous giggle. 'Look at him. Now what's he doing?'

But he was doing nothing, merely standing impassively at the edge of the trees, waiting.

THERE didn't seem to be much else for them to do except follow him, which wasn't easy, given his speed across the ground, the roughness of the forest floor, the handicap of O'Brian's injured leg. Kelso carried the camera case. Once or twice they seemed to lose him, but never for long. He must have kept stopping to let them catch up.

After a few minutes they came back out on to the track, but further up, roughly midway between the abandoned Toyota and the empty settlement.

He didn't pause. He led them straight across the snowy track and into the trees on the other side.

This was not good, thought Kelso, as they passed out of the grey light and back into the shadows. Surreptitiously, without slackening pace, he put his hand into his pocket and tore a page out of his yellow notebook, screwed it into a ball and dropped it behind him. He did this every fifty yards or so – hare and hounds: an old school game – only now he was hare *and* hound.

O'Brian, panting at his back, whispered, 'Nice work.'

They emerged into a small clearing, with a wooden cabin in the centre. He had built this well – and recently, by the look of it – cannibalising the old encampment for his materials. Why he had done this, Kelso never discovered. Perhaps the other place was too full of ghosts. Or, maybe he wanted a spot even more secluded, and more easily defensible. In the silence, Kelso thought he could hear running water and he guessed they must be near the river.

The cabin was made of the familiar grey timber, with one small window and a door to suit his height, set a yard above the ground and approached by four wooden steps. At the base of these he picked up a branch and prodded deep into the snow. There was a spurt of white powder as something jumped and snapped. He withdrew the branch. Clamped around the end was a large animal trap, the rusty metal teeth stuck deep into the wood.

He laid this carefully to one side, climbed the steps to his door, unfastened the padlock and went inside. After a brief exchange of looks with O'Brian, Kelso followed, ducking his head to pass through the low entrance, emerging into the one small room. It was dark and cold and he could smell the insanity – he inhaled the lonely madness, as sharp and sour as the lingering stink of unwashed flesh. He put his hand to his mouth. Behind him he heard O'Brian suck in his breath.

Their host had lit a kerosene lamp. The whitened skulls of a bear and a wolf shone from the shadows. He put the notebook on the table, next to a half-eaten plate of some dark and bony fish, put a pot of water on the hob and bent to rekindle the old iron stove, keeping his rifle close to hand.

Kelso could imagine him an hour ago: hearing the distant sound of their car on the track, abandoning his meal, grabbing his gun and heading for the forest, his fire doused, his trap set –

There wasn't a bed, merely a thin mattress, leaking stuffing, rolled and tied with string. Beside it was an ancient Soviet-made transistor radio, the size of a packing case, and next to that a wind-up gramophone with a tarnished brass horn.

The Russian unfastened the satchel and took out the notebook. He opened it at the picture of the girl gymnasts in Red Square and held it up for them: there, you see? They nodded. He set it down on the table. Then he pulled on a length of greasy leather hanging round his neck and kept on pulling until he hauled from somewhere deep in the fetid folds of his clothes a small piece of clear plastic. He offered it to Kelso. It was warm from the heat of his body: the same picture, but folded very small, so that only Anna Safanova's face was visible.

'You are the ones,' he said. 'I am the one you seek. And now: the proof.'

He kissed the home-made locket and lowered it back into his clothes. Then, from the belt of his greatcoat, he drew out a short, wide-bladed knife with a leather hilt. He turned it, showing them the sharpness of the edge. He grinned at them. He kicked back the bit of carpet at his feet, dropped to his knees and prised up a crude trapdoor.

He reached down and pulled out a large and shabby suitcase.

HE unpacked his reliquary like a priest, reverently placing each object on the crude wooden table as if it were an altar.

The holy texts came out first: the thirteen volumes of Stalin's collected works and thoughts, the *Sochineniya*, published in Moscow after the war. He showed the title page of each book to Kelso and then to O'Brian. All of them were signed in the same way – 'To the future, J. V. Stalin' – and all, clearly, had been read and re-read endlessly. On some of the volumes, the spines were badly cracked or hanging off. The pages were swollen by markers and bent corners.

Then came the uniform, each part carefully wrapped in

yellowing tissue paper. A pressed grey tunic with red epaulets. A pair of black trousers, also pressed. A greatcoat. A pair of black leather boots, gleaming like polished anthracite. A marshal's cap. A gold star in a crimson leather case embossed with the hammer and sickle, which Kelso recognised as the Order of Hero of the Soviet Union.

And then came the mementoes. A photograph (in a wooden frame, glazed) of Stalin standing behind a desk: signed, like the books, 'To the future, J. V. Stalin'. A Dunhill pipe. An envelope containing a lock of coarse grey hair. And finally a stack of gramophone records, old 78s, as thick as dinner plates, each still in its original paper sleeve: 'Mother, the Fields are Dusty', 'I'm Waiting For You', 'Nightingale of the Taiga,' 'J. V. Stalin: Speech to the First All-Union Congress of Collective Farm Shock Workers, February 19 1933', 'J. V. Stalin: Report to the Eighteenth Congress of the Communist Party of the Soviet Union, March 10 1939' . . .

Kelso couldn't move. He couldn't speak. It was O'Brian who took the first step. He glanced at the Russian, touched himself on his chest, gestured at the table, and received in return a nod of approval. Tentatively, he reached out to pick up the photograph. Kelso could see what he was thinking: the likeness was indeed striking. Not exact, of course – no man ever looks exactly like his father – but there was *something* there, no doubt about it, even with the younger man's beard and straggling hair. Something in the cast of the eyes and the bone structure, perhaps, or in the play of the expression: a kind of ponderous agility, a genetic shadow that was beyond the skills of any actor.

The Russian grinned again at O'Brian. He picked up his knife and pointed at the photograph, then mimed hacking at his beard. Yes?

For a moment, Kelso wasn't sure what he meant, but O'Brian did. O'Brian knew at once.

Yes. He nodded vigorously. Oh, yes. Yes, please.

The Russian promptly scythed away a great swathe of coarse black facial hair and held it out, with childish pleasure, for their inspection. He repeated the stroke, again and again, and there was something shocking about the way he did this, in the casual manipulation of the razor-edged knife – this side, that, and then the throat – in the careless self-mutilation of it. *There is nothing*, thought Kelso, with a flash of certainty, *there is no act of violence this man is not capable of.* The Russian reached behind his head and grabbed his hair into a thick ponytail and sliced it off as close to the roots as he could. Then he crossed the cabin in a couple of strides, opened the door of the iron stove, and flung the mass of hair on to the burning wood where it flared for an instant before shriveling to dust and smoke.

'Bloody hell,' whispered Kelso. He watched, disbelieving, as O'Brian began opening the camera case. 'Oh no. Not that. You can't be serious.'

'I can.'

'But he's mad.'

'So are half the people we put on television.' O'Brian pushed a new cassette into the side of the camera and smiled as it clicked home. 'Showtime.'

Behind him, the Russian had his head bent over the bowl of hot water steaming on the stove. He had stripped to a dirty yellow vest and had lathered his face with something. The rasp of the knife-blade on his bristle made Kelso's own flesh ache.

'Look at him,' said Kelso. 'He probably doesn't even know what television *is*.'

'Fine by me.'

'God.' Kelso closed his eyes.

The Russian turned towards them, wiping himself on his shirt. His face was blotchy, beaded with pinheads of blood, but he had left himself a heavy moustache, as black and oily as a crow's wings, and the transformation was stunning. Here stood the Stalin of the 1920s: Stalin in his prime, an animal force. What was it Lenin had predicted? *'This Georgian will serve us a peppery stew.'*

He tucked his hair under the marshal's cap. He slipped on the tunic. A little loose around the front, perhaps, but otherwise a perfect fit. He buttoned it and strutted up and down the room a couple of times, his right hand circling modestly in an imperial wave.

He picked up a volume of the *Collected Works,* opened it at random, glanced at the page and handed it to Kelso.

Then he smiled, held up a finger, coughed into his hand, cleared his throat and began to speak. And he was good. Kelso could tell that straight away. He was not merely word perfect. He was better than that. He must have studied the recordings, hour after hour, year after year since childhood. He had the familiar, flat, remorseless delivery; the brutal, incantatory beat. He had the expression of heavy sarcasm, the dark humour, the strength, the *hate*.

'This Trotsky–Bukharin bunch of spies, murderers and wreckers,' he began slowly, 'who kow-towed to the foreign world, who were possessed by a slavish instinct to grovel before every foreign bigwig, and who were ready to enter his employ as a spy –' his voice began to rise ' – this handful of people who did not understand that the *humblest* Soviet citizen, being free from the fetters of capital, stands head and shoulders above any high-placed foreign *bigwig* whose neck wears the yoke of capitalist slavery –' and now he was shouting ' – who needs this *miserable* band of venal *slaves*, of what value can they be to the people, and whom can they demoralise?'

He glared around, defying any of them – Kelso with the open book, O'Brian with the camera to his eye, the table, the stove, the skulls – any one of them to dare to answer him back.

He straightened, thrusting out his chin.

'In 1937 Tukhachevsky, Yakir, Uborevich and other fiends were sentenced to be shot. After that, the elections to the Supreme Soviet of the U.S.S.R. were held. In these elections, 98.6 per cent of the total vote was cast for the Soviet power!

'At the beginning of 1938 Rosengoltz, Rykov, Bukharin and other fiends were sentenced to be shot. After that, the elections to the Supreme Soviets of the Union Republics were held. In these elections 99.4 per cent of the total vote was cast for the Soviet power! Where are the symptoms of demoralisation, we would like to know?'

He placed his fist on his heart.

'Such was the *inglorious* end of the opponents of the line of our Party, who finished up as *enemies of the people!*'

'*Stormy applause*,' read Kelso. '*All the delegates rise and cheer the speaker. Shouts of "Hurrah for Comrade Stalin!" "Long live Comrade Stalin!" "Hurrah for the Central Committee of our Party!"*'

The Russian swayed before the rhythm of the dead crowd. He could hear the roars, the stamping feet, the cheers. He nodded modestly. He smiled. He applauded in return. The imaginary tumult rang around the narrow cabin and rolled out across the snowy clearing to split the silent trees.

Chapter Twenty-seven

FELIKS SUVORIN'S AIRCRAFT dropped through the base of low cloud and banked to starboard, following the line of the White Sea coast.

A stain of rust appeared in the snowy wilderness and spread, and he began to make out details. Drooping cranes, empty submarine pens, derelict construction sheds ... Severodvinsk, it must be – Brezhnev's big nuclear junkyard, just along the coast from Archangel, where they built the subs in the 1970s that were supposed to bring the imperialists to their knees.

He stared down at it as he fastened his seatbelt. Some mafia middlemen had been sniffing around up here, about a year ago, trying to buy a warhead for the Iraqis. He remembered the case. Chechens in the taiga! Unbelievable! And yet they would manage it one day, he thought. There was too much spare hardware, too little supervision, too much money chasing it. The law of supply and demand would mate with the law of averages and they would get something, sometime.

The wingflaps shuddered. There was a whine of cables. They descended further, yawing and pitching through the snowstorm. Severodvinsk slid away. He could see grey discs of freezing water, flat blank swampland, white-capped trees and more trees, running away for ever. What could live down there? Nothing, surely? No one. They were at the edge of the earth.

The old plane trundled on for another ten minutes, barely fifty yards above the forest ceiling, and then ahead Suvorin saw a pattern of lights in the snow.

It was a military airfield, secluded in the trees, with a snow plough parked at the edge of the apron. The runway had just been cleared but already a thin white skin was beginning to form again. They came in low to take a look then lifted once more, the engine straining, and turned to make a final approach. As they did so, Suvorin had a tilting glimpse of Archangel – of distant, shadowy tower blocks and filthy chimneys – and then in they came, bouncing off the runway, once, twice, before settling, turning, the propellers conjuring miniature blizzards from the snow.

When the pilot switched off the engine there was a quality of silence that Suvorin had never experienced before. Always in Moscow there was something to hear, even in the so-called still of night – a bit of traffic, maybe, a neighbour's quarrel. But not here. Here the quiet was absolute, and he loathed it. He found himself talking just to fill it.

'Good work,' he called up to the pilot. 'We made it.'

'You're welcome. By the way, there's a message for you from Moscow. You're to call the colonel before you go. Make any sense?'

'Before I go?'

'That's it.'

Before I go where?

There wasn't enough room to stand upright. Suvorin had to crouch. Drawn up beside a big hangar he could see a line of bi-planes painted in arctic camouflage.

The door at the back of the plane swung open. The temperature dropped about five degrees. Snowflakes billowed up the fuselage. Suvorin grabbed his attaché case and jumped down to the concrete. A technician in a fur hat pointed him towards the hangar. Its heavy sliding door was pulled a quarter open. Waiting in the shadows, next to a couple of jeeps, sheltering from the snow, was a reception committee: three men in MVD uniforms with AK-74 assault rifles, a guy from the militia and, most bizarrely, an elderly lady in thick male clothing, hunched like a vulture, leaning on a stick.

SOMETHING had happened, Suvorin could tell that right away, and whatever it was, it was not good. He knew it when he offered his hand to the senior Interior Ministry soldier – a surly-lipped, bull-necked young man named Major Kretov – and received in reply a salute of just sufficient idleness to imply an insult. And as for Kretov's two men, they never even bothered to acknowledge his arrival. They were too busy unloading a small armoury from the back of one of the jeeps – extra magazines for their AK-74s, pistols, flares and a big old RP46 machine gun with cannisters of belt-fed ammunition and a metal bipod.

'So, what are we expecting here, major?' Suvorin said, in an effort to be friendly. 'A small war?'

'We can discuss it on the way.'

'I'd prefer to discuss it now.'

Kretov hesitated. Clearly he would have liked to tell Suvorin to go to hell, but they had the same rank, and besides he hadn't quite got the measure yet of this civilian-soldier in his expensive western clothes. 'Well, quickly then.' He clicked his fingers irritably in the direction of the gangly young militia man. 'Tell him what's happened.'

'And you are?' said Suvorin.

The militia man came to attention. 'Lieutenant Korf, major.'

'So, Korf?'

The lieutenant delivered his report quickly, nervously.

Shortly after midday, the Archangel militia had been notified by Moscow central headquarters that two foreigners were believed to be in the vicinity of the city, possibly seeking to make contact with a person or persons named Safanov or Safanova. He had undertaken the inquiry himself. Only one such citizen had been located: the witness Vavara Safanova – he indicated the old woman – who had been picked up within ninety minutes of receipt of the telex from Moscow. She had confirmed that two foreigners had been to see her and had left her barely an hour earlier.

Suvorin smiled in a kindly way at Vavara Safanova. 'And what were you able to tell them, Comrade Safanova?'

She looked at the ground.

'She told them her daughter was dead,' cut in Kretov, impatiently. 'Died in childbirth, forty-five years ago, having a kid. A boy. Now: can we go? I've got all this out of her already.'

A boy, thought Suvorin. It had to be. A girl wouldn't have mattered. But a boy. An heir –

'And the boy lives?'

'Reared in the forest, she says. Like a wolf.'

Suvorin turned reluctantly from the silent old woman to the major. 'And Kelso and O'Brian have gone into the forest to find this "wolf", presumably?'

'They're about three hours ahead of us.' Kretov had a large-scale map spread over the hood of the nearest jeep. 'This is the road,' he said. 'There's no way out except back the way they went, and the snow will hold them up. Don't worry. We'll have them by nightfall.'

'And how do we reach them? Can we use a helicopter?'

Kretov winked at one of his men. 'I fear the major from

Moscow has not adequately studied our terrain. The taiga is not well supplied with *helicopter pads*.'

Suvorin tried to stay calm. 'Then we reach them how?'

'By snow plough,' said Kretov, as if it was obvious. 'Four of us can just fit in the cab. Or three, if you prefer not to wet your fancy footwear.'

Again, and with difficulty, Suvorin controlled his temper. 'So what's the plan? We clear a way for them to drive back into town behind us, is that it?'

'If that proves necessary.'

'If that proves necessary,' repeated Suvorin, slowly. Now he was beginning to understand. He gazed into the major's cold grey eyes, then looked at the two MVD men who had finished unloading the jeep. 'So what are you people running nowadays? Death squads, is that it? It's a little bit of South America you've got going up here?'

Kretov began folding up the map. 'We must move out immediately.'

'I need to speak to Moscow.'

'We've already spoken to Moscow.'

'*I* need to speak to Moscow, major, and if you attempt to leave without me, I can assure you that you will spend the next few years *building* helicopter pads.'

'I don't think so.'

'If it comes to a trial of strength between the SVR and the MVD, be aware of this: the SVR will win every time.' Suvorin turned and bowed to Vavara Safanova. 'Thank you for your assistance.' And then, to Korf, who was watching all this, goggle-eyed: 'Take her home, please. You did well.'

'I told them,' said the old woman suddenly. 'I told them nothing good could come of it.'

'That may be true,' said Suvorin. 'All right, lieutenant, off you go. Now,' he said to Kretov, 'where's that fucking telephone?'

O'BRIAN had insisted on shooting another twenty minutes of footage. By sign language he had persuaded the Russian to pack up his relics and then to unpack them again, holding each object up to the camera and explaining what it was. ('His book.' 'His picture.' 'His hair.' Each was dutifully kissed and arranged on the altar.) Then O'Brian showed him how he wanted him to sit at the table smoking his pipe and to read from Anna Safanova's journal. ('*Remember Comrade Stalin's historic words to Gorky: "It is the task of the proletarian state to produce the engineers of human souls . . ."*')

'Great,' said O'Brian, moving around him with the camera. 'Fantastic. Isn't this fantastic, Fluke?'

'No,' said Kelso, 'it's a bloody circus.'

'Ask him a couple of questions, Fluke.'

'I shall not.'

'Go on. Just a couple. Ask him what he thinks of the new Russia.'

'No.'

'Two questions and we're out of here. I promise.'

Kelso hesitated. The Russian stared at him, stroking his moustache with the stem of his pipe. His teeth were yellowish and stumpy. The underside of his moustache was wet with saliva.

'My colleague would like to know,' Kelso said, 'if you have heard of the great changes that have taken place in Russia and what you think of them.'

For a moment, he was silent. Then he turned from Kelso and stared directly into the lens.

'One feature of the history of the old Russia,' he began,

'was the continual beatings she suffered. All beat her for her backwardness. She was beaten because to do so was profitable and could be done with impunity. Such is the law of the exploiters – to beat the backward and the weak. It is the jungle law of capitalism. You are backward, you are weak – therefore you are wrong; hence, you can be beaten and enslaved.'

He sat back, sucking on his pipe, his eyes half closed. O'Brian was standing directly behind Kelso, holding the camera, and Kelso felt the pressure of his hand on his shoulder, urging him to ask another question.

'I don't understand,' Kelso said. 'What are you saying? That the new Russia is beaten and enslaved? But surely most people would say the opposite: that however hard life might be, at least they now have freedom?'

A slow smile, directly into the camera. The Russian removed his pipe from his mouth and leaned forwards, jabbing it at Kelso's chest.

'That is very good. But, unfortunately, freedom alone is not enough, by far. If there is a shortage of bread, a shortage of butter and fats, a shortage of textiles, and if housing conditions are bad, freedom will not carry you very far. It is very difficult, comrades, to live on freedom alone.'

O'Brian whispered, 'What's he saying? Does it make sense?'

'It makes a kind of sense. But it's odd.'

O'Brian persuaded Kelso to ask a couple more questions, each of which drew similar, stilted replies, and then, when Kelso refused to translate any more, he insisted on taking the Russian outside for a final shot.

Kelso watched them for a minute through the narrow, dirty window: O'Brian making a mark in the snow and then walking towards the cabin, returning, pointing to the line, trying to make the Russian understand what he wanted him to do. It was almost as if he had been expecting them, Kelso thought. *'You are the ones,'* he had said. *'You are truly the ones . . .'*

'This is the book of which it is spoken . . .'

He had been educated, obviously – indoctrinated, perhaps, a better word. He could read. He seemed to have been brought up with a sense of destiny: a messianic certainty that one day strangers would appear in the forest, bearing a book, and that they, whoever they were – even if they were a couple of imperialists – *they would be the ones . . .*

The Russian was apparently in a great good humour, bringing his index finger up close to his eye and wiggling it at the camera, grinning, stooping and making a snowball, tossing it playfully at O'Brian's back.

Homo Sovieticus, thought Kelso. Soviet man.

He tried to remember something, a passage in Volkogonov's biography, quoting Sverdlov, who had been exiled with Stalin to Siberia in 1914. Stalin wouldn't associate with the other Bolsheviks, that was what had struck Sverdlov. Here he was: unknown, almost forty, had never done a day's work in his life, had no skills, no profession, yet he would simply go off on his own to hunt or fish, and 'gave the impression that he was waiting for something to happen'.

Hunting. Fishing. *Waiting.*

Kelso turned from the window and quickly slipped the notebook back into the satchel, stuffed the satchel into his jacket. He checked the window again, then stepped over to the table and began leafing through Stalin's *Collected Works*.

It took him a couple of minutes to find what he was looking for: a pair of dog-eared pages in different volumes, both passages heavily underlined with black pencil. And it was as he thought: the Russian's first answer was a direct quotation from a Stalin speech – to the All-Union Conference of Managers of Socialist Industry, February 4 1931, to be exact – while the second was lifted from an address to three thousand Stakhanovites, November 17 1935.

The son was speaking the words of the Father.

He heard the sound of Stalin's boots on the wooden steps and hastily replaced the books.

SUVORIN followed one of the MVD men out of the hangar and across the runway towards a single-storey block next to the control tower. The wind tore through his coat. Snow leaked through the tops of his shoes. By the time they reached the office he was freezing. A young corporal looked up as they came in, without interest. Suvorin was beginning to feel thoroughly sick of this tin pot, backwoods town, this *Archangel.* He slammed the door.

'Salute, man, damn you, when an officer comes into the room!'

The corporal leapt up so quickly he knocked over his chair.

'Get me a line to Moscow. Now. Then wait outside. Both of you wait outside.'

Suvorin didn't start to dial until they had gone. He picked up the chair and righted it and sat down heavily. The corporal had been reading a German pornographic magazine. A stockinged foot poked out glossily from beneath a pile of flight logs. He could hear the number ringing faintly. There was heavy static on the line.

'Sergo? It's Suvorin. Give me the chief.'

A moment later, Arsenyev came through. 'Feliks, listen.' His tone was strained. 'I've been trying to reach you. You've heard the news?'

'I've heard the news.'

'Unbelievable! You've talked to the others? You must move quickly.'

'Yes, I've talked to them, and I mean to say, what is this, colonel?' Suvorin had to put his finger into his other ear and shout into the receiver. 'What's going on? I've landed in the middle of nowhere and I'm looking out of the window here at three cut-throats loading a snow plough with enough firepower to take out a battalion of NATO –'

'Feliks,' said Arsenyev, 'it's out of our hands.'

'So what is this? Now we are supposed to take our orders from the MVD?'

'They're not MVD,' said Arsenyev quietly. 'They're Special Forces in MVD uniforms.'

'Spetsnaz?' Suvorin put his hand to his head. Spetsnaz. Commandos. Alpha Brigade. *Killers.* 'Who decided to turn them loose?'

As if he didn't know.

Arsenyev said, 'Guess.'

'And was His Excellency drunk as usual? Or was this a rare interlude of sobriety?'

'Have a care, major!' Arsenyev's voice was sharp.

The snow plough's heavy diesel cracked into life. The revving engine shook the double glass, briefly obliterating Arsenyev's voice. Big yellow headlights turned and flashed through the snow then began moving ponderously across the runway towards Suvorin.

'So what are my orders exactly?'

'To proceed as you think fit, using all force necessary.'

'All force necessary to achieve what?'

'Whatever you think fit.'

'Which is what?'

'That's for you to decide. I'm relying on you, major. I'm allowing you complete operational freedom –'

Oh but he was a wily one, wasn't he? The wiliest. A real survivor. Suvorin lost his temper.

'So how many are we supposed to kill then, colonel? One man is it? Two? *Three?*'

Arsenyev was shocked. He was profoundly disturbed. If the tape of the call was ever played back – which it would be, the following day – his expression would be obvious for all to hear. 'Nobody said anything about killing, major! Has anyone there said such a thing? Have I?'

'No, you haven't,' said Suvorin, finding within himself a depth of sarcasm and bitterness he didn't know he possessed, 'so obviously whatever happens is my responsibility alone. I haven't been guided by my superior officers in any way. And neither, I am sure, has the exemplary Major Kretov!'

Arsenyev started to say something but his voice was drowned out by the roar of the engine being revved again. The snow plough was nearly up against the window now. Its blade rose and fell like a guillotine. Suvorin could see Kretov in the driver's seat, passing his finger across his throat. The horn sounded. Suvorin waved at him irritably and turned his back.

'Say again, colonel.'

But the line was dead and all attempts to reconnect it failed. And that was the sound that Suvorin afterwards could never quite get out of his ears, as he sat squashed in the jumpseat of the snow plough, bouncing into the forest: the cold, implacable buzz of a number unobtainable.

Chapter Twenty-eight

THE SNOW HAD eased and it was much colder – it must have been minus three or four. Kelso pulled up his hood and set off as fast as he could towards the edge of the clearing. Ahead of him through the trees his paper trail of yellow markers blossomed every fifty yards in the snowy undergrowth like winter flowers.

Getting out of the cabin had not been easy. When he had told the Russian they needed to go back to their car – 'only to collect some more equipment, comrade,' he had added, quickly – he had received a look of such glinting suspicion he had almost quailed. But somehow he held the other man's gaze and eventually, after a final, searching glance, he was given a brief nod of permission. And even then O'Brian had lingered – 'you know, we could do with one more shot from over here . . .' – until Kelso had grabbed him hard by the elbow and steered him towards the door. The Russian watched them go, puffing on his pipe.

Kelso could hear O'Brian, breathing hard, stumbling after him, but he didn't stop to let him catch up until they were out of sight of the hut.

O'Brian said, 'You got the notebook?'

Kelso patted the front of his jacket. 'In here.'

'Oh, nice work,' said O'Brian. He performed a little victory shuffle in the snow. 'Jesus, this is a story, isn't it? This is a hell of a story.'

'A hell of a story,' repeated Kelso, but all he wanted was to get away. He resumed his walk, but more urgently now, his legs aching with the effort of pushing through the snow.

They came out on to the track and there was the Toyota, a hundred yards away, wrapped in a wet, white layer more than an inch deep, thicker towards the rear where the wind was blowing from, and as they came closer they could see that the surface was beginning to crystalise to ice. It was still tilting forwards, its back tyres almost clear of the snow, and it took them a while to locate all the damage. The Russian had fired three bullets into the car. One had blown off the lock on the back door. Another had opened up the driver's side. A third had gone through the hood into the engine, presumably to silence the alarm.

'That crazy sonofabitch,' said O'Brian, staring at the ugly holes. 'This is a forty-thousand-dollar vehicle –'

He squeezed behind the steering wheel, put the key in the ignition and turned it. Nothing. Not even a click.

'No wonder he didn't mind if we came back to the car,' said Kelso, quietly. 'He knew we weren't going anywhere.'

O'Brian had started looking worried again. He struggled out of the front seat and sank deep into the drift. He waded round to the back, lifted the rear door and blew out a long sigh of relief, his breath condensing in the cold air.

'Well, it doesn't look as though he's damaged the Inmarsat, thank Christ. That's something.' He glanced around, frowning.

Kelso said, 'Now what?'

O'Brian muttered, 'Trees.'

'*Trees?*'

'Yeah. The satellite's not straight above our heads, remember? She's over the equator. This far north, that means you need to keep the dish at a real low angle to send a signal. Trees, if they're close up – they, ah, well, they kind of *get in the way.*' He turned to Kelso, and Kelso could have murdered him then: killed him just for the nervous, sheepish grin on his big, handsome, stupid face. 'We're gonna need a space, Fluke. Sorry.'

A space?

Yeah. A space. They would have to return to the clearing.

O'BRIAN insisted they took the rest of the equipment back with them. That, after all, was what Kelso had told the Russian they were going to do, and they didn't want to make him suspicious, did they? Besides, no way was O'Brian going to leave over a hundred-grand's-worth of electronic gear sitting in a shot-up Toyota in the middle of nowhere. He wasn't going to let it out of his *sight*.

And so they struggled back along the track, O'Brian in the lead carrying the Inmarsat and the heavier of the big cases, with the Toyota's battery, wrapped in a black plastic sheet, jammed under his arm. Kelso had the camera case and the lap-top editing machine and he did his best to keep up, but it was heavy going. His arms ached. The snow sucked at him. Soon, O'Brian had turned into the forest and was out of sight, while Kelso had to keep stopping to transfer the damned bloody swine of an edit case from one hand to the other. He sweated and cursed. On his way back through the trees he stumbled over a hidden root and dropped to his knees.

By the time he reached the clearing, O'Brian already had the satellite dish connected to the battery and was trying to twist it into the right direction. The trajectory of the antenna pointed directly at the snowy tops of some big firs, about fifty yards away, and he was hunched over it, his jaw working with anxiety, holding the compass in one hand, pressing switches with the other. The snow had almost stopped and there was a faint blueness to the freezing air. Behind him, framed against the shadows of the trees, was the grey wooden cabin – utterly still, deserted apparently, apart from the thread of smoke rising from its narrow iron chimney.

Kelso let the cases drop and leaned forwards, his hands on his knees, trying to recover his breath.

'Anything?' he said.

'Nope.'

Kelso groaned.

A bloody circus –

'If that thing doesn't work,' he said, 'we're here for the duration, you realise that? We'll be stuck here till next April with nothing to do except listen to extracts from Stalin's *Complete Works*.'

It was such an appalling prospect, he actually found himself laughing, and for the second time that day, O'Brian joined in.

'Oh man,' he said, 'the things we do for glory.'

But he didn't laugh for long, and the machine stayed silent.

AND it was in this silence, about thirty seconds later, that Kelso thought he heard again the faint sound of rushing water.

He held up his hand.

'What?' said O'Brian.

'The river.' He closed his eyes and raised his face to the sky, straining to hear. 'The river, I *think* –'

It was hard to separate it from the noise of the wind in the trees. But it was more sustained than wind, and deeper, and it seemed to be coming from somewhere on the other side of the cabin.

'Let's go for it,' said O'Brian. He snatched the pair of crocodile clips off the battery terminals and began rapidly rolling up the cable. 'Makes sense, if you think of it. Must be how he gets about. A boat.'

Kelso hoisted the two cases and O'Brian called out, 'Watch yourself, Fluke.'

'What?'

'Traps. Remember? He's got this whole wood wired.'

Kelso stood, looking at the ground, uncertain, remembering the spurt of snow, the snap of the metal jaws. But it was hopeless to worry about that, he thought, just as there was no way they could avoid passing directly by the door of the cabin. He waited for O'Brian to finish packing up the Inmarsat, and then they started walking together, treading warily. And Kelso could sense the Russian everywhere now: at the window of his squalid hut, in the crawlspace underneath it, behind the stack of cordwood piled against the back wall, in the dank and mossy water barrel and in the darkness of the nearby trees. He could imagine the rifle trained on his back and he was acutely aware of the softness of his own skin, of its babyish vulnerability.

They reached the edge of the clearing and followed the perimeter of the forest. Dense undergrowth. Fallen, rotted logs. Strange white fungoid growths like melted faces. And occasionally, in the distance, crashes, as the wind shifted and brought down falls of frozen snow. It was impossible to see much further than a hand's reach. They couldn't find a path. There was nothing to do but plunge between the trees.

O'Brian went first and had the worst of it, lugging the two heavy cases and the big battery, having to twist his bulky body sideways to edge through the narrow gaps, sometimes left, sometimes right, ducking abruptly, no free hand to protect his face from the low branches. Kelso tried to follow in his footsteps and after half a dozen paces he was conscious of the forest swinging shut behind them like a solid door.

They stumbled on for a few minutes in the semi-darkness. Kelso wanted to stop and transfer the edit machine to his other hand but he didn't dare lose sight of O'Brian's back and soon he had forgotten about everything except the pain in his right shoulder and the acid in his lungs. Trickles of sweat and melted snow were running into his eyes, blurring his vision, and he was trying to bring his arm up to wipe his forehead on his wet sleeve when O'Brian gave a shout and lurched forwards, and suddenly – it was like passing through a wall – the trees parted and they were in the light again, standing on the ridge of a steep bank that fell away at their feet to a tumbling plain of yellowish-grey water a clear quarter-mile across.

IT was an awesome sight – God's work, truly – like finding a cathedral in the middle of a jungle – and for a while neither man spoke. Then O'Brian set down his cases and the battery and took out his compass. He showed it to Kelso. They were on the northern bank of the Dvina facing almost exactly due south.

Ten yards below them, and a hundred yards to their left, dragged clear of the water and covered in a dark green tarpaulin, was a small boat. It looked as though it had been taken out for the winter, and that would make sense, thought Kelso, because already ice was beginning to extend out into the river – a shelf maybe ten or fifteen yards across that seemed to be widening even as he watched.

On the opposite bank there was a similar strip of whiteness, and then the dark line of the trees began again.

Kelso raised his binoculars and inspected the far shore for signs of habitation but there was none. It looked utterly forbidding and gloomy. A wilderness.

He lowered the binoculars. 'Who're you going to call?'

'America. Get them to call the bureau in Moscow.' O'Brian already had the case of the Inmarsat open and was slotting together the plastic dish. He had taken off his gloves. In the extreme cold his hands looked raw. 'When's it gonna be dark?'

Kelso looked at his watch. 'It's nearly five now,' he said. 'An hour perhaps.'

'Okay, let's face it, even if the battery holds on this thing and I get through to the States and they fix us a rescue party – we're stuck here for the night. Unless we take some pretty dramatic action.'

'Meaning?'

'We take his boat.'

'You'd steal his boat?'

'I'd borrow it, sure.' He sat on his haunches, unwrapping the battery, refusing to meet Kelso's eyes. 'Oh, come on, man, don't look at me like that. Where's the harm? He's not going to need it till the spring anyhow – not if the temperature keeps on dropping like this – that river'll be iced over in a day or two. Besides, he shot up our car, didn't he? We'll use his boat – that's fair.'

'And you can work a boat, can you?'

'I can work a boat, I can work a camera, I can make pictures fly through the air – I'm fucking superman. Yeah, I can sail. Let's do it.'

'And what about him? He'll just stand there, will he, while we do it? He'll wave us off?' Kelso glanced back the way they had come. 'You realise he's probably watching us right now?'

'Okay. So you go keep him talking while I get everything ready.'

'Oh, thank you,' said Kelso. 'Thank you very much indeed.'

'Well, at least I've had a fucking idea. What's yours?'

A fair point, Kelso had to concede.

He hesitated, then focused his binoculars on the boat.

So this was how the Russian survived – how he made his occasional forays into the outside world. This was how he acquired the fuel for his lamp, the tobacco for his pipe, the ammunition for his guns, the battery for his transistor radio. What did he use for money? Did he barter what he caught or trapped. Or had the encampment been set up in the 1950s with a treasury of some sort – NKVD gold – which they had been eking out ever since?

The boat was concealed in a small depression, protected from the river by a low screen of trees: to anyone drifting by, she would be invisible. She was resting on her keel, propped up to port and starboard by logs – a sturdy-looking vessel, not big, room for four people, at a pinch. A bulge at her stern suggested an outboard motor, and if that was the case, and if O'Brian could make it work, they might reach Archangel in a couple of hours – less, probably, with the current flowing so fast through its narrowing channel.

He thought of the crosses in the cemetery, the dates, the obliterated faces.

It did not look as though many people had ever left this place.

It was worth a try.

'All right,' he said, reluctantly, 'let's do it.'

'That's my boy.'

When he stepped back into the trees, he left O'Brian

aiming the antenna across the river, and he had not gone far when he heard behind him the blissful, rising note of the Inmarsat locking on to the satellite.

THE snow plough was coming on fast now, thirty, forty miles an hour, rushing down the track, throwing up a great white bow wave of freezing surf that went smashing into the trees on either side. Kretov was driving. His men were jammed together next to him, nursing their guns. Suvorin was hanging on to the metal moorings of the jump seat at the back of the cab, the barrel of the RP46 poking into his thigh, feeling sick from the vibration and the diesel fumes. He marvelled at the complexities that had overwhelmed his life in so short a time, and pondered nervously the wisdom of the old Russian proverb: 'We are born in a clear field and die in a dark forest.'

He had plenty of time for his thoughts because none of the other three had addressed a word to him since they left the airfield. They passed chewing gum to one another and TU-144 cigarettes and talked quietly so he couldn't hear what they were saying above the racket of the engine. An intimate trio, he thought: clearly a partnership with some history. Where had they been last? Grozny, maybe, taking Moscow's peace to the Chechen rebels? ('*The terrorist gunmen all died at the scene . . .*') In which case this would be a holiday for them. A picnic in the woods. And who was giving them their orders? *Guess . . .*

Arsenyev's joke.

It was hot in the cab. The single windscreen wiper batted away the pawprints of snow with a soporific beat.

He tried to shift his leg away from the machine gun.

Serafima had been on at him for months to get out of the

service and make some money – her father knew a man on the board of a big privatised energy consortium and, well, let's just say, my dear Feliks, that – how should we put this? – a number of *favours* are owed. So what would that be worth, papa, exactly? Ten times his official salary and a tenth of the work? To hell with Yasenevo. Perhaps it was time.

A heavy male voice started grunting from the radio. Suvorin leaned forwards. He couldn't make out exactly what was being said. It sounded like co-ordinates. Kretov was holding the microphone in one hand, steering with the other, craning his neck to study the map on the knee of the man sitting next to him, watching the road. 'Sure, sure. No problem.' He hung up.

Suvorin said, 'What was that?'

'Ah,' said Kretov, in mock-surprise, 'you're still here? You got it, Aleksey?' This was to the man with the map, and then, to Suvorin, 'That was the listening post at Onega. They just intercepted a satellite transmission.'

'Fifteen miles, major. It's right on the river.'

'You see?' said Kretov, grinning at Suvorin in the mirror. 'What did I tell you? Home by nightfall.'

Chapter Twenty-nine

KELSO CAME OUT of the trees and walked towards the wooden cabin. The surface of the snow had frozen to a thin crust and the wind had picked up slightly, sending little twisters of powder dancing across the clearing. Rising from the iron chimney the thin brown coil of smoke jerked and snagged in the breeze.

'*When one approaches Him, do so openly.*' That was the advice of the maidservant, Valechka. '*He hates it when people creep up on Him. If a door has to be knocked upon, knock upon it loudly . . .*'

Kelso tried his best to make his rubber boots thump on the wooden steps, and he hammered on the door with his gloved fist. There was no reply.

Now what?

He knocked again, waited, then raised the latch and pushed open the door, and immediately, the now-familiar smell – cold, close, *animal*, with an underlay of stale pipe tobacco – rose to overwhelm him.

The cabin was empty. The rifle was gone. It looked as though the Russian had been working at his table: papers were laid out, and a couple of stubby pencils.

Kelso stood just inside the doorway, eyeing the papers, trying to decide what to do. He checked over his shoulder. There was no sign of movement in the clearing. The Russian was probably down at the river's edge, spying on O'Brian. This was their only tactical advantage, he thought: the fact that there were two of them and only one of him and he couldn't watch them both at once. Hesitantly, he stepped over to the table.

He only meant to look for a minute, and probably that was all he did – just long enough to run his fingers through it all:

A pair of passports – red, stiff-backed, six inches by four, lion-crested, marked 'PASS' and 'NORGE', issued in Bergen, 1968 – a young couple, identical-looking: long hair, blond, hippyish, the girl quite pretty in a washed-out kind of way; he didn't register their names; entered the USSR via Leningrad, June 1969 –

Identity papers – old-style, Soviet Union, three different men: the first, a youngish, jug-eared fellow in spectacles, a student by the look of him; the second, old, in his sixties, weathered, self-reliant, a sailor perhaps; the third, bug-eyed, unkempt, a gypsy or a drifter; the names a blur –

And, finally, a stack of sheets, which, as he fanned them out, he saw were six sets of documents, of five or six pages each, pinned together and written in pencil or ink, in various hands – this one neat, that one hesitant, another a wild and desperate scrawl – but always, at the top of the first sheet, in neat Cyrillic capitals, the same word: 'Confession'.

Kelso could feel the freezing draught from the open door shifting the hairs on the back of his scalp.

He replaced the pages carefully and backed away from them, his hands raised slightly as if to ward them off, and at the doorway he turned and stumbled out on to the steps. He sat down on the weathered planking and when he raised the binoculars and scanned the rim of the clearing he found that he was shaking.

He stayed there for a couple of minutes, recovering his nerve. It occurred to him that what he ought to do – the calm, rational, sensible thing: the not-leaping-to-any-hysterical-conclusions kind of thing, that a serious scholar would do – was to return and briefly make a note of the names for checking later.

So when he had satisfied himself for the twentieth time that not a soul was moving in the trees, he stood and ducked back through the low door, and the first thing he saw on re-entry was the rifle propped against the wall, and the second was the Russian, sitting at the table, perfectly still, watching him.

'He possessed in a high degree the gift for silence,' according to his secretary, *'and in this respect he was unique in a country where everybody talks far too much . . .'*

He was still in full uniform, still in his greatcoat and cap. The gold star of the Order of Hero of the Soviet Union was pinned to his lapel and shone in the dull light of the kerosene lamp.

How had he done that?

Kelso started gabbling into the silence. 'Comrade – you – I'm startled – I – came to find you – I wanted –' He fumbled with the zipper on the front of his jacket and held out the satchel. 'I wanted to return to you the papers of your mother, Anna Mikhailovna Safanova –'

Time stretched. Half a minute passed, a minute, and then the Russian said, softly, 'Good, comrade,' and made a note on the sheet of paper beside him. He indicated the table and Kelso took a pace towards it and laid the satchel down, like an offering placed to appease some unreliable and vengeful god.

Another endless silence followed.

'Capitalism,' said the Russian eventually, putting down his stub of pencil and reaching for his pipe, 'is thievery. And imperialism is the highest form of capitalism. Thus it follows that the imperialist is the greatest thief of all mankind. Steal a man's papers, he will. Oh, easily! Pick the last kopek from yer pocket! Or steal a man's boat, eh, comrade?'

He winked at Kelso and continued staring at him as he struck a match, sucking the fire into the bowl of his pipe, producing great spurts of smoke and flame.

'Close the door would you, comrade?'

It was beginning to get dark.

If we have to stay here the night, thought Kelso, we shall never leave.

Where the hell was O'Brian?

'Now,' the Russian continued, 'and this is the decisive question, comrade: how do we protect ourselves from these capitalists, these imperialists, these thieves? And we say the answer to this decisive question must be equally decisive.' He extinguished the match with one shake and leaned forwards. 'We protect ourselves from these capitalists, these imperialists, and these stinking, crawling thieves of all mankind only by the most ferocious vigilance. Take, for example, the Norway couple, with their serpenty smiles – crawling on their maggoty bellies through the undergrowth to ask for "directions, comrade," if you please! On a "walking holiday" if you please!'

He waved their open passports in Kelso's face and Kelso had a second glimpse of the two young people, the man in a psychedelic headband –

'Are we such *fools*,' he demanded, 'such backward *primitives*, not to recognise the capitalist–imperialist thief–spy when it worms its way among us? No, comrade, we are not such backward primitives! To such people we administer a hard lesson in socialist realities – I have their confessions here before me, they denied it at first but they admitted it all in the end – and we need say no more of them. They are as Lenin predicted they would be: dust on the dunghill of history. Nor need we say anything of him!' He waved a set of identity papers – the older man. 'And nor of him! Nor him!' The faces of the victims flashed briefly. '*That*,' said the Russian, 'is our decisive answer to the decisive question posed by all capitalists, imperialists and stinking thieves!'

He sat back with his arms folded, smiling grimly.

The rifle was almost within Kelso's reach but he didn't move. It might not be loaded. And even if it was loaded he wouldn't know how to fire it. And even if he fired it he knew he could never injure the Russian: he was a supernatural force. One minute he was ahead of you, one minute behind; now he was in the trees and now he was here, sitting at his table, poring over his collection of confessions, making the occasional note.

'Worse by far however,' said the Russian after a while, 'is the canker of the right-deviationism.' He relit his pipe, sucking noisily on the stem. 'And here Golub was the first.'

'Golub was the first,' repeated Kelso, numbly.

He was remembering the row of crosses: T. Y. Golub, his face blacked out, died November-the-something, 1961.

The essence of Stalin's success was really very simple, he thought, built around an insight that could be reduced to a mere three words: *people fear death.*

'Golub was the first to succumb to the classic conciliationist tendencies of the right-deviationism. Of course, I was merely a child at the time, but his whining still clamours in my ears: "Oh, comrades, they are saying in the villages that Comrade Stalin's body has been removed from his rightful place next to Lenin! Oh, comrades, what are we going to do? It is hopeless, comrades! They will come and they will kill us all! It's time for us to give up!"

'Have you ever seen fishermen when a storm is brewing on a great river? I have seen them many a time. In the face of a storm one group of fishermen will muster all their forces, encourage their fellows and boldly put out to meet the storm: "Cheer up, lads, hold tight to the tiller, cut the waves, we'll pull her through!" But there is another type of fishermen – those who, on sensing a storm, lose heart, begin to snivel and demoralise their own ranks: "What a misfortune, a storm is brewing; lie down, boys, in the bottom of the boat, shut your eyes; let's hope she'll make the shore somehow."'

The Russian spat on the floor.

'Chizhikov took him out into the dark part of the forest that very night and in the morning there was a cross and that was the end of Golub and that put an end to the bleatings of the right-deviationists – even that old hag his widow put a sock in her mouth after that. And for a few years more, the steady work went on, under our four-fold slogans: the slogan of *the fight against defeatism and complacency*, the slogan of *the struggle for self-sufficiency*, the slogan of *constructive self-criticism is the foundation of our Party*, and the slogan of *out of the fire comes steel*. And then the sabotage began.'

'Ah,' said Kelso. 'The sabotage. Of course.'

'It began with the poisoning of the sturgeon. This was soon after the trial of the foreign spies. Late in the summer this was. We came out one morning and there they were – white bellies floating in the river. And time without number we discovered that food had been taken from the traps and yet no animals were caught. The mushrooms were shrivelled, useless things – scarcely a *pood* to be had all year – and that had never happened before, either. Even the berries on the two-*verst* track were gone before we could pick them. I

discussed the crisis confidentially with Comrade Chizhikov
– I was older now, you understand, and able to take a hand
– and his analysis was identical to mine: that this was a classic
outbreak of Trotskyite wreckerism. And when Yezhov was
discovered with a flashlight – out walking, after curfew: the
swine – the case was made. And this,' he held up a thick pile
of barely legible scrawl and slapped it against the table, 'this
is his confession – you can see it, here, in his own hand – how
he received his signals by torch-transmission from some
spiderish associates he had made contact with while out
fishing.'

'And Yezhov – ?'

'His widow hanged herself. They had a child.' He looked
away. 'I don't know what became of it. They're all dead now,
of course. Even Chizhikov.'

More silence. Kelso felt like Scheherazade: as long as he
could keep talking, there was a chance. Death lay in the
silences.

'Comrade Chizhikov,' he said. 'He must have been a –' he
nearly said *'a monster'* – a formidable man?'

'A shock-worker,' said the Russian, 'a Stakhanovite, a
soldier and a hunter, a red expert and a theoretician of the
highest calibre.' His eyes were almost closed. His voice fell to
a whisper. 'Oh, and he *beat* me, comrade. He beat me and he
beat me, until I was *weeping* blood! On instructions that were
given to him, as to the manner of my upbringing, by the
highest organs: "You are to give him a good shaking every
now and again!" All that I am, he made me.'

'When did Comrade Chizhikov die?'

'Two winters ago. He was clumsy and half-blind by then.
He stepped into one of his own traps. The wound turned
black. His leg turned black and stank like maggoty meat.

365

There was delirium. He raged. In the end, he begged us to leave him outside overnight, in the snow. A dog's death.'

'And his wife – she died soon afterwards?'

'Within the week.'

'She must have been like a mother to you?'

'She was. But she was old. She couldn't work. It was a hard thing to have to do – but it was for the best.'

'*He never ever loved a human being,*' said his schoolfriend, Iremashvili. '*He was incapable of feeling pity for man or beast, and I never knew him cry . . .*'

A hard thing –

For the best –

He opened one yellow eye.

'You are shifty, comrade. I can tell.'

Kelso's throat was dry. He looked at his watch. 'I was wondering what had become of my colleague –'

It was now more than half an hour since he had left O'Brian by the river.

'The Yankee? Take my tip there, comrade. Don't trust him. You'll see.'

He winked again, put his finger to his lips and stood. And then he moved across the cabin with an extraordinary speed and agility – it was grace, really: one, two, three steps, yet the soles of his boots barely seemed to connect with the boards – and he flung open the door and there was O'Brian.

And later Kelso was to wonder what might have happened next. Would it all have been treated as some terrific joke? (*'Your ears must be flapping like boards in this cold, comrade!'*) Or would O'Brian have been the next interloper in the miniature Stalinist state required to sign a confession?

But it was impossible to say what might have happened, because what did happen was that the Russian suddenly pulled O'Brian roughly into the cabin. Then he stood alone at the open door, his head tilted to one side, nostrils dilated, sniffing the air, listening.

SUVORIN never even saw the smoke. It was Major Kretov who spotted it.

He braked and pointed to it, put the snow plough into first gear, and they crawled forwards for a couple of hundred yards until they drew level with the entrance to the track. Halfway along it, the sharp white outline of the Toyota's roof showed up clear against the shadows of the trees.

Kretov stopped, reversed a short distance, and left the engine idling as he scanned the way ahead. Then he swung the wheel hard and the big vehicle lurched forwards again, off the road and down the track, clearing a path to within a few paces of the empty car. He turned the engine off and for a few moments Suvorin heard again that unnatural silence.

He said, 'Major, what *are* your orders, exactly?'

Kretov was opening the door. 'My orders are plain Russian good sense. "To stuff the cork back in to the bottle at the narrowest point."' He jumped down easily into the snow and reached back for his AK-74. He stuffed an extra magazine into his jacket. He checked his pistol.

'And this is the narrowest point?'

'Stay here and keep your backside warm, why don't you? This won't take us long.'

'I won't be a party to anything illegal,' said Suvorin. The words sounded absurdly prim and official, even to his ears, and Kretov took no notice. He was already beginning to move off with his men. 'The westerners, at least,' Suvorin called after them, 'are not to be harmed!'

He sat there for a few more seconds, watching the backs of

the soldiers as they fanned out across the track. Then, cursing, he shoved the front seat forwards and squeezed himself into the open door. The cab was unexpectedly high off the ground. He leapt and felt himself jerked backwards, heard a tearing sound. The lining of his coat had snagged on a bit of metal. He swore again and detached himself.

It was hard to keep up with the other three. They were fit and he was not. They had army boots and he had leather-soled brogues. It was difficult to maintain his footing in the snow and he wouldn't have caught them at all if they hadn't stopped to inspect something on the ground beside the track.

Kretov smoothed out the screwed-up yellow paper and turned it this way and that. It was blank. He balled it up again and dropped it. He inserted a small, flesh-coloured miniature receiver, like a hearing-aid, into his right ear. From his pocket he took out a black ski-mask and pulled it over his head. The others did the same. Kretov made a chopping motion with his gloved hand towards the forest and they set off again: Kretov first with his assault rifle held before him, turning as he walked, ducking this way and that, ready to rake the trees with bullets; then one soldier, then another, both keeping up the same wary surveillance, their faces like skulls in the masks; and finally Suvorin in his civilian clothes – stumbling, slipping, in every way absurd.

CALMLY the Russian closed the door and collected his rifle. He pulled out a wooden box from beneath the table and filled his pockets with bullets. In the same unhurried manner, he rolled back the carpet, lifted the trapdoor and leapt, cat-like, into the space.

'We stand for peace and champion the cause of peace,' he said. 'But we are not afraid of threats and are prepared to answer the instigators of war blow for blow. Those who try to attack us will receive a crushing repulse to teach them not to poke their pig snouts into our Soviet garden. Replace the carpet, comrade.'

He disappeared, closing the trapdoor after him.

O'Brian gaped at the floorboards and then at Kelso.

'What the fuck – ?'

'And where the hell have *you* been?' Kelso grabbed the satchel and quickly stuffed it back into his jacket. 'Never mind him,' he said, rolling back the carpet. 'Let's just get out of here.'

But before either of them could move a skull appeared at the cabin windows – two round eyes and a slit for a mouth. A boot kicked wood. The door splintered.

THEY were made to stand against the wall – shoved against the rough planked wall – and Kelso felt cold metal jabbed into the nape of his neck. O'Brian was a bit too slow on the uptake so he had his forehead banged against the planking, just to mend his manners and teach him a little Russian.

Their wrists were trussed tightly behind their backs with thin plastic.

A man said roughly, 'Where's the other?' He raised the butt of his rifle.

'Under the floorboards!' shouted O'Brian. 'Tell 'em, Fluke, he's under the fucking floorboards!'

'He's under the floorboards,' said a well-educated voice in Russian that Kelso thought he recognised.

Heavy boots clumped on the wooden floor. Turning his head, Kelso saw one of the masked men walk to the end of the cabin, point his gun at the ground and casually begin firing. He flinched at the deafening noise in the confined space and when he looked again the man was walking backwards, spraying bullets into the floor in neat rows, his weapon leaping in his hands like a pneumatic drill. Wood chips sprouted, ricocheted, and Kelso felt something strike the side of his head, just below his ear. Blood started trickling down his neck. He turned the other way and pressed his cheek to the wall. The noise stopped, there was a rattle of a fresh magazine being fitted, then it started again, then stopped. Something crashed to the floor. There was a stink of cordite. Acrid smoke made him clench his eyes and when he opened them again he could see the blond-headed spy from Moscow. The spy shook his head in disgust.

The man who had been firing kicked aside the shredded carpet and lifted the trapdoor. He shone a flashlight down through the rising dust, then clambered into the hole and disappeared. They could hear him moving around beneath their feet. After thirty seconds he reappeared at the door of the cabin, pulling off his mask.

'There's a tunnel. He's got out.'

He produced a pistol and gave it to the blond man.

'Watch them.'

Then he gestured to the other two and they clattered out into the snow.

Chapter Thirty

SUVORIN FELT WET. He glanced down and saw that he was standing in a puddle of melted snow. His trousers were sodden. So was the bottom of his overcoat. A piece of frayed silk lining trailed on the floor. And his shoes – his shoes were leaking and scuffed – they were *ruined.*

One of the two bound men – the reporter: O'Brian, wasn't that his name? – started to turn and say something.

'Shut up!' said Suvorin, furiously. He clicked off the safety catch and waved the gun. 'Shut up and face the wall!'

He sat down at the table and wiped his damp sleeve across his face.

Absolutely *ruined . . .*

He noticed Stalin glowering at him. He picked up the framed photograph with his free hand and tilted it to the light. It was signed. And what was all this other stuff? Passports, identity papers, a pipe, old gramophone records, an envelope with a piece of hair in it . . . It looked as though someone had been trying to perform a conjuring trick. He sprinkled the hair into his palm and rubbed it between his thumb and forefinger. The fibres were dry, grey, coarse, like a clump of bristles. He let them fall and wiped his hands on his coat. Then he laid the pistol on the table and massaged his eyes.

'Sit down,' he said, wearily, 'why don't you?'

Outside in the forest there was a long jabbering burst of gunfire.

'You know, he said sadly to Kelso, 'you really should have caught that plane.'

*

'WHAT happens next?' said the Englishman. It was obviously difficult for them to sit properly. They were on their knees, next to the wall. The stove had gone out. It was getting very cold. Suvorin had slid one of the records out of its paper sleeve and put it on the turntable of the ancient gramophone.

'It's a surprise,' he said.

'I am an accredited member of the foreign press corps –' began O'Brian.

The crack-crack of a high velocity rifle was answered by a heavier bang.

'The American ambassador –' said O'Brian.

Suvorin wound the handle of the gramophone very fast – anything to block out the noise from outside – and placed the needle on the record. Through a hailstorm of crackles, a tinny orchestra struck up a wavering tune.

More gunfire. Someone was screaming, far away, through the trees. Two shots followed in rapid succession. The screaming stopped and O'Brian started whining, 'They're going to shoot us. They'll shoot us, too!' He struggled against the plastic wire and tried to rise, but Suvorin put his wet shoe on O'Brian's chest and gently pushed him down again.

'Let us,' he said, in English, 'at least try to act like civilised men.'

This was not what I dreamed for myself, either, he wanted to say. It formed no part of my life's dreams, I do assure you, to arrive in some stinking madman's hovel and hunt him down like an animal. Honestly, I believe you would find me an amusing fellow, if only circumstances were different.

He made an effort to follow the beat of the music, conducting with his forefinger, but he couldn't find any rhythm, there seemed to be no sense to it.

'You'd better have brought an army,' said the Englishman,

'because if it's just three against one out there, they don't stand a chance.'

'Nonsense,' said Suvorin, patriotically. 'They're our special forces. They'll get him. And yes, if necessary, they *will* send an army.'

'Why?'

'Because I work for frightened men, Dr Kelso, some of whom are just about old enough to have been touched by Comrade Stalin.' He frowned at the gramophone. What a racket. It sounded like howling dogs. 'Do you know what Lenin called the Tsarovich, when the Bolsheviks were deciding the fate of the Imperial Family? He called the boy "the living banner". And there's only one way, Lenin said, to deal with a living banner.'

Kelso shook his head. 'You don't understand this man. Believe me – you should see him – he is criminally insane. He's probably killed half a dozen people over the past thirty years. He's nobody's banner. He's crazy.'

'Everyone said Zhirinovsky was crazy, remember? His foreign policy towards the Baltic States was to bury nuclear waste along the Lithuanian border and blow it into Vilnius every night using giant fans. He still got twenty-three per cent of the vote in the ninety-three election.'

Suvorin couldn't stand this unearthly, bestial music a moment more. He lifted the needle.

They heard a solitary shot.

Suvorin held his breath for an answering salvo.

'Perhaps,' he said doubtfully, after waiting a long while, 'I should think about calling up that army –'

'THERE are traps,' said Kelso.

'What?'

Suvorin was at the doorway, peering tentatively into the twilight. He looked back into the cabin. He had looped some rope around their wrists and attached it to the cold stove.

'He's put down traps. Be careful where you tread.'

'Thank you.' Suvorin planted his foot on the top step. 'I'll be back.'

His plan – and that was a good word, he thought, that had a certain ring to it: his *plan* – was to get back to the snow plough and use the radio to summon reinforcements. So he headed towards the entrance to the clearing, the only fixed point he had. There were good footprints to follow here, although it was getting dark, and he must have been midway along the rough path when he felt the explosion and a second later he heard it, a great rush of snow marking the passage of the shock wave as it travelled through the forest. Cascades of crystal pattered down from the higher branches and bounced off into space, leaving tiny clouds of particles hanging in the air like puffs of breath.

He spun around, the gun held out in a double grip, pointing uselessly in the direction of the blast.

He panicked then and began to run – a comic figure, a jerking marionette – trying to bring his knees up as high as they would go to avoid the sucking, clinging snow. His breath was coming in sobs.

He was so intent on keeping going he almost tripped over the first body.

It was one of the soldiers. He had been caught in a trap – a huge trap: a bear trap, maybe – so big and powerfully sprung, the jaws of it had actually clamped into the bone above his knee. There was a lot of blood smeared around in the flattened snow, blood from the shattered leg and blood from a big head wound that gaped through the back of the knitted ski-mask like a second mouth.

The corpse of the other soldier was a few paces further on. Unlike the first man, he was lying on his back, his arms outstretched, his legs arranged in a perfect figure 4. There was a puddle of blood on his chest.

Suvorin put down his gun, took off his gloves and checked the pulses of both men – although he knew it was useless – pulling aside the layers of clothing to feel their warm, dead wrists.

How had he ambushed them *both*?

He looked around.

Like this, probably: he had laid the trap on the path, buried in the snow, and had lured them over it; the man in the lead had missed it, somehow, the man in the rear had been caught – that was the screaming – and the lead man had turned to help only to find their quarry behind them – that was what was cunning: they wouldn't have expected that. And so he had been shot full in the front, and then the second man had been taken out at leisure, executioner-style, with a bullet at point-blank range in the back of the head.

And then he had taken their AK-74s.

What kind of creature *was* this?

Suvorin knelt by the head of the first soldier and pulled off his ski-mask. He took out his ear-piece and pressed it to his own ear. He thought he could hear something. A rushing sound. He found the little microphone attached to the inside cuff of the dead man's left hand.

'Kretov?' he whispered. 'Kretov?' But the only voice he could hear was his own.

Then the gunfire started up again.

*

THE fire was like a red dawn through the trees, and when Suvorin stepped out on to the track he could feel the heat of the burning snow plough, even at a range of a hundred yards. The fuel tank must have exploded and the inferno had melted the winter all around it. The vehicle stood blazing in the centre of its own scorched spring.

The gunfire was continuing sporadically, but that wasn't Kretov returning fire. That was boxes of ammunition, exploding in the cab. Kretov himself was sitting down, doubled over in the centre of the track, beside the RP46, as dead as his comrades. He looked as though he had been shot while trying to set up the machine gun. He had got as far as mounting it on to the bipod but he hadn't had time to open the cannister of ammunition.

Suvorin went up to him and touched his arm and Kretov toppled over, his grey eyes open, a look of astonishment on his broad, pink face. Suvorin couldn't see a wound, not at first, anyway. Perhaps the heroic major of the Spetsnaz had simply died of fright?

Another loud bang from the direction of the fire made him look up, to find himself being watched by Comrade Stalin, in his generalissimo's uniform and cap.

The GenSec was some way up the track, standing before the fire, his left hand on his hip, his right holding a rifle almost casually across his shoulder. His shadow was long in proportion to his squat torso. It danced and flickered on the churned snow.

Suvorin thought he would choke on his own heart. They looked at one another. Then Stalin started marching towards him. And *marching* – that was the word for the way he walked: quickly, but without hurrying, swinging his arms up across his barrel chest, left-right, left-right: look lively there, comrade, here I come!

Suvorin fumbled in his pocket for his pistol and realised he had left it in the trees, beside the first two corpses.

Left-right, left-right – the living banner, kicking up the snow –

Suvorin didn't dare look at him an instant longer. He knew that if he did he would never move.

'Why is your face so shifty, comrade?' called the advancing figure. 'Why can't you look Comrade Stalin directly in the eyes?'

Suvorin swung the barrel of the RP46, his memory toiling back twenty years, to his compulsory army training, shivering on some godforsaken range on the outskirts of Vitebsk. *'Cock gun by pulling operating handle to the rear. Pull rear sight base to the rear and lift cover. Lay belt, open side up, on the feed plate so that the leading round contacts the cartridge stop and close cover. Pull trigger and gun will fire . . .'*

He closed his eyes and squeezed the trigger and the machine gun jumped in his hands, sending a couple of dozen bullets sawing into a birch tree at a range of twenty yards.

When he dared to check the track again Comrade Stalin had disappeared.

IF Suvorin's memory served him right, the ammunition belt of the RP46 carried 250 rounds, which the gun would dispatch at a rate of, say, 600 rounds per minute. So, given he'd already used a few, he probably had something less than thirty seconds of firepower with which to cover 360 degrees of track and forest, with night coming on and the temperature plunging to a level that would kill him in a couple of hours.

He had to get out of the open, that was for sure. He couldn't keep on like this, scrambling round and round like a tethered goat in a tiger shoot, trying to see through the gloom of the trees.

He seemed to remember some abandoned wooden huts at the far end of the track. They might provide a bit of cover. He needed to get his back against a wall somewhere, needed time to *think*.

A wolf howled in the forest.

He disconnected the machine gun from the bipod and hoisted the long barrel up on to his shoulder, the ammunition belt heavy on his arm, his knees almost buckling under the weight, his feet sinking deeper into the snow.

The full-throated howling came again. It was not a wolf at all, he thought. It was a man – a man's exultant shout: a blood cry.

He started wading up the track, away from the burning snow plough, and he sensed that there was someone walking parallel with him through the trees, keeping an easy pace, laughing at his ponderous attempt at flight. He was being played with, that was all. He would be allowed to get within a few paces of his destination, then he would be shot.

He came out of the neck of the track and into the abandoned settlement and headed for the nearest wooden building. The windows were out, the door had gone, half the roof was missing, it stank. He put down the gun and crawled into the corner, then turned and dragged the weapon after him. He wedged himself against the wall and pointed the barrel at the door, his finger on the trigger.

KELSO heard the big explosion, gunfire, a long pause, and then the short and heavy clatter of a much bigger weapon opening up. He and O'Brian were on their feet by now, frantically trying to find some way of cutting the rope that bound them to the stove chimney. Each sound from the forest drove them to more desperate efforts. The thin plastic was digging into his wrists, his fingers were slippery with blood.

There was blood on the Russian, too, when he appeared in the doorway. Kelso saw it as he came towards them, unsheathing his knife – smeared across his face, on his forehead and on either cheek, like a hunter who had dipped himself in his kill.

'Comrades,' he reported, 'we are dizzy with success. Three are dead. Only one still lives. Are there more?'

'More coming.'

'How many more?'

'Fifty,' said Kelso. 'A hundred.' He tugged against the rope. 'Comrade, we must get clear of this place, or they will kill us all. Even you cannot stop so many. They are going to send an army.'

ACCORDING to Suvorin's watch, about fifteen minutes had elapsed.

The temperature was plunging as the light faded. His body began to vibrate with the cold – a steady, violent shaking he couldn't stop.

'Come on,' he whispered. 'Come on and finish the job.'

But nobody came.

Comrade Stalin's capacity for springing surprises was truly endless.

THE next thing Suvorin heard was a distant click, followed by a whirr.

Click-whirr. Click-whirr.

Now what was he doing?

Suvorin found it hard to move at first. The frost had locked his joints and starched his wet clothes to board. Still, he was on his feet in time to hear the mysterious click-whirr turn suddenly into a cough and then a roar as an engine started.

No, no, not an engine exactly: a motor – an outboard motor –

He was baffled for a moment, but then he realised.

'Fifteen miles, major. It's right on the river . . . '

WELL, the RP46 didn't get any lighter, nor the snow any easier, and now he had the oncoming darkness to contend with, but he tried. He made a valiant effort.

'Bastard, bastard, bastard,' he chanted as he ran, following the pulse of the revving outboard as it led him through the fifty yards or so of trees that screened the deserted fishing settlement from the river.

He crashed through the last barrier of undergrowth and came out on to the crest of a bank that sloped down steeply to the water's edge. He stumbled along the ridge, heading upstream. Some pieces of electronic equipment lay spread out in the snow. Grey ice extended for a little distance and the black water rushed beyond his reach – an immensity of it: he couldn't see the trees on the opposite shore. And already the little boat was heading towards the centre, and turning now, carving a great white sickle of spray in the darkness. He could just make out three crouched figures. One seemed to be trying to struggle to his feet, but another pulled him down.

Suvorin dropped to his knees and unshouldered the machine gun, fumbling to close the cover on the ammunition belt, which promptly jammed. By the time he had it free and ready to fire the boat had rounded the curve of the river – and then he couldn't see it any more, he could only hear it.

He put down the gun and bent his head.

Beside him, like a space probe landed on some hostile planet, the antenna of a satellite dish pointed low across the Dvina to the dissolving horizon. One set of cables connected the dish to a car battery. Another was linked to a small grey box labelled 'Transportable Video & Audio Transmission Terminal'. Even as he watched, a row of ten red zeros in a digital display winked at him briefly, faded and died.

He had an overwhelming sense of emptiness, squatting there, as if some malevolent force had erupted from this place and escaped for ever, a comet trailing darkness.

For perhaps half a minute he listened to the sound of the outboard motor and then that too was gone and he was left alone in the utter silence.

Chapter Thirty-one

THE FIGURE SUVORIN had seen trying to rise in the boat was O'Brian – *my gear!*, he shouted, *the tapes!* – and the figure who had pulled him down was Kelso – *forget the bloody gear, forget the tapes.* For a moment the boat rocked dangerously, and the Russian cursed them both, and then O'Brian moaned and sat down quickly and put his head in his hands.

Kelso couldn't make out anyone on the shore as they roared away from it. All he could see was the sky pulsing red above the tips of the darkening firs where something big was burning fiercely, and then very quickly a bend in the river obliterated even that and he was conscious only of speed – of the racket of the outboard motor and the rushing current hurtling them downstream through the forest.

He was thinking with great clarity now, everything else in his life irrelevant, everything narrowed to this one single point: survival. And it seemed to him that all that counted was to put as much distance as possible between themselves and this spot. He didn't know how many men were left alive behind them, but the best he reckoned they could hope for was that a search party wouldn't set out till the morning. The worst scenario was that the blond-headed man had radioed for help and Archangel would already be sealed.

There was no food or water in the boat, just a couple of oars, a boathook, the Russian's suitcase, his rifle, and a small tank that smelled as though it was leaking cheap fuel. In the darkness he had to hold his watch up very close to his eyes. It was just after half-past six. He leaned over and said to O'Brian, 'What time did you say the Moscow train left Archangel?'

O'Brian lifted his head long enough from his despair to mutter, 'Ten past eight.'

Kelso twisted round and shouted above the engine and the wind, 'Comrade, could we get to Archangel?' There was no reply. He tapped his watch. 'Could we get to the centre of Archangel in an hour?'

The Russian didn't seem to have heard. His hand was on the tiller and he was staring straight ahead. With his collar turned up and his cap pulled down, it was impossible to make out his expression. Kelso tried shouting again and then gave up. It was a new kind of horror, he thought, to realise that they probably owed their lives to him – that he was now their ally – and that their futures were at the mercy of his unfathomable mind.

THEY were heading roughly north-west and the cold was being hammered into them from all sides – a Siberian wind at their backs, the freezing water beneath their feet, the rushing air on their faces. O'Brian remained monosyllabic, inconsolable. There was a light in the prow, and Kelso found himself concentrating on that – on the shifting yellow path and the roiling water, black and viscous as it began to solidify.

After half an hour the snow resumed, the flakes huge and luminous in the dark, like falling ash. Occasionally something knocked against the hull and Kelso spotted lumps of ice drifting in the current. It was as if winter was clutching at them, determined not to let them go, and Kelso wondered if fear was the reason for the Russian's silence. Killers could be frightened, like anyone else, perhaps more than anyone else. Stalin lived half his life in a state of terror – scared of aeroplanes, scared of visiting the front, never eating food unless it had been tasted for poison, changing his guards, his routes, his beds – when you had murdered so many, you knew how easily death could come. And it could come for them here very easily, he thought. They would run into an ice barrier, the water would freeze behind them, they would be trapped; the ice-crust would be too thin to risk crawling across, and here they would die, covered for decency under a shroud of snow.

He wondered what people would make of it. Margaret – what would she say when she learned her ex-husband's body had been found in a forest nearly a thousand miles from Moscow. And his boys? He cared what they would think: he wouldn't miss much, but he would miss his sons. Perhaps he should try to scrawl them a heroic final note, like Captain Scott in Antarctica: 'These rough notes and our dead bodies must tell the tale –'

He thought that perhaps he didn't fear dying as much as he had expected he would, which surprised him as he had little physical courage and no religious faith. But a man would have to be a rare fool – wouldn't he? – to spend a lifetime studying history without acquiring at least some sense of perspective on his own mortality. Perhaps that was why he'd done it – devoted so many years to writing about the dead. He'd never thought of it that way.

He tried to imagine his obituaries: *'never quite fulfilled his early promise . . . never published the major work of scholarship of which he was once judged capable . . . the bizarre circumstances of his premature death may never be fully explained . . .'* The memorialising articles would all be the same and he would know every one of their grudging, time-serving authors.

The Russian opened the throttle wider and Kelso could hear him, muttering to himself.

*

ANOTHER half hour passed.

Kelso had his eyes closed and it was O'Brian who saw the lights first. He nudged Kelso and pointed, and after a second or two, Kelso saw them as well – high gantry lights on the chimneys and cranes of the big wood pulp factory on the headland outside the city. Presently more lights began to appear in the darkness on either bank and the night sky ahead became fractionally paler. Perhaps they would make it after all?

His face was frozen. It was hard to speak.

He said, 'Got the Archangel map?'

O'Brian turned stiffly. He looked like a white marble statue coming to life and as he moved small slabs of frozen snow cracked and slid off his jacket into the bottom of the boat. He dragged the city plan out of his inside pocket and Kelso shifted forwards off the thin plank that served as a seat, fell on to his hands and knees, and crawled awkwardly to the prow. He held the map to the light. The Dvina bulged as it came into the city, and a pair of islands split it into three channels. They needed to keep to the northern one.

It was a quarter to eight.

He moved back to the stern and managed to shout, 'Comrade!' He made a chopping motion with his hand to starboard. The Russian gave no sign of having understood but a minute later, as the dark mass of the island emerged out of the snow, he steered to the north of it and soon afterwards Kelso made out a rusty buoy and beyond that a line of lights in the sky.

He cupped his hand to O'Brian's ear. 'The bridge,' he said. O'Brian pulled down his hood and squinted at him. 'The bridge,' repeated Kelso. 'The one we came over this morning.'

He pointed and very quickly they were passing beneath it – a double-bridge, half-rail, half-road: heavy ironwork dangling stalactites of ice, a strong smell of sewage and chemicals, the drumming of vehicles overhead – and when he looked back he could see the headlights of traffic moving slowly through the snow.

The familiar shape of the Harbour Master's building appeared ahead of them on the starboard side, with a jetty stretching out and boats moored to it. They hit an invisible sheet of thick ice and Kelso and O'Brian were bounced forwards. The engine cut out. The Russian restarted it and reversed, then found a channel which must have been cut by a bigger boat earlier in the evening. There was still ice but it was thinner and it splintered as their prow sliced into it. Kelso looked back at the Russian. He was standing now, peering intently at the dark corridor, his hand on the tiller, taking them in. They came alongside the jetty and he put the outboard into reverse again, slowing them, stopping. He cut the motor and leapt nimbly on to the wooden planking, holding a length of rope.

O'BRIAN was out of the boat first, with Kelso after him. They stamped and brushed the snow off themselves and tried to stretch some life back into their frozen limbs. O'Brian started to say something about finding a hotel, maybe, calling the office, but Kelso cut him off.

'No hotel. Are you listening to me? No office. And no bloody story. We're getting out of here.'

They had thirteen minutes to catch the train.

'And him?'

O'Brian nodded to the Russian who was standing quietly, holding his suitcase, watching them. He looked oddly forlorn – vulnerable, even, now that he was out of his home territory. He was obviously expecting to come with them.

'Christ almighty,' muttered Kelso. He had the map open. He didn't know what to do. 'Let's just go.' He set off along the jetty towards the shore. O'Brian hurried after him.

'You still got the notebook?'

Kelso patted the front of his jacket.

'D'you think he's got a gun?' said O'Brian. He glanced back. 'Shit. He's following us.'

The Russian was trotting about a dozen paces behind them, wary and fearful, like a stray dog. It looked as though he had left his rifle behind in the boat. So what would he be armed with, wondered Kelso? His knife? He pushed his stiff legs forwards as hard as he could.

'But we can't just leave him –'

'Oh yes we bloody can,' said Kelso. He realised O'Brian didn't know about the Norwegian couple, or any of the others. 'I'll explain later. Just believe me – we don't want him anywhere near us.'

They almost ran off the jetty and came into the big bus park in front of the Harbour Master's building – a bleak expanse of snow, a few sorrowful orange sodium lights catching the whirling flakes, nobody else about. Kelso struck north, slithering on the ice, holding on to the map. The station was at least a mile away and they were never going to make it in time, not on foot. He looked around. A ubiquitous, boxy, sand-coloured Lada, spattered with mud and grit, was emerging slowly from the street to their right, and Kelso ran towards it, flapping his arms.

In the Russian provinces, every car is a potential taxi, most drivers willing to hire themselves out on the spur of the moment, and this one was no exception. He swerved towards them, throwing up a fountain of dirty snow, and even as he pulled up he was winding down his window. He looked respectable enough, muffled against the cold – a school-teacher, maybe, a clerk. Weak eyes blinked at them through thick-framed spectacles. 'Going to the concert hall?'

'Do us a favour, citizen, and take us to the railway station,' said Kelso. 'Ten dollars US if we catch the Moscow train.' He opened the passenger door without waiting for an answer and tipped forward the seat, shoving O'Brian into the back, and suddenly he saw that this was their chance, because the Russian, caught by surprise, had fallen behind slightly, and was making heavy progress through the snow with his case.

'Comrade!' he shouted.

Kelso didn't hesitate. He rammed back the seat and got in, slamming the door.

'Don't you want –' began the driver, looking in his mirror.

'No,' said Kelso. 'Go.'

The Lada skidded away and he turned to look back. The Russian had set down his case and was staring after them, seemingly bewildered, a lost figure in the widening vista of the alien city. He dwindled and disappeared into the night and snow.

'Can't help but feel sorry for the poor bastard,' said O'Brian, but Kelso's only emotion was relief.

'"Gratitude,"' he said, quoting Stalin, '"is a dog's disease."'

THE Archangel railway station was at the northern edge of a big square, directly opposite a huddle of apartment blocks and wind-blasted birch trees. O'Brian threw a $10 bill in the direction of the driver and they sprinted into the gloomy terminal. Seven wood-fronted ticket kiosks with net curtains, five of them closed, a long queue outside the two that were open, a baby crying. Students, backpackers, soldiers, people of all ages and races, families with their home-made luggage – huge cardboard boxes trussed with string – children running everywhere, sliding on the dirty, melted snow.

O'Brian pushed his way to the front of the nearest line, spraying dollars, playing the westerner: 'Sorry, lady. Excuse me. There you go. Sorry. Gotta catch this train –'

Kelso had an impression of a fortune changing hands – three hundred, four hundred dollars, murmurs from the people standing round – and then, a minute later, O'Brian was striding back through the crowd, waving a pair of tickets, and they ran up the stairs to the platform.

If they were going to be stopped then this would be the place. At least a dozen militia men were standing around, all of them young, all with their caps pushed back like Imperial Army privates off to war in 1914. They stared at Kelso and O'Brian as they hurried through the terminal, but it was no more than the frank stare that all foreigners received up here. They made no move to detain them.

No alert had been issued. *Whoever is running this show,* thought Kelso, as they came back out into the open air, *must be convinced we're already dead –*

Doors were being closed all the way along the great train; it must have been a quarter of a mile long. Low yellow lighting, snow falling, lovers embracing, army officers hurrying up and down with their cheap briefcases – he felt they had stepped back seventy years into some revolutionary tableau. Even the giant locomotive still had the hammer and sickle welded to its side. They found their carriage, three cars back from the engine, and Kelso held the door open while O'Brian darted across the platform to one of the babushkas selling food for the journey. She had a wart on her cheek the size of a walnut. He was still stuffing his pockets as the whistle blew.

The train pulled away so slowly it was hard at first to tell it was moving. People walked alongside it down the platform, heads bent into the snow, waving handkerchiefs. Others were holding hands through the open windows. Kelso had a sudden image of Anna Safanova here, almost fifty years ago – *'I kiss mama's dear cheeks, farewell to her, farewell to childhood'* – and the full sadness and the pity of it came home to him for the first time. The people ambling along the platform began to jog and then to run. He stretched out his hand and pulled O'Brian aboard. The train lurched forwards. The station disappeared.

Chapter Thirty-two

THEY SWAYED ALONG the narrow, blue-carpeted corridor until they found their compartment – one of eight, about halfway down the carriage. O'Brian pulled back the sliding wooden door and they lurched inside.

It was not too bad. A thousand roubles per head in 'soft' class bought two dusty, crimson banquettes facing one another, a white nylon sheet, a rolled mattress and a pillow neatly folded on each; a lot of laminated, imitation-wood panelling; green-shaded reading lamps; a little fold-up table; privacy.

Through the window they could see the spars of the iron bridge clicking past but once they were across the river there was nothing visible in the snowstorm except their own reflections staring back at them – haggard, soaking, unshaven. O'Brian drew the yellow curtains, unfastened the table and laid out their food – a grubby loaf, some kind of dried fish, a sausage, tea-bags – while Kelso went in search of hot water.

A blackened samovar stood at the far end of the corridor, opposite the cubicle of the carriage's female attendant, their *provodnik*: a hefty, unsmiling woman, like a camp guard in her grey-blue uniform. She had rigged up a little mirror so she could keep an eye on everyone without stirring from her stool. He could see her watching him as he stopped to study the timetable that was fixed to the wall. They had a journey of more than twenty hours ahead of them, and thirteen stops, not counting Moscow, which they would reach just after four in the afternoon.

Twenty hours.

What were their chances of lasting that long? He tried to calculate. By mid-morning at the latest, Moscow would know that the operation in the forest had been bungled. Then they would be bound to stop the only train out of Archangel and search it. Perhaps he and O'Brian would be wiser to get off at one of these earlier stops – Sokol, maybe, which they would reach at 7 a.m., or, better still, Vologda (Vologda was a big town) – get off the train at Vologda, get to a hotel, call the American Embassy –

He heard a sliding door open behind him and a businessman in a smartly cut blue suit came out of his compartment and went in to the lavatory. His neatness made Kelso aware of his own bizarre appearance – heavy waterproof jacket, rubber boots – and he hurried on down the corridor. It would be best to stay out of sight as much as possible. He begged a couple of plastic cups off the grim-faced guard, filled them with scalding water, and made his way unsteadily back to their sleeping-berth.

THEY sat opposite one another, chewing steadily on the dry, stale food.

Kelso said he thought they should get off the train early.

'Why?'

'Because I don't think we should risk being picked up. Not before people know where we are.'

O'Brian bit off a piece of bread and considered this.

'So you really think – back there in the forest – they'd've shot us?'

'Yes I do.'

O'Brian had apparently forgotten his earlier panic. He began to argue but Kelso cut him off impatiently. 'Think about it for a minute. Think how easy it could have been. All the Russians would have had to say is that some maniac took us hostage in the woods and they sent in the special forces to rescue us. They could have made it look as though he'd murdered us.'

'But nobody would've believed that –'

'Of course they would. He was a psychopath.'

'What?'

'A psychopath. This is why I didn't want to bring him with us. Half the people in that cemetery, he put there. And there were others.'

'Others?' O'Brian had stopped eating.

'At least five. A young Norwegian couple, and three other poor bastards, Russians who just happened to take a wrong turning. I found their papers while you were down at the river. They'd all been made to confess to spying, and then they were shot. I tell you, he's a sick piece of work. I only hope to God I never have to see him again. So should you.'

O'Brian seemed to be having difficulty swallowing. There were bits of fish stuck between his teeth. He said quietly, 'What d'you think's going to happen to him?'

'They'll get him in the end, I imagine. They'll close down Archangel until they find him. And I don't blame them, to be honest. Can you imagine what Mamantov and his people would do if they got hold of a man who looks like Stalin, talks like Stalin and comes with a written guarantee that he's Stalin's son? Wouldn't they have had some fun with that?'

O'Brian had slumped back in his seat, his eyes shut, his face stricken, and Kelso, watching him, felt a sudden twinge of unease. In the rush of events he had entirely forgotten Mamantov. His gaze shifted from O'Brian to the wire luggage rack where the satchel was still carefully wrapped inside his jacket.

He tried to think, but he couldn't. His mind was shutting down on him. It was three days since he'd had a proper sleep – the first night he'd sat up with Rapava, the second he'd ended in the cells beneath Moscow militia HQ, the third had been spent on the road travelling north to Archangel. He ached with exhaustion. It was all he could do to kick off his boots and begin making up his meagre bed.

'I'm all in,' he said. 'Let's work something out in the morning.'

O'Brian didn't answer.

As a flimsy precaution, Kelso locked the door.

IT must have been another twenty minutes before O'Brian finally moved. Kelso had his face to the wall by then and was drifting in the hinterland between sleep and wakefulness. He heard him unlace his boots, sigh and stretch out on the banquette. His reading lamp clicked off and the compartment was in darkness save for the blue neon night light that fizzed above the door.

The immense train rocked slowly southwards through the snow and Kelso slept, but not well. Hours passed and the sounds of the journey mingled with his uneasy dreams – the urgent whisperings from the compartments on either side; the *slop slop slop* of some babushka's slippers as she shuffled past in the corridor; the distant, tinny sound of a woman's voice over a loudspeaker as they stopped at the remote stations throughout the night – Nyandoma, Konosha, Yertsevo, Vozhega, Kharovsk – and people clumping on and off the train; the harsh white arc lights of the platforms shining through the thin curtains; O'Brian restless at some point, moving around.

He didn't hear the door open. All he knew was that

something rustled in the compartment for a fraction of a second, and then a hard pad of flesh clamped down over his mouth. His eyes jerked open as the point of a knife began to be inserted into his throat, at that point where the flesh of the under-jaw meets the ridged tube of the windpipe. He struggled to sit up but the hand pressed him down. His arms were somehow pinned beneath the twisted sheet. He couldn't see anyone but a voice whispered close to his ear – so close he could feel the hot wetness of the man's breath – 'A comrade who deserts a comrade is a cowardly dog, and all such dogs should die a dog's death, *comrade* –'

The knife slid deeper.

KELSO was awake in an instant – a cry rising in his throat, his eyes wide, the thin sheet balled and clenched between his sweating hands. The gently swaying compartment was empty above him, the blue-edged darkness faintly tinged by grey. For a moment he didn't move. He could hear O'Brian breathing heavily and when eventually he turned he could see him – head lolling, mouth open, one arm flung down almost to the floor, the other crooked across his forehead.

It took another couple of minutes for his panic to subside. He reached over his shoulder and lifted a corner of the curtain to check his watch. He thought it must be still the middle of the night, but to his surprise it was just after seven. He had slept for the best part of nine hours.

He raised himself up on to his elbow and pushed the curtain a fraction higher and saw at once the head of Stalin floating towards him, disconnected in the pale dawn beside the railway track. It drew level with the window and passed away very quickly.

He stayed at the window but saw nobody else, just the

scrubby land beyond the rails and the faint gleam of the electricity lines strung between the pylons seeming to swoop and rise, swoop and rise as the train trundled on. It wasn't snowing here, but there was a cold, bleached emptiness to the emerging sky.

Someone must have been holding up a picture, he realised. Holding up a picture of Stalin.

He let the curtain drop and swung his legs to the floor. Quietly, so as not to wake O'Brian, he tugged on his rubber boots and cautiously opened the door to the empty corridor. He peered both ways. Nobody about. He closed the latch behind him and began walking towards the rear of the train.

He passed through an empty carriage identical to the one he had just left, all the while glancing at the passing landscape, and then 'soft' class gave way to 'hard'. The accommodation here was much more crowded – two tiers of berths in open compartments down one side of the corridor, a single row arranged lengthwise on the other. Sixty people to a car. Luggage crammed everywhere. Some passengers sitting up, yawning, raw-eyed. Others still snoring, impervious to the waking carriage. People queuing for the stinking toilet. A mother changing a baby's filthy nappy (he caught the sour reek of milky faeces as he pushed past). The smokers huddled at the open windows at the far end of the carriage. The scent of their untipped tobacco. The sweet coldness of the rushing air.

He went through four 'hard' carriages and was on the threshold of the fifth, and had decided this would be the last – had concluded he was worrying about nothing: he must have dreamt it, the countryside was empty – when he saw another picture. Or, rather, he realised it was a pair of pictures coming towards him, one of Stalin, the other of

Lenin, being held aloft by an elderly couple, the man wearing medals, standing on a slight embankment. The train was slowing for a station and he could see them clearly as he passed – creased and leathery faces, almost brown, exhausted. And a couple of seconds later he saw them turn, suddenly years younger, smiling and waving at someone they had just seen in the carriage Kelso was about to enter.

Time seemed to decelerate, dreamily, along with the train. A line of railway workers in quilted jackets, leaning on their pick-axes and shovels, raised their gloved fists in salute. The carriage darkened as it drew alongside a platform. He could hear music, faintly, above the metallic scrape of the brakes – the old Soviet national anthem again –

Party of Lenin!
Party of Stalin!

– and a small band in pale blue uniforms slid past the window.

The train stopped with a sigh of pneumatics and he saw a sign: VOLOGDA. People were cheering on the platform. People were running. He opened the door to the carriage and there facing him was the Russian, still in his father's uniform, asleep, sitting no more than a dozen paces away, his suitcase wedged in the rack above his head, a clear space all around him, passengers standing back, respectful, watching.

The Russian was beginning to wake. His head stirred. He batted something away from his face with his hand and his eyes flickered open. He saw that he was being observed and carefully, warily, he straightened his back. Someone in the carriage started to clap and the applause was taken up by the others, spreading outside to the platform where people had crammed up against the window to watch. The Russian stared around him, the fear in his eyes giving way to bewilderment. A man nodded encouragingly at him, smiling, clapping, and he slowly nodded back, as if gradually beginning to understand some strange foreign ritual, and then he started to applaud softly in return, which only increased the volume of adulation. He nodded modestly and Kelso imagined he must have spent thirty years dreaming of this moment. *Really, comrades,* his expression seemed to say, *I am only one of you – a plain man, rough in my ways – but if venerating me in some way gives you pleasure –*

He wasn't aware of Kelso watching him – the historian was just another face in the crowd – and after a few seconds Kelso turned and began fighting his way back through the jostling throng.

His mind was in a turmoil.

The Russian must have got on board the train in Archangel, a minute or so after them – that was conceivable, if he had copied what they'd done and flagged down a car. That he could understand.

But this?

He knocked into a woman who was pushing her way roughly along the corridor, struggling with a pair of carrier bags, a red flag and an old camera.

He said to her, 'What's happening?'

'Haven't you heard? Stalin's son is with us! It's a miracle!' She couldn't stop smiling. Some of her teeth were metal.

'But how do you know?'

'It's been on the television,' she said, as if this settled matters. 'All night! And when I woke, his picture was still there and they were saying he'd been seen on the Moscow train!'

Someone pushed into her from behind and she was pitched into him. His face was very close to hers. He tried to disentangle himself but she clutched on to him, staring hard into his eyes.

'But you,' she said, 'you know all this! You were on the television, saying it was true!' She threw her heavy arms around him. Her bags jabbed into his back. 'Thank you. Thank you. It's a miracle!'

He could see a bright, white light moving along the platform behind her head and he scrambled past her. A television light. Television cameras. Big grey microphones. Technicians walking backwards, stumbling over one another. And in the middle of this mêlée, striding ahead towards his destiny, talking confidently, surrounded by a phalanx of black-jacketed bodyguards, was Vladimir Mamantov.

IT took Kelso several minutes to claw and squeeze his way back through the crowds. When he opened the door to their compartment O'Brian had his back to him and was staring through the window. At the sound of Kelso entering, he wheeled round quickly, his hands up, his palms outwards – pre-emptive, guilty, apologetic.

'Now, I didn't know this was going to happen, Fluke, I swear to you –'

'What have you done?'

'Nothing –'

'What have you *done?*'

O'Brian flinched and muttered, 'I filed the story.'

'You *what?*'

'I filed the story,' he said, sounding more defiant now. 'Yesterday, from the river bank, while you were talking to him in the hut. I cut the pictures to three minutes forty, laid a commentary, converted them to digital and sent them over the satellite. I nearly told you last night, but I didn't want to upset you –'

'*Upset me?*'

'Come on, Fluke, for all I knew the story might not have gone through. Battery could've failed or something. Gear could've been shot up –'

Kelso was struggling to keep pace with all that was happening – the Russian on the train, the excitement, Mamantov. They still hadn't left Vologda, he noticed.

'These pictures – what time would they have been seen here?'

'Maybe nine o'clock last night.'

'And they would have run – what? Often? "On the hour, every hour"?'

'I guess so.'

'For *eleven hours?* And on other channels, too? Would they have sold them to the Russian networks?'

'They'd've *given* them to the Russians, as long as they were credited. It's good advertising, you know? CNN probably took them. Sky. BBC World –'

He couldn't help looking pleased.

'And you also used the interview with me, about the notebook?'

The hands came back up, defensively.

'Now, I don't know anything about that. I mean, okay, they *had* it, sure. I cut that and sent it back from Moscow before we left.'

'You irresponsible bastard,' said Kelso, slowly. 'You do know Mamantov's on the train?'

'Yeah. I saw him just now.' He glanced nervously at the window. 'Wonder what he's doing here?'

And there was something in the way he said this – a slight

falseness of tone: a pretence at being offhand – that made Kelso freeze. After a long pause he said, quietly, 'Did Mamantov put you up to this?'

O'Brian hesitated and Kelso was conscious of swaying slightly, like a boxer about to go down for the final time, or a drunk.

'Christ almighty, you've set me up –'

'No,' said O'Brian, 'that's not true. Okay, I admit Mamantov called me up once – I told you we'd met a few times. But all of this – finding the notebook, coming up here – no: that was all us, I swear. You and me. I knew nothing about what we'd find.'

Kelso closed his eyes. It was a nightmare.

'When did he call?'

'At the very beginning. It was just a tip. He didn't mention Stalin or anything else.'

'The very beginning?'

'The night before I showed up at the symposium. He said: "Go to the Institute of Marxism-Leninism with your camera, Mr O'Brian" – you know the way he talks – "find Dr Kelso, ask him if there is an announcement he wants to make." That was all he said. He put the phone down on me. Anyway, his tips are always good, so I went. Jesus –' he laughed ' – why else d'you think I was there? To film a bunch of historians talking about the archives? Do me a favour!'

'You irresponsible, duplicitous bloody *bastard* –'

Kelso took a step across the compartment and O'Brian backed away. But Kelso ignored him. He'd had a better idea. He dragged down his jacket from the luggage rack.

O'Brian said, 'What're you doing?'

'What I would have done at the beginning, if I'd known the truth. I'm going to destroy that bloody notebook.'

He pulled the satchel out of the inside pocket.

'But then you'll ruin the whole thing,' protested O'Brian. 'No notebook – no proof – no story. We'll look like complete assholes.'

'Good.'

'I'm not sure I can let you do that –'

'Just try and bloody stop me –'

It was the shock of the blow as much as the force of it that felled him. The compartment turned upside down and he was lying on his back.

'Don't make me hit you again,' begged O'Brian, looming over him. 'Please, Fluke. I like you too much for that.'

He held out his hand, but Kelso rolled away. He couldn't get his breath. His face was in the dust. Beneath his hands he could feel the heavy vibrations of the locomotive. He brought his fingers up to his mouth and touched his lip. It was bleeding slightly. He could taste salt. The big engine revved again, as if the driver was bored of waiting, but still the train didn't move.

Chapter Thirty-three

IN MOSCOW, COLONEL Yuri Arsenyev, clumsily juggling technologies, had a telephone receiver wedged between his shoulder and his ear, and a television remote control in his plump hands. He pointed it at the big television screen in the corner of his office and tried hopelessly to raise the volume, boosting first the brightness and then the contrast before he was at last able to hear what Mamantov was saying.

'. . . *flew up here from Moscow the moment I heard the news. I am therefore boarding this train to offer my protection, and that of the Aurora movement, to this historic figure, and we defy the great fascist usurper in the Kremlin to try to prevent us from reaching together the once and future seat of Soviet power . . .*'

The past twelve hours had already delivered a succession of unpleasant shocks to the chief of the RT Directorate, but this was the greatest. First, at eight o'clock the previous evening, there had been the anxious call reporting that Spetsnaz HQ had lost all communication with Suvorin and his unit in the forest. Then, an hour later, the first television pictures of the lunatic raving in his hut had begun to be broadcast (*'Such is the law of capitalism – to beat the backward and the weak. It is the jungle law of capitalism . . .'*) Reports that the man had been seen on the Moscow sleeper had reached Yasenevo just before dawn and a scratch force of militia units and MVD had been assembled at Vologda to stop the train. And now this!

Well, to take a man off under cover of darkness in some piddling little halt like Konosha or Yertsevo – that was one thing. But to storm a train in daylight, in full view of the media, in a city as big as Vologda, with V. P. Mamantov and his Aurora thugs on hand to put up a fight – that was something else entirely.

Arsenyev had called the Kremlin.

He was therefore hearing Mamantov's ponderous tones twice – once via the television in his own office and then again, a fraction later, coming down the telephone, filtered through the sound of an ailing man's laboured breathing. In the background at the other end of the line someone was shouting, there were general sounds of panic and commotion. He heard the clink of a glass and a liquid being poured.

Oh, please, he thought. *Not vodka, surely. Please. Not even him. Not this early in the morning –*

On the screen, Mamantov had turned and was boarding the train. He waved at the cameras. The band was playing. People were applauding.

Holy mother –

Arsenyev could feel the lurching of his heart, the clenching of his bronchial tubes. Getting air into his lungs was like sucking mud through a straw.

He took a couple of squirts on his inhaler.

'No,' grunted the familiar voice in Arsenyev's ear, and the line went dead.

'No,' wheezed Arsenyev, quickly, pointing at Vissari Netto.

'No,' said Netto, who was sitting on the sofa, also holding a telephone, patched through on a secure military circuit to the MVD commander in Vologda. 'I repeat: no move to be made. Stand your men down. Let the train go.'

'The right decision,' said Arsenyev, replacing the receiver. 'There could have been shooting. It wouldn't have looked good.'

Looking good was all that mattered now.

For a while Arsenyev said nothing as he contemplated, with increasing unease, this final fork in his life's road. One route, it seemed to him, took him to retirement, pension and a dacha; the other to almost certain dismissal, an official inquiry into illegal assassination attempts and, quite possibly, jail.

'Abandon the whole operation,' he said.

Netto's pen began to move across his pad. Deep in their fleshy sockets, like a pair of berries in dough, Arsenyev's little eyes blinked in alarm.

'No, no, no, man! Don't write any of this down! Just do it. Pull the surveillance off Mamantov's apartment. Remove the protection from the girl. Abort the whole thing.'

'And Archangel, colonel? We've still got a plane waiting up there for Major Suvorin.'

Arsenyev tugged at his thick neck for a few seconds. In his perennially fertile mind, the form of an unattributable briefing for the foreign media was already beginning to take shape: *'reports of shooting in the Archangel forest . . . regrettable incident . . . rogue officer took matters into his own hands . . . disobeyed strict orders . . . tragic outcome . . . profound apologies . . .'*

Poor Feliks, he thought.

'Order it back to Moscow.'

IT was as if the train had been held in check too long, so that when the brakes were finally released it lunged forwards and then stopped abruptly, and O'Brian, like the clapper of a bell, was slammed into the front and back of the compartment. The satchel flew out of his hands.

Very slowly, creaking and protesting, and with the same

infinitesimal speed as when they left Archangel, the locomotive began to haul them out of Vologda.

Kelso was still on the floor.

'No notebook – no proof – no story –'

He dived for the satchel and scooped it in one hand, got the fingertips of his other up on to the door handle, and was attempting to rise when he felt O'Brian grab his legs and try to drag him back. The handle tipped, the door slid open and he flopped out on to the carpeted corridor, kicking backwards frantically with his heels at O'Brian's head. He felt a satisfying contact of hard rubber on flesh and bone. There was a howl of pain. The boot came off and he left it behind like a lizard losing the tip of its tail. He limped away down the corridor on his stockinged foot.

The narrow passage was clogged with anxious 'soft' class passengers – *'Did you hear?' 'Is it true?'* – and it was impossible to make quick progress. O'Brian was coming after him. He could hear his shouts. At the end of the carriage the window of the door was open and he briefly considered hurling the satchel out on to the tracks. But the train hadn't cleared Vologda, was travelling much too slowly – the notebook was bound to land intact, he thought: was certain to be found –

'Fluke!'

He ran into the next carriage and realised too late that he was heading back towards 'hard' again, which was a mistake because 'hard' was where Mamantov and his thugs had boarded – and here, indeed was one of Mamantov's men, hastening down the corridor towards him, pushing people out of his way.

Kelso grabbed the door handle nearest him. It was locked. But the second handle turned and he almost fell into the empty compartment, locking the door after him. Inside it was shaded, the curtains closed, the berths unmade, a stale smell of cold, male sweat – whoever had occupied it must have got off at Vologda. He tried to open the window but it was stuck. The Aurora man was battering at the door, shouting at him to open up. The handle rattled furiously. Kelso unfastened the satchel and tipped out the contents and had his lighter in his hand as the lock gave way.

THE blinds of Zinaida Rapava's apartment were drawn. The lights were off. The television screen flickered in the corner of her tiny flat like a cold blue hearth.

There had been a plainclothes guard outside on the landing all night – Bunin to start with, and then a different man – and a militia car parked ostentatiously opposite the entrance to the apartment block. It was Bunin who had told her to keep the blinds closed and not to go out. She didn't like Bunin and she could tell he didn't like her. When she asked him how long she would have to stay like this, he had shrugged. Was she a prisoner, then? He had shrugged again.

She had lain in a foetal curl on her bed for the best part of twenty hours, listening to her neighbours coming home from work, then some of them going out for the evening. Later, she heard them preparing for bed. And she had discovered, lying in the darkness, that as long as something occupied her eye, she could prevent herself seeing her father: she could block out the image of the broken figure on the trolley. So she had watched television all night. And at one point, hopping between a game show and a black-and-white American movie, she had lighted on the pictures from the forest.

' . . . *freedom alone is not enough, by far . . . It is very difficult, comrades, to live on freedom alone . . .*'

407

She had watched, hypnotised, as the night went on, how the story had spread like a stain across the networks, until she could recite it by heart. There was her father's lock-up, and the notebook, and Kelso turning the pages (*'it's genuine – I'd stake my life on it'*). There was the old woman pointing at a map. There was the strange man walking across the forest clearing and staring into the camera as he spoke. He ranted part of a hate-filled speech and that had nagged at her memory for a while in the early hours, until she remembered that her father had sometimes played a record of it when she was a child.

(*'You should listen to this, girl – you might learn something.'*)

He was frightening, this man, comic and sinister – like Zhirinovsky, or Hitler – and when it was reported that he had been seen on the Moscow train, heading south, she felt almost as if he were coming for *her*. She could imagine him stamping down the halls of the big hotels, his boots hammering on the marble, his coat flying behind him, smashing the windows of the expensive boutiques, hurling the foreigners out on to the pavements, looking for her. She could see him in Robotnik, overturning the bar, calling the girls whores and shouting at them to cover themselves. He would paint out the western signs, shatter the neon, empty the streets, shut down the airport –

She knew they should have burned that notebook.

It was later, when she was in the bathroom, naked from the waist up, splashing cold water into her red eyes, that she heard from the television the name of Mamantov. And her first thought was, naïvely, that he had been arrested. After all, that was what Suvorin had promised her, wasn't it?

'We're going to find the man who did this terrible thing to your father, and we're going to lock him up.'

She grabbed a towel and darted back to the screen, hastily drying her face, and scrutinised him, and, oh yes, she knew it was him right enough, she could believe it of *him* – he looked a pitiless, cold bastard, with his wire-framed glasses and his thin, hard lips, and his Soviet-style hat and coat. He looked capable of anything.

He was saying something about 'the fascist usurper in the Kremlin' and it took her a minute to realise that actually he wasn't being arrested. On the contrary: he was being treated with respect. He was moving towards the train. He was boarding it. Nobody was stopping him. She could even see a couple of militia men, watching him. He turned on the step to the carriage and raised his hand. Lights flickered. He flashed his hangman's smile and disappeared inside.

Zinaida stared at the screen.

She searched through the pockets of her jacket until she found the telephone number Suvorin had given her.

It rang, unanswered.

She replaced the receiver calmly enough, wrapped the towel around her torso and unlocked her door.

Nobody was on the landing.

She went back into the flat and lifted the blind.

No sign of any militia car. Just the normal Saturday morning traffic beginning to build for the Izmaylovo market.

Afterwards, several witnesses came forward who claimed to have heard the sound of her cry, even above the noises of the busy street.

KELSO was overpowered with humiliating ease. He was pushed back on to the banquette, the satchel and the papers were taken from him, the door was wedged shut, and the young man in the black leather jacket took the seat opposite him, stretching one leg across the narrow aisle to prevent his prisoner from moving.

He unzipped the jacket just far enough to show Kelso a shoulder holster, and Kelso recognised him then: Mamantov's personal bodyguard from the Moscow apartment. He was a big, baby-faced lad, with a drooping left eyelid and a blubbery lower lip, and there was something about the way he let his boot rest against Kelso's thigh, cramming him against the window, that suggested hurting people might be his pleasure in life: that he needed violence as a swimmer requires water.

Kelso remembered Papu Rapava's slowly twisting body and began to sweat.

'It's Viktor, isn't it?'

No reply.

'How long am I supposed to stay here, Viktor?'

Again, no answer, and after a couple more half-hearted attempts to demand his release, Kelso gave up. He could hear the sound of boots in the corridor and he had the impression that the whole of the train was being secured.

After that, not much happened for several hours.

At 10.20 they stopped as scheduled at Danilov and more of Mamantov's people poured aboard.

Kelso asked if he could at least go to the lavatory.

No answer.

Later, outside the city of Yaroslavl, they passed a derelict factory with a rusting Order of Lenin pinned to its windowless side. On its roof, a line of youths was silhouetted, their arms raised high in a fascist salute.

Viktor looked at Kelso and smiled, and Kelso looked away.

IN Moscow, Zinaida Rapava's apartment was empty.

The Klims who lived in the flat beneath afterwards swore they had heard her go out soon after eleven. But old man Amosov, who was fixing his car in the street directly across from the block, insisted it was some time after that: more like noon, he thought. She went straight by him without uttering a word, which wasn't unusual for her – she had her head down, he said, and was wearing dark glasses, a leather jacket, jeans and boots – and she was heading in the direction of the Semyonovskaya metro station.

She didn't have her car: that was still parked outside her father's apartment.

The next authenticated sighting came an hour later, at one o'clock, when she turned up at the back of Robotnik. A cleaner, Vera Yanukova, recognised her and let her in and she went directly to the cloakroom where she retrieved a leather shoulder bag (she showed her ticket; there was no mistake). The cleaner opened up the front entrance for her to leave, but she preferred to go out the way she had come, thus avoiding the metal detectors which were switched on automatically whenever the door was unlocked.

According to the cleaner, she was nervous when she arrived, but once she had the bag she seemed in good spirits, calm and self-possessed.

Chapter Thirty-four

DID KELSO FALL asleep? He afterwards wondered if he might have done, for he had no real recollection of that long afternoon until he heard footsteps in the corridor and the sound of someone knocking softly on the door. And by then they were into the northern fringes of Moscow and the flat October light was already falling on the endless iron and concrete of the city.

Viktor idly swung his foot off the banquette and stood, hitching up his trousers. He removed his knife from the mechanism of the lock and slid back the door a fraction, then pulled it all the way, coming stiffly to attention, and suddenly Vladimir Mamantov was across the threshold and into the compartment, bringing with him that same odd odour of camphor and carbolic that Kelso remembered from his apartment. The same clump of dark bristles still nestled in the cleft of his chin.

He was all false smiles and apologies: so sorry if Kelso had been inconvenienced in any way, such a pity they had not been able to meet much earlier in the journey, but he had had other, more pressing matters to attend to. He was sure that Kelso understood.

His overcoat was unbuttoned. His face was sheened with sweat. He tossed his hat on to the banquette opposite Kelso and sat down next to it, grabbing the satchel, removing the documents, gesturing to Viktor to take the seat next to Kelso, calling to the second bodyguard he had left in the corridor to close the door and not to let anyone in.

This was not the Mamantov Kelso had met seven years ago

on his release from prison. This was not even the Mamantov from earlier in the week. This was Mamantov in his prime again. Mamantov rejuvenated. Mamantov *redux*.

Kelso watched him as his thick fingers checked through the notebook and the NKVD reports.

'Good,' he said, briskly, 'excellent. Everything is here, I think. Tell me: were you really were planning to destroy all this?'

'Yes.'

'All of it?'

'Yes.'

He looked at Kelso in wonderment and shook his head.

'And yet you are the one who is always bleating about the need to open every historical document for inspection!'

'Even so, I'd still have destroyed it. In the interests of stopping you.'

Kelso felt the increasing pressure of Viktor's elbow in his ribs, and he knew that the young man was longing for an opportunity to hurt him.

'Ah! So history is only to be permitted where it suits the subjective interests of those who hold the records?' Mamantov smiled again. 'Has the myth of so-called western "objectivity" ever been more completely exposed? I can see I shall have to take these documents back into my possession for safe-keeping.'

'Take them back?' said Kelso. He couldn't keep the incredulity out of his voice. 'You mean you had them before?'

Mamantov inclined his head graciously.

Indeed.

MAMANTOV had replaced the papers in the satchel and had fastened the straps. But he couldn't quite bring himself to leave. Not yet. After all, he had waited so long for this moment. He wanted Kelso know. It was fifteen years since Yepishev had first told him about this 'black oilskin notebook' and he had never lost faith that one day he would find it. And then, like a miracle, in the very darkest hours of the cause, who should turn up on the membership lists of Aurora but the very same Papu Rapava whose name had cropped up so often in the KGB's files? Mamantov had summoned him. And at long last – hesitantly, reluctantly at first, but eventually out of loyalty to his new chief – Rapava had told him the story of the night of Stalin's stroke.

Mamantov had been the first to hear it.

That had been a year ago.

It had taken him a whole nine months to get into the garden of Beria's mansion on Vspolnyi Street. And do you know what he had had to do? No? He had had to set up a property company – Moskprop – and *buy* the goddamn place off its owners, the former KGB, although that hadn't been too hard because Mamantov had plenty of friends at the Lubyanka who, in return for a percentage, were happy to sell state assets for a fraction of their true value. Some might call it corruption, or even robbery. He preferred the western term: privatisation.

The Tunisians had been kicked out, finally, under the terms of their lease, in August, and Rapava had led him to the exact spot in the garden. The toolbox had been retrieved. Mamantov had read the notebook, had flown to Archangel, had followed exactly the same trail as Kelso and O'Brian into the heart of the forest. And he had seen the potential at once. But he also had the sense – the genius, he would almost call it, but he would leave that judgement to others – the *wit*, let's say, to recognise what Kelso had just so aptly proved: that history, in the end, is a matter of subjectivity not objectivity.

'Suppose I had returned to Moscow with our mutual friend, convened a press conference and announced he was Stalin's son. What would have happened? I'll tell you. Nothing. I would have been ignored. Derided. Accused of forgery. And why?' He jabbed his finger at Kelso. 'Because the media is in the grip of cosmopolitan forces that loathe Vladimir Mamantov and all he stands for. Oh, but if Dr Kelso, the darling of the cosmopolitans – ah, yes, if *Kelso* says to the world, "Behold, I give you Stalin's son," then that is a different matter.'

So the son had been prevailed upon to wait a few weeks longer, until some other strangers would appear bearing the notebook.

(And that explained a lot, thought Kelso: the odd sense he had experienced in Archangel that people had been somehow waiting for them – the communist official, Vavara Safanova, the man himself. *You are the ones, you are truly the ones; and I am the one you seek . . .*')

'And why me?' he asked.

'Because I remembered you. Remembered you wheedling your way in to see me when I was fresh from Lefortovo after the coup – your fucking arrogance, your certainty that you and your kind had won and I was finished. The shit you wrote about me . . . What was it Stalin said? "To choose one's victims, to prepare one's plans minutely, to slake an implacable vengeance, and then to go to bed . . . there is nothing sweeter in the world." Sweet. That's it. Nothing sweeter in the world.'

ZINAIDA Rapava arrived at Moscow's Yaroslavl Station a few minutes after four o'clock. (What exactly she had been doing in the three hours since leaving Robotnik the authorities were never able to determine, although there were unconfirmed reports of a woman matching her description being seen at the Troekurovo cemetery, where her mother and brother were buried.)

At any rate, at five past four, she approached an employee of the Russian railway network. Afterwards he couldn't say why she stuck in his mind when so many others were milling around that day: perhaps it was the dark glasses she was wearing, despite the perpetual sunken gloom beneath the hooded arches of the railway terminus.

Like the rest, she wanted to know which platform the Archangel train would be arriving at.

The crowds were already beginning to build, and Aurora stewards were doing their best to keep them in order. A gangway had been roped off. A platform had been erected for the cameras. Flags were being distributed – the Tsarist eagle, the hammer and sickle, the Aurora emblem. Zinaida took a little red flag, and maybe it was that, or maybe it was the leather jacket that made her look like a typical Aurora activist, but whatever it was she secured a prime position, at the edge of the rope, and nobody bothered her.

She can be glimpsed, occasionally, on some of the videotape of the crowd, taken before the train arrived – cool, solitary, waiting.

THE train was trundling past the suburban stations. Curious Saturday afternoon shoppers looked to see what all the fuss was about. A man held up a child to wave but Mamantov was too busy talking to notice.

He was describing the way he had lured Kelso to Russia – and that, he said, was the touch he was proudest of: that was a ruse worthy of Josef Vissarionovich himself.

He had arranged for a front company he owned in Switzerland – respectable, a family firm: it had been exploiting the workers for centuries – to contact Rosarkhiv and offer to sponsor a symposium on the opening up of the Soviet archives!

Mamantov slapped his own knee with mirth.

At first, Rosarkhiv hadn't wanted to invite Kelso – imagine that! they thought he was no longer of 'sufficient standing in the academic community' – but Mamantov, through the sponsors, had insisted, and two months later, sure enough, there he was, back in town, in his free hotel room, all expenses paid, like a pig in shit, come to wallow in *our* past, feeling superior to *us*, telling *us* to feel guilty, when all the time the only reason he was there was to bring the past back to life!

And Papu Rapava, asked Kelso, what had he thought of this plan?

For the first time, Mamantov's face darkened.

Rapava had claimed to like the plan. That was what he'd said. To spit in the capitalists' soup and then to watch them drink it? Oh yes please, comrade colonel: that had appealed to Rapava very much! He was supposed to tell Kelso his story overnight, then take him directly to Beria's old mansion, where they would retrieve the toolbox together. Mamantov had tipped off O'Brian who promised to turn up with his cameras at the Institute of Marxism–Leninism the next morning. The symposium was to provide the perfect launch pad. What a story! There would have been a feeding frenzy. Mamantov had the whole thing worked out.

But then: nothing. Kelso had called the following afternoon and that was when Mamantov had learned that

Rapava had failed in his mission: that he had told his story right enough, but then had run away.

'Why?' Mamantov frowned. 'You mentioned money to him, presumably?'

Kelso nodded. 'I offered him a share in the profits.'

A look of contempt spread across Mamantov's face. 'That *you* should seek to enrich yourself – that I'd expected: that was another reason I selected you. But that *he* should?' He shook his head in disgust. 'Human beings,' he murmured. 'They always let you down.'

'He might have felt the same about you,' said Kelso. 'Given what you did to him.'

Mamantov glanced at Viktor and something passed between the older man and the younger in that instant – a look of almost sexual intimacy – and Kelso knew at once that the pair of them had worked on Papu Rapava together. There must have been others but these two were at the centre of it: the craftsman and his apprentice.

He felt himself beginning to sweat again.

'But he never told you where he'd hidden it,' he said.

Mamantov frowned, as if trying to remember something. 'No,' he said, softly. 'No. He came of strong stock. I'll grant him that. Not that it matters. We followed you and the girl the next morning, saw you collect the material. In the end, Rapava's death changed nothing. I have it all now.'

Silence.

The train had slowed almost to walking pace. Beyond the flat roofs, Kelso could see the mast of the Television Tower.

'Time presses,' said Mamantov suddenly, 'and the world is waiting.'

He picked up the satchel and his hat. 'I've given some thought to you,' he said to Kelso, as he stood and began buttoning his coat. 'But really I can't see that you can harm us. You can withdraw your authentication of the papers, of course, but that won't make much difference now, except to make you look a fool – they're genuine: that will be established by independent experts in a day or two. You can also make certain wild allegations about the death of Papu Rapava, but no proof exists.' He bent to examine himself in the small mirror above Kelso's head, straightening the brim of his hat in readiness for the cameras. 'No. I think the best thing I can do is simply leave you to watch what happens next.'

'Nothing's going to happen next,' said Kelso. 'Don't forget I've talked to this creature of yours – the moment he opens his mouth, people will laugh.'

'You want to bet on it?' Mamantov offered his hand. 'No? You're wise. Lenin said: "The most important thing in any endeavour is to get involved in the fight, and in that way learn what to do next." And that's what we're going to do now. For the first time in nearly ten years we're going to be able to start a fight. And such a fight. Viktor.'

Reluctantly, and with a final, wistful glance at Kelso, the young man got to his feet.

The corridor was crowded with figures in black leather jackets.

'It was love,' said Kelso, when Mamantov was halfway out of the door.

'What?' Mamantov turned to stare at him.

'Rapava. That was the reason he didn't take me to the papers. You said he did it for the money, but I don't think he wanted the money for himself. He wanted it for his daughter. To make it up to her. It was love.'

'Love?' repeated Mamantov incredulously. He tested the

word in his mouth as if it was unfamiliar to him – the name of some sinister new weapon, perhaps, or a freshly discovered world capitalist–zionist conspiracy. 'Love?' No. It was no use. He shook his head and shrugged.

The door slid shut and Kelso collapsed back in his seat. A minute or two later he heard a noise like a high wind roaring through a forest and he pressed his face to the window. Up ahead, across an expanse of track, he could see a shifting mass of colour that gradually became more defined as they drew alongside the platform – faces, placards, waving flags, a podium, a red carpet, cameras, people waiting behind ropes, Zinaida –

SHE spotted him at the same instant and for a few long seconds their eyes locked. She saw him start to rise, mouthing something, gesturing at her, but then he was borne away and out of sight. The procession of dull green carriages, spattered with mud from the long journey, clanked slowly past then juddered to a halt, and the crowd, which had been festively noisy for the past half hour, was suddenly quiet.

Youths in leather jackets leapt from the train immediately in front of her. She saw the shadow of a marshal's cap move behind one of the windows.

The gun was out of her bag by now and hidden inside her jacket and she could feel the cold comfort of its shape against her palm. There was a ball of something very tight within her chest but it wasn't fear. It was a tension longing to be released.

In her mind she could see him very clearly, each mark upon his body a mark of his love for her.

'Who is your only friend, girl?'

There was a movement in the doorway of the carriage. The two men were coming out together.

'*Yourself, papa.*'

They stood together on the top step, waving, close enough for her to touch. People were cheering. The crowd surged at her back. She couldn't miss.

'*And who else?*'

She pulled out the gun very quickly and aimed.

'*You, papa. You –*'

THE POWER OF READING

Visit the Random House website and get connected with information on all our books and authors

EXTRACTS from our recently published books and selected backlist titles

COMPETITIONS AND PRIZE DRAWS Win signed books, audiobooks and more

AUTHOR EVENTS Find out which of our authors are on tour and where you can meet them

LATEST NEWS on bestsellers, awards and new publications

MINISITES with exclusive special features dedicated to our authors and their titles

READING GROUPS Reading guides, special features and all the information you need for your reading group

LISTEN to extracts from the latest audiobook publications

WATCH video clips of interviews and readings with our authors

RANDOM HOUSE INFORMATION including advice for writers, job vacancies and all your general queries answered

Come home to Random House
www.rbooks.co.uk